AFTER SILENCE

Jessica Gregson

Deixis Press

First published in 2022 by Deixis Press
www.deixis.press
ISBN 978-1-8384987-6-4

Cover design by Libby Alderman
paperyfeelings.co.uk

Typeset using Baskerville
Cover font: Awesawez by Gabriela Christine,
chosen in honour of Tanya Savicheva

AFTER SILENCE

Jessica Gregson

Deixis Press

In memory of my uncle, Richard Gregson,
who knew how to put on a show.

After silence, that which comes nearest to
expressing the inexpressible is music.

–Aldous Huxley

Nothing is different; thin snow beats
Against the dining-room window-pane.
I am totally unchanged,
But a man came to see me.

I asked: "What do you want?"
He said: "To be with you in hell."

–Excerpt from 'The Guest', AA Akhmatova,
translated by DM Thomas

LYCHKOVO

18 August 1941, mid-afternoon

Katya woke from nothing with her mouth closed on a gasp. This sudden coming back to herself, from something that wasn't sleep: there were no words for it, uncoiling into her body, finding it already moving without her will. She saw her hand first, its five fingers as alien as an undersea creature, unrecognisable, pressed against flesh, red with blood. The feel of it, slick and hot, its unmistakable soft-firmness. Then her hearing, returning with a flood, and her own voice, mid-sentence: "...it's all right, it's all right."

A hand landed on her shoulder and Katya turned. She didn't know the face, but somehow associated it with wooden boards, open trucks and glances not met, a collection of independent impressions, clattering together like the shifting of stones, trodden on. The face spoke: "They're coming back." The eyes in the face were frantic, and the voice seemed to come from very far away, echoey and slowed down. *They're coming back*. Katya's heart shuddered at the words, but she couldn't have said why. Arms gestured overhead, and something gleamed in the smoke-choked sky, a metallic wink.

Katya got to her feet. The shape at her feet was just a shape, not a body, not a child. Railway carriages lay on their sides, their timbers splintered, and she had a wild urge to laugh at them, as shattered and broken as toys. She coughed instead, and when she started she found she couldn't stop, her throat ablaze with a rich copper tang. When she spat, she spat blood. Flames crawled up the side of the station building, languorous and unhurried. The noise was unimagined, people and machines grinding their gears together, the sound of the world heaving up its timbers and reforming in an utterly unfamiliar configuration. A plane flew low overhead, and in the pilot's seat Katya glimpsed a face as pale and blank as a petal. A noise, then, like pebbles in a bucket, but these were not stones. The woman whom Katya did not recognise pulled her back, down, and between the carriages of the train. Dust rose from the ground in plumes. A boy of perhaps eleven ran past, stopped, and fell with abandon, his arms flung heavenward, doing nothing to break his fall. Katya considered fear and discarded it as useless. The ground was cold against her belly, and she rested her face on her blood-streaked hands.

After some time the sound stopped, and Katya got up. She saw the world in a series of still images, unconnected to one another. Broken glass, blood, bodies. Sounds meant nothing. Yet her feet moved, and she was driven by a nameless imperative. Mounting the steps of one of the few railway carriages left standing, she didn't understand what she saw: a pile of thin, flimsy mattresses, a pair of women huddled on top. "Is it over?" the younger of the pair asked, wild-eyed. "Is it over? Is it over?" Katya didn't know what she meant – this was all there was; how could it be over? – but she heard herself answer: "I don't know. It's gone quiet."

The women moved. Katya could see that the younger one was shaking down every inch of her body, though her face was calm, aside from her darting eyes. The older one was cut badly on her forehead, the blood clotting in her eyebrow as she swiped at it viciously, seeming to take its incessant trickle as an affront. As they unstacked the mattresses, the children came into view: the smallest ones, four or five, their faces smeared and damp but well past tears now. They were so quiet, clinging onto a motley collection of items: a doll, a coat, a grease-stained package wrapped in brown paper and string, the last remnants of home.

"We should take them out of here," the older woman said.

"We should," said Katya. The voice that came out of her mouth sounded like the voice of a woman in control, someone who knew what she was doing. She was a vehicle driven by someone else.

"Is it safe?" the younger woman asked. Her voice trembled as much as her body, each syllable juddering into the next.

"We're no safer here," the older woman said. Her voice was firm. "Smell that smoke! The carriage could go up in minutes."

"The fields," said Katya. As she spoke, an image of a field floated into her mind, warm brown and furrowed, the fecund smell of earth. It was as if she was understanding for the first time what a field was. The older woman nodded.

They each helped with the children: six of them, all around the same age, four boys and two girls. The older woman carried two, one slung on each hip with a grim sort of ease. Katya led two by the hand, trying to hurry them as much as possible while their small feet stumbled over the wrecked ground. One of the small girls was missing a shoe, her white sock grey with grime and puddling around a chubby ankle, and Katya got halfway through the thought *her mother's not going to be pleased about that* before her mind jumped to another track. The shaky woman had the last two children by the hand, dark-haired boys with solemn faces who looked like twins, but as soon as the woman got onto the platform her legs went out from under her and she sank to the ground, as inevitable as a building subsiding. Looking around her, she seemed unable to get her breath. Her hands let go of the boys and went to cover her face.

"The children," said Katya. Her voice was flat. The woman nodded, her face still hidden, but she didn't move. Flanked on either side by a child, it was a tableau that Katya couldn't make any sense of. She had to look after the children, though, she knew that. Hitching the grubby-socked girl onto her hip, she held out her free hand to the small boys and they came to her, unquestioning. The woman still didn't move, perhaps could not. With her full skirt billowing over her legs she looked like an amputee. Again, Katya had to swallow down a laugh.

The aeroplanes could still be heard in the distance; Katya could not tell whether they were approaching or departing. Neither could the woman with the cut head, and so they told the children, silent and biddable, to lie down in the ditch at the edge of the field until they were sure it was safe. She and the older woman kept watch, not speaking. There was something, now, tugging at the edge of Katya's awareness, something that she was supposed to do, or supposed to be, an unscratchable itch, irritating and insistent. She didn't have time to worry about it now. She had to keep the children safe. The older woman spread a blanket over the children, and for a moment Katya wondered why: the day was still warm, the sun spilling wastefully over the ground. Then she realised that the woman wasn't trying to keep the children warm: she was trying to keep them hidden. The whine of an engine cut through the heavy air, and without thinking, both Katya and the older woman flung themselves into the ditch, putting their bodies between the children and the sky. Katya smelled the rich, heady scent of the soil. The sun was smooth on her back and she felt calm. Beneath her, a child moved, and a hand pushed its way into hers. "It's all right, Nadya," Katya said, through the dirt on her lips, "Mama's here. You're safe."

Nadya.

A small girl with dimples like thumbprints. Her older sister, straight-backed and resolute. The feathery float of their hair. Katya's children. Memory unspooling backwards, Katya's heart leaped, twisted and started to hammer. The planes didn't matter now, nor these children curled up in the ditch, these strange, wrong children. *The girls, her girls.* Katya got up, stumbled up the slope, and started to run.

I: ALLEGRETTO

WAR

CHAPTER ONE

I: 8 September 1941

Wake up.

Katya opened her eyes. The air felt right this morning. It would be today; she was certain. The morning tasted good on her lips, and it had the right heft in her hands.

If they were to come, she would have to be ready. Every morning, the preparations that she had made for them the day before made her shake her head at her own stupidity. To think that she had thought the girls would want *pelmeny*, when it was obvious that they would be craving *syrniki* with jam! To think that she had set out their best dresses, when of course they would be tired and cold and want nothing more than to be wrapped in their oldest, softest clothes! Yesterday's foolishness always astounded her, but it didn't matter. Today she would get it right; today they would come.

The rules were complex and they often changed. There were certain things that Katya was not allowed to do. She could not look at the photograph that hung on the wall, last summer near Vyborg, Nadya and Tanya water-slick and grinning, their hair so heavy with damp that it looked almost black. To look at it was to invite in a knife-blade of sorrow that made her gasp, even though there was certainly nothing to be sad about; to take down the picture would be worse. The streets of the city held numerous dangers, things that she had to ignore or avoid. The paper-pasted windows were one thing, the schools another. Children: she could not look a child in the face, and if alone she would cross the road for the sake of her own safety, to stop herself from shuddering to pieces – but mostly she was not alone; mostly she was with Lidiya or Elena, and worse than having to pass within arm's length of a child was to open herself up to Lidiya's questions.

Katya dressed quickly, but with care: a dress that Tanya had once said, off-hand, that she liked to see her mother wear. She pinned up her hair in a way that made it look thicker and fuller than it was, and set the kettle on the stove to boil for tea. As she waited, she checked again that all was as it should be, laid out with the precision of a museum. The girls' clothes were ready for them. Katya had even searched out a favourite frock of Nadya's, old and too small but a vivid green that Nadya had loved – it had been put aside to give to Elena for Masha, but that didn't matter now; Katya was sure she could make it fit Nadya still. The food, too: Katya had never had much of an appetite, and in recent days had been eating less and less, subsisting on bread and oil and a little macaroni, so as to keep for the girls the foods that they liked best. There was talk of shortages already, but Katya had not seen any evidence in the shops, which still carried the same array of goods as before the war; it was all a fuss about nothing, anyhow, Yevgeny had said so, and Yevgeny was sure to know. Yevgeny would have – he would have –

"You ready?"

Lidiya. Katya was certain she had never spoken more than twenty words to her *before*, and most of those had just been standard, muttered greetings on the unfortunate occasions that they had met on the stairs. But these days, with two apartments empty now – the Tsvetkovs never having returned from their dacha, and old Ksenia Shirokova gone to join her daughter in Novosibirsk at the start of the war – those remaining in the building rattled around much more than they used to, and this seemed to mean rattling into one another, more often than not: Ilya Nikolayevich, upstairs; the Ignatiyevs across the hall from Katya, Elena moon-faced and anxious since Semyon had insisted on volunteering as soon as war was declared – and Lidiya, sharp-eyed and sharper-tongued, whose presence had always felt to Katya like sandpaper on the skin. This new – whatever it was, not quite intimacy, certainly not friendship, but something else, a binding together – it was unwarranted, unwanted, but creepingly welcome. Since the day that Katya had come back to the apartment, alone, Lidiya had been the one person who had never once *asked*, which meant that Katya had never once had to *say*: either what she knew to be true, or what everyone else believed. Instead, Lidiya knocked on her door every morning, sometimes with Elena, sometimes alone, not even waiting to be invited in now, putting her head inside and calling for Katya to come and queue for food. It still seemed like a game, the ration cards and the lines outside the shops – Nadya would enjoy the novelty of it, although Tanya would take it too seriously. Katya would have to be careful to keep her from worrying; after all, Tanya would be upset enough about –

That was another thing that wasn't allowed. "You're early this morning," she said to Lidiya.

"The queues are getting longer."

"I know. Just let me drink my tea first, all right?" Belatedly, Katya realised her rudeness; she was so unaccustomed to treating Lidiya as a guest. "Would you like a cup?"

Lidiya combined a nod and a shrug, economically implying that she didn't much care either way. Katya poured a cup, passed the sugar, sipped her own tea. Lidiya's was gone in two gulps, and, impatient, she drummed her fingers on the table, the careful soundlessness of it more irritating than the sound of tapping would have been.

"All right," Katya said, relenting. There was half an inch of bitter, tepid liquid left in her cup. "Let's go."

The mood in the queue was close to jolly: almost all women, the occasional man looking shame-faced or defiant, daring anyone to question why he hadn't signed up. Lidiya and Katya barely spoke; they had little enough to talk about, and most of the topics they would normally have covered were deemed off-limits by silent collusion. Instead, Katya listened to the talk that eddied around her. One woman imparted news from the Front, her air of self-importance telegraphing that most of what she said was invented. Another repeated the same story about a German spy that Katya had heard at least twice before, always having happened to the colleague or the cousin or the sister-in-law of the speaker. A third told her friend about how her neighbour had reappeared, just a week or two ago, blackened by soot, battered and exhausted, having made her way back from the Front by horse-cart and train and on foot, her nine-year-old son with her –

The girls would walk. Tanya would take Nadya by the hand and they would walk, they would stay far from the roads because they were scared, and at night they would sleep in ditches or under trees or in barns, burrowing under the dry, clean straw with its fresh, rural smell. Tanya knew enough about the movement of the sun that they would go in the right direction, and once they reached the edge of the city they would ask people, they would find their way, they would turn into the street and count their way to the building and they would mount the stairs. They would mount the stairs and they would knock on the door and their mother wouldn't be there to meet them.

"I have to go."

Lidiya frowned. "What? Don't be stupid, we're only five from the front."

Katya had already stepped to one side, hoisting her handbag onto one shoulder. The woman behind her moved up into her place, with a jealous sidelong look. Pushing her ration card into Lidiya's hand, Katya couldn't quite meet Lidiya's gaze.

"I'll be at home. Pick up my ration for me, all right?"

"Are you ill? Do you need me to come with you?"

Right now – *right now* the girls were in the hallway, knocking on the locked door, sitting on the step to wait. Katya could see them, their knees grimy beneath their skirts, the set of Tanya's jaw and the querulous tremble of Nadya's lower lip.

"I'm fine, I promise. Just – I'll see you at home."

As Katya walked, the hope pushed its way into her stomach, up her throat, clouding around her heart, making breathing difficult. She had never thought that incipient happiness would feel so much like panic. She could not run: that was another rule. Instead, she pressed her handbag tight against her ribs, walking with a loping, stiff-legged stride that would have been comical in any other circumstance. Turn, turn again, and there was the corner. Perhaps they had not yet gone inside, perhaps she would see them on the street, still, with their dull gold hair above their pale dresses. But no: they must be indoors, then, mounting the stairs, or already waiting outside the apartment. Katya could not run, but the heels of her shoes knocked loudly on the steps and she looked up for the two fair heads peering over the banister. Her hand on the rail was damp with sweat, and her heart felt less like it was beating than squeezing into a tighter and tighter ball inside her. She was so certain, she had been so certain that she could just about make out the shadows of the girls in the empty hall, their watery, insubstantial outlines, when the air-raid siren began its howl and wiped out everything but itself.

When Lidiya came home, Katya was so stiff with cold and stillness that she wasn't sure she could stir from the step. Lidiya didn't look surprised to find her sitting there; the advice was to stay in the hallway during raids, if you couldn't make it to a shelter. Lidiya wasn't to know that Katya hadn't yet been inside her apartment.

"So, you're all right," Lidiya said, eschewing greetings. "Sorry I've been such an age. I was in the shelter near the Pioneer Palace and every time I went to move the bloody siren went off again. Well, you know."

"I suppose it's starting in earnest, now." Katya didn't care. During the raid fear had swept through her like a tide, more like something that was happening to her than something that she was feeling. Now she felt as brittle and hollow as sea-wrack.

"Not just that," Lidiya said grimly. She extended a hand to Katya. "Come up onto the roof."

It was clear from the charred taste of the air that the city was ablaze, so the smoke, when Lidiya pointed to it, was not unexpected.

"What did they hit?" Katya asked. Lidiya snorted.

"*Think* about it, Katya! What's over in that direction, and would burn easily?"

Katya thought, with all the dry detachment of a child working out an algebra puzzle – but when the answer came to her, she felt an unexpected chill in the pit of her stomach.

"The warehouses."

Lidiya nodded. "That's right. Badaev. They must have been aiming right for them, and now they'll burn for days."

Katya said nothing. They watched the clouds, heavy-bellied with sugar and grain and fat, the city's stores going up in smoke. It could only have been her imagination, but at the back of her throat Katya could taste a burnt, bitter sweetness.

II: 17 October 1941

Katya realised she had been foolish. Of course the girls wouldn't come back into the city straight away. Of course someone in the countryside would have spotted two children roaming alone, and taken them in. Katya had heard, by now, of some of the children who had been on the evacuation trains, whose tongues had been tied and whose words had been stopped by the horror of what they had seen; they hadn't been able to speak for weeks, not even able to pronounce their own names. It was a horrible thought, Tanya and Nadya silent and frightened, but it was less horrible than any alternative, and that made it true. If they had been with Yevgeny when it had happened, if they had *seen*, why wouldn't the fear be so much that they couldn't tell of it?

They could still come at any moment. Perhaps they had recovered enough to tell people where they belonged, or perhaps the family who had rescued them – Katya hoped they were kind, conjuring up a plump, rosy-cheeked peasant woman straight out of a fairy-tale – had become refugees themselves, trailing into the city. She still had to be ready, she still had to be prepared for them. It was becoming harder to go out of the apartment, because Katya never knew when she would be assailed with the certainty that *now, right now, they were coming now*. The more often that certainty was wrong, the more likely it was that the next time would be right. The queues were the worst, because that was when she had the least to distract her, and the most time to think.

It was cold for October, unsettlingly so, if Katya let herself take the time to consider it: the sort of cold that waited for you to open your mouth so that it could climb down your throat and settle inside you, making itself comfortable in the spaces between your ribs, the unplumbed depths of your lungs, the marrow of your bones. In the queue, people were quieter than normal, shrugging themselves deeper into their jackets. Still, when the first flakes of snow drifted out of the white sky, silent and unannounced, there was no one who didn't seem shocked by their arrival.

"No," Lidiya said, in flat denial. "It's too early, surely? It *must* be."

"It won't settle," Elena said. Her certainty was unconvincing. "We're bound to have a few weeks yet."

They both turned to Katya, as if waiting for her to arbitrate. *Snow*. Last winter, Nadya had clamoured to be pulled all over the city in a sled, and Tanya had taken the job on herself as much as possible, trying not to laugh as Nadya pretended to whip her like a horse and demand she go faster. Katya had promised them a new sled this year, as even Nadya's feet had started to drag on the ground. And *there* it was, now: that certainty, that compulsion that had started to feel more like sickness, like swooning, the stark fact that she had to get home, she couldn't remain where she was any longer. Katya took a step to the side, out of the line.

"*No*," Lidiya said again, but this time she was staring at Katya as she said it. Elena looked nonplussed as Lidiya's arm shot out, grabbing Katya's hand in a grip so tight that it was nearly painful.

"What's wrong?" It never did any good to play dumb for Lidiya, but Katya couldn't think of another tactic.

"Shouldn't I be asking you that?" Beneath her make-up, flawless as ever, Lidiya's face was unreadable.

"I don't feel well," Katya said, glib and unconvincing.

"Then you should stay here where we can keep an eye on you."

"But I – if I – "

"Is it a headache, Katya?" Elena asked, solicitous. She didn't normally queue with Katya and Lidiya; she had only come today because Ilya Nikolayevich was looking after the children. "I've been getting them too, sometimes. They say it's from the hunger."

"It's not a headache," Lidiya said. Her eyes didn't move from Katya's face.

"I just need to go home, that's all." Katya was past caring whether she sounded rude. They couldn't keep her there; she had to – she *had* to –

Inexorable, Lidiya tugged on Katya's hand, and Katya was drawn forward, back into the queue. It was a shock: Katya had realised, in a bland, emotionless way, that the food shortages had made her weaker; it was another thing to have it demonstrated so clearly, her powerlessness against Lidiya's will. With neat, spare movements, Lidiya tucked Katya's arm into her own, a posture that would appear to an onlooker as nothing more than simple friendliness, but Katya could see the tendons corded in Lidiya's neck. "You don't need to go anywhere."

And the fight dropped out of Katya, as suddenly and as completely as a wave receding. In its absence, she felt impossibly feeble. She started to shake, every bone knocking against the next. To remain upright and breathing felt a challenge. Lidiya said nothing; Elena only watched, perplexed. Still the snow came down, gentle and persistent, flecks of white settling on the shoulders of Elena's coat, on Lidiya's eyelashes, on Katya's own lips. Three years ago: *Tanya catching snowflakes on her tongue, Nadya's little hands, baby-plump, reaching out to touch them.* Katya waited, braced herself, but it didn't come. Lidiya was right: she didn't have to go anywhere. Quite the opposite – she felt rooted to the spot, buried deep in the Leningrad soil. Still, when the queue started to move, she found she was able to move with it.

By the time they walked home, the three of them, rations in hand, the city, already half-vanished under sandbags and camouflage nets, was further disappearing under a layer of snow. Sounds were muffled; Leningrad's breath seemed bated. For whole moments at a time, it was possible to forget what the snow signified, and see only its harmless, familiar beauty. Then they remembered.

III: 15 November 1941

One week after the encirclement, and things were becoming disordered. They said it was to do with the hunger, the way that people's minds no longer worked properly. In Katya, it manifested mostly in a loss of any sense of time, past and present jumbled and indistinct. She could not reliably distinguish things that had happened that day from things that had happened a day or a week before. Trying to cast her mind back, it skipped like a stone on flat water, incidents and events with little relation to one another. When had it been that she had started to eat the food she had hoarded for the girls' return, sharing it out with the others that remained in the building? She couldn't recall; all she knew was that it was nearly gone, and no new stores had come into the house to replace it. Nor could she remember the precise moment when the shelling had become routine, a simple fact to be reacted to: although her whole body still thrilled to the terror of it, the fear was now purely physical. Katya could not pinpoint the time when the six of them remaining in the building had ceased to be a loose collection of individuals who just happened to share living space, and become instead a collective: when had it been that Lidiya had first shouldered her way into Katya's kitchen, summoning Ilya and Elena and the children to join in the supper she had made from their pooled rations? The first time that Ilya Nikolayevich, grey and stooped and courteous, had knocked on her door to invite her to join the rest of them listening to Anna Akhmatova or Olga Bergholz speak the city into poetry? The first time she herself had heard the air raid siren and her first thought had been to cross the hallway to Elena's apartment, to make sure she had help with the children? Katya had not willed it, herself; she often had a powerful wish to be left alone, to remain alone, never to have to speak to anyone else ever again, but Lidiya would not let it be.

Katya had known that the girls would come back, and now they had, but not in a way that Katya would have wished it. She had started to see them at times unexpected, moments impossible. At first it had just been a glimpse out of the corner of her eye, the muted gleam of their hair. Then, sometimes, at a distance, there they would be on the street ahead of her, turning into an alleyway where Katya did not want to go, but where she was compelled to follow, only to find them vanished. She only ever saw them up close in half-light: in the bright white flashes from the shells the girls were revealed, suddenly, in front of Katya, silent and watchful, dressed exactly as they had been the last time she had seen them, and gone again the next time the sky burst with light. Katya knew that they were not real, that they were a hallucination brought on by grief and hunger and the horror of the winter's settling over the city like a noose around its neck – it was easy to tell herself that when they were not there in front of her, or dancing at her elbow, just beyond her field of view. At those times, they were unignorable. Katya feared them and longed for them in equal measure. Unlikely as they were, all sorts of unlikely things had come shimmering out of the gloom in the broken city. Hunger had stopped people from dreaming, and so the city had started to dream awake. *Real* had stopped having any meaning that could be hammered down.

Things were being lost, threads coming untied. Katya noticed it in others, too, the way that Lidiya, now, would sometimes break off in the middle of a sentence, seemingly forgetting what she had been saying. Ilya was slower, more hunched, with a habit of taking deep, rattling breaths as if trying to summon strength back into his body; Elena, instead, seemed emptied of affect, her normal courtesy and goodwill gone. Even towards Serezha and Masha, although she seemed to be going through the motions of childcare, she wasn't nearly as free with affection as she had once been. Katya could only guess at the changes in herself; she felt fundamentally altered, sundered and unwholesome. If all it had taken was will, she wouldn't have chosen to wake up every day, but there was something running through her, a wire strung taut, and she found herself awake and moving before she could stop herself. There was no reason to go on, and yet she couldn't seem to help it, sweeping up the shattered glass in the apartment following an air raid, hunting out strips of plywood to place at the gaping windows to keep out the wind. The plywood had already started to vanish from other windows as people began the hunt for firewood, and Katya wondered, in an abstracted, considering way, how long her own would last.

Purpose helped, and for that reason Katya liked the fire watch. She would have liked it better if Lidiya had allowed her to do it alone, but Lidiya never would, and Katya knew why – as much as she tried to hide it, Lidiya had guessed how little it would take for Katya to be willing to let go of everything, to renounce. Sometimes it felt as if all she was waiting for was a chance, and yet chances slipped past, again and again, gone before she could grasp them.

The city was still beautiful at night, despite everything. If you half-closed your eyes you could believe that the fires were electric lights, and the explosions fireworks. From the roof of the building they could watch the bombs falling as if watching a film in the cinema, rather than the reality of people's lives being wrecked. The moon and stars seemed fixed, permanent. Lidiya complained – Lidiya always complained, a subsonic grumble that seemed to cheer her up, and which Katya had learned to tune out – about fire watch, the antiquated equipment, buckets and sand, axes and helmets, none of which would be any use against an incendiary bomb, but even as she complained, Katya knew that without something to do, Lidiya would be lost.

Midnight. *It is worse doing nothing than doing something.* This is what Katya thinks, and so she looks forward to fire watch as much as she can look forward to anything, as a relief from the sickening, gut-churning tedium. And then it is fire watch, and she realises again that it is something that is also a kind of nothing, a nothing-something, which is boring but also horrifying, heartbeat slowed to the speed of ice, each thump scouring through the channels of her body like a glacier, her blood cooling in the night, in the silence.

It will always be now. This is what Katya thinks then: *it will always be this moment.* Time is not passing. It is a single minute which is an hour which is all the days and nights of her life, all the days and nights of everybody's lives. The world is holding its breath. Time is running backwards, rivers flowing uphill, the graves disgorging their dead. She is thankful when the aeroplanes come and the bombs fall, lighting up the sky like a smile: at least they are proof that something is changing. Then the explosions, somewhere to the north: Vasilievsky, Petrograd.

Katya looks at the snow crusted onto the edge of the roof, and as she looks she feels herself shrink. She has become molecular in size, and every crystal of the snow can fit into her outstretched hand. And then she is shooting up, monstrously large, one leg on Ostrovsky Island, one foot in the Neva, astride the city. *No.* She closes her eyes. This is part of it, the starvation sickness: the altered perception, the waking dreams. It is easier to keep at bay in the daylight, when other people are around. At night, in the silence, it is too easy to forget what is real. Katya looks up. There is the sharp-toothed sliver of the moon, its bright face tucked into the night sky, hiding the city from the enemy. Elsewhere, on the Mainland, people are looking at that moon, people in Moscow, in Stalingrad, in Tashkent; further: in Berlin, in London, in Tokyo, in New York, they are watching the moon and it is the same moon that is shining down on the Neva, Lake Ladoga, the Baltic Sea. It cannot be right. The moonlight swallows Katya whole.

It was nearly dawn when the bomb dropped. Katya had felt this so many times in the past few months, and yet always in the first immense, silent second she was back in Lychkovo, the first explosion when the world drew in before flinging itself outwards. She heard Lidiya cry out beside her and grab her hand as the sound came like a chthonic growl, working its way up through the guts of the building, shaking every timber and every brick. The ground beneath them shuddered and swayed, the very earth cut loose from its moorings. The sky was busy with red and orange clouds, and when Katya breathed in, she breathed in smoke and dust, choking. Lidiya pulled her upright and they ran downstairs, feet slipping on the stairs. Ilya Nikolayevich was already standing in the hallway, his expression a mixture of irritation and alarm.

"Direct hit across the road," Lidiya shouted, and Katya was glad that one of them had been paying attention; she hadn't been able to see anything for dust. "Half the building's gone. We need to get out in case this one goes, too."

There was no need to knock on the doors; nobody could have slept through the explosion. Elena was blinking, half-awake, holding Masha by the hand; Lidiya took charge of Serezha and hustled them down the stairs, outside, towards the shelter. The street was full of people running, tripping over the personal possessions that the half-vanished building had spewed into the road. Katya saw blankets, a clock, a bucket. Papers, some singed and some burning, tumbled in the wind like leaves. As they walked there came another explosion, further away than the first, but still close enough to rock the ground. Katya saw one of the buildings further down the road bloom fire. It spat out its windows. She saw the girls standing, watching, and she ran.

Lidiya caught her. Lidiya always caught her and for a moment, there in the street, they fought, silently. Neither of them had any strength for it, but Lidiya's will was stronger than anything else Katya had ever encountered. The world flickered and flashed, and suddenly Katya was in the shelter, the length of her leg pressed against Lidiya's. They sat in the near-dark, no sight, no sound, no speech. All that remained was smell: smoke, bad weather, the shelter's damp – and Lidiya's arm tight around Katya's shoulders. She couldn't remember how they had got there. Lidiya's touch felt like an embrace, but when Katya looked into her face she didn't see anything that she had seen there before, concern or pity or sympathy. She only saw anger.

"You're not the only one to have lost somebody," she told Katya in a hissing whisper. Katya couldn't quite catch her breath. Across the room, Ilya held Masha in his lap, murmured a story into Serezha's ear, while Elena sat staring at nothing.

"I know that."

"You don't act like you do." Lidiya's left hand moved convulsively, tightening into a fist and relaxing. Her nails were ragged and bloody. "If you want to die, you have plenty of opportunity. But you came back from Lychkovo, and you're still alive. You've got something that thousands of people would have wanted. What happened to Yevgeny and the girls was tragic, but you're still alive. *You're still alive*. Now do something about it."

❧

CHAPTER TWO

12 September 1941

The thing Trofim hadn't expected about the army was the way that it provided a constantly shifting definition of *worst*. For over a year now, Trofim's idea of *worst* had consisted of the dizzying whiteness of pine forests in winter, the feathery sound of fresh snow sliding off branches, the heart-stopping crack of a gunshot, and above and below and around all the rest of it, a profound, weighty silence like the earth's held breath. Now the *worst* had changed: the fiery colours of early autumn, the smell of wood-smoke and rotting leaves, the inexorable growl of tanks, the clatter of automatic fire, and the sort of full-throated screaming that comes only from the most intense kind of pain.

When Trofim came to himself, his vision was filled with colour, deep aquatic blue and rich, burnished gold, tessellated like a Byzantine mosaic. It was so improbably beautiful that he thought for a moment that he would weep, and that, to his mild surprise, seemed to indicate that he wasn't actually dead, although that had been his initial assumption. Memory unwound, but it gave him little enough to grab hold of, just a tumult of noise and motion, and the occasional image, free of context but sharp as crystal: the calm, impassive face of a German officer, his raised hand holding a grenade; flames, translucent and trembling in the sunlight, as they licked the roof of a burning cottage; Arkady Ilych, one of the other trumpeters in the regimental band, wearing a look of disgruntlement on the half of his face he had left. None of that explained how he had got there; none of that explained how quiet it was.

The blue and gold resolved themselves into a swaying pattern of autumn leaves and sky, and the soothing cool at Trofim's back resolved itself into damp earth. There was something lying across his chest, uncomfortable and restrictive: an arm. Trofim pushed it off, with some effort, and sat up. This action caused the world to rock and sway alarmingly, but when his surroundings finally arranged themselves Trofim found that he was in a wood, and that the arm that had been across his chest belonged to a Red Army soldier who was most definitely, emphatically dead. Beyond the soldier was a trio of corpses, all dressed in Red Army uniforms, all missing their boots – one also missing his head. Trofim had always been secretly, shamefully squeamish, but this sight bothered him far less than he would have expected. His vision was slightly occluded, and on lifting his hand to his left eye, Trofim found that his eyelashes were clotted with blood. Pain roared in then, a monstrous presence that was both universal and sharply, tightly focussed behind Trofim's left ear. His fingers found a gash, sticky with dried blood, disappearing into his hair, and a lump the size of an egg. Another pain insinuated itself below his ribcage, on his right hand side: Trofim decided that he must have been hit in the head, fallen onto his side and then kicked onto his back. He was rather proud of this deduction.

When he got to his feet the pain was so immense that Trofim was sure for a moment that he was going to vomit; when he did not, he felt absurdly pleased with himself. Standing, he took stock of his situation as much as the clamour in his head would allow. His own boots were gone, but the damp earth felt good on his blistered feet. His left eye stung viciously; he needed to wash the blood out of it, and when he caught the gentle, liquid sound of running water on the air, he couldn't help grinning: this all seemed to be working out rather neatly. The stream, when he found it, was narrow, its water peat-dark but clear; Trofim knelt by its side and scooped up water to bathe his eye, scrubbing at it with the least grimy patch of sleeve he could find. Blotting his face dry, finally able to open his left eye properly, Trofim looked up through a veil of white, writhing clouds to see the barrel of a rifle trained on his head.

The man holding the gun was short and stocky, several days' beard growth and a Red Army uniform as filthy as Trofim's own, but he had a powerful sense of self-containment, as if he knew exactly what he was doing. Trofim had lost count of the number of times he had had a gun pointed at him over the past few years, but this was the first time it had been done with such an air of concentrated insouciance.

"Trofim Romanovich Pavlenko, Sergeant, 71st Army," Trofim gabbled. At the sound of Russian, the man visibly relaxed, shifting a little, though Trofim noticed the barrel of his rifle lowered only slightly.

"That's a relief. It's getting harder and harder to tell these days, what with the Fascists stripping the uniforms off our dead." He frowned. "Of course, if *I'd* been a Fascist in a Red Army uniform, you'd have given yourself away as soon as you started speaking Russian."

"If you'd been a Fascist in a Red Army uniform, you'd have shot me before I even had the chance to speak," Trofim offered. The man cocked his head, as if conceding the point, and then grinned.

"What if we'd *both* been Fascists in Red Army uniforms?"

This tickled a laugh out of Trofim. It felt oddly normal, standing in the woods with this man, exchanging casual remarks, surrounded by the dead. Finally lowering his gun completely, the man extended a hand to Trofim and, when Trofim took it, used it as leverage to pull himself across the stream. Closer now, the man squinted at Trofim. "Actually, you look familiar."

"I'm one of the company musicians, you might have – "

"Ah, right. I expect I've seen you in one of the concerts. I'm Sasha Yelizarov. Also 71st Army, Junior Lieutenant in the rifles. Though I assume I'm either going to get court martialled or promoted after this." He looked around himself and sighed. "This is a right fuck up."

Trofim supposed that was as good a way of putting it as any. "What happened to you?"

"Hard to tell. A few of us got cut off from the rest, and came under heavy fire as we tried to make our way back. I was the only one to come out of it." He spoke with an almost clinical precision, entirely lacking in any emotion. "I've been hiding out here for a couple of hours. You're the first from our side that I've seen. Alive, that is. And you?"

"I don't know, really. It's all a bit confused." Trofim tried to cast his mind back: what was the last thing he remembered, before waking up, staring at the sky? A Soviet tank on fire, the indescribable stench of it; Arkady Ilych bawling out a half-remembered prayer before a bullet took off half his head. When Trofim tried to speak, horribly, humiliatingly, he found his tongue snarled up in his mouth; the words he wanted to say came out as a useless clatter of sounds. Sasha's eyebrows lifted; he put a hand on Trofim's shoulder and, with strength surprising for someone several inches shorter than Trofim, pushed him down. Trofim sat, feeling suddenly boneless. The sense of lunatic wellbeing that had cushioned him since he woke retreated with a tidal relentlessness, and Trofim was left stranded and gasping. He closed his eyes; it didn't help. Sasha pushed something into his right hand, and when Trofim opened his eyes he found he was holding a lit cigarette. He wanted to tell Sasha that he didn't smoke, not out of any moral high-mindedness but because you needed a clear set of lungs to blow into a trumpet – but he didn't trust himself to shape even the first word of an explanation. Instead he lifted the cigarette to his lips and took a deep, desperate drag.

By the time the cigarette had burned down to a stub, Trofim had just about collected himself. He rehearsed the words in his head, and then spoke them, clear and distinct: "I used to stammer, when I was a child," he said to Sasha, by way of explanation. Sasha shrugged, as if to indicate that it didn't matter much to him whether Trofim could string together a sentence or not; perhaps kindly, he didn't dispute Trofim's *used to*. "I think I must have been knocked unconscious, somehow. When I woke up, everyone was either gone or dead."

Sasha nodded. "I guess you were lucky – the Fascists must have assumed you were dead. Good thing you didn't wake up when they were taking your boots off you. You must have been a convincing corpse – to be honest, when you came staggering out of the woods a few minutes ago with your face covered in blood, I wouldn't have been surprised if you'd turned out to be an *upir*." He shifted slightly closer, peering at Trofim's face. "Give us a look."

Obligingly, Trofim dipped his head, keeping very still as Sasha parted the hair behind his ear and probed the cut there. Flakes of dried blood drifted past his field of vision. Presently Sasha leaned back.

"I expect you could do with a few stitches, but it's not too bad. Looks like it's from shrapnel – you were lucky not to lose your head outright." He got to his feet, and held out a hand to Trofim. "If you're feeling all right, we should get going."

All right: Trofim conceded that how he felt was some sort of approximation, given the circumstances. He hauled himself upright, relieved to find the world careening around him much less than when he'd first awoken. "Get going where?"

"Unless you want to get shot for desertion, back to the rest of our lot, as quick as we can."

This hadn't even occurred to Trofim. An enormous weight of weariness descended upon him, and for a moment he couldn't imagine why Sasha wouldn't just leave him alone to live in this forest for the rest of his life. But Sasha was already scanning the landscape, hitching his knapsack up on his back; he had a momentum that Trofim felt unable to interrupt, and a way of asking questions that were really statements, demanding to be agreed with.

"That way's east," Sasha said, pointing. "Best guess is that the rest of our lot are that way."

They didn't speak. Trofim used all the frayed remnants of his concentration simply to follow in Sasha's footsteps, and Sasha seemed sunk in an internal world of his own making. From time to time they caught the smell of smoke, the distant rattle of gunfire; more rarely came the soft report of footsteps, and the outline of a voice, speaking a language too faint to define. At those moments Sasha would catch onto Trofim's shoulder, hold his finger to his lips for silence, and they would stand, their eyes on one another, until the sounds faded and it was safe to go on. Sasha had a talent for stillness, Trofim noticed, relaxed in his own body, while he himself seemed to develop a repertoire of itches and discomforts the moment he knew he couldn't move to ease them. There were bodies, too, fewer of them and further apart, but Sasha eyed them carefully in a way that Trofim didn't understand until he approached one and – while Trofim, shamefully queasy, looked away –

unlaced the dead man's boots. "They should be about your size," Sasha said when he was done, handing them over to Trofim. "Put them on."

When night fell, it did so with a disconcerting abruptness, the long shadows of the trees running together like spilled ink to form an impenetrable darkness. For the first time in hours, Sasha spoke.

"We should probably bed down for the night. No point blundering about and getting ourselves lost."

Trofim didn't point out that *lost* implied that they had a direction and a destination, neither of which he was certain of. When he sat down next to Sasha, Trofim found his body was still rocking with the rhythm of walking. They ate an unpleasant, cobbled-together sketch of a meal, the remnants of Sasha's rations, as Trofim's had been filched, along with practically everything else, while he'd been unconscious: dry macaroni, a bit of salt, a scrap of sausage. Trofim wished for a fire, but knew without asking that Sasha wouldn't agree to such an obvious marker of their position.

"We'll sleep in shifts," Sasha said. By the light of a match, he scrutinised Trofim's face as shadows leaped up his own. "You look done in. I'll take first watch, you get some rest."

Trofim was only too happy to obey. He felt he had never been so tired. Wrapping himself in his greatcoat, his head on his empty knapsack, when Sasha's hand squeezed his shoulder to wake him it was as if no time had passed, and he hadn't moved an inch.

"What time is it?"

"Nearly four." Sasha's voice was a thread in the darkness.

"You shouldn't have let me sleep so long."

"You needed it. I just need to get my head down for a couple of hours. Wake me when it gets light."

Upright, his back against the trunk of a tree, Trofim took account of himself. Sleep had wrought a minor miracle; he felt much more rooted in his body than he had the day before. The pain in his head had calmed to a low growl. There was something restful in sitting, waiting for the dawn, which stole into the forest with a drained, greyish light; it illuminated Sasha's sleeping face, pinched with exhaustion, and Trofim hesitated to wake him until the light turned golden, announcing unambiguous morning. Trofim touched Sasha's shoulder, but Sasha only breathed out a curse and hunched further into himself; when Trofim gripped Sasha's upper arm more firmly, Sasha gave a yelp – awake in a moment, he sat up, rubbing his eyes. "Morning," he said, yawning.

"What's wrong with your arm?"

Sasha grimaced. "I caught a bullet yesterday – maybe the day before. Nothing too bad, it's mostly just a graze."

"Let me look at it."

"What are you, a doctor?"

"One of my sisters is a nurse, actually. She insisted on teaching me some basic first aid when I first joined up."

Deft and a little daring, Trofim rolled up Sasha's sleeve before Sasha could refuse, exposing the improvised bandage underneath. It was bloody and begrimed. "You keep it like this and it'll get infected. We need to wash it out."

Sasha had a little water left in his canteen; now that it was light, he deemed it safe enough to light a fire on which to boil it. When the water was ready, Trofim peeled back the bandage and couldn't suppress a wince at the pulped flesh beneath. It wasn't as bad as it could have been, but nor was it the graze that Sasha was claiming. Sasha himself stared straight ahead, unmoving; when Trofim touched his skin he was conscious of a very faint tremor, and the sensation of heat: probably Sasha was already running a slight fever, infection setting in. Looking closer, Trofim could see scraps of fabric caught in the wound. He swore. "Do you have a knife?"

Silent, Sasha handed it over. Trofim held the blade over the fire until it started to blacken, and judged it as good enough; he set to work, picking the shreds of material out of Sasha's arm. When he had gone as far as he could he rinsed it with the water, and then, remembering, searched in his knapsack for a small glass bottle that the looters had overlooked, evidently deeming it useless. "Hold still," he told Sasha, and poured some of its contents onto the wound; Sasha jerked back, and a cloyingly sweet smell filled the air.

"What the fuck is that?"

"It's cologne. They were passing it out to use as antiseptic – they'd run out of the normal stuff."

"I smell like a cheap whore," Sasha said.

"Trust me, it's an improvement," Trofim ventured; Sasha gave a grin that became a wince as Trofim bound up his arm again with a strip torn off his own shirt.

"Fuck, that hurt like a bitch."

"I think it might be getting infected," Trofim said fretfully. "You should really take a course of sulfa…"

"And do you happen to have any stashed about your person? No? Then there's no point worrying about it." Sasha rolled down his sleeve in brisk, spare movements. "Though perhaps I should put some of that revolting cologne on the cut on your head."

Trofim allowed it: it burned fiercely, and the smell was even worse up close, but when the pain died down the wound felt cleaner. By the time he'd rearranged his knapsack and buttoned his greatcoat, Sasha was already standing, clearly anxious to be off.

"East?" Trofim asked.

"East," Sasha confirmed. They started to walk.

It was just before midday when they reached the village. It wasn't the first village they had seen, but it was the first one that was quiet, its buildings whole, no evidence of fighting. If it had been up to Trofim he would have walked straight in, not much caring whether it was held by the Soviets or by the Fascists; Sasha's words, *if we don't want to get shot for desertion,* had been playing uncomfortably in his head, and he wasn't sure, by this point, who would give them the warmer welcome. But Sasha insisted they wait, watching from the edge of the woods, flat on their bellies in the leaf litter. Trofim breathed in the rich, fecund scent of the forest in autumn. He could feel his heart pounding against the earth. For the first few minutes they saw nothing other than a middle-aged peasant woman going to tend to a cow, but then a door opened and a trio of men appeared, talking animatedly; the uniforms they wore were the same as Trofim and Sasha's own, and the words that reached them on the chill breeze were Russian. Next to Trofim, Sasha rolled onto his back, closing his eyes, his face slack with relief. "Thank god," he said quietly. "Thank god."

They entered the village slowly, their hands up – to be shot by their own side by mistake at this stage would be an ignominious end. The trio of men received them without emotion, and Trofim let Sasha do the talking, explaining how they had both become separated from their regiment, how they had found each other in the woods, how they had walked east. When Sasha had finished, the oldest of the three men, a Major whom the others referred to as Borya, nodded.

"Same old story. We've got thirty or forty stragglers in this village alone, from all sorts of regiments. Orders are to shoot them for desertion, but that strikes me as a wilful waste of manpower."

"Thank you," Sasha said drily.

"I'm in touch with command. We're to move off tomorrow morning, early, join the rest of them. You got here just in time. Might even be a bit of lunch left over, if you're lucky."

An *izba* had been handed over to the soldiers – or appropriated by them, it was hard to tell – two rooms, carved wood around the windows, painted a once-bright blue. To Trofim's city-bred eyes, it looked perversely picturesque. Inside was a motley collection of men, a variety of ranks and backgrounds, some playing cards, some talking, some asleep. "We'll stay here tonight," the Major said. Some of the men looked up; one or two raised a hand in greeting, and Sasha nodded back, while Trofim dropped his eyes. "It'll be a bit of a squeeze, but you should fit, as long as you stay pretty still when you're sleeping. There's a *banya* out the back, too, and the water's been heated, if you want to wash," the Major added, "which I'd advise, given that the two of you smell like a brothel's latrine."

Clean and fed, Trofim was slightly embarrassed by his desire to stick close to Sasha, although Sasha didn't seem to mind. One of the other stragglers, a thin, nervy man who had evidently had some slight medical training, had been pressed into service as a medic, and, on the Major's instructions, dressed the gash on Trofim's head and inspected the wound on Sasha's arm. "You cleaned it well," he said to Sasha, who inclined his head towards Trofim.

"It was him. If it had been up to me, it probably would have dropped off by now."

The medic grunted. "I'd give you red streptocide if I had any," he said, "but I don't. Perhaps when we move tomorrow."

"I feel fine," Sasha said, patently lying; he looked pale and shaky to Trofim, and had barely picked at the paltry meal that they were offered. As soon as the medic left them alone, he stretched out under a tree, pulled his cap down over his eyes and dropped into a fitful sleep, while Trofim played a desultory and largely silent game of cards with one of the other soldiers, a dull-faced boy named Viktor, for want of anything better to do. The events of the past few days kept breaking over him like waves; he badly wanted to talk about them, but it felt crass to do so to people who had gone through much the same but were just quietly getting on with things. When evening fell, two of the village women came to cook for the soldiers, boiling water over a fire in the yard, peeling potatoes and chopping onions with a practical economy of movement; their eyes lowered, Trofim couldn't tell whether they were helping willingly or under duress. After fetching food for Sasha, Trofim went to wake him, and was relieved to find that the sleep seemed to have done him a bit of good – at least his skin had lost its earlier ashen cast. Trofim himself felt better for the food, the bath, the company, and better still when a bottle of cheap cognac was produced and shared around. A few of the men had started raggedly to sing when one gave a cry, ran into the *izba* and reappeared with an accordion. It was clear that he didn't really know how to play it; all that came out of the instrument were a few half-hearted whines, which the men around him gamely tried to use as the basis for a song. Next to Trofim, Sasha sat up.

"Fuck your mother," he said in amused disgust, his voice carrying. "Give it here."

Trofim had noticed Sasha's seemingly unconscious ability to command, and he was pleased to note that he wasn't the only one susceptible to it: there was something about Sasha that made people want to do what he said. Shrugging, the man passed over the accordion, and Sasha settled it around his shoulders, flexing his fingers over the buttons. With unmistakable assurance, he played a chord, opened his mouth, and started to sing: "If there is war tomorrow…"

The men joined in in a trickle, and then in a gush. Sasha played awkwardly, trying to keep his injured arm as still as possible, but he didn't stop. 'If there is War Tomorrow' was followed by 'The Blue Scarf', 'Wide Is My Motherland' and finally 'Katiusha'. When Sasha went to put the accordion down, the men shouted in disappointment, but Sasha just shrugged. "I got shot in the arm a day ago. That's your lot for now." He held the accordion out to the man who had offered it to him, but the man shook his head.

"You keep it. It's not mine, anyway. I found it in one of the villages we passed through."

Sasha looked at him narrowly: "*Found* it," he repeated, as if tasting the words. The man flushed.

"You know how it is..."

"Thanks," Sasha said, in clear dismissal; the man slunk away, flushed. Sasha turned over the accordion in his hands, examining the state of the wood, the mother-of-pearl inlays. "This is a nice one," he said, mostly to himself.

"Where did you learn to play?" Trofim asked.

"My father used to play. He taught me when I was a kid. I was the only one of us who was interested." The music had helped, Trofim thought, more than the rest or the food – Sasha's eyes were brighter and there was colour in his cheeks. Trofim thought of his trumpet, then, just for a moment, the sharp joy of building music from nothing, and the ease in playing that he'd never found in speaking – but there was a bright pain behind the thought, and Trofim shut it down as quickly as he could.

They turned in early that night, as the Major told them they'd be starting before dawn the next day. When the men started moving inside the *izba*, however, Sasha shook his head.

"I'll kip out here."

"Don't be stupid," the Major said. "It may be crowded in there, but we can make room."

"There's no need," Sasha said, looking mutinous. "We slept outside last night, and it'll be warm enough by the fire."

"I'll stay out too," Trofim offered. "The air's clearer out here." It was true: the stove inside the *izba* was belching out a thick, black smoke that felt smothering.

Shrugging, the Major told them to suit themselves and not blame him if they froze to death overnight. Left alone, Sasha looked at Trofim for a moment, his expression unreadable; Trofim looked blandly back. Borya had had a point: it was colder than it had been the night before, a crisp wind racing down from the north, and against his will, Trofim shivered.

"You should go in," Sasha said quietly.

"I'm all right," Trofim said. He pulled his greatcoat more tightly around him, and shifted a little closer to the fire. "You shouldn't get chilled, though, if you're running a fever."

"I don't feel cold," Sasha said, and then: "I don't like sleeping in places I can't get out of easily." The words weren't confessional, but his tone of voice was, unmistakeably so. Trofim suspected this was the closest Sasha ever came to an admission of fear.

"I suppose that makes sense," Trofim said, carefully light. Curling up on his side, he closed his eyes. Sleep teased him, tossing him on its gentle swell without ever swallowing him completely. The words of 'Katiusha' kept looping through his head: *the apple and pear trees were blooming…Katiusha was walking, singing a song about her true love*. When he opened his eyes again Sasha was still sitting, silhouetted against the soft bruise grey of the sky. The end of his cigarette glowed like a tiny, crimson star. He half turned towards Trofim and his eyes glinted, flat, in the fading firelight.

"What instrument do you play, Trofim?"

"Trumpet," Trofim said, his mouth clumsy with weariness. "Or I did. It got lost, over the last few days." *Along with everything else.* It didn't matter. Trofim closed his eyes again. He trembled on the very lip of unconsciousness, tugged down into the dark.

"We'll find you a new one," Sasha said, the ends of his words trailing like comets. Trofim was asleep before he could answer.

CHAPTER THREE

I: 30 December 1941

Katya woke to find her death next to the bed, squatting by her pillow. As always, it was gone before her eyes were fully open; mostly she could only see it in snatches, glimpses of its dark shape out of the tails of her eyes, and more often it couldn't be seen at all, the only sign of its presence a curious density of the air where it stood. This was her grandmother's superstition, something Katya had always mocked, now visited upon her – but not only upon her, upon all of them still alive in the city. Katya knew that they all had similar companions at their elbows; she had noticed Lidiya, sometimes, turning her head quickly as if trying to look something in the face when there was nothing there but shadows.

In two days the year would be over. Lidiya had fixed on having a new year's celebration, which struck Katya as the most stubborn temptation of fate: a challenge laid down for the new year to be worse than the old one. Lidiya, as always, was resolute. The children needed it, Lidiya insisted, if nothing else: a sign that, despite the lack of food, the lack of heat, the shelling and the fear and the corpse-strewn streets, some things went on as normal. Katya suspected that the children wouldn't be fooled by such transparent pretence, but she said nothing. Lidiya needed a plan, something to hold onto.

The celebration would be in Elena's apartment – for the sake of the children, Lidiya said, again, though also, unspoken, because Elena would not or could not leave her bed, now. With an enthusiasm that bordered on feverish, Lidiya had stockpiled, prospected, speculated, brokered deals, and finally procured a scanty collection of items that would constitute the feast: some barley, a handful or two of dried fish, a bottle of something purporting to be wine. One of Lidiya's friends was to come to the party on New Year's Eve itself, and there was a rumour that she had a few pieces of chocolate. Two days to go, and Lidiya, a gaunt-faced general, sent them on errands: Ilya, with a sledge, to borrow a gramophone from a colleague; and Katya to exchange the sugar Lidiya had carefully hoarded for a few grams of bread, to compensate for the near-empty bakeries. Normally, they would not split up; normally, they would go about the city at least in pairs, for there was safety in numbers. From inside the building, the stories they heard seemed nightmarish enough to be doubted: wild-eyed men with axes, NKVD offices with their back rooms filled with boxes containing the clothes of children who had disappeared. In the streets…in the streets it felt different.

All December the shells had rained down and then the snow and then the shells again. Encrusted in layers of ice and soot, buildings burned sluggishly, and the canals were obsidian black, frozen veins through Leningrad's body, which would bleed ichor if the ice were cracked. The city looked like an old man, sagging and ramshackle. Through every second window gleamed daylight, the sign of a roof lost or a wall destroyed. In other windows the glow was red, for fire, from incendiary bombs or a *burzhuika* placed too close to curtains or bedding. There was no water to extinguish them; all anyone could do was wait for them to burn themselves out. Flames lapped at the windows of an apartment that was somehow familiar to Katya; it took her fogged brain a moment to remember that it was the block where Natasha had lived, before she had left for Moscow.

The woman Katya was meeting was one of the living ghosts of the city, her eyes looking inward, her face yellowed and waxy. There was something in her stance as she waited by the Obvodny Canal that made her seem timeless, as if she had been waiting for hundreds of years before Katya's arrival, and would wait for hundreds more. Lidiya had told Katya the woman's name but it had slipped right out of Katya's head again, forgotten, as soon as it had been spoken. The woman's coat was stained with diesel, her mouth working constantly, as if searching for something to chew. Katya knew that feeling, the desperate desire just to sink one's teeth into something, whether edible or not. The woman took from Katya the sugar in its twists of paper, and passed back the greasy, damp parcel of bread. Four hundred grams: an unimaginable amount, an extravagance. It came to Katya from a distance, the recollection that the ration at the start of the war had been six hundred grams, but that must be wrong, she must be mistaken, surely nobody could ever eat that much? The two women's eyes did not meet, and Katya was thankful; she avoided mirrors as much as she could, these days, and she knew that the woman's face could have been her own. As she turned away, Katya dared to close her fingers around the packet of bread, feeling its edges. She could cram it into her mouth right now, but she wouldn't. Some did; she had seen them outside the bakeries, both hands forcing the bread down their throats. For Katya, though, ritual was still important: three meals a day, eaten with cutlery, bread cut into tiny portions that she would place into her mouth and suck until they dissolved. Lidiya had taught her a trick, a few weeks ago, placing her bread on a saucer rather than on a plate. "You see," Lidiya had said, with evident pride, "it looks much bigger now," and "I couldn't possibly eat all that," Katya had replied, making Lidiya snort with surprised amusement. She herself laughed now, remembering it, a strange human sound in the silent street. As she walked, she chanted in her head something that she had read on one of the leaflets the Germans had dropped on the city: *finish your bread, you'll soon be dead.* As soon as she realised it she stopped herself: that was wrong; superstitious as it seemed, she wouldn't invite death in. But the chant came back as soon as her feet were moving again: *finish your bread, you'll soon be dead. Finish your bread, you'll soon be dead.*

Katya walked. It came to her that she was no longer sure where she was going or where she had come from. There was something in her hand, and she looked and found that it was bread, but as soon as she looked away she forgot again, only certain of its solidity and the way her fingers curved around it. She should eat it, but she shouldn't; there was a reason why she shouldn't and she couldn't remember what it was, but she knew that it was important. She was walking. She had always been walking. Her joints clicked and burned: her hips, her knees, her ankles. The air slid into her lungs as clean and sharp as a knife, then out in a cloud. She stopped before realising she had done so. A gorgeous warmth stole over her, a sense of wellbeing. Past and future vanished into the dazzling white: all life, all time dwindled to a single moment, an infinite now. She was standing by railings, looking into a park, and the blunt shapes of benches and flowerbeds and trees under snow seemed inexpressibly beautiful. Straight-backed against the railings sat a corpse, covered in a light tracery of ice. It was a woman, perhaps Katya's age, perhaps younger. Her eyes were closed and her face bore an expression of peaceful renunciation. Her hands were rounded as if they were holding something, but they only formed a cup for the ceaseless snow.

Katya sat down next to the woman. It seemed the only decent thing to do, to offer company. She was deliciously, deliriously tired. The opportunity to rest felt like the greatest gift imaginable. She was sat in the snow but all she could feel was its softness, not the cold of it. It was yielding. Even the railings against her back felt soft and right, as if they had been put there just to support her. She closed her eyes, but when she did that the ground seemed to tilt. She opened them again. There she was, her padded coat, her filthy gloves, the bread clutched in her hand. She should eat it. She could not. She did not want to. The world seemed suddenly full of light.

A pair of *valenki* boots appeared, at Katya's eye level. They shuffled past, stopped, turned and came back. Katya's vision shifted, and shifted again. Things became mere shapes, then grasped again their meaning: the legs became posts, columns and returned to legs. A face loomed from above, wide and white as the moon.

"You're alive."

Katya chose not to dignify that with a response. Of course she was. The stranger's breath was warm on her face, and she had a sense, suddenly, of how cold she must be, and how cold she didn't feel.

"You need to get up," the stranger said. Katya shook her head. She was comfortable, just taking a little rest. There was a hollow in the snow that had been made just for her. She had never felt so safe or so cosseted.

"You need to get up, or you'll die," the stranger said. Katya could not tell if the stranger was a man or a woman, just a blank pale face poking out of layer upon layer of clothes. The voice was oddly toneless. It spoke of death as if it were nothing, merely offering it as an inevitability.

"I'm resting," Katya said, or thought she said. Her mouth didn't seem to be working properly, her tongue swollen and her teeth like chips of ice. She looked up, past the sexless, ageless face into the flat white sky. Snow swirled, white on white. Black edged her vision, threatening to flood in, paper dipped in ink. The stranger put a hand on Katya's shoulder, but the padding of Katya's coat was so thick that she barely felt it as any more than a distant pressure.

"Do you want to end up like her?" the stranger asked. The hand moved from Katya's shoulder to her cheek, turning her head, forcing her to look at the dead woman next to her. The dead woman's skin was laced with ice, her lips blue. There was a half-smile on her face. Only the dead could smile with such simple peace. "She sat down and died with bread in her hands, just like you."

And the stranger was right. Katya's death was there, standing right behind her, its hands inches away from her throat. Something lit up deep in her belly, a gnawing pain, a small flame. She couldn't lift her hand, and yet she lifted her hand. The stranger took it with an unearthly strength. Clutching her bread under her arm, Katya pulled, hardly knowing if she was trying to pull herself up or the stranger down. She slipped one foot under herself and then the other, braced her knees, stood stooped and then upright. Breath roared through her lungs; her skin sang with cold.

"Where do you live?" the stranger asked. Katya told her. They walked together in silence, hand gripped in hand. It was as if Katya had never stopped and sat, her walk uninterrupted. Her death was still there, but it had dropped back a few paces. A manageable distance. When they reached the intersection of Borovaya Ulitsa the stranger stopped.

"I live to the south. Will you be all right from here?"

Katya nodded.

"Good luck," the stranger said, and walked away. It wasn't until Katya got home that she realised she had never said thank you. She wasn't certain she wanted to.

II: 2 January 1942

Katya woke: in the gaps between the plywood boards, light was seeping into the purpled sky. There was a sound on the stairs, a repetitive drag-thump, drag-thump, and Katya's heart leaped into listless motion. *Breathe*, she told herself, and then realised that she already was.

When she opened her front door she found Lidiya and Ilya on the landing, carrying a corpse wrapped in a sheet. Katya's mouth was dry, not from shock, but from the long disuse of night.

"Who – " she began. Her tongue stuck to the roof of her mouth. She released it and started again. "Who is it?" The question was unnecessary. The day before, four adults had been alive in the building. Now, Lidiya and Ilya were standing in front of her, and the third was Katya herself. There was only one person that it could be.

"I was worried when I didn't see the children this morning," Lidiya said. She held Elena's wrapped feet in her hands, as casually as if she were holding a parcel of bread. "She must have died in the night. Serezha was rubbing her chest, trying to wake her up."

Katya nodded. She knew that Lidiya's words were somehow horrifying, but they made no emotional impression. "What are you going to do with her?"

"I don't want to put her outside. Who knows how long it'll take them to collect the body – the children might see."

"Put her in the apartment opposite yours," Katya said. "The Tsvetkovs aren't coming back anytime soon. And with the windows broken it's cold enough that – " She didn't want to finish the sentence. No matter how hardened she had become, there were still some things she was reluctant to say out loud.

"And people won't be able to – to get at her," Ilya said. They all knew what he meant.

"Let me help," said Katya. Ilya's arms were shaking violently and Katya took over his position by Elena's head. They had wrapped her in a makeshift shroud, a shiny blue bedspread that was too flimsy to be useful for warmth. Under the slippery fabric Katya felt the distinctive soft-hardness of something dead. *I am holding a body*, she told herself. Nothing. *Elena's body*. She forced herself to find a memory of Elena. They had never been particularly friendly *before*, but Masha and Nadya had been close in age, often playing together: Katya remembered Elena as a simple, stolid woman, her arms folded in the doorway as she watched Masha and Nadya pat their hands together on the stairs.

"Ready?" Lidiya asked. Ilya had subsided onto the bottom step, his head in his hands. Katya looked at him and then away, down at her hands, into Lidiya's face.

"Ready," Katya said.

Elena's husband Semyon came on Sunday. He had walked from his volunteer station with a pail of buckwheat tucked under his grimy greatcoat, and when he couldn't get an answer at his own apartment he banged on Katya's door with the flat of his hand, loudly enough that even Lidiya, downstairs, was roused.

"Where is my family?" Semyon demanded. There was something in his voice Katya could not place, a tremor, a tension. She couldn't answer. Standing behind Semyon, Lidiya met Katya's eyes. She opened her mouth to speak. Her face did not change. "Where is my wife?"

"She died," Lidiya said baldly. As soon as the words were out her eyebrows lifted, just a fraction, in a way that Katya had come to understand as signalling regret. Lidiya made use of this expression a lot, her mouth always leaping ahead of the rest of her.

For a moment Semyon didn't move. Instead, his internal structure seemed to shift, folding in on himself, buckling like overstrained metal. He swung around to face Lidya, then turned back to Katya.

"Is it – ?"

"It's true," Katya said. There was something else she should say, she was sure. "I'm sorry." *That* was it. The words felt like they had travelled a great distance to arrive at her lips.

"Do you want to come downstairs?" Lidiya asked. Her tone had softened in a way that would have been imperceptible to anyone who did not know Lidiya very well. Katya was still unused to finding herself in that category. "I can't offer you much – well, I can't offer you anything. But the children – they've been staying with me."

Masha and Serezha were asleep, curled up together like puppies by the stove. Semyon didn't wake them, just stood over them, watching, his hands hovering inches from their bodies. Lidiya and Katya looked on from the doorway until Semyon turned his back and came to join them in the kitchen, sitting heavily at the table. For want of something to do, Katya made tea, as she would have for any other guest in any other time. In Katya's head, the tea was the tea that she had grown up with, scalding, black and bittersweet. These days, tea was boiled water flavoured with a little salt. The heat of it was important, the steam that rose off it was as hot and cloying as if it had been real tea, and Katya was able to pretend up until the moment that it hit the back of her throat.

"Is she – " Semyon began. He swallowed visibly and started again. "Her body, did you – ? What did you – ?"

"It's in the empty apartment opposite," Lidiya said. "We thought it was better than…"

"Yes," Semyon said.

"We would have taken her to the cemetery," Lidiya said, defensive, "but these days you can't even get anyone to dig a grave without bribing them with bread, and I thought that any spare bread would be better given to the children."

"Of course," Semyon said. He had a quiet courtesy that seemed to disarm Lidiya; Katya wondered why she had never noticed that about him before. "I wouldn't expect you to do that. But I'm glad that – that she's safe. You hear things…"

"In the spring, things will be easier," Katya said, mouthing words she didn't believe.

"Yes. Yes." Semyon stared at his hands, spread on the table. The skin around his fingernails was ragged and torn. A scratch ran from his right forefinger to his wrist and disappeared below his cuff. "And the children? Did they see her after – after – "

"No," Lidiya said, too loudly. Her eyes darted to Katya's again and for a second Katya felt a wild laugh trapped behind her breastbone: for all her self-declared lack of scruples, Lidiya was a shockingly bad liar. But Semyon seemed not to have noticed – or perhaps had chosen not to. Lidiya licked her lips, and said, haltingly, "They were asleep when we found your wife. They must have – when they went to sleep the night before, she still would have been alive. They didn't see anything."

"Good, good." Semyon spoke as if distracted. "And now…" he looked at Lidiya and then at Katya, anxious. "You have been taking care of the children until now, but my wife has a sister in Petrograd. Or had a sister, I don't know – you never know – "

"They will stay here," Lidiya said sharply. Semyon looked surprised and Lidiya, embarrassed, cleared her throat. "I mean, of course it's up to you. But they are welcome – and this place is familiar to them. It's safe." She reached out a hand across the table, stopping short half an inch from where Semyon's fingers were still spread. "We will take care of them. I promise – I *swear* to you."

For a moment, Semyon looked uncertain. He stared into Lidiya's face as if trying to search for the lie behind the words, and then turned to Katya.

"My girls used to play with your children," Katya said. Her tongue felt clumsy.

"I remember." He did not ask where her children were. Perhaps Elena had told him what had happened; perhaps he knew enough not to question an absence any more. "All right. If you're sure, I would be happy for them to stay here."

Again, silence. It was easier to bear now, the weight of it.

"I should tell you," Lidiya said abruptly, "we didn't register the death. We thought – it's still so early in the month. The ration cards – for the sake of the children, we thought – "

Katya had rarely seen her so discomfited, but Semyon just nodded slowly, considering. "That is right. For the children, they must have as much food as possible. Serezha, he looks so terribly thin. Both of them do."

"We do our best," Lidiya said.

Semyon nodded again, his thoughts clearly elsewhere. "I would like to see my wife," he said at last. Lidiya's eyes flickered, meeting Katya's for a moment before looking back at Semyon.

"Are you certain?"

"You think I haven't seen the dead before?" Semyon laughed, a frightening sound. "At the Front, we're losing men every day. And here – the streets are full of them."

"It's different when it's your own," Lidiya said. Semyon shrugged.

"Nevertheless."

Katya had the key, and so she let him in, glad, suddenly, that they'd laid down Elena's body with some care. Before she closed the door, Katya saw Semyon kneel down, push away the slippery blue fabric, lay his palm against his wife's cheek. Something, some emotion pooled in Katya's chest, spilling down her arms. That was it: not the burial or the registration of the death, but the ability to touch it, sit with it side by side and truly know it. It was the same feeling that she had had when watching a mother, mid-December, her dead child clutched in her arms, wailing aloud outside the clerk's office where they would write the name of the baby in freezing ink: a greedy emotion, a longing. Only afterwards did Katya identify the feeling as envy.

III: 15 January 1942

Katya and Lidiya walked together to the Neva. As they lined up by the holes in the ice, they were surrounded by other women, the only ones who still had strength to spare; they had left Ilya watching the children, but Katya knew that he wouldn't have had the strength to hold the buckets that she and Lidiya were carrying. The other women held pots, pails and pitchers, anything that could carry water. They formed chains, passing the water from hand to hand. Sometimes a pot slipped from fingers numb with cold. Sometimes a woman cried. More often she stared at the dropped pot in disbelief, and went back to scooping and passing the water. The banks were a cascade of ice. More than once, Katya had seen a woman fall while climbing back up from the river; more than once, that woman had failed to get back up. This time the two of them made it, clinging to one another, and only a little of the water spilled: this was what passed for luck these days.

On the way home, Katya, holding a pitcher, watched ice spread across its surface like cobwebs. Back at the apartment, they would thaw it on the stove and boil it for good measure, a step that Katya would happily bypass were it not for Lidiya's strictures. Hunger was a constant but thirst still took her unawares; if Lidiya hadn't been watching her she would have gladly licked at the ice as it started to melt, water running off it in droplets. But: *cholera*, Lidiya would say. *Typhus*. *Dysentery*. As if those words meant anything, weighed against immediate need.

Today, Lidiya tied her pail to her with string. It struck Katya with a trickle of fear: normally Lidiya would not betray any weakness, any hint that she trusted herself less than she should. Back at the building, they counted as they climbed the front steps, at first only to themselves, but Katya heard the numbers that Lidiya muttered under her breath, echoing the words in her own head, and so they counted together, out loud. Eight steps to go: it was impossible, as impossible as if it were a thousand. *Six*. Katya did not trust herself to take her hand off her pitcher of water to clutch the railing. She was bent forward at an angle she knew would be laughable in someone else, in other circumstances. Five steps from the top. Katya couldn't move her feet. "Let's stop," said Lidiya. Her voice was quiet and soft-edged. Katya examined Lidiya's face to see whether she was stopping for Katya's sake or for her own; in the frail winter light it was impossible to tell. Katya bent and put her pitcher down. Straightening, she untied Lidiya's bucket and put it down next to the pitcher. She took Lidiya's hands, clumsy in her mittens. Katya could no longer tell where her own body ended and Lidiya's began. She held Lidiya's hands and listened to her breathe. Lidiya leaned forward. Her forehead pressed against Katya's shoulder. Katya could smell Lidiya's hair, thick and unwashed, and the hint of perfume that clung stubbornly to the collar of her coat. Katya held her. She closed her eyes against the dark, warmed her face with her own breath. Perhaps they would stay there forever, perhaps they would freeze like that and whenever Ilya Nikolayevich would pass them on the steps, he would admire the noble women who had died while fetching water for him.

"Come on," Lidiya said into Katya's neck. They pulled apart and started to climb.

IV: 28 January 1942

These days, there were lists. Whenever her mind was idle, Katya ran through them: the list of things that were lost. The list of food that they had. The list of things that they could sell. The list of deaths, the list of bombings, the list of shellings. The list of people she knew who were still alive.

The paradox made it particularly bitter: the ration rising but the bakeries closing down, the frozen pipes meaning that it was impossible to get enough water to bake the bread. A human chain carried buckets from the Neva; it was never going to be enough. Ration cards were useless. Perhaps in November or December Katya had thought, once or twice, looking at her ration, that it would almost be better to have no food at all than to have such a mockingly small amount. She had been wrong. Her tongue swelled in her mouth, her joints ached, she could barely stand without falling. The children slept most of the time, waking up wailing from dreams of feasts. Their stomachs were round and hard, their skin weak as paper. Katya, Lidiya and Ilya pooled the things that they had never wanted to sell: a pair of earrings that had been Katya's grandmother's, a handsome fur hat of Ilya's, Lidiya's wedding ring. They drew lots, and it fell to Ilya to go out. When he came back his face was ravaged. In his hands he had a few hundred grams of bread, some scraps of meat that were more bone than flesh, three potatoes. "It was all they would give me," he said. He sounded shattered. "I went to every stall on the market, but no one would offer me more than this."

It would last them a day, maybe two. Katya's stomach writhed at the sight of the food, her mouth started to water, and yet she felt a powerful revulsion, wanting and not wanting at the same time. The pile of food in Ilya's hands marked precisely how long they had to live.

"Maybe the bakeries will start running again," Ilya said dully, speaking with routine, unfelt optimism. Katya barely heard him.

"We've sold everything that we had left," she said. *Everything that anyone would buy.*

"No, we haven't," Lidiya said. She stood, stumbled, and righted herself, pulling her coat more tightly around her.

"What do you mean?" Ilya asked at the same time as Katya demanded, "Where are you going?" A sense of dread came on her, heavy and powerful.

"To the Front," Lidiya said. She spoke with certainty, but her gaze hovered above Katya and Ilya's heads. "It's not so far. I can walk it, if I go slowly. And you know what people are saying – the men, there… they'll pay."

"Oh, Lidiya…"

"You can't," Katya said. An image came to her of a scene she'd never known she'd witnessed: Lidiya's face turned to Lev's, open and joyful, her shoulder tucked under his arm.

"What else is there?"

Neither Katya nor Ilya answered. There was no answer to give.

"If it was just us, that would be one thing. But there are the children. I can't – I've been thinking about it for days. If I know there's something I can do, I can't not do it. You can't ask me not to."

"I'll come with you," Katya said impulsively. Lidiya shook her head.

"Somebody has to stay with the children."

"Ilya can do that, I could – "

"*I don't want you coming with me*," Lidiya snapped. Katya dropped her eyes, silent. Gentler, Lidiya added, "It's not you. I mean…I mean that I don't want anyone there that I'll have to see afterwards. If I go on my own it'll be easier to forget."

~

Lidiya was gone for nearly six hours. In her absence, together in Lidiya's apartment, Katya and Ilya barely spoke. The apartment was too quiet, the children sleeping too soundly, the air clotted with waiting. Katya started on one of her lists: things that could have happened. Lidiya could have been attacked. She could have fallen and been unable to get up. She could have simply decided to leave them. She wasn't coming back.

When Lidiya opened the door it was nearly two in the morning. Her face had been whipped into redness by the wind, there was ice in her hair and along her eyelashes. She held two loaves of bread, a jar of sauerkraut, two fish, and she put them down on the kitchen table with exaggerated care. Ilya looked at Katya, his face full of fear and disbelief. He opened his mouth, and Lidiya shook her head. "Please don't," she said quietly. For once, there was no edge to her voice. She took a pot, filled it with the dark, dirty water from the pail under the table, and put it on the stove. "I need to wash."

V: 30 January 1942

Some days, the past and the present seemed too close, one overlaying the other. Lidiya sat by the window, leaning her head into what little light there was. Watching her, Katya remembered Yevgeny, the way that the air had always seemed heavier around him. "*Aktrissulya*," he said once, watching Lidiya walk down the street. Katya had heard the sneer in his voice, the dismissal, and she had smiled, too, glad of the reassurance that her husband found Lidiya as trivial as she did herself. Time shifted: Lidiya was back at the window in Katya's apartment, sitting at the table, the kitchen scissors in her hand. She held them out to Katya blade first, in the way that Katya had been taught not to do.

"Cut it," Lidiya commanded.

"What?"

Lidiya rolled her eyes. No matter how weakened she was, it seemed she always had energy to spare for sarcasm. "My hair, of course. It has to come off, not worth the trouble and energy of washing it. It's been revolting for months, and it's coming out in handfuls anyway. I'll do yours after if you want."

Lidiya's hair. Katya had envied it, in the same half-hearted way she had envied everything about Lidiya – something that was so far away that it was almost impossible to want. Even now, while Katya's hair hung in drab hanks against her cheeks, Lidiya's was still, somehow, coaxed into waves. Katya wouldn't take the scissors.

"Are you sure? It still looks…"

"Oh, for god's sake." Lidiya seized a handful of hair and closed the blades of the scissors around it. The noise they made was clean and crisp. Katya closed her eyes momentarily, witness to an execution, and when she opened them Lidiya sat, her left hand full of hair, wild-eyed and lopsided. "There. You have to finish me off now. I look like a lunatic."

Lidiya's hair was soft and fine and, as she had warned, thick with grease and soot and ash. It weighed heavy in Katya's hands, and gave off a smell that was half perfume, half acrid. Katya started to cut, laying each discarded lock on the table with almost exaggerated care, and had only done half of Lidiya's head before she had to stop, her arms shaking and weak. It took nearly an hour, and Lidiya's crop was staggered and uneven. She ran her fingers through it, light hairs falling into her face, and she blew them off her lips. Her neck exposed, Katya could see every bone in Lidiya's spine, the crystalline edge of her jaw. Lidiya didn't ask for a mirror.

"Thanks. Want me to do you?"

Katya's reluctance surprised her. She had never much cared for her hair, but it was part of her costume, something she had always worn. Suddenly, savagely, she wanted rid of it.

"Go on."

CHAPTER FOUR

24 January 1942

It was the third night that Vasya had woken up shouting, and although Dima had carefully constructed a series of walls and bunkers to hold back fear, this time he couldn't stop it from rippling through him. The cold lent weight to the air, as if Dima had just to move his arms and crystals of frost would fall like shards of glass. The noises that Vasya was making weren't quite words but his distress was clear, and Dima knew that he should go to him, perhaps shove him closer to the stove, but for five seconds, then ten, he couldn't make himself move: his own warmth covered his body like a blanket, and the thought of giving it up made him almost angry. Fifteen seconds, twenty. Dima moved.

He felt for his watch: somewhere between six and seven. Steeling himself, Dima crept out of bed, wrapped his blanket around his shoulders, crossed the bare foot or so between his bed and Vasya's, huddled on either side of the *burzhuika*, as it gave out its meagre threads of warmth into the bitter room. Vasya had stopped shouting now, but the sounds he was making instead were worse: a series of low, steady moans that were halfway to keening. The first movements of the day were always the hardest: Dima felt the brittleness of his own bones, fought down the horribly familiar sense that they were seconds away from splintering inside him. He sat on the edge of Vasya's bed, breathed in the thick scent of Vasya's body, fumbled for and grasped his shoulder, wondering if the bony feel of it would ever stop coming as a shock.

"Vasya – Vasya, wake up."

The springs of the bed squealed as Vasya shifted. His hand still on Vasya's shoulder, Dima felt Vasya's spine start to round as his knees pulled in tighter to his chest. Vasya spoke again, a harsh-sounding word that Dima didn't catch, redolent with distress. Dima had had these dreams himself, sometimes, of food and drink just out of reach, or worse, of eating incessantly without any sense of satiety.

"Vasya, come on." Dima spoke louder this time, squeezing Vasya's shoulder. He didn't dare shake him; he had become superstitious about sudden movements, the damaging potential of shock, the possibility of rattling someone into pieces. Vasya sighed, breathing out silence, his body tautening.

"Dima?" His voice was clotted.

"You were yelling," Dima whispered. *Again*, he didn't add.

"Oh god," Vasya said. He drew himself into an even tighter ball. "Oh god, oh god."

"It's all right," Dima said mechanically, feeling foolish and overly conscious of the worthlessness of comfort. Still, those were the things that you had to say. Waking up was always the worst; days mostly got better from there, except when they didn't. Vasya didn't need reminding of that.

"I was dreaming – oh *god*. Is there anything?" Vasya's voice was edged with wildness. Dima didn't have to ask what he meant. *Anything* meant food, something that both of them had stopped referring to by name. There was nothing, or as good as nothing, and they both knew it, but still they asked, as if the question alone could summon sustenance from the frozen air.

"Wait," Dima said. His own stomach had awoken now, curled high in his abdomen, just below his ribs. It knocked against his bones, a stubborn stone. He reached towards his own bed, felt for his pillow and found, beneath it, wrapped in newspaper, the corner of yesterday's bread he had saved, as he always did, mostly just for the sake of knowing that there was more. It was much less than a mouthful, a triangle of crust that oozed water and tasted like nothing edible, and yet as Dima held it tears pricked his eyes at the thought of giving it up. *Preposterous*. He unwrapped it, and before he could think twice about it, pressed it to Vasya's lips.

"Here. Eat it, quick."

Vasya's mouth moved against Dima's hand, and Dima lay down behind him, his chest pressed against the length of Vasya's spine: warmth was at a premium, almost as sought after as food. Dima closed his eyes, shifted his head so that one ear was against Vasya's back, heard him chew and swallow. A sudden vicious impulse came, to pry Vasya's mouth open, pull out the sodden remnants of the bread. *You need him*, Dima told himself. They both knew it: after love, after dignity and humanity and fellow-feeling, need was what was left. The paper was still crumpled in his hands, and Dima smoothed it slowly, moistened a fingertip and ran it along the peaks and troughs, the wrinkles and the furred edges. The bread was too damp these days to leave much behind in the way of crumbs, but it was a calming act, making sure there was nothing edible left to be discarded. He was tempted to put the paper itself in his mouth, to chew it and swallow it, but he had done this before and the foul taste of the ink and the clawing cramps it had given him were fresh in his memory. When Dima was sure that the paper was bare he folded it carefully, placing it on the floor beside the bed. He would gather it later with the rest of the rubbish, and Vasya would laugh at him for doing so, as if tidiness mattered any more. At least, Dima hoped Vasya would laugh.

"Shit," Vasya said. His voice surprised Dima in the darkness; Vasya's silence had been so complete that Dima had assumed he'd fallen back to sleep. He sounded more awake now, as if he'd started to pull the scraps of himself together. "That was your bread, wasn't it? You shouldn't have given it to me."

Dima shrugged. "You need it more than I do."

"Don't be stupid. Don't pretend you're not hungry."

"It's not as bad for me."

Vasya didn't dispute it. Neither of them knew why some people suffered worse than others, but Dima had always been skinny, and perhaps that was part of it. Vasya, on the other hand – Dima remembered the heft of his shoulders from a year before, the tight feel of his coat as it strained across his back, now sagging loose. It took more fuel to keep a body like Vasya's going.

"It's still early, not even seven. You should go back to sleep," Dima said. He felt the bones shift as Vasya shook his head.

"I…don't think that would be a good idea."

"Don't, Vasya."

"I think I might be done, Dima."

"*Don't.*"

Dima didn't shout, but the word came out with a piercing violence that silenced them both. In the small of his back, the base of his lungs, the tips of his fingers, Dima felt panic, lurking, ready to pounce. He shook it off.

"We'll find something."

"*What*, Dima? There's nothing to find!"

"Perhaps Pavel has something…"

"You know he doesn't. You know he's dependent on *us* most of the time."

"Or we could go to the Haymarket."

"With what?"

"There's – "

"*No*, Dima."

It was Dima's customary offer, and Vasya's customary response. Dima wondered occasionally what he would do if Vasya ever said yes.

"We'll find something." Cheerfulness was Dima's job, one of the few things he could give Vasya in return for the myriad things Vasya had done for him. "Are you sure you checked Slava's room properly?"

"I checked."

"Maybe I should check again."

"I told you, Dima, there's nothing to find."

"Perhaps." Dima sat up, clenching his fists tightly as the world swung around him, finally settling. "But sometimes I can find things. You know that."

Vasya snorted, and the sound of it was a tiny flame lit up inside Dima. "That you can. Go and search, then, if it makes you feel better."

It did. Dima had a sense, somehow, both that this was the worst that things had been, and also that there was a way out, if he could only do the right set of things in the right order. Purpose helped: he didn't feel tired at all, as if it had been swallowed by everything else, and the hunger and the cold girded him as they sometimes did, wrapping themselves around his bones and holding him together, holding him upright. He had no need to dress, for he slept in his clothes, but he knotted the blanket around his shoulders like a cape.

"Good luck," Vasya said. Perhaps Dima was imagining it, but there seemed to be something a little stronger in Vasya's voice. This was what they were good at, bolstering each other up.

Dima hadn't been into Slava's room *since*, but he remembered the layout from before the war, when he and Vasya would sometimes visit of an evening, and Vasya and Slava would drink vodka and talk in half-riddles about people they half-knew while Dima would smile and nurse a single glass for as long as he could pass unnoticed. Slava had changed since the Blockade, in the same way that many people had: he had stopped greeting Vasya and Dima, had started locking his door assiduously, and sometimes at night Dima had heard scraping sounds through the wall, as if something were being placed across the entrance as a barricade. Dima was sure that Slava had been hiding something, hoarding something, but the day after Slava hadn't come home, Vasya had managed to jimmy the lock and spent over an hour searching the place before coming out despairing and empty-handed: there was nothing, he insisted, nothing but the few filthy and tattered clothes that Slava hadn't been wearing, and a pile of blankets. They had divided the blankets into two piles, one for Vasya and one for Dima, and while Vasya had flung his half straight onto his bed, Dima had insisted on washing his share, appalled by their faint reek of someone else's skin. They had taken days to dry and now smelled slightly scorched, from hanging too close to the stove, but it was an improvement.

Slava's room was so cold it made Dima's chest seize, and it took a moment for him to catch his breath again. When he did, he lowered himself to the floor. This was what he had meant when he said that he searched differently; most people, he was sure, were too reliant on their eyes, and ignored the other clues that the world offered. If there was anything hidden here, Dima was certain that he would find it. Starting with the patch of wall right beside the door, Dima spread his fingers against it, palm flat. It felt smooth, and a tentative tap revealed no hollowness. Placing his right hand below his left, Dima felt again, and again, and again. It was the sort of slow, methodical action that would have driven him half-crazy in normal times, but now it was strangely soothing. Dima's heart slowed from its normal staccato race, and his blood pooled in his wrists, his elbows, his knees. He shifted, flattened his hands, tapped.

It was past eight by the time he found it, the slight irregularity in the wall and the papery echo that spoke of something hidden. He had to bite his lips to stifle a laugh, or a crow: he had known, he had been right! Slava must have done a good job of covering it up, or Vasya would've found it, a depression in the wall behind the table which might have been there already, or which might have been created as a hiding place, a brick or two removed; Dima's fingernails scrabbled to find purchase and then lifted: newspaper, he thought, it must have been layered on thick and then painted to match the rest of the wall, but easy to remove for access. When the hole was exposed he stopped, his hands balled in his lap. Dima had a natural aversion to reaching into small spaces, a fear of dangers that he could not see, a fear of damage to his hands – and this, now, was something else, because worse than reaching in and finding something unexpected would be reaching in and finding nothing. If this had been Slava's hiding spot, there was nothing to say that he hadn't cleared it out before he'd been killed, or died, or vanished, or whatever he'd done. Dima took a deep breath, lifted his left hand, walked the pads of his fingers along the rough, crumbling brick he had exposed. When the tip of his index finger knocked against something cold and smooth he sobbed, just once, a tender swell of emotion that came from nowhere and vanished as quickly as it had appeared. His eyes dry, his hands steadier than they had been for hours, Dima removed the contents of Slava's store: three glass bottles, their contents moving in an oily gurgle, and a packet wrapped in paper that crackled in his hands.

A sudden dizziness rushed over Dima, as if whatever had been holding him together for the past hours had left him, job done. He dug his nails into his palms and bit down hard on his lower lip, using pain to tether himself to consciousness, concentrating on the slow swooping beat of his heart. He hated most the nausea that came with these waves of weakness, the way that his stomach would heave mockingly, as if it had something to expel. It was at times like this that he couldn't help thinking of the things he mostly tried to ignore: how long it had been since he had eaten (twelve hours), how long it had been since he had eaten anything other than bread (five days), how long it had been since he hadn't felt hungry (a length of time that felt immeasurable). When his hands had stopped shaking, Dima twisted the cap off one of the bottles and raised it to his face: the clean, sharp smell of vodka. Then the packet: the scent that rose from the open paper was almost unbearable in its sweetness. *Biscuits.* Running his finger down the outside of the packet, Dima counted: nine. He couldn't help it: with his thumbnail he scratched the uppermost biscuit, and lifted his thumb to his mouth, letting the powdery, sugary crumbs dissolve on his tongue. For a second he allowed himself to think it: *you don't need to tell Vasya about the biscuits. Show him the vodka, tell him that's all there was. He'll be happy enough with that.* And then he forced himself to remember: the way that Vasya always passed both portions of bread to Dima so that he could weigh them in his hands and decide which one to take. The way that Vasya never complained when Dima gave into his baser impulses and took the ration that felt infinitesimally larger. Dima wrapped the biscuits again, twisting the paper as tightly as he could, and tucked the bottles into the waistband of his trousers. His legs felt as liquid as the vodka, so he hauled himself onto his knees, crawling to the door. He would stand when he reached it; he wouldn't allow Vasya to see him like this, but if they were going to the Haymarket to trade, he would need every shred of energy that he could save.

The silence in their own room unnerved Dima, but then he heard it, over the roar of blood in his own ears: the tattered edges of Vasya's breathing. He had evidently fallen asleep again, against his better judgement. Dima had no qualms about waking him this time, revelling in the sound of Vasya's indrawn breath as he caught sight of the bottle that Dima was holding.

"Oh my *god*." The same words he had used earlier, but his tone couldn't have been more different. One of Vasya's hands gripped Dima's free one, squeezing it.

"And there are two more bottles – I put them on the table. And a packet of biscuits." Dima heard the childish note of triumph in his own voice but couldn't suppress it. Vasya laughed, an indescribable sound.

"You're going to be insufferably smug after this, aren't you?"

"I thought you could keep one of the bottles, and we'll trade the other two at the Haymarket. And eat the biscuits, of course." He steeled himself. "There were twelve, but I couldn't help it, I scoffed three straight away when I found them. So you get six, I get three of the ones that are left."

"Dima," Vasya said warningly. Dima fought to keep his face as still as he could. This was a downside of being unable to see: he could never control what other people were reading into his face; it operated as a one-way signal. Turning to the table, his face half hidden, he carefully unwrapped the biscuits, counting out three for himself, six for Vasya. He held out Vasya's share, wordless, and felt Vasya's refusal hanging between them, unspoken and impossible.

"I'll have the crumbs, all right?" he said at last. Still Vasya said nothing, did not take the biscuits Dima was offering him. Dima's arm started to shake. He felt perilously close to crying, all of a sudden; he wanted to stamp his foot and beat his fists on the floor. "Don't make me say it, Vasya," he said, hating the pleading note that had crept into his voice, sharp as a file. *I need you strong. I need you alive.* The silence stretched. Dima lowered his arm, and Vasya caught it. For a moment neither of them moved, and then Vasya took the biscuits from Dima's hand. "Thank you," he said quietly.

~

Prices had changed, but prices always changed. The air in the Haymarket was dense, too many voices, too much hope for too little reason. The smells were smothering and Dima struggled not to wrinkle his nose. Crowds like this were always a challenge; it wouldn't be so bad if he didn't mind appearing blind, but he made things more difficult for himself because he always wanted to pass. The concentration it took to let go of Vasya's elbow and make his own way according to sound and smell and touch was lacking these days; after only a few minutes a headache started building, right behind his eyes. Dima wanted to sleep, or at least to sit down and have no one speak to him for some time. Instead, he folded his hands into loose fists, the calloused pads of his fingers rubbing against the ball at the base of his thumb. It was calming, a reminder of his body.

Vasya had insisted they both have a small glass of vodka before leaving – for warmth, Vasya said. Vasya always had a reason. It worked, though; perhaps in part because Dima was unaccustomed to it, but he could still feel the heat trails the vodka had burned down his throat and into his stomach. He felt only slightly queasy. The vodka and the biscuits had revitalised Vasya almost beyond recognition; on reaching the Haymarket he had commanded Dima to hang back while he himself plunged into the crowd. Dima knew, although Vasya would never say, that Dima was a liability to negotiations: trailing a blind man gave off a desperation that Vasya needed to hide in order to get the best deal he could.

"Dima!" Dima couldn't help but smile; although Vasya's voice was hoarse and weak, the cadence was just the same as it had been in better times, when he was proud of something and wanted to show it off. Dima could never get used to the idea that Vasya might ever want to show off to *him*. Grasping Dima's shoulder, Vasya turned him slightly. "Dima, this is Shura. He has food – he's agreed to give us fifty grams of ground meat for the two bottles of vodka. His apartment is just around the corner – he's going to take us there."

Fifty grams of meat: Dima's mouth started to water at the very thought. He held out his hand towards where Shura must be, by Vasya's shoulder. "Shura. Pleased to meet you."

A hand grasped his, and Dima's skin prickled in alarm. This wasn't right, this hand, with its smooth skin and its curved lines; it was *plump*. In the last few months Dima had grasped many hands, but none that had felt like this. This was the hand of a healthy man, but there were no healthy men left in Leningrad.

"You are blind, Dima?" Shura asked. His voice was oleaginous; it made Dima's own stick in his throat. "That must make things very difficult for you both."

"We get by," Dima snapped. This was wrong, this was very wrong.

"I'm sorry, I didn't mean to – "

"No, no," Vasya jumped in with an utterly unconvincing laugh. "It's quite all right. Dima, can I talk to you for a moment?"

"Vasily, I haven't much time. If you don't want to exchange with me, there are plenty who do."

"Just a minute, Shura, honestly!" Vasya's voice held fear, desperation, inexpertly concealed beneath bluster. He took Dima's shoulder and hustled him, not gently, a few metres away, to where Dima assumed was out of Shura's earshot. "What the fuck are you doing, Dima?"

"I don't trust him."

Vasya's sigh was almost a hiss. "Dima, we don't have time for this."

"Why him? The market's full of people…"

"Because he's offering us the best deal! By far the best!"

"And you don't wonder why?" *You don't trust the fat ones*; Dima had heard Vasya say it often enough. They both knew what it meant, even if Vasya, in his need and his hunger, had forgotten, or forced himself to forget.

"He's small, Dima. Maybe five, six inches smaller than me. If he – if it came to it, I could take him, easily."

"Six months ago, maybe." Dima said it quietly, not wishing to be cruel. Vasya pretended he hadn't heard. "And why do we have to go to his apartment, anyway? Why can't he bring the meat here? We'll wait."

"Didn't you hear what I just said? He's small, Shura is. You think people are too good to steal other people's food? It happens, it's been happening."

"It's probably rat, anyway."

"So what if it is? It wouldn't be the worst thing."

"And what if it's – what if it's *that*?"

"*Then I would eat it!*" Vasya didn't shout, not quite, but his voice was forceful enough that Dima had to fight the urge to take a step back. "And so would you. Because if we don't, we are both going to die." Vasya reached out and gripped Dima's arm just above the elbow, as if to soften his words. "I can go alone, if you want. You can wait here, if you're scared."

Scared. The word was a goad and Dima knew it, and yet he couldn't help rising to it. "I'm not *scared*. Of course I'll come."

The apartment wasn't just around the corner. As Dima walked, he counted, so much of a habit now that he could no sooner have stopped than sawn off his own legs. The bottles of vodka swirled and sloshed in his trouser pockets, one on each side: they had agreed months ago that Dima should always carry anything precious, as Vasya was liable to get distracted in animated conversation and fail to notice an urchin lifting whatever he had stashed about his person. Vasya and Shura talked as they walked, a low murmur of conviviality that Dima deliberately tuned out. He hated this. It was not often that he disobeyed his instincts, and every atom of his body rebelled against it. *You would have believed me before*, Dima said to Vasya silently. It was true: in normal circumstances Vasya trusted Dima's views of people almost more than Dima did himself, and though Vasya never would have admitted it sober, Dima knew that Vasya thought of his judgements as bordering on the supernatural, no matter how often Dima tried to explain that it was just a question of paying attention, a different kind of attention.

"We're here," Shura said, evidently for Dima's benefit. The air thickened as they turned off the main street, into a courtyard. "This is the building. The apartment's on the top floor." Just the sound of his voice, the complacent ooze of it, raised Dima's internal alarms, but he said nothing. The headache that had been rumbling behind his eyes had shifted, slipping back to the base of his skull where it met his spine. Sand complained underfoot as they mounted the metal steps; the front door was propped open. The building had a smell about it that hit Dima in the chest – smoke, damp, the sharp scent of cold stone, all undercut with something unsettling, a sweet-sour smell that managed to entice and repel at once. One flight of stairs, two: Dima's knees felt rusty, his muscles turned to water. Ahead, he could hear the light tap of Shura's feet, and the heavy trudge of Vasya in the too-big galoshes he had appropriated after his own had given out. The higher they climbed, the closer the air seemed around them. Halfway up the tenth flight of stairs Dima heard Shura's footsteps stop on the landing. Without thinking, he reached out and grabbed the back of Vasya's jacket, stopping him where he was.

"This is it," Shura said. There was a cheerfulness in his voice that clanged, hollow. A key slipped into a lock, tumblers fell in a clatter, but the door didn't open. "Come on," Shura said. Vasya started to move; Dima held on.

The door swung open with a flood of warmth, and that smell, that gorgeous, sickening smell filled the hallway. "Come on!" Shura said again to Vasya, his voice sharper now. Vasya's body jerked against Dima's grip as Shura grabbed Vasya's arm, tugging it.

"Wait, what are you – " said Vasya, unease in his voice at last, and at the same time Dima heard Shura call behind him, in the same rough tone, any need to ingratiate gone: "Give us a hand here, there's two – "

"*Fuck!*" A tussle; something – someone – fell. "Go, go, go!" Vasya was shouting, but Dima didn't wait to be told. *This is why you count*: the thought came clearly as he took the steps two, three at a time, landed heavy on the landing, reached for the wall and turned. *Twelve steps in the next flight*. Landing, again. Turn, move. Vasya's footsteps behind him, clumsier than his own; behind that someone else, maybe Shura, maybe another, maybe both. *First floor*. Dima's legs felt stronger than they had in months, his lungs blown out like balloons as he ran. Despite the danger and the horror there was something joyous about simply *doing* something, action and reaction; absurdly, he wanted to laugh, or shout in wild exultation. On the final flight now; the cold of the outdoors and its fresh bright smell: Dima felt he could never get enough of it. He'd moved faster than he'd thought possible, his feet hitting the top doorstep as he heard the thunder of footsteps – Vasya's, the others' – on the landing above – and of course that was when he slipped on the treacherous, glassy ice that he was normally so careful of, pitching sideways. There was nothing to grab, and so Dima fell, his hands tucked under his arms for protection, hitting the ground hard. He had perhaps a second to decide: scramble to his feet and keep running, or lie still and hope to escape notice? His back was pressed against the smooth stone of the building's exterior, and his face against ice; shifting a hand, he felt something distinctly: a foot, frozen solid, stripped of its shoes and socks. That was where he was, then, squashed between the building and the pile of ice and debris and corpses that could be found in most courtyards these days. The footsteps were nearly upon him. Dima closed his mouth and held his breath.

Vasya, first: Dima could hear the ugly way in which his breath dragged in and out of his mouth; even before the war he'd never been the fittest of men, relying more on his size and bulk than on agility. For a split second his footsteps slowed, and Dima knew he was looking around for him. *Go, you stupid fucking bastard*, he told Vasya in his head, and Vasya seemed to take heed. "Fuck, fuck!" Vasya spoke the words like a mantra, half sobbing, and ran.

The footsteps behind Dima didn't pause: just one set, now, not the light tap of Shura's feet but a heavier thud, and Dima was viciously glad, hoped that Vasya had hurt Shura, hoped he'd hurt whoever this fucker was too if he managed to catch up with him. The footsteps died away, moving back in the direction of the market, as Dima finally allowed himself to breathe out. Vasya would be safe; he had got far enough by now, Dima was sure, that now nothing could be done to him without anyone else seeing. Dima just had to take care of himself now, heave himself to his feet and get gone before whoever had been pursuing Vasya came back. *Now, then*, he told himself, and squirmed upright, reached for the edge of the steps and hauled himself up. No time to check himself for injury; his legs felt serviceable enough and for the moment that was all that mattered. So where – ? This wasn't a part of town he knew well; he didn't think he had ever been on this street before, and the only way back to the Haymarket that he was sure of was the route that Vasya and his pursuer had taken. Still, if he stayed where he was, he was just as trapped in the courtyard as he would have been in the apartment. *Move*, Dima told himself, *it doesn't matter where, just go. You'll work it out*. And he moved.

It was two hours before he got home and, as Dima had hoped, Vasya was there before him. He didn't need to be able to see to know that Vasya had been crying; it was evident in the raggedness of his voice, and Dima knew by now that, unlikely as it seemed, Vasya had a hair-trigger for tears even at the best of times, despite his tough man exterior. Before Dima had even managed to close the door behind him Vasya was across the room, squeezing him in a rib-cracking bear hug, muttering *oh,*

thank god, oh, thank god over and over again. Vasya's face was pressed into Dima's shoulder; Dima had never quite been able to accept the idea that he was taller than Vasya these days.

"Shut up, you idiot. I'm fine."

Vasya drew back, his hands on Dima's shoulders, and there was a brief moment of silence as Vasya pulled himself together. "What the fuck happened to you, then? You were ahead of me coming down the stairs – I've never seen you move that fast – and then the second I was outside you'd vanished. I would've stayed to look, but…"

"But that would've been even stupider than you usually are. I slipped coming out of the building, fell behind that big pile of…" *Of bodies.* Dima's voice faltered; he forced himself to carry on: "that big pile of snow and ice. And I thought that since I was down, I should just stay down – I assumed anyone chasing us wouldn't hang about to look for me when he had you in his sights."

"You were right. Though once I was back on the street I knew I was all right. There was no way they were going to do anything right out in the open like that." Vasya fell silent, and Dima squirmed a little; this was the silence of scrutiny. "Are you all right?"

Dima shrugged. "More or less. No serious harm done. Anyway – " he changed the subject as quickly as he could, unconvinced of his own ability to keep up a convincing pretence for any length of time. Digging into his coat pockets, he brought out two packets wrapped in paper. "Present!" he said, holding them out to Vasya.

"What– ? Oh, bread, I suppose. I'd forgotten you had the ration cards."

That was a lie and both of them knew it; it wasn't the sort of thing you forgot. Dima let it pass.

"Yes, I stopped off at a bakery on the way home. Open it."

The paper rustled as Vasya did so. For a moment he said nothing. "But this is – this is bigger, surely?"

"They raised the ration today."

"Are you serious?"

"Absolutely. I don't know what's happened – maybe it's something to do with the Ice Road – but the ration's gone up again. They were saying that there might be things other than bread available over the next few days." Dima smiled, remembering. "They were sobbing, the women in the bakery – they were so happy. About three hundred grams of bread."

"So what's this, then?"

Dima heard Vasya shake the other packet. He always rather liked it when Vasya did something like that, made the same sort of physical gesture that he'd make to someone who could see.

"Have a look."

Vasya did so. "Oh fuck, is that – "

"Buckwheat. Yes. One of the women in the bakery exchanged it for me, for one of the bottles of vodka. The other broke in my pocket when I fell – sorry about that."

"I thought I could smell alcohol on you." There was something in Vasya's voice again, something close to tears. It made Dima panic: he was certain he was only a hair's breadth away from bawling himself, and if Vasya were to express any emotion, it'd set him off.

"I know it's not meat, but – "

"Yeah, I don't think I really feel like meat any more."

Nor did Dima. "It should keep us going for a few days, though, shouldn't it? There's a little salt in there too. The woman who exchanged – I think she felt sorry for me. She has a blind brother, evacuated to Moscow. Kept asking me what I was doing, still here in the city."

"What did you tell her?"

"I never know what to say when people ask. Tell them that it never occurred to me to leave? Makes me sound like a fool." Absently, Dima touched his hand to the damp patch on his right thigh, and raised it to his face, grimacing. Vasya was right; he did smell of vodka. "I need to wash."

"I'll put some water on to heat, then."

The door opened and swung closed as Vasya went into the kitchen. Feeling for the edge of his bed, Dima sat, and not a moment too soon: the shaking started again, shuddering its way up from the soles of his feet, rattling his bones against each other. Dima pressed his lips together, crossed his arms over his chest and waited for it to stop: it was unpleasant, embarrassing but no worse than a hundred other physical indignities that had been visited upon him over the past six months. This was the third time, the first being in the bakery when – much to his horror and shame – his legs had gone completely from under him, he'd had to sit on the filthy floor for several minutes and endure the concerned clucking of a small army of elderly ladies before he'd been able to rise; the second time had been halfway between the bakery and the apartment, but at least he had felt it coming that time, and had been able to lean against a wall until it passed. He supposed it was shock, or something like it, but strangely, despite his body's betrayal, he felt quite well in himself – better than he had for days, if not weeks. The bright feeling of purpose that had blazed through him was still there. It was good to know that something had happened, that things could still happen, that there was something more than the grinding boredom of cold and hunger and constant, bone-deep fear.

"Water's on – oh, *shit.*" Vasya was next to him in seconds, his arm tight around Dima's shoulders, holding him upright. As humiliating as it felt for Vasya to see him weakened, Dima had to own that the arm was comforting – and, of course, that Vasya had seen him in worse states.

"Don't worry – it's just the shakes. It'll go in a minute." It was already retreating, even as Dima spoke, the violent tremors fading to a faint, sustained shivering that could have been easily explained away by the chill air. *You could have been killed*, Dima said to himself, cold and clear. He had to ask.

"Vasya – when they opened the door to the apartment, what did you see?"

Vasya huffed out a breath, and his grip on Dima's shoulders loosened. For a moment Dima was sure Vasya wouldn't answer. "Meat," Vasya said at last, his voice bland. "Just – meat. A lot of meat. Too much."

"Do you think it was – "

"I don't – I don't know. There was nothing to show that it was. It could have been beef, or mutton, I suppose. Horse. But where – " Vasya shut his mouth sharply enough that Dima could hear the click of his teeth. "Let's not talk about it, all right?"

"All right."

"Though if I ever see that cocksucker Shura again…"

Dima let him run. Vasya's threats had the comforting quality of a familiar lullaby. He started to undress, slowly shucking off layer after layer – the padded jacket, the knitted sweaters underneath, the shirt below that. Vasya would mock him for what he called Dima's 'obsession' with cleanliness – Dima didn't like to think about how long it had been since Vasya last bathed properly – but there were things, Dima thought, there were *things* that you didn't compromise on, no matter what.

"Fuck, what happened to your shoulder?" Vasya sounded shocked.

"Oh – " Dima raised his hand to touch it, finding Vasya's fingers already there, gentle. "Am I bruised?"

"You're *purple*. From here – " Vasya drew his fingertip from the edge of Dima's shoulder down nearly to his elbow " – to here."

"It must be from when I fell. You know..." Dima demonstrated, hands tucked under his arms. "I can't put my hands out to break my fall. Too risky. Better to damage anything else." He shrugged the shirt all the way off, and Vasya wrapped a blanket around his shoulders as soon as he did so.

"You look fucking freezing," he said roughly. "It's making me cold, just looking at you."

This was Vasya's *I'm sorry*, Dima realised. He was relieved; he wasn't sure if he could cope with the torrent of apologies that Vasya was liable to come out with. "Water's probably heated by now," he said, and then, "you know, Shura didn't ask to see the vodka. I didn't think of it at the time, but why would he make a deal to exchange for something he hadn't even seen?"

"I'm an idiot," Vasya said, with a blustering bravado that made Dima smile.

"No, you're not. But just...just listen to me next time, all right?"

The words hung in the air between them for a moment, then dropped. They wouldn't mention it again.

❧

CHAPTER FIVE

I: 5 March 1942: 7.05am, Leningrad Front

"Do you smell that, boys?" Andrei Ivanovich demanded, breathing deep and slapping his open palms off his greatcoated chest in deliberate theatricality. The crust of bread clutched in one hand – part of their paltry breakfast ration – did not add to his gravitas.

Sasha rolled his eyes. "An intriguing miasma of overfull latrines and improperly buried corpses. The smell of the battlefield. Delightful, Andriusha."

"You have no romance in your soul, Sasha. The smell of *spring* is on the air. It might still be twenty below zero, but when you start to smell that, you know that spring is coming. It's unmistakable."

Trofim agreed, though he couldn't say it. The war had done something to his voice, bringing back its childhood unreliability. Nine out of ten times it worked fine when he had to use it, but that one time when it failed him was crushing in its humiliation, and so the fear of the thing had become worse than the thing itself. The only person he could talk freely in front of these days seemed to be Sasha – not because Trofim didn't stammer in front of him, but because Sasha had such a peculiarly calming way of dealing with it: he didn't mock it, like some did, or ignore it, like others, but just silently acknowledged it, and waited for Trofim to say what he wanted to say. It still surprised him that Sasha seemed to assume that it was worth waiting for.

The Leningrad Front had taken on a grinding monotony that Trofim found comforting and maddening by turns. When they had first been reassigned here, in November, Trofim had found that his proximity to where he had grown up provoked a sense of panicked vertigo that threatened to choke him. From where they had dug in, motionless in the immense, heart-stopping silence of the winter, they could see the outline of the city, and Trofim hadn't been able to stop himself from guessing at the geography that lay beneath the lazy curls of smoke that shells and bombs sent up like flags: how close were they to his parents' flat in Vasilievsky? These days, it was easy enough to blur his focus and see it as just another front, just another battlefield – easier still now that his parents were gone, evacuated over the Ice Road and presumably now with his sister Diana in Moscow, though letters were so hard to come by that Trofim still didn't know for sure. He tried to avoid thinking about it as much as he could.

"In any case," Andrei went on, "I wanted to remind you. They're broadcasting Shostakovich's latest from Kuibyshev this evening. Thought you might want to listen, get some of the others along. The Leningrad Symphony, he's calling it. Good for morale."

Sasha looked at Trofim; Trofim looked away. He had mentioned this to Sasha himself, in a casual, off-hand way designed to carefully convey that he didn't much mind whether or not he listened to the Symphony. It was true that Trofim had never been a great admirer of Shostakovich; his own musical taste tended more towards the eighteenth century, straightforward melody and good, strong parts for the brass section. But since he had heard, back in September, that Shostakovich was working on a symphony for Leningrad, excitement had crawled up the back of his throat whenever he thought of it. "Sure," Sasha said at last. "We'll listen. I've got a couple of bottles of vodka stashed away, too. I'll bring them along."

"Good man," Andrei said, slapping Sasha on the shoulder. As he went to go, Sasha stopped him.

"Trofim's got a good new joke about a *politruk*. Tell him, Trofim."

Oddly, Trofim was never beset by his stutter when telling jokes; it was the certainty of the words, more like reciting a poem, or singing. "There's a company sat around the fire," he began, obediently, "and the *politruk*'s telling jokes. Everyone's laughing, except one man, who's sitting there looking miserable. Doesn't even smile. So the *politruk* starts asking questions. Has he had bad news from home? Is he sick? Has his girl finished with him? No, no, no, nothing wrong. Finally, the *politruk* gets angry, and asks the man straight out: why weren't you laughing? And the man says: this isn't my company. You're not my *politruk*."

The laugh didn't just come from Sasha, but also from the two men sitting closest to them, gnawing on their bread. After a beat, Andrei joined in too, sounding a little strained. "Until this evening, boys."

"Nice one, Trofim," Sasha said, still grinning, when Andrei was out of earshot.

II: 5 March 1942: 11.15am, Kazachy Baths

The opening of the city's baths was an event: the first chance of a proper, thorough clean for months. Dirt had formed a carapace that needed steam and warmth to break through. Lidiya became almost wild at the prospect, sniffing out rumours, chasing them down from the Kazachy Baths to the Mytninskaya and back again, forcing Katya to do likewise. Despite the beguiling idea of cleanliness, the thought of displaying her winter-worn body to the world gave Katya a lurch of revulsion, no matter how much she told herself that other people's bodies would be as ravaged as her own. The thought of showing Lidiya that she minded was even worse.

In the queue, towels flung over their shoulders and soap in their pockets, Lidiya kept up the litany of complaints that Katya had come to understand as a form of self-comfort: Lidiya was lost without something at which to be angry; happily, this was something the war was always able to provide. Katya had learnt to tune it down to a low rumbling mutter, obscurely restful. Nudging Katya with her shoulders, Lidiya spread her hands, palms upwards, displaying the blisters that Katya had seen several times before.

"...and how they *expect* us to shovel ice when our hands are in this sort of state..." She fixed Katya with an irritated eye. "You're lucky you've got a way out of it now."

A way out of it. "What do you mean?"

"The orchestra, of course. You must have heard the announcements on the radio?"

They had started just a few days earlier: the Radio Committee Orchestra was calling for all musicians alive in Leningrad to report. The word *musician*: it didn't fit, slid through Katya's hands like water. Years ago, it was true, she had played with the Radio Committee Orchestra, one of their second violins – before Nadya was born; two small children at home had made her job feel like an indulgence. Lidiya was still looking at her, and Katya knew from bitter experience that Lidiya wouldn't let go of this, wouldn't look away.

"I've heard them. I just – I didn't think it was to do with me."

"Don't be ridiculous."

"I'm not a musician any more."

"Nobody's anything any more." Lidiya waved an illustrative hand over the queue. "Look at these walking dead. You think any of these women are anything more than a bag of bones and an angry stomach, these days?" A woman in front of them turned, scowling; Lidiya continued, regardless. "That's not the point. The point *is* that things are never going to get better if people don't start remembering what they were before."

Katya said nothing. The woman was still glaring at them; Katya raised her eyebrows and offered her a slight, apologetic shrug, to which the woman nodded shortly in acknowledgement and turned away.

"Well?" Lidiya demanded.

"There's nothing to talk about, Lida." Katya heard the hard edge to her own voice, surprising Lidiya into silence. At the front of the queue, two women were admitted; Katya and Lidiya advanced a pace, stood, waited. To Katya's surprise, Lidiya didn't speak, didn't push.

Inside the baths, Katya angled her body away from Lidiya's, trying to hide without looking like she was hiding. Winter had freed her bones and loosened her skin, but below the curve of her ribcage her stomach still pouched, patterned silver from two pregnancies. The lines were a comfort, a reminder that the girls had been real, once, but they flamed red in the wet heat of the bath house and Katya's skin was mottled and slack, barely human. Out of the corner of her eye, she caught Lidiya looking, and Katya's throat closed. She shifted her shoulders in a futile attempt to mask her body.

"I'll do your back," Lidiya said blandly. Katya suffered Lidiya pouring on the water, scrubbing her with soap that smelled thick and dead. "Now me," Lidiya ordered, turning. Half cringing, Katya poured water, lathered and scrubbed. *This is not a person*, she told herself. It made it manageable, and was easier to believe of a body so emaciated. Dark balls of Lidiya's skin came away under Katya's fingers, and her ribs pressed through her back, their shadows like thick lines of charcoal drawn by a bold hand.

"Whatever you thought I was thinking when I was looking at you, you were wrong," Lidiya said. Her tone was casual, her eyes closed. *Keep scrubbing*. Katya moved her arm, up and down, back and forth. She said nothing.

"I had three miscarriages. Before my husband…went away."

Katya scrubbed. Lidiya's words took a long time to register. She remembered, suddenly, acidly, saying to Yevgeny, "Of course the *aktrissulya* wouldn't want to have children, they'd spoil her figure."

"I'm sorry."

Under Katya's hands, Lidiya shrugged. "It happens. That's what I said the first time, anyway. The second time it was harder to believe. As for the third…" For a moment Lidiya was silent. "You think it's impossible for anyone to envy you. I would watch you, sometimes, when you were with your girls. And I would remember the way you looked at me. I couldn't square the two with each other. I couldn't understand how you could look at me like that, when you had what you had."

"The girls are gone." It was routine now, every time they were mentioned. Katya had to remind herself.

"Yes. And here we are. Just the two of us." Lidiya barked a laugh. "It wasn't your fault, you know, what happened. None of it. And so I just wonder when you're going to stop punishing yourself."

They didn't speak for the next half hour. Katya concentrated on the smooth feel of the tepid water running over her hands, the clouds of steam that half-obscured her and almost allowed her to pretend that she was alone. From the darkness voices echoed, quiet and tame. She rinsed, and watched as the grime of the winter, her own filthy skin sluiced away. Beside her Lidiya did likewise, screwing her eyes shut as she rinsed off her hair, shaking it out like a wet dog. They walked out together, blinking at the glare of daylight, and Katya looked down at the skin of her wrists, shocked by its glow and its translucence. When she ran an experimental fingertip across it, its smoothness felt inhuman. Beside her, Lidiya looked as red-eyed and disgruntled as a baby.

"By the way," she said, as casually as if she was resuming a conversation after a lull of only a minute or two, "given that you've had two children and practically starved to death over the winter, I just wanted to say: you have very impressive breasts."

Katya choked, her face splitting into a grin before she had time to think about it. Considering and discarding responses, she tried a shrug, Lidiya-style, and it seemed to fit. "Thanks."

III: 5 March 1942: 5.30pm, Ulitsa Marata

"I wish you'd play something other than those bloody exercises, Dima." Vasya sounded a little plaintive. Dima lowered his bow, the muscles across his shoulders and down his arms giving off shivering sparks of pain. His hands were shaking badly, and the familiar surge of terror came: that he would damage the Guarneri, that he would drop it. Barely trusting himself to breathe, he set the violin down on the bed, the bow beside it. He would clean it and put it away when he felt more certain of himself.

"The exercises are important," he told Vasya. He knew Vasya didn't really care, but Dima wanted to explain anyway. "You wouldn't win a single boxing match if you didn't practise sparring, right? This is the same."

"No poor bastard has to watch me sparring," Vasya said.

"And you don't have to listen to me practising, either," Dima said, a little acidly. He had never practised at home before the Blockade; one of the advantages of his erstwhile job as an accompanist in a ballet school was that they let him use the studios out of hours as much as he wanted. The walls of the communal apartment were paper-thin, and Dima hated the idea of disturbing people. Now, there wasn't anyone left but him and Vasya, and Vasya could damn well put up with it. He did sympathise, though, more than Vasya would have guessed. For weeks, when the winter had been at its worst, Dima hadn't been able to lift his violin at all, and now, he meted out his strength, knowing to the minute how much he would be permitted. Although he longed to play music, real music, he knew that the only sensible thing to do with the limited resources allowed him was to concentrate on building his technique back up from the winter's depredations. He had managed thirty-five minutes today, up five minutes from the day before – a small triumph that made him grin. Perhaps later, when the shaking had stopped, he might treat himself to a tune.

From Vasya's bed came the unmistakable sounds of him heaving himself to his feet, hunting in his pockets for his keys. "I should head off," he said. "You sure you don't want to come?"

"I'm all right here, thanks."

"Pasha'll miss you."

"I doubt it," Dima said, grinning. It was true and it wasn't, he knew. "You're just going to sit around drinking and smoking and talking about people I don't know, as usual. Besides..." He gestured in the approximate direction of the radio.

"Pasha'll probably want to listen too," Vasya said. "We could all – "

"You'll hate it," Dima said. "I don't want to have to listen to you complaining about it. I'd probably deck you."

Vasya laughed, the same bright, hoarse *ha* that he had made before the war. It gladdened Dima to hear it. A lot gladdened Dima these days: the slightly silken feel of the air as it softened into spring; the fact that Vasya had the strength to walk the kilometre to Pasha's without needing Dima to lean on; the increased rations, the better quality of the bread, the returning strength that straightened and tautened his body. There was nothing like near-death, Dima thought, to reinvigorate a person.

"Bye, then," Vasya said, squeezing Dima's shoulder as he passed on his way to the door. That was another pleasing thing: that farewells no longer had that leaden feeling that they had had when things were at their worst; that the assumption had returned that people would see each other again. The door clicked and slammed, and Vasya's footsteps faded – slower than they had been before the Blockade, but faster than they had been a month ago, even a week. Dima smiled to himself. He touched his watch – still an hour to go yet, but Dima reached for the table where the radio receiver stood and flicked it on, just in case. The thought of missing it filled him with a prickling anxiety. Over the radio came the quiet, crackling sound of Olga Bergholz, her slight hesitation before she spoke the words that Dima could reel off by heart now, having heard them so many times during the winter: *Can I endure it? Can I bear it? / You'll bear it. You'll last out. You will.* They were as soothing as a fairy tale. He might, he thought, treat himself to a tiny glass of Vasya's vodka while he listened to the Symphony. It seemed appropriate. Feeling for the bottle and glass that he knew lay beside Vasya's bed, Dima took them to the kitchen, washed all traces of stickiness off the glass with water from the pail, and dried it fastidiously. The pour of the vodka had a creamy sound to it, and the smell of it burned the back of Dima's throat. He wasn't going to start enjoying drinking any time soon, but it was the best way he could think of to mark an occasion.

IV: 5 March 1942: 7.20pm, Leningrad Front

For something that Trofim had wanted to listen to, he seemed to be expending an absurd amount of energy on not listening to it. From the very start of the opening movement, that relentless, martial melody, Trofim had felt something inside him splinter. This was the first time he had listened to music in months – *serious* music, the sort of music that might make you feel something. He wasn't sure that he could bear it.

Instead, he studied the faces of the men crammed into Andrei's dugout, clustered around the small radio that sat on his desk. Andrei himself seemed to be more focussed on the vodka than on the music, but the rest of the faces seemed rapt, silent, turned like flowers towards the pool of light spilling from Andrei's lamp. Sasha was across the other side of the room, sat next to Viktor, whose mouth was slightly agape, as if that would aid his hearing. Trofim remembered Viktor from when they'd first met him, back in that *izba* in the middle of the forest, caked in grime and seemingly incapable of stringing together a sentence without a single profanity. He had latched onto Sasha immediately, and Trofim had never been able to complain about his omnipresence when he knew he had done exactly the same thing. He was sometimes regretful, however, that the price of Sasha's friendship was having to put up with the rest of Sasha's friends.

He had nearly made it through the first movement. Trofim allowed himself to relax, just a little, before he realised what a mistake that was. As soon as he stopped trying not to listen, the music came flooding in – that first motif again, but different now, less warlike, more pastoral, gentle, strings and woodwinds, and Trofim realised, suddenly, like a swoon, that he was on the verge of weeping. He had to get out, he had to get outside. Leaving his glass of vodka on the dirt floor, he muttered something deliberately incomprehensible, stepped over and past the men huddled on the ground, and shouldered his way through the heavy blanket that stood in for a door. Outside, he leaned against the earth wall and took stock of himself. From the middle distance came the clamour of gunfire, but other than that the evening was remarkably quiet. It felt as if something was swelling somewhere behind Trofim's lungs, crushing the rest of him into pieces: the sensation was intense and intolerable. Trofim put his hands over his face, opening his eyes and concentrating on the red blurs where the light slipped in through his fingers. He wasn't crying so much as just leaking, a seemingly inexhaustible supply of salt water. From behind him he could hear the muffled hum of the music, the clink of glass, a low tumble of voices.

The curtain ruffled; without looking, Trofim knew that it would be Sasha emerging. Trofim dropped his hands, and as he unobtrusively blotted at his face, Sasha stood at a careful distance, far enough away that both of them could pretend Trofim's weakness went unwitnessed.

"Here," Sasha said at last, holding out Trofim's discarded vodka in one hand and a lit Belomor in the other. Trofim took both, grateful and greedy. Above them, the sky was clear, the wind cold and sharp as a whip. The last light was being wrung out of the day.

"What do you think of it?" Trofim asked. His voice sounded clear enough, steady enough to pass muster.

"Well. I don't know much about music – "

"You don't need to know anything about music to know what you like."

Sasha smiled, conceding the point. "It's – powerful. Not comfortable to listen to. But it sounds like it means something."

Trofim nodded. He took a slug of the vodka and a drag on the cigarette, masochistically revelling in the doubled burn.

"You miss it," Sasha said. It wasn't a question.

Trofim nodded again. It was more complicated than that, but distance made it simpler. He hadn't touched a trumpet in months, now, not since his own had been lost or stolen during that desperate, frantic retreat; not since they had been reassigned to the Leningrad Front and he had chosen to sign back on as an ordinary rifleman. He had thought, then, *what is the point of music, when things are like this?* He still didn't know. He still woke up almost every morning with his finger against the dip in his upper lip, touching the callus that was slowly softening there. In the gathering darkness Trofim could feel Sasha's keen eyes on his face; he had heard him say, once, to Andrei, *I don't know why anyone would be here if they could be anywhere else*, something that Andrei had responded to with sputtering justifications.

"What would you have done, if you hadn't joined the army?" Trofim asked.

Sasha gave a short laugh. "I expect I would've been a criminal. Or dead. Or in the Gulag." He twitched one shoulder in a sketch of a shrug. "I never had any education after I was eleven or so. Can read and write and add up, and not much else. There weren't a lot of options."

Trofim couldn't help conjuring up the question Sasha didn't ask, had never asked. He was adept, usually, at putting it out of his mind, but sometimes that alternate life dropped into his head, fully formed: graduating from the Conservatoire; a normal orchestra rather than a military band; maybe a wife; maybe, by now, even a family. Everything he refused to allow himself to want; he felt the longing would double him over.

Sasha's hand touched his shoulder. "Let's go back inside," he said. "The second movement will be starting."

V: 5 March 1942: 8.00pm, Ulitsa Pravda

Over the winter, they had all stopped locking their doors. Although nominally they still lived separately – Ilya on the top floor, Katya in the middle and Lidiya with the children on the ground floor – since they had started pooling food in October or November, meals had been taken communally in Katya's kitchen, which Lidiya claimed was the best-equipped – and more often than not since January, Lidiya and the children had been bedding down in Katya's living room, Lidiya claiming it was warmer than downstairs. Katya didn't mind as much as she thought she would've, though she was blackly amused at having stumbled into the sort of communal apartment that Yevgeny's influence had always allowed her to guiltily avoid.

She had minded this evening, though, when Lidiya and Ilya and the children barged into her living room and switched on the radio. "The Symphony," Lidiya had said in explanation.

"You don't even like music," Katya pointed out.

Lidiya shrugged. "True enough. But this is different."

"What if I don't want to listen?"

"But we *always* listen to the radio in Auntie Katya's apartment, don't we, Masha?" Lidiya was shameless. "Anyway, if you don't want to listen you've got a whole other room to sit in. We'll tell you when it's over."

Lidiya could be relentless, but she also had a cunning cleverness of her own, and she always seemed to know when to stop pushing. She didn't ask Katya why she didn't want to listen; she didn't cajole, and she didn't turn up the volume so that Katya was blasted by it against her will. Katya sat alone on her bed, hearing the faint hum of the strings and the patter of the drums curling under her door. She wanted to put her ear to the door, to try and hear more. She wouldn't let herself.

Before the winter, Katya had put her violin away, wrapped in an old coat of Tanya's, pushed to the back of a shelf. She had pushed the thought of it back, too, down inside herself, further down even than the girls, tucked behind her heart. She wasn't punishing herself, she was sure that Lidiya had been wrong about that – it was just that the violin was an access to joy that she didn't deserve.

In the dim light of her bedroom, the clean skin at Katya's wrists kindled and glowed when she reached for the bundle on the shelf. She didn't think she could have brought herself to touch it before she had washed. Tanya's coat: it still held the scent of her, faintly, probably because it had been worn so often; the fresh smell of soap, pencil shavings and the tang of snow. The last time Tanya had worn it, the start of the previous winter, her arms had poked three inches past the ends of the sleeves, and Katya had put it away for Nadya to grow into.

She laid the bundle on the bed and knelt beside it, unwrapping the cloth, exposing the case. There had been a time when her fingers would nag her to play, when music would erupt inside her and she couldn't rest until she had given it voice. Then came the war and then the winter, when the thought of music had made her feel so fragile, as if she could crack wide open with the bitter beauty of it. In the coldest months there had been a group of musicians in an apartment on Volodarskogo Prospekt; they would play together, the tattered ends of their melodies reaching the streets, and Katya had started to walk a block out of her way just to avoid hearing them. She had felt sick and glad when Lidiya had told her that they had fallen silent.

She opened the case. The felt bed on which the violin lay was deep blue and lustrous, a colour that Katya hadn't seen for such a long time, something that she could barely have imagined with her eyes closed. The instrument itself was the colour of warm honey. Katya lowered her head, her nose close to the strings, and breathed in the piny scent of rosin. Close up, she could see the shower of dust that lay under the strings, and the calligraphic loops of the wood grain under the thick layer of varnish. It was a dream, this artefact, something so beautiful and so self-indulgent. Katya picked up the violin, easing it free of the case. She was afraid to touch it. It felt like something living, too precious, needing care that she was unable to give it. Her heart crashed in her chest and her hands trembled; how could it be that she had once handled it so easily, almost as if it were part of her own body? When she felt calm enough, Katya cradled the scroll of the violin, running her hand over the pegs. She took the bow in her fingertips, tightening the horse hair until it was ready to play. Attaching the chin rest, she lifted the violin and closed her eyes. The orchestral opening of the andante movement of Tchaikovsky's D major violin concerto: it came from somewhere inside her, but not inside her head; somewhere deeper, behind her ribs, lodged between her lungs, throbbing with every breath. Katya raised her right hand, holding her bow. It did not touch the strings. The fingers of her left hand started to move; she heard the *tap-tap* sound of them clicking against the fingerboard, while the melody swelled inside her, riding on her blood, her pulse the surest metronome she knew. It was the sort of piece that she had always felt slightly ashamed of liking, over-emotional and slushy; the crisp, clean precision of the baroque was more pleasing, the feeling that she was picking up a challenge that had been thrown down. Yet at that moment she couldn't imagine ever again playing something that hadn't been composed by a Russian.

As suddenly as it had started, the music fell away, and Katya was left feeling foolish, holding an instrument she didn't understand, her body in a position she barely recognised. Her arms ached, and she moved quickly to lay down the violin and bow before she dropped them. She had been stupid, she knew; months of starvation had left her so depleted that any unnecessary movement could exhaust her to the core. To pick up the violin was one thing, but to pretend to play? As soon as she felt safe to do so, she put the violin back in its case, careful to wipe the strings clean of rosin, although the bow hadn't touched them. *Now put it back on the shelf*, Katya told herself. *Put it back*. She didn't move. From outside her bedroom door, from the radio set and from Kuibyshev, there came the distinct sound of applause.

VI: 5 March 1942: 8.30pm, Ulitsa Marata

Dima took the smallest possible sip of his vodka, barely enough to dampen his lips, and he had the pleasing idea that it had somehow evaporated before it hit his gullet. He laid his head on the table, breathed in its scent of wood and the sweetness of old, spilled alcohol. The radio receiver was inches away from his head, and he fancied that its vibrations were stirring his hair. He couldn't have listened to this with Vasya here; he couldn't have borne his questions and his comments. There were times when you just needed to be quiet in your own head. Dima imagined Shostakovich conducting his own Symphony, the Symphony that he had written for the city where he had grown up, the city that Dima had pushed his way into and declared as his own. When he had first come here, he had dreamed of meeting Shostakovich, perhaps in the Conservatoire, to which in these dreams Dima had miraculously been granted access; perhaps in the street, identified by some uncanny sixth sense. Dima had dreamed of shaking his hand, of finding the words that he needed to make the man understand how important his music was to him. Perhaps they would attend a football match together. Perhaps they would become friends. Perhaps Shostakovich would be beguiled by their twin names, and perhaps his own poor sight would lend him sympathy for Dima's situation. Perhaps he would use his influence to get Dima accepted in the place he most wanted to go – a proper orchestra. Dima had been younger then, sixteen or seventeen, and as he'd got older he'd recognised those imaginings as the child's dreams they were. But there was still a place at the core of him that believed in this connection he had invented out of nothing. There was Kuibyshev, an orchestra, a rostrum, a man in a tailcoat and a pair of thick spectacles, and there was Dima, his cheek against warm pine and his body flooded with music, and there was something running back and forth between the two, a current that was invisible and intangible but no less powerful for that. As the strings came soaring out of the darkness at the start of the third movement, Dima's heart twisted inside him and he felt a happiness that made him ache. Against the scarred surface of the table, his fingers began to move.

VII: 20 March 1942: Evening, Leningrad Front

Sasha, Trofim knew, had a way of arranging things. After the retreat, he had arranged for Trofim and Viktor to be reassigned to the same unit as him, and ever since then he had constantly managed to arrange the little things that mattered most – slightly increased rations, a bottle of vodka or of cognac, Andrei's lenience in his lectures and his lessons. That Sasha had managed to arrange for a trumpet should have been a surprise in nothing but scale, and yet still Trofim couldn't quite manage to grasp it.

"Present," Sasha said blandly, handing over the case.

Not daring to believe it, Trofim opened it up. The trumpet that was lying inside was greenish, tarnished, and the dank smell of mildew rose up from the case's felt lining.

"It's not in the best condition," Sasha said, "but I assumed you'd know how to bring it back to life."

"I – " Trofim couldn't string together the words. He lifted up the instrument, let the light play off its dulled gleam. He didn't dare put it to his lips. "How did you – ?"

He expected Sasha to prevaricate, but instead Sasha looked a little embarrassed. "I've been asking around for a while. Someone told me that one of the signalmen might have one of these. He was friends with a trumpeter in one of the military bands who died of dysentery over the winter. I persuaded him to hand it over." He shrugged. "I'm sorry I didn't follow it up before now. Just…other things kept getting in the way, a bit, over the winter. But I did promise you, back when we first met. Last night reminded me."

Vivaldi's Concerto for Two Trumpets in C Major was singing in Trofim's head – always a favourite, for times of triumph. He knew he didn't have the breath for it, and he knew that this trumpet would take some coaxing to get anywhere near the golden sound he wanted. He touched his finger to his top lip. "Thank you," he said to Sasha, clear and quiet.

"Well," Sasha said. Gratitude always seemed to make him uncomfortable. He turned to go, and then half-turned back, speaking to Trofim over his shoulder. "By the way. Word is that they're calling up anyone in the army with musical training to reinforce the Radio Committee Orchestra. Rehearsals to start in early April. They're planning to do a performance of Shostakovich's Leningrad Symphony in the city, sometime in the summer. So I signed you up."

"But – " *I'm not in a military band any more*, Trofim said in his head. The words wouldn't come. There was something knotted under his breastbone and the feel of it changed with each heartbeat: pleasure, anger, shame. Playing for himself was one thing; playing publicly was quite another – and although he had never gone so far as to say aloud that he wasn't a musician any more, he'd thought he'd made it clear that his hands, now, were shaped for a rifle and not for a trumpet. He was angry that Sasha had failed to understand this, and ashamed that he hadn't been able to make it clearer – and there, too, was that knife blade of pleasure, so sharp that it was near painful, his body remembering with eagerness how it would feel to play.

CHAPTER SIX

I: 5 April 1942

It had started to creep back in, the music, on the quickening of blood and the warmer air. Katya had awoken that morning with her wrists aching, a sure sign she had been playing in her sleep. As she prepared her morning tea, she caught herself humming – but she hadn't exactly intended to come to the rehearsal. Even when she had picked up her violin and left the apartment, making sure that Lidiya didn't see her go, she couldn't have said for sure that she was going to the Radio House. Perhaps she would just walk, perhaps she would sit somewhere for a few minutes, her violin on her bony lap, breathing in the soft spring air, and then go back home again.

And arriving at the Radio House after all, Katya was suddenly certain that she had made a mistake: the wrong place, or the wrong day. She recognised no one in that collection of matchstick men, hollow-eyed, some faces still blackened by soot. One or two of the women were made up garishly, clad in bizarre selections of items that seemed to have been flung on, haphazard. And then, with a shudder, Katya caught the eye of Gennady Maksimovich and everything slipped into focus. These were people whom she knew. Familiarity had softened the changes the winter had wrought in Lidiya and Ilya, whereas Katya had seen none of these musicians since the start of the Blockade. Her own foolishness nauseated her: the idea of an orchestra had been something rarefied, beautiful, but reality made it impossible. These people weren't musicians; they were refugees. If it hadn't taken all her strength to get to the Radio House in the first place, she would have turned tail and fled.

It takes time to recognise someone half-starved, to furnish the bare lines of skull and jaw with flesh. When the man next to her, violin in hand, turned to greet her, it took Katya a long, silent moment before his name bloomed in her head.

"Daniil Aaronovich?"

A mouth on a death's head: it opened and gave a mirthless chuckle. "Don't sound so disbelieving. You're not looking yourself, either."

"I know, of course. I'm sorry."

"You want to play, then?"

Katya shrugged. "What else is there to do?"

"The rations will be better. They say that they will feed us in the cafeteria every day after rehearsals. There was a time when I would have said I only cared about the music. Now I only care about food. I would play anything for the sake of a bit of food."

"Where are the others?" Katya asked. One by one, the other musicians were starting to tremble into focus, and Katya could pick out the people she had known, projecting smiles and swaggers and personalities onto the dead who were standing around her. The conductor, Karl Ilych Eliasberg, looking as if he could fit another of himself inside the oversized jacket he was wearing, wearily counted heads. Of an orchestra of a hundred people, there were fewer than twenty there.

"You know where they are. In the cemeteries, like everyone else." Daniil raised a grimy hand, fingers extended. "Galina Andreyovna died at the start of the war. Her apartment block was one of the first hit. Mischa Ribin starved over the winter, and his wife, Anna. Some of us got together to check on them. We would walk across the city every day, to make sure that they were still alive." He shrugged. "But attention doesn't keep someone alive." He looked into Katya's face. "What about you? Where have you been? Did your family…"

"We were evacuated," Katya said quickly, before he could ask. His face twisted with a mixture of envy and pity for those who had got out, those who had been too weak to stay. It angered her. "We were on one of the trains at Lychkovo," she said, "when the Fascists attacked. Yevgeny was killed. I haven't seen the girls since." That was as much as she could say about it.

"I'm sorry."

Katya envied Daniil's bitterness, a shield. She took the opportunity to try it out for herself. "I'm not the only one to have lost someone."

"At least I never had anyone much to lose. No wife or children, in any case."

"Your parents?" Katya recalled them vaguely: a thin, fretful mother and an expansive, genial father who welcomed his son's musician friends into the apartment to rehearse. Or was he also a musician? Katya couldn't remember. Everything was tangled.

"They went to my sister in Sverdlovsk almost as soon as it all started. They were terrified, tried to make me go with them, said Leningrad was too close to the border…you hear about what's been happening since the Fascists invaded. In Dubno, in Vilna – you know, my family's from near Dubno, my parents only came to Leningrad when I was a child. All their brothers and sisters are still there. Were. You think: how lucky we left. And then: this is lucky?"

"Better to be alive," Katya said, because it was what you were supposed to say. She wasn't sure she believed it. Daniil looked unconvinced.

"Perhaps. Or perhaps better a quick death than a slow one."

They fell silent. Katya couldn't remember the last time she'd had such a lengthy conversation with someone outside her apartment. Across the room, a woman sat down abruptly on the floor, her head between her knees, and Katya remembered Marina Davidovna from *before*, a friend of Natasha's from the Conservatoire with an enviable figure, a round, sweet face, and a way of lowering her eyelashes and looking at men from underneath them. Katya had been jealous of her, then, and now all she could feel was an amorphous sense of pity, for Marina and for Daniil and for all of them.

"I heard he didn't want to be evacuated, Dmitri Dmitriyevich," Daniil said. That was something Katya remembered clearly: Daniil's casual use of Shostakovich's name, as if the two of them were friends, although as far as she knew they were barely acquainted. "A friend of mine was with him in the Conservatoire's fire-fighting brigade, until they made him leave. Strange, isn't it, that the first performance was to a group of people who've probably never seen the city? And now they want to do it here. They're talking about a series of concerts over the summer, but it's obvious that the Symphony is what it's all about."

"It's impossible," Katya said flatly. She was sure of it, even though it was the very reason she had come here. "There are far too few of us, and we're much too weak. We need four times the numbers, even assuming anyone here can play for more than a minute or two."

Daniil nodded. "I know, of course. And if *we're* saying this, what about the brass players, and the woodwinds? No one has the breath to play for five minutes, let alone for four movements. But I'll pretend it's possible for the sake of the food."

It was a rehearsal in nothing but name. Most of the musicians were exhausted just from the walk to the Radio House; they lacked the strength to play, and Karl Ilych could not stand up for long enough to conduct. Katya listened with a sense of almost amused disbelief as Karl Ilych urged them to round up any musicians they knew were left in the city; he himself had been to Smolny to persuade them to release musically trained soldiers from the Leningrad Front. What was this peculiar collusion that music could still be possible, let alone a performance of the Symphony? This would be nothing more than physical labour, as simple and heartless as digging a trench. Katya should give it up, they all should; the extra rations couldn't be worth how much more energy they would waste in trying to scratch music out of silence. And yet there it was, that tingle in her fingertips and her palms, that looseness in her wrists. Her body wanted to play.

~

The boy who stood outside the Radio House was blind. It only became clear to Katya in the way he turned his face to follow sounds; the blankness in his eyes was not too different from the blankness on the faces of the starving. Leningrad was a city of the blind, a city of the dead. This boy was different, though. There was life in his face. In his right hand he held a stick, and in his left a violin case.

Katya nearly walked straight past him when he reached for her arm. You couldn't walk anywhere in the city these days without someone begging for help that was impossible to give. It wasn't worth the guilt of stopping to hear what they were asking: for bread, for a shoulder to lean on. But although the boy was thin to the point of emaciation, he looked healthier than most. The spring was better than the winter, it was true, but just three days ago Katya had seen a man sit down on a bridge, close his eyes, and die, as if it was a decision. This boy did not look like him.

"Have you come from the rehearsal?" the boy asked. He spoke quietly, as if he didn't want anyone to overhear.

"It was hardly a rehearsal. Barely anyone had the strength to hold their instruments, let alone play," Katya said. "But yes, I was there."

"Were there many of you?"

"Perhaps fifteen, twenty at the most. Most are dead, or close to it. Some evacuated, some at the Front." Katya looked down at the violin case in the boy's hand. "Did you come here to play?"

The boy smiled, sheepish. "I was too nervous to come inside. I heard people speaking, and it sounded as if everyone knew each other. I thought perhaps they wouldn't need me, that I wouldn't be welcome."

"We need everyone we can get," Katya said. The 'we' had come out unbidden. "Have you…have you played in orchestras before?"

"Of course. I played in the Orchestra for the Blind before the war, but no one is left, now. Most were evacuated. I was too stubborn, or too stupid. And then I kept hearing the calls on the radio, about the rehearsal today. My friend told me that there were posters, too, asking musicians to report. I've always wanted to play in a real orchestra, and I wondered if they would be desperate enough to take me now."

The Orchestra for the Blind: Katya had never heard of it. That unfamiliar prickle behind her breastbone – that was curiosity, she realised. It had been months since she had felt it. "How do you follow a conductor, if you can't see?" Perhaps it was wrong to speak so bluntly, but tact took energy.

"In the Orchestra for the Blind, the conductor has a stick that he bangs on the ground, and we follow the beat." The boy grimaced. "It's far from ideal, of course, and I wouldn't pretend that the musical standards are particularly high. But I've practised playing with sighted musicians, for chamber music. You've probably never listened closely enough to know – you don't need to – but you can tell when someone's about to start playing. The way that they breathe changes. You can hear them sit up straight. As soon as the conductor lifts his baton, the whole orchestra seems to hush. That's how I know when it's time to start." He sighed a little. "My friend's going to kill me, that I didn't get up the guts to go inside. But next time – "

"Tomorrow, same time," Katya supplied. Karl Ilych had said to spread the word, after all. The boy nodded, decisive.

"All right. I'll be there." With a swift grin, he tucked his stick under his arm and extended a hand in Katya's approximate direction. "I'm sorry, I should introduce myself. I'm Dima. Well, Dmitri Aleksandrovich Kaverin, but…Dima."

Some impulse made Katya remove her glove before putting her hand into his. His palm was dry and warm. "Ekaterina Yefimovna Kiryanova. Katya." Uncertain, she wasn't sure whether to offer would be insulting or appreciated. "Do you – do you need any help getting anywhere? I could perhaps…"

Dima's smile broadened. "I don't *need* any help, but it would be nice to have some company." He turned, gestured south down Nevsky Prospekt. "I'm going this way."

"So am I."

The silence that fell as they walked was surprisingly easy. Knowing that he could not see her staring, Katya watched Dima with naked fascination. He seemed to negotiate the world he couldn't see with such facility, swiping his stick along the pavements and ghosting his fingertips along the walls of buildings. He had been right: he didn't need her help, and slowly Katya allowed herself to relax, dropping the arm she had been ready to offer.

"Have you always been…?" she began, and then stopped, unsure whether *blind* was a word that it was polite to use.

"Blind, you mean?" Dima asked. His tone was light. Katya was stung with embarrassment.

"Yes. Sorry, I shouldn't have asked."

"It's all right to ask. Makes it easier for me to ask you personal questions back." He smiled in a way that seemed oddly open to interpretation. Katya, unsure if he was teasing, felt a blush rise as high as her collarbones, her jawline, waiting to see if it needed to continue as far as her cheeks.

"But no, I wasn't born blind. I had a bad case of measles when I was two and a half, that's when I lost my sight."

"I'm sorry," said Katya, but Dima shook his head.

"Don't be. As far as I'm concerned I've never been any other way; I don't know what I'm missing, really."

"Don't you – don't you remember seeing anything, then?"

"I have one memory," Dima said. He stopped short, turning his face towards her. At another time, Katya would have worried that they looked strange, the wrecked woman and the young, animated boy, standing stock still in the middle of the pavement. Dima spoke with his hands, even encumbered as they were with his stick and violin case, making every sentence a small performance. Katya couldn't stop watching him. Every time she told herself to look away, to examine instead the texture of the filthy snow under her feet or the shamefully ragged state of her own fingernails, her eyes were drawn back to his face, his hands. They were long and almost absurdly elegant, the fingers that protruded from his tattered cuffs, the nails clipped short and kept scrupulously clean. Katya wondered why he didn't wear gloves, and then remembered the way he used his fingertips to find his way. Every time he started to speak Katya was taken aback. Her thoughts were so loud in her head that she kept forgetting that Dima was real in front of her. He was so alive that he seemed half-imaginary, impossible, a fever dream.

"I only remember one thing, from before I went blind," he said, smiling as if his blindness was a joke he was playing on the rest of the world. "It's…a box. A warm-coloured box." He shrugged, sketching a shape with his hands. "When I told my brother about it, he said he thought it was the cupboard that was beside our bed when I was a little boy, a wooden cabinet where our mother used to store our clothes."

"That's all you can remember?"

"You would think it would be more than that, wouldn't you? Or at least if I only got one memory, it would be something more meaningful. I don't know, like a sunset, or my mother's face." Dima laughed. Katya wasn't quite sure what he was laughing at, but she felt her chest tremble in sympathetic amusement, although the laugh didn't quite make it out of her mouth. "But perhaps it was the last thing I saw before I went blind. That's what I think. I must have spent a lot of time in bed when I was ill, mustn't I, maybe lying on my side, staring at the cupboard? No wonder I remember it."

They walked on. Past the Anichkov Bridge, Dima tucked his stick under his arm, shifting his violin case to his other hand.

"Don't you need it?" Katya asked, surprised.

"Not really. I only carry it around so that kind ladies will feel sorry for me and offer to walk me home." He was grinning, but Katya felt tripped up, wrong-footed.

"Are you making fun of me?" she asked. As soon as the words were out she could tell how childish they had sounded.

Dima started. There was an expression on his face that Katya couldn't begin to make sense of. For a moment he said nothing. "I'm not making fun of you," he said, mildly, at last. "I'm making fun of myself, really. No, I don't need the stick from here. I know these streets very well. I only take it with me when I'm going somewhere a little less familiar. To stop me from tumbling into the Fontanka." He gestured with the arm that was holding his violin. "I live just down there, Ulitsa Marata."

"I'm in the other direction," Katya said. She felt surprisingly regretful. There was something sustaining about Dima. It seemed easier to walk when he was beside her. Her knees ached naggingly, and she realised that she had not noticed the pain since they had left the Radio House together.

Dima looked a little regretful himself. "Ah, I'm sorry. I should never have given it away that I don't really need your help to get me home." He stretched out a hand, and Katya shook it. "It was very nice to meet you, Katya. If you see me loitering outside the Radio House tomorrow, give me a kick and make me come inside, all right?"

"All right," Katya agreed. Her smile felt strange and unpractised.

Dima turned to go. Katya did likewise, then turned back. She watched Dima making his way down the street, deftly skirting the holes in the road. Every so often he would stretch out his left hand and touch, very lightly, the buildings that lined the pavement, but aside from that quirk, he walked with such confidence and assurance that Katya felt sure a casual observer would be hard-pressed to tell that he was blind. He had only gone ten or fifteen metres before he turned, smiling.

"I know you're still there," he called.

Katya froze. For a moment she was sufficiently flustered that she considered just walking away, but Dima had already started back towards her, and it would have felt too cruel to flee from a blind man.

"What – how did you know?"

He shrugged. "I'm good at being blind. With a bit of practise you can pick up on all sorts of things. Movement, and stillness." He waved a hand behind his back. "I just felt – there was stillness there, behind me. I knew you hadn't gone. Were you waiting to see if I was going to totter into the road? Now that the trolleybuses aren't running it's not so dangerous." He held out his arm to her. "But if you're so worried about me, you can walk me home after all."

Half an hour later, Katya let herself into the apartment building. Her legs were shaking; she had gone twenty minutes out of her way to walk Dima to his door, and she couldn't understand it at all; it wasn't as though she could spare the energy. She tried to tread quietly, but she could never be quiet enough: Lidiya stuck her head out of her apartment as Katya passed. "So?" she demanded, without preamble.

"So, what?"

"So, did you go?"

Lidiya's arms were wet to the elbows, dripping onto the hallway floor. "I'm bathing Serezha," Lidiya explained. "Come in and talk to me while I finish."

Resistance was useless; Katya put her violin down by the door and did as Lidiya commanded. In the bathroom, Lidiya knelt by the bath, and Katya sat on the toilet seat. She gave a half smile to Serezha, and then looked away: she hated to see him naked, the way that all his bones looked bundled together under the tautness of his skin. It was painful to watch; Katya was amazed that Lidiya, who was much closer to Serezha than she was, could bear it with such equanimity.

"Are you going to answer me?" Lidiya asked over her shoulder. She carefully soaped between Serezha's toes, as he looked down, silent. His lack of energy was frightening: a tiny old man.

"Yes, I went," Katya said, goaded.

"And?"

"And I'll go back tomorrow."

"Well, then!" Lidiya sounded pleased. Rinsing the suds off Serezha, she splashed a little water at his face, which raised a feeble giggle. As she let out the plug, he splashed her back. Katya passed her a towel, and Lidiya dried Serezha as quickly as possible: the room was icy, and he was shivering. Together, they manhandled Serezha into the clothes that Lidiya had laid out on the edge of the basin – trousers, thick woollen socks, a man's shirt that was probably one of his father's, and a knitted jumper that Katya recognised as an old one of Tanya's. She must have given it to Elena the previous winter, when Tanya had outgrown it, to be passed back for Nadya in due course. For a moment, Katya couldn't bring herself to loosen her fingers, but she forced herself to put the jumper into Lidiya's outstretched hand.

"Right, you're done," Lidiya told Serezha. He limped out of the bathroom, his gait unsteady, as Lidiya watched, frowning. "I'm worried about him," she told Katya. "He's not putting on weight fast enough, now that the rations are increasing. Masha's already so much better than she was over the winter, but he…"

She turned towards Katya as if intending to go on, but catching sight of Katya's expression, Lidiya raised her eyebrows sharply. She took Katya's face in her hands and gazed into it, as Katya, confused, tried to pull away.

"Lida – stop it! What are you doing?"

"There's light in your face," Lidiya said. She looked at Katya for another long moment before releasing her. "There's light in your face for the first time since August. If this is what music does for you, for god's sake keep doing it."

II: 6 April 1942

At that moment, Katya thought it was a good thing that Dima was blind, because he couldn't see that everyone watching him was expecting him to fail. No one else had needed any sort of audition to join the orchestra; most of them had known one another for years, knew each other's levels of musical competence, and the orchestra was desperate enough for musicians that even those whose skills were less than ideal were being welcomed with open arms. Dima was a different matter. He claimed to have led the first violins in the Leningrad Orchestra for the Blind, but Katya had seen the scepticism on the faces around her and knew that no one had heard of it any more than she had. Katya felt sorry for him, sympathy mixed with a half-acknowledged twinge of fondness. The winter had drained so many people of life, but Katya had started to notice that some people seemed to have deeper wells of vitality than others. On the street, they might be as grey and thin and drawn as anyone else, but something in them caused them to burn slightly more brightly. Lidiya was like this, and so was Dima. There was something buoyant in him, something that tugged inescapably upwards.

They had left it to Gennady Maksimovich, the leader of the second violins, to decide Dima's fate; the first violins were considered out of the question. Katya knew Genya from her days in the orchestra: a kind, no-nonsense man. She had a sense that he wouldn't even be humouring Dima if he hadn't had one eye on the battalions of strings the Leningrad Symphony would need: a minimum of sixteen first violins and fourteen seconds, all of whom would have to be strong enough to perform. Looking around her, Katya was doubtful that many of the string players could even lift their instruments. Her own arm shook just holding her case. The calls were still going out on the radio, and Karl Ilych had announced that the musicians from the Front would join the rehearsals as soon as the paperwork was finalised, but it seemed unlikely that anyone coming to rehearsal from the Front would be much stronger than the civilians. She wanted Dima to succeed: there was comfort in the idea of his bright, warm presence in her section. She doubted he would.

Dima had prepared well. He had clearly known that he wasn't going to be accepted unconditionally, and when Genya asked him to play something for them he smiled and acquiesced. The entire string section, scant as it was, gathered round, for lack of anything better to do, welcoming anything that put off the time when they would have to heft their own instruments and play; Genya went to offer Dima a music stand before realising how redundant that would be. Dima opened his violin case, and a sudden charge of interest crackled on the air, lifting the spectators out of their customary apathy.

"Is that a Guarneri?" someone asked from behind Katya. Someone else – Daniil? – clicked his tongue.

"Of course not, fool. It couldn't – "

"It's a Guarneri – a del Gesù," Dima said calmly. Katya liked the way that he spoke, how he was always careful to angle his head in the direction where he thought the speaker stood. He never got it quite right, which was somehow endearing. She watched the way he handled the instrument, a mixture of certainty and gentleness. It was clear that it was part of his own body.

"Where did you get it?" Daniil demanded. His tone was rude, his emphasis on *you*, the implication that Dima didn't deserve such an instrument. Dima didn't flinch, though Katya felt strangely wounded by proxy.

"It was a gift, from my first teacher, Arseny Grigorevich Stepanov."

Katya didn't recognise the name, but Genya clearly did. His eyebrows tilted and he shifted slightly. Katya wasn't sure if he was reconsidering Dima, or was simply taken off-guard. "I used to know him," he said to Dima, his tone soft. Dima smiled.

"I know. He spoke about you sometimes."

"Is he – ?"

"I haven't spoken to him since 1936," Dima said. His meaning was clear. No one questioned it. They watched as he lifted the instrument, utterly unselfconscious, and tuned it. He applied rosin to the hairs of his bow. He started to play.

It was a good choice. Katya had expected Dima to choose something flashy and technically difficult, the sort of piece that only impresses those who know little about music. Instead, he had chosen the Largo movement of Respighi's D major violin sonata. It was a piece Katya knew well; she had played it herself at the Conservatoire, but hearing it from Dima was like hearing it for the first time. Her spine stiffened, and her toes curled inside her shoes. Her skin rippled like grass under wind. Katya looked around to see if her reaction was unusual. Everyone around her seemed unusually still, concentrated, more real. Dima made the violin sound human. It didn't sing; it spoke. He moved as he played. Katya could remember that from when she had first learned to play, feeling as if the music was filling her from the toes up, the need to dance almost irresistible. She had suppressed it for fear of looking foolish. Dima didn't have any conception of what *looking foolish* might mean, and as a result avoided it altogether.

When he finished, no one spoke for a moment. Katya felt as if her entire body was stretched with a delicious tension. She forced her shoulders to drop, and her spine to soften and round. Genya cleared his throat.

"Well, you can obviously play," he said. "How about something a little more technically challenging?" Katya wasn't sure if he was still testing Dima, or just wanted to hear him play again as much as she did. Dima grinned, wolfish, but stayed silent. His violin spoke for him, as he launched immediately into Paganini's first caprice, L'Arpeggio. Technically, it was perfect, but Katya could have named a dozen people off the top of her head who could play it just as well, herself included. What was extraordinary was his manner, the meaning of it. Dima played the piece as a joke: it was clear from the outset that he recognised the cliché of the showy challenge that he was throwing down. His face was carefully neutral, but each phrase from his fingers radiated irony. Next to her, someone laughed, an involuntary sound that was as startled as it was pleased. Katya watched Genya's face, the way his lips were pressed together to prevent a smile that Dima couldn't see anyway. As if in response, Dima sped up a fraction, and, finishing, dropped an experimental and sketchy bow in Genya's general direction.

"All right, all right," Genya said. He was laughing, his bones jangling against one another. There was something a little frightening about seeing merriment on a face as ravaged as his. Dima stopped, smiling and a little breathless. The feeling in the room had relaxed; Dima had been admitted amongst them. Katya wasn't sure if he realised it himself yet, but he looked pleased enough from the sheer exhilaration of playing for a new audience.

"You play beautifully," Genya conceded at last. "I can see a lot of Arseny Grigorevich in your style. You were obviously taught well. And there's something else, too – your lyricism is very impressive. But I still don't see how a blind man can fit in with an orchestra. How do you learn music, and how do you follow a conductor?"

"May I sit?" Dima asked politely. Katya saw that he was having difficulty catching his breath; his vitality, his liveliness served to mask his physical weakness, but did not make up for it. She was closest, and when no one else moved, she dragged a chair over to him, and took his hand, placing it on the chair's back.

"Thank you, Katya," Dima said. Seated, he braced his arms against his knees. They were shaking. His face was calm: he was used to being betrayed by his body, as they all were. "I can read braille music," Dima explained at last, "but mostly I learn by memory. Even with braille music, you still have to be able to memorise a piece, as of course you can't read braille and play at the same time."

"And you can memorise whole symphonies?" Genya sounded sceptical, but Dima didn't react.

"Yes. It's not uncommon. I've been blind since I was very young. In the absence of sight, blind people have to develop very good memories. This city, for example: I have a map of it in my head, although I've never seen it, and I have to have that map, because I don't have the option of getting lost, looking up and seeing the Peter and Paul Fortress and working out where I am from there. It's the same with music. For shorter pieces, I only need to hear them once before I can play them back, as long as they're not too complex. For longer ones, it takes a few more tries, but it doesn't take as long as you'd think to get the notes down. I heard you were going to do Glazunov's Triumphal March for the first concert," he added, "and I know that. I've played it before."

"You know we're to perform Shostakovich's latest symphony," Genya said haltingly. "I've not yet seen the score, but apparently it's a monster, and of course there's only the one copy, so it'll be a while before we can start rehearsing it. We'll have to learn it quickly, and you'll have no recordings to practise with. Do you think you could do that, without being able to see a score? The rest of the orchestra will copy out their own parts, but I doubt that anyone will be able to help you translate it into braille."

"I can do it by ear," Dima said. His certainty made him believable. "If I sit in my section the first time it's played, I will be able to pick it up quickly. If other members of the section are practising their parts at home, I can practise with them. I promise you, I can do it."

"And how about following the conductor? How can you do that?" Something subtle had changed in Genya's tone. Katya could tell that he wanted Dima to convince him.

"That's more difficult, of course. I've never played in an orchestra with sighted people before, but Arseny Grigorevich and I used to play together a great deal, and I've played a lot of chamber music with sighted musicians. It's not easy, but I can compensate a great deal with my hearing. I notice smaller sounds because I have to. Did you know that people's breathing changes when they're just about to play? There's an inhalation, as if they're about to speak. You can feel the tension change." He shrugged, a little helplessly. "It's very difficult to explain, and of course it's not foolproof. I would have to be very careful to hold back until I was sure. But I think I could do it. I would at least like to try."

Genya nodded slowly, and then flushed, having obviously forgotten that Dima could not see him. "All right," he said. "We do need everyone that we can get at this time, and you seem to be in better health than most of the rest of us. We'll try you out on the first concert, and see how it goes."

The smile on Dima's face was so broad that he looked like a child. "Thank you," he said, but Genya was already walking away. Stretching his arms, flexing his fingers one by one, Dima levered himself upright, turning his face towards Daniil, who was asking him a question about his instrument with grudging respect. Katya could wait, she would wait until after the rehearsal to congratulate him; she may have been the first to find him, but she had no claim on him; any proprietorial pride she had was surely misplaced. And yet: *thank you, Katya*, he had said, when she had brought him the chair. He hadn't been able to see her, and yet he had known who she was. He had known who she was.

LYCHKOVO

18 August 1941, early afternoon: Demyansk

How to pinpoint the moment of the change, from tedium to terror? One minute Katya was fretting about trivialities – that new stain on the hem of Nadya's dress; how had that got there? – and then next, panic slipped over her like a shiver and the world shifted sideways, just a little, just enough for it to look utterly alien.

The platform was so warm that it soaked through the soles of her shoes, and Yevgeny's face was as serious as she'd ever seen it.

"We have to move the children," he said. Uncomprehending, Katya tightened her grip on Nadya and Tanya's shoulders, and then, "the Fascists are dropping paratroopers, trying to cut us off," Yevgeny explained, which was when Katya understood that he meant more than Tanya and Nadya: all of the thousands of children that thronged the train station would have to leave, not by train to Mga or Novgorod, as had been the plan, but by any means possible to Lychkovo, the last rail line open, the only way out.

Anything that could carry people was hastily pressed into service. The truck into which Katya and the girls were loaded was ancient and lumbering, twenty, even thirty years old; they sat on wooden benches open to the sky, which was still blue, still clear, oblivious, but there was a hum, now, strung on the air, the distant sound of aeroplanes that meant that the war had made an abrupt move from the theoretical to the real. Katya had thought she had known what was going to happen: people had spoken of nothing else in the weeks since the declaration of war, holding their breaths, waiting for it to begin, as if the war was going to be gently ushered in, rather than dropped into their laps. Reality was as different from what Katya had imagined as a drawing done with her eyes closed.

Nadya clung close to her mother, large-eyed and silent, while Tanya feigned a grave unconcern; Katya did her best to keep them distracted, their eyes on her and not looking up into the wide, warm sky, because she dreaded what they might see there. She could hear it now, the noise of the planes getting louder, but as long as they were unseen and unacknowledged Katya could pretend it was nothing but the agitated hum of bees: a lazy, late-summer sound. She was grateful to Tanya for not saying aloud what Katya knew that she had realised: that something had gone wrong. Katya didn't know where Yevgeny was now: presumably somewhere at the head of the convoy, with the other officials. There was another woman in the truck with them, one of the Party representatives managing the evacuation and whom Katya faintly recognised; she and Katya carefully avoided each other's eyes. The other children in the truck were quiet. Katya would have expected screaming and crying, but they seemed to wordlessly trust the few adults in their midst to keep them safe. These children, city children in their best clothes, some begrimed from several days of travel: they had never known danger, and had no context to fit it into. The amount of them made Katya feel slightly vertiginous, and she looked at one and then another in turn, imagining where they were from, what their mothers looked like, what had been the last thing they had said to their children when they had loaded them onto the trains in Leningrad that morning, or yesterday, or several days ago. *Be good. Don't forget me. Hold onto your doll.*

And then, suddenly, Lychkovo: a relief and a nightmare at once: the platform thronged with children, as bright as flowers. Their mothers and fathers had dressed them with such care before sending them away, so that they would arrive at their destinations aglow with cleanliness and health, so that whoever was to take them in at the end of the journey would be more inclined to love them. The train was already there, waiting to be loaded, waiting to leave. As the buzzing got louder, Katya found it harder and harder to tell whether it was inside or outside her own head. A bee bobbed its way through the crowds, and for a moment Katya felt passionate relief. *That was all it was!* But it wasn't. The aeroplanes were visible, now, glinting in the sky like treasure. They were metal, and the children's faces were magnets, drawn inexorably up towards them. The aeroplanes were lower than Katya had ever known them, the fist-sized bolts that held them together clear to see. The crowd held its breath, and fear spread out its arms. One small boy opened his throat, his voice a weapon, and the other children followed. Katya could hear the woman who had been in the truck with her speaking to the children, who turned to face her as if she could stand between them and the aeroplanes: "It's all right! It's not the enemy! They're our planes!" They were not.

Yevgeny was suddenly at Katya's elbow, conjured out of nothing. "We have to get the children onto the trains," he said to Katya, as if that weren't blisteringly obvious. The older children had already taken the initiative and were scrambling up the metal stairs, bags and parcels in hand, but the younger ones didn't know what to do, and couldn't be told. Behind Katya, a group of boys of about twelve or thirteen started to help, taking the tiny cases from the hands of infants and pushing them into the carriages. It shamed Katya. "I should help," she told Yevgeny.

"No, you should stay with the girls! We need to stay together – "

But Tanya had hold of Yevgeny's hand now. Her face was still calm, almost eerily so, but she would not let go. Her father had always been the centre of Tanya's world, the pole she swung to, and Katya knew that Nadya would follow her older sister into hell. "They feel safer with you," Katya whispered to Yevgeny, telling the truth and hating it. "We'll never get loaded if someone doesn't help get the little ones on. You take the girls, and I'll find you on the train."

"Mama," said Nadya, her voice uncertain.

Katya pressed a kiss to the dimple in the very centre of Nadya's cheek, and rubbed her hand over Tanya's hair, still baby soft. "It's all right, girls. You'll be safe with Papa. I'll only be a few minutes."

The boys looked younger the closer Katya came to them, and they turned to her as if she had some sort of authority. "The planes…" one said, as if she hadn't noticed. They were too old to lie to, and so Katya told them what she hoped to be the truth. "They're low enough to see us, they know it's only women and children. They must be heading for the Front."

Behind her, the aeroplanes turned. "They're dropping something," someone said. The voice sounded disembodied, and a waterfall ran through Katya's head, a list of the things that could be falling from the sky: leaflets, snowflakes, gifts. The earth heaved like a shrug, and Katya's head filled to the brim with silence as thick and deep as water.

❧

II: MODERATO (POCO ALLEGRETTO)

MEMORIES

CHAPTER SEVEN

I: 15 April 1942

Spring brought broad, golden skies; it brought the continuing thaw, the resumption of a certain kind of life in the city, however tentative and circumscribed. It brought the resurrection of the trolleybuses, and when the first one swept past her in the streets with a noise like a river breaking its banks, it brought tears to Katya's eyes and her heart to her mouth. It brought the thaw of the pipes, water flowing again; it brought threads of green pushing up through the cracked pavements and lacing the skeletal trees, sweet new leaves that people would gather for food. And April brought music.

Katya had been right: there was little enough joy in it. Rehearsals were slow and painful. The trickle of musicians brought in from the Front swelled the orchestra's numbers, but the men were largely bone-pale and shattered, little stronger than anyone else. Karl Ilych had difficulty in making himself understood, and Katya could not tell whether he was unclear, or whether the orchestra, stupefied by hunger and cold, was unable to take in complex instructions. The music stuttered and faltered; again, and again, Karl Ilych would demand it, section by section: the Glazunov, the Tchaikovsky started to knit itself together, fragment by fragment, but towards the end of each rehearsal it was fraying at the edges again. Even the strongest among them, Dima,

Daniil, the soldiers, would be limp and trembling with spent effort when it was time to leave, both from the physical drain and the mental strength it took to listen and to concentrate for that amount of time. Spring was curative, but it couldn't erase the winter's damage: people still died, in the bombing and the shelling, and of illness, of hunger. In the eyes of Karl Ilych this was no excuse for poor performance, and the rest of the orchestra followed his lead. He had no compunction about stripping the ration of anyone who failed to come to rehearsal, no matter the reason: weakness, illness, bereavement. Some buckled in the face of this rigour, but Katya found it bracing: it made her sit up straighter, work harder, wanting to please. Sometimes, at the very tips of her fingers, she could feel herself making a sound that came close to deserving the name of music. That was a fierce, sharp comfort.

The other comfort was Dima. *Some people burn more brightly*, Katya had thought, when she first met him, comparing the flame of his energy to Lidiya's. But if Lidiya was a blowtorch, Dima was a bonfire. He drew people to him, flocking round, warming themselves. Although he was friendly with everyone, from the start he created his own orbit, and people fell in like satellites: Daniil, with half-reluctant fascination; Marina, life starting to spark in her face; one of the young soldiers who had been released from duty to attend rehearsals, a fair, shy-looking trumpeter named Trofim, who seemed strangely ill at ease with the other army musicians; herself. She never would have presumed, but Dima pulled her in, sought her out, sat beside her in the second violins and in the cafeteria at lunch, and even her silence, sometimes mulish and sometimes exhausted, didn't seem to dissuade him. They had started to walk together as a matter of course, from the Radio House down Nevsky Prospekt, as far as the Vladimirskaya Church, an arrangement that every day Katya expected to change, but it never did: if she left before Dima he would catch her up, using effort she knew he could ill afford; if she left after him she would find him waiting. His friendship was insinuating and insistent, in a way that Katya might have resented, had it come from someone she liked less.

That Dima was a talker was clear from the start, but what took Katya longer to notice was his skill in teasing other people out, a clever barter of confidences. Her own close-mouthed nature was a habit held long enough that she wasn't immediately susceptible, but those who had simply been ground into silence under the fist of the winter, Katya noticed, started to open their mouths again, looking almost taken aback at what they said and what they wanted to say. Conversation was one of a thousand luxuries lost through the Blockade, and it wasn't until it started to come back, halting and clumsy at first, that Katya realised that she had missed it – not to be a part of, never that, but just to have around her, the quiet purr of it, noise and life.

"Were your family musicians, Dima?" Marina asked over lunch. Dima nearly choked on a mouthful of barley, making a visible effort to swallow it down.

"Good god, no! Did you have some image of me as – I don't know, a demure and well-behaved little boy, obediently practising scales before I could even walk?"

Marina laughed. The sound of it was starting to sound less alien to Katya's ears. "Not…quite." It was clear from her face that she had thought just that, and clearer still that at Dima's words she had realised how unlikely that image was.

"No, I was a horrible little boy. Vile. Music – it was a surprise, to me as much as to anyone. It was a lifeline, a parachute. Before that – I used to be a brawler."

Daniil snorted a little in soft disbelief, the sort of near-silent comment Katya was coming to learn that Dima wouldn't let anyone away with. "What, you don't believe me?" He pantomimed affront, holding out his hands, half-fisted, palms down. "Look. Scarred knuckles."

Daniil looked, and so did Katya: sure enough, across Dima's knuckles was a tracery of old scar tissue, white and pink, as fine as lace.

"How can you fight someone you can't see?"

"Easy. Same way you do anything else if you can't see: listen hard, use your wits. My brother taught me how, when I was six, before I went away to school. There were some kids in the village who used to tease me, you know, for being blind, and my brothers would fight them for me, but I wanted to be able to do it myself. Alik, my brother – he was closest in age to me, just a couple of years older – he taught me how to listen, how to follow his voice and the other noises he made and swing towards them. And he moved my hands for me, back and forth, so my muscles would know how to punch. I'd play it over in my head, practising. You have to get good at things like that, if you're blind. Let your body remember."

He paused for breath, lifted a spoonful of watery broth to his mouth. There was something in the way Dima told a story, Katya thought, that folded you into it. It wasn't that he was a particularly gifted storyteller, or that the words he chose were finer or cleverer than anyone else's; it was that he assumed that people wanted to hear what he had to say, and so they did.

"Did it work, then? Your brother's training?" Daniil asked.

"Well. Yes and no. The next time Alik and I were out together, and the village kids started up at me…"

"What would they say?" Marina asked.

"It varied. Most common was they'd come running up to me, tap me on the shoulder and tell me we were playing tag. Then they'd run away, and there'd be laughter. The first time, I had no idea what they were laughing at, but Alik told me that they were imitating the way I turned around, trying to find them." Dima laughed himself, and although Katya listened for it, she couldn't discern any bitterness. "It must have been pretty funny. I probably would have done the same in their place. But the good thing about that was that they had to come up close to me to do it. If they'd just shouted from the other side of the road, I couldn't have done anything, but as soon as they tapped my shoulder, I knew where they were. That day, I remembered what Alik had said. This boy came running – Volodya, he was always the worst of them – and I heard him speak, and I felt the tap on my shoulder. Everything went very still inside my head. I could tell from his voice where he was standing, my arms knew where they had to go to grab his arm, and I did."

II: 1925

Dima grabbed the arm. It was exactly where Alik had said it would be, but everything else about it was wrong. The arm was huge, the limb of a monster, unimaginably different from Alik's spindly ones, and Dima's head span with frantic, intuitive geometry: if the arm was like *that*, the chest would be *there*, and the head... The space at Dima's other shoulder felt empty: Alik had slipped away, as Dima had asked him to do, and yet Dima filled up with panic as surely as if someone had poured it in through his ear. They had planned this, Dima had insisted that he wanted to do this alone, but he hadn't *known*. Alik had said that Volodya was a big boy, but Dima had only had the most muddled and half-baked idea of what that meant. *Now* he knew. *Now* he was scared.

He only had a second. Volodya was already starting to pull away with a laugh that sounded disbelieving; as soon as he did that, Dima wouldn't know where he was, and he would be alone, and he had stepped out of the role of passive blind boy and he was sure that wasn't going to bring him anything good. He pushed the panic as far back as he could: it was warm and spongy, and he hid it behind his teeth. Just as Volodya yanked himself free of Dima's grasp, Dima kicked. This hadn't been part of the plan: Alik had told him to punch Volodya in the softest part of his belly, but Dima had made the mistake of grabbing Volodya with his stronger right hand, and his legs felt like a better bet than his feeble left. The kick was inexact, a wide arc in the approximate direction of the thick trunk of Volodya's body, wide enough to unbalance Dima and throw him off guard. He was lucky. The side of his boot connected with a part of Volodya's body that was gristly and bony. The noise it made was a cheerful clack, like the slam of a door. Volodya howled and toppled, Dima on top of him. A world opened up, of struggling, yielding flesh and the tender treachery of skin. The panic changed to exultation, roaring through Dima like a wave. He moved in for the kill.

He got a pounding, but the heady joy of those few seconds where Volodya was fearful and squirming beneath him cancelled out all the pain of the two blacked eyes, the split lip, the body marbled with bruises, and his mother's hysterical disapproval and disappointment when Alik, who had been lurking, proud and worried, at the corner of the street, led Dima home. And it worked. The next time he and Alik passed the boys in the street there was no tap on the shoulder, no invitation to play tag, just blissful silence. The time after that, Volodya came up to Dima and shook his hand.

III: 1926

Dima had never understood what people meant when they talked about colours, but school at least taught him the meaning of grey. It was in every breath he took, in the taste of the food, the tone of voice of the staff who spoke to him. It was in the rough blankets he ran his hands over at night, the squeak of the mattresses on the long rows of beds, the snatched gasps of the one child who inevitably couldn't hold back his tears and was trying his best to hide them.

Dima was seven years old, and he was angry. It was a feeling that he didn't understand: he knew the quick blossoming of rage that he'd felt when Volodya and the others used to tease him, and he knew the flush and prickle of irritation when Alik's knee landed in his ribs for the third time in one night, but this sick, dogged anger that squatted low in his belly was new to him, and he didn't know what to do with it. Dima had never thought to resent his blindness any more than he resented the hair that stood up on his head and wouldn't be smoothed down, or the way that his brothers snored, or his mother's quick temper that moved from blows to embraces within seconds. But now Dima understood what it meant: it meant school, it meant losing his family, it meant being defective, it meant sharing a building with hundreds of boys and girls like him, who were just as sad and angry as he was, and who were willing to take that sadness and anger out on anyone who brushed up against them. Dima didn't think about it; he just became one of them.

The boy in the next bed was called Piotr, and Dima hated him immediately, just because he was there. He hated the damp way Piotr sniffed at night, and he hated the dull clomps of his feet hitting the ground as he heaved himself out of bed in the morning, and he hated the hot stink of urine when Piotr wet the bed, which he did most nights. Most of all, though, Dima hated Piotr's voice, which was thick and slow. The stench of difference came off Piotr: Dima recognised it immediately, and so did the rest of the boys. Put a group of children together and within a day they will have sorted themselves out from strongest to weakest, through a series of arcane rules that none of them could explain, but which most of them understand implicitly. In this sorting Piotr came out bottom, and if he didn't realise it, everyone else did. Piotr opened his hands in friendship and got only fists in return. On the first morning, when Dima was groping for his clothes in a pre-dawn darkness that he could feel on his skin, Piotr asked his name. His words came slowly, as if they'd been built out of clay. Dima sensed friendliness, and confusion. A bag of tears hung in the back of Dima's throat, threatening to burst at any moment. The only way he could stop them from coming was to give them to someone else.

"Shut up," he said to Piotr. His voice trembled on the first word, but cruelty was a thread of iron running through him. It uncurled his spine, making him stand up straighter. "Don't ever talk to me. *Idiot.*"

Dima couldn't see Piotr's reaction, but he felt his puzzled recoil, and rejoiced in it. As long as there was someone feeling worse than he was, Dima thought that perhaps he could face the day.

What he didn't yet know was that aggression and hatred could be almost as much of a bond as love. Piotr was an idiot, and Dima hated him, but he was Dima's idiot, and it was Dima's hatred. His anger was always there, ready to crawl up the back of his throat and out of his mouth, crouched in the joints of his shoulders and willing to flood into his fists. Dima couldn't sleep for the sound of Piotr's sodden sniffs, and so he should have been glad at the hiss from the bed on Piotr's other side, telling him to shut up and that he was a cretin and should be in a school for mental defectives, not a school for the blind. He should have been gladder at the thump of something thrown at Piotr's bed, and gladder still at the scuffle of footsteps and the sound of a fist connecting with the soft tissue of Piotr's face. Instead, the anger came, bright as a searchlight, and just as directed. Dima launched himself out of bed, sure-footed. He had fought a lot at home, and he had always lost, but the idea of fighting another blind boy had never occurred to him until now. He wasn't afraid, because losing wasn't losing if you didn't mind the salt tang of blood against your teeth and the hot throb of a bruise. His hands found Piotr's bed, the sandpaper blankets, the struggling, wriggling bodies. His first punch landed on Piotr, and he realised his mistake at Piotr's whimper of pain and resignation. The resignation only made Dima angrier. He grabbed the other boy by his flimsy pyjamas, caught him off guard and they fell, Dima underneath. The floor snatched the air from his lungs, but his anger was stronger than it. They wrestled in silence. Dima was hit once, twice. The other boy gasped through clenched teeth: "stop your bloody sniffing, cretin," and laughter erupted in Dima's chest as he realised that the boy thought he was still fighting Piotr. He hadn't realised that blind people could be so stupid. The laughter gave him strength as he heaved the boy over onto his back, straddled him and hit him three times in a way that he had learned at Alik's hand: two in the face, one in the guts. The boy whooped once and was quiet.

"Leave him alone," said Dima. The silence in the dormitory was loud, pulsing against Dima's ears. The boy underneath him wasn't trying to throw Dima off any more, and Dima's anger retreated somewhat. A fearsome peace erupted inside him, and he raised his voice. "That goes for all of you. Leave him alone."

Getting to his feet, he felt his way back to his bed and lay down. There was blood on his lips and he licked it off, wondering if he would get in trouble in the morning for bleeding on the pillow; it was the sort of thing his mother used to shout at him for. In the next bed, Piotr sniffed, and Dima sighed. "Shut up, Piotr," he said warningly. For a moment, Piotr didn't say anything, and then, as quiet as an exhalation: "Thanks."

~

Dima fought most days, because it pushed his anger away and filled his mind with cleaner things. When he fought, he was purely physical. His arms, his ribs, his legs, his face, a series of lines and planes, designed with purpose. He lost often: many of the other boys were bigger, they'd been there longer, they had brokered alliances, but the important thing, Dima knew from his encounters with Volodya, was to be willing. Anyone who cringed from a fight would become a target. Anyone who stood up to one – no matter the outcome – would earn a modicum of respect. Alone, Dima ran his fingers over the scabs on his knuckles, the lumps and swellings on his face and head. They pleased him. They reminded him that he was still there, and that although he couldn't see anyone, he could still be seen.

One more angry child in a school full of them didn't make much difference to those in charge. Dima was mostly ignored, except when it was impossible for the staff to do so. Fighting in the dormitory or outside was acceptable because the teachers could pretend not to see; fighting in the classroom was not. Dima learned this quickly, but he couldn't always help himself; there was such violent gladness in it, that silent shout of the body, and he was happy to be provoked.

The day was cold. Dima could feel the frost on the air, lacing the insides of the windows, and he enjoyed the heat that the blossoming bruises brought to his skin. He wasn't entirely sure where he was, except that he'd been taken out of class after knocking another boy out of his seat for calling Piotr an imbecile, and he had been yanked so roughly through the hallways of the school that he had lost his bearings. As well as the inevitability of punishment, fighting in class was never wise because of the number of potential hazards – chair and desk legs crammed close together, and too many other boys who couldn't move swiftly enough to get out of the way. Dima hadn't meant to really hurt the other boy, but the desks had sharp edges and Dima had felt him go limp under his hands. A shudder had gone through him then, from his ribs out, certain he'd killed him and was going to be sent to Solovki immediately. But the boy's chest had continued to rise and fall with the calm motion of a rocking boat. This had done little to mollify their teacher, Vladimir Igorevich; apparently knocking someone unconscious wasn't much better than killing them in his general worldview, and so Dima had been whisked out of the room, half-dragged, half-carried down a corridor and put in a room to await further judgement. Now, he was alone, and he was cold. The bright burn that flashed through him when he fought was fading, and he was starting to wonder what was going to happen to him next.

Dima had heard the click and tumble of the lock when Vladimir Igorevich had left him alone, but he tried the door anyway: useless. In a way, Dima was relieved: pride would have demanded he try to escape if it had been possible, but no matter how clearly he imagined himself striding out bravely over the fields and somehow making it back to his family, he knew that he would be lost within minutes, and simply at risk of a worse thrashing. Besides, Dima could never bring himself to picture actually arriving home to the family who had sent him away in the first place.

Standing by the door, he listened for footsteps, *tac-tac* on the slippery floor. Nothing. Fear fought with anger fought with boredom, and boredom won. It usually did. Dima began to explore the site of his confinement. His fingers were his emissaries to the outside world; he sent them on their errand. A wall, smooth, and his fingertips slid along it the way they did on the wall above his bed. He edged along, knocking into something that stood shoulder-high: a desk of some sort, its lid pitted and splinter-scabbed. A classroom, then. Moving further into the room there was something else, wooden and slippery and monolithic. Dima had not felt an object like this before. Underneath his palm the wood curved like water, and his fingers found a hinge and a join, something that could be opened. A kind of cupboard, perhaps? He should leave it alone; he knew he would only be in more trouble if he was found interfering with things when they came back to get him, but he was hungry with curiosity. Fitting his fingers into the groove, he pushed and lifted, and it – whatever it was – opened. He didn't know what he might find, papers perhaps, those weighty sheaves of paper that the teachers were always making Dima run his fingers over, explaining that the paper *said* something, although that idea was patently ridiculous – but no paper fell slithering to the floor. Inside, instead, was a huge set of teeth.

Dima stopped short, frozen. His heart seized up in his chest. Some slumbering wooden beast was about to bite off his fingers, he was certain, but the creature didn't move. For a long moment he stood, still and breathless, his fingers resting on the teeth, and he realised they had a spring to them, nudging up against his fingers. Instinct made him push back. Everything changed.

All fear vanished, and he pressed again. The piano note rang out like a bell. So *this* was it, *this* was what made the music that they sang along with in class! He had never thought much about the instrument that produced it, although Dima quite liked the singing: his favourite was the song about the train, which pushed forward to communism. He was fairly shaky on what communism was, but he had taken a train on his way to school, and he had been enchanted by the snorting, hissing strength of it and its irresistible sway. In his head, he heard the song's melody and, tentative, he pressed the key again, then the one to the right of it. That was higher. In a flash, he understood. He groped for the seat that must be there and found a stool, scrambling up onto it, settling so his fingers were spread along the keys. Within moments, he had picked out the melody of the song, humming through his teeth as he went. There it was, below his hands, but there was something missing: it felt too thin. Speculatively, wanting to see what would happen, Dima pressed down two keys at once. The sound doubled and thickened, but it didn't sound quite right when he pressed adjacent keys; the sounds shivered against each other in discomfort. He moved a finger one key along. There, *that* was better: those sounds seemed fonder of one another. Dima played the melody again, both hands moving this time, trying to work out which sounds went together and which did not. He played again. One of the fresh scabs on his knuckles cracked open, and a stripe of blood ran down his finger. He sucked it off absently. He played again.

By the time Vladimir Igorevich came back to deal with him, Dima just about had it down, so tantalisingly close that even when he heard the key turn in the lock and the door swing open, he didn't stop, waiting for the hand that would land on his shoulder and pull him away. It didn't come. Relishing good luck he couldn't quite believe, Dima played to the end of the song and fell silent, waiting. When Vladimir Igorevich spoke, he sounded more surprised than angry.

"Dmitri, why didn't your parents tell us about your music lessons?"

"I haven't had any music lessons."

Dima heard him sigh, his breath pushing harsh out of his mouth, the noise he always made when Dima was about to get in trouble, and while Dima didn't mind getting in trouble, there was something galling about getting in trouble when he hadn't actually done anything wrong for once. "It's true, I promise!"

"All right, maybe *lessons* is the wrong word, but your parents taught you how to play the piano?"

"No, we don't have one at home. My father used to play the accordion sometimes." *When he was drunk*, he added in his head, knowing enough not to say that part out loud, although he wasn't entirely sure what *drunk* meant, other than loud and tearful and musical.

"So where did you learn to play?"

"I didn't. It's…it's easy, isn't it?" Dima was confused. It *was* easy. You heard the sounds in your head and then you played them, in the same way that you heard the words in your head and then you spoke them.

"Most people don't think so."

"What about people who can see?"

"Even them."

This was a new idea. Dima knew that he was good at fighting for a blind kid, but that only got him so far. He hadn't thought it was possible to be as good at something as people who could see, and hadn't even known how completely he'd accepted that idea until he considered that it might not be so.

"Come with me," Vladimir Igorevich said. His hand finally landed on Dima's shoulder, but it was much gentler than Dima had expected. As if sensing his relief: "Don't think I've forgotten about your punishment," Vladimir Igorevich added warningly.

"Is Kolya all right?" Dima asked, in what he hoped was a meek voice.

"He's in the infirmary with a lump like a plum on his forehead, but he'll live."

The room Vladimir Igorevich led him to was unfamiliar, on a corridor Dima hadn't walked down before, and as soon as the man in the room spoke, Dima knew that he wasn't someone that he'd met before. The voice had a croak to it that was almost inhuman. It sounded like it was coming from deep inside the man, and it made Dima quake a little. He stood up taller to compensate.

"Show Arseny Grigorevich what you were playing, Dima," Vladimir Igorevich said. He guided Dima over to the piano, but Dima squirmed away as he tried to help him onto the stool. He could do the rest himself.

As soon as he touched the keys, a feeling of power surged through him. Dima smiled. The song rang out clear in his head, and he felt for the note where it needed to start. He pressed a key at random, and the sound made his skin tremble. This was different from the piano in the classroom, which had sounded like old bells in a bag. This was like singing. Walking his fingers up the keys, counting in his head, he found the note he wanted, and, ignoring the murmured conversation between Vladimir Igorevich and Arseny Grigorevich, Dima started to play.

When the song was finished, there was silence. Dima twisted himself around on the stool, addressing himself to the place where the croak had come from. "That's all," he said, feeling oddly apologetic.

"Vladimir Igorevich says you've never had lessons," the croak replied. Dima examined the voice, trying to discern what it might be thinking. Normally he could tell if a speaker was angry or happy or sad or scared, no matter how hard they were trying to hide it, but the croak was impossible to read.

"No, Arseny Grigorevich."

"That's evident. Your technique is atrocious." He paused for a moment, and then asked, "And you've never played a piano before today?"

"No, Arseny Grigorevich."

"Vladimir Igorevich, you can go now," the croak said, and Dima almost laughed. He had spoken to Vladimir Igorevich like Vladimir Igorevich spoke to his pupils! The door whispered as Vladimir Igorevich left, and Arseny Grigorevich shifted away from Dima. There was a noise like wings beating, and Dima waited.

"Listen carefully," said the croak, and Dima did.

Something hissed, and a piano piece began to play. Dima listened as hard as he could. It wasn't something he had heard before, but the melody was simple and pleasant. By the second time it was repeated, Dima was humming along, and by the third, his fingers were moving against his legs.

When it was over, Arseny Grigorevich asked, "Do you think you could play that for me? Just the melody, at first."

Eager, Dima turned back to the keyboard. That was easy. He wanted to rush through the notes to show Arseny Grigorevich what he could do, but he forced himself to count against the beat of his heart, playing the tune as closely as possible to the way that it had sounded. It wasn't perfect: it was missing some notes that seemed to fit between the keys that sat next to each other, but Arseny Grigorevich neither helped him nor rushed him, and before long Dima pushed his fingers forward and found the double layer of keys that contained the sounds he needed. The second time he played it, it was perfect.

"And do you think you could add the other hand?" Arseny Grigorevich asked. Dima wasn't sure, but he nodded anyway, keen to please. In his head, he heard again the hiss before the music began, and he found that if he thought hard enough about it he could find the shadow-harmony that lay beneath the melody. His hands on the keys, he played it once, stumbling, halting, and then again. Happiness lodged in his chest like a ball of fire, eclipsing anger for the first time in months. His knuckle was bleeding again, and his hands hurt, but he didn't want to stop until it was right.

When he had finished, Arseny Grigorevich asked whether he would like to learn how to play properly, and Dima said yes. There was a tremor in Arseny Grigorevich's voice that Dima couldn't identify. Arseny Grigorevich told him that he needed to remember that a lot of what he learned would be boring and wouldn't make sense at first, but in the end he would be able to play far more beautiful things than he could have imagined. "Like what?" Dima asked, and Arseny Grigorevich moved him over on the stool, settling heavily beside him. Music exploded into the room like a flock of birds. Dima was transfixed. His heart felt swollen. He hadn't thought that this was possible. He knew, suddenly, how it felt to want something more than anything else, more than the things he'd thought he wanted, more than the things that he was supposed to want.

When the music stopped, Arseny Grigorevich took Dima's hands in his own. For a moment neither of them said anything, and then, "No more fighting," Arseny Grigorevich said. He spoke with an authority that made argument impossible. Dima agreed in a heartbeat.

IV: 15 April 1942

"Just like that?" Trofim asked. Rehearsal was over; outside the Radio House Dima leaned against the wall, mustering his strength for the walk home. He had asked Katya to wait; it had seemed rude to refuse. Despite his pallor and the shaking of his hands, Dima seemed unwilling or unable to stop talking; it occurred to Katya that sound, whether speech or music, was the flare he sent up from the wilderness of his blindness. At Trofim's question, Dima grinned, shrugging.

"Ah. Not quite. Much easier to make a promise like that than to keep it, don't you find?" He pushed off from the wall and stood a moment, feet apart, whether bracing himself or testing himself, Katya was unsure. "Better go," he said to her. "Vasya'll be getting worried."

❧

CHAPTER EIGHT

I: 1927

Music was better than fighting. Most of the time Dima didn't even have to remind himself of this: music wrought a change in him that he couldn't have imagined. The piano was so different from the music he had known before, his father's slurred singing over the wheeze and honk of his accordion, and the formulaic songs they sang at school – but quite aside from that, there was the power he felt when he played, the intoxicating sense of being good at something for the first time. Arseny Grigorevich had warned him that the exercises would be boring to start with, but he was wrong. From the very first time he stumbled through a set of tortuous, tedious Hanon exercises and found himself improved the next day, Dima understood that they were building blocks, necessary tools. Dima hadn't known this feeling since Alik had taught him to fight, but it turned out there was more than one thing in the world worth working at.

All day, music sang in Dima's head. He woke up to it, it whispered in his ear while he was trying to do his lessons. It clanged louder in the yard when he was exercising, because he didn't have to listen to anyone else then. The best time was at night, when he lay in bed. When he had first come to school, he had had trouble sleeping: he was used to noise, the snores and mutters of his brothers and the clatter of his father coming home late, but that was familiar noise, family noise, and the snorts and snuffles of unfamiliar boys was something else. Now, something had cracked open inside him, an intoxicating buoyancy, and he moved constantly to the beat and sway of it, his blanket a giant keyboard on which he played himself to sleep.

Arseny Grigorevich was a hard taskmaster, never sparing his disapproval if he felt that Dima's playing wasn't up to par, and not above the occasional smack with a ruler over the back of Dima's knuckles if Dima was being particularly dense or wilful. Still, lessons remained a treat: music aside, there was something warming about being the sole focus of an adult's attention, even if that attention took the form of anger and irritation. On coming to school, Dima had been swallowed up into a heaving sea of children just like him, and now, thanks to nothing but chance and luck, he had been spat back out again. In his first lesson, Arseny Grigorevich had taken Dima's hands and placed them on the keyboard, bending his fingers so that they were at the correct angles, positioning his wrists until everything was just right, and from that moment Dima had felt nothing but a rather desperate, flailing love for him – partly for the doors that Arseny Grigorevich was unlocking, but mostly due to the simple fact that Arseny Grigorevich was the only adult to have touched Dima with gentleness, rather than in punishment, since his family.

It had been a year, now; a year since he had found the piano and over a year since he had left home, but Dima was only fleetingly aware of seasons passing, the snows giving way to the fresh whiff of spring, the heavy heat of summer like a cloak on his shoulders, and then autumn again with its smell of healthy decay. Dima hadn't gone home for the summer; it had hurt, a stubborn ache, to be left behind with a group of bitter, abandoned boys, the hard core of the school's trouble-makers, but Dima had the sense that if he hadn't found music, the absence of his family would have near destroyed him. As it was, at least his lessons were undisturbed.

By December, school was so cold it stole the breath right out of the body. Dima had cut the fingers off an old pair of gloves to practise in, but Arseny Grigorevich wouldn't let him wear them in lessons, saying that they obscured his clear view of Dima's hands. Today, the two of them were to play together for the first time: Arseny Grigorevich said that it was important that Dima accustom himself to playing with other people, if he ever wanted to be taken seriously as a musician. Dima had only the murkiest impressions of Arseny Grigorevich as separate from himself; he could just about comprehend that Arseny Grigorevich's life did not suspend itself the second Dima walked out the door, only to spring into action again once he returned, but beyond that, all he had gathered was that Arseny Grigorevich himself had been a violinist first and foremost, back when he was a musician rather than a teacher. It wasn't something that interested Dima overmuch; he had heard the violin before, of course, when Arseny Grigorevich played him crackling recordings on his monstrous gramophone, but he had always been straining to make out the piano line, and the violin had sounded dull and whining compared to the keyboard's rich cascade of sound. Dima had been practising the Schubert duet for weeks, playing it over and over on his blanket at night, and so he arranged himself on the piano stool with a degree of confidence: the introduction was note-perfect, chiming exactly as it did in his head. Arseny Grigorevich took a breath, moved his arms, and the first note broke the air.

Dima stopped. He knew it was wrong, but he was astounded. The instrument sounded human, its voice like a cry or a moan, miles away from the hoarse complaint that he had heard on the recordings. Arseny Grigorevich stopped too. "Dmitri…"

"Sorry," Dima said quickly. He began again, and this time managed to keep playing when Arseny Grigorevich came in, by virtue of intense concentration alone, forcing his fingers from one key to the next. When they had finished, "Well," said Arseny Grigorevich consideringly, about to launch into his customary litany of critiques, but Dima dared to interrupt him.

"Please, Arseny Grigorevich," he said, "may I touch it?"

There was a silence, but it wasn't an angry one. One of the things Dima liked best about Arseny Grigorevich was the way that he seemed to always reach for the meaning behind Dima's words, ready to punish when he knew Dima intended cheekiness, and to overlook when Dima spoke out of turn through pure enthusiasm. Dima heard Arseny

Grigorevich move, and when he spoke again, his voice came from lower and closer to Dima: he was kneeling beside the piano stool.

"You must be very careful," Arseny Grigorevich said warningly. It was only years afterwards that Dima appreciated what a privilege it was for Arseny Grigorevich to allow him to handle his instrument, a Guarneri del Gesù of enormous worth; to put it in the hands of a careless eight-year-old was madness. But Dima knew how to be careful when it mattered. He had little idea of what to expect, what a violin was and how it worked. Dima held it in his lap, sensing Arseny Grigorevich's hands inches away, ready to catch it if he slipped. He didn't slip. In silence, he ran his hands over the shape of it, the unimagined curves of its body, the dusty lines of the strings, up to the tight curl at the top which felt like the snails that Alik used to put into his hands to tease. Tentative, feeling his way, Dima plucked at a string. The sound was disappointing, weak and thin, utterly unlike the full-throated song that Arseny Grigorevich had teased from the instrument. This was not the piano; this was not something that Dima could instantly make sense of.

"Like this," Arseny Grigorevich said, relenting. He took the violin from Dima's lap, and as Dima sat, passive, he felt the instrument tucked under his chin. Steadying it with one hand, Arseny Grigorevich took Dima's left hand with his free one, placing it on the neck of the instrument. Dima's arm trembled slightly with the strain, full stretch.

"It's far too big for you, of course, but it gives you the idea." With brisk gentleness, Arseny Grigorevich arranged Dima's fingers so that they were touching the strings. Into Dima's right hand something else was placed, something that felt like a long stick. "This is the bow," said Arseny Grigorevich. He led Dima's fingers along it: wood, and then something that felt like hair. Dima flinched, and Arseny Grigorevich laughed, an unpractised, grudging sound. "It's hair from a horse," he explained. "To play the violin, you have to rub the hairs against the strings."

Dima didn't move. The moment felt too important to risk spoiling it with a mistake. "Try it," said Arseny Grigorevich, granting him permission. Dima raised the bow.

It could not have been more different from the first time he had touched a piano. The bow skittered across the strings like something living, producing an unearthly squeal that was nothing like music. Anger flashed through Dima. He wouldn't let the violin think that he couldn't master it. He raised the bow again and lowered it to the strings, just touching. The first try, he had barely swiped at the strings, afraid of pressing too hard. This time, to punish the instrument, he applied more pressure. The violin groaned. It wasn't the beautiful, throbbing moan that Arseny Grigorevich had produced, but it was closer. Dima tried again, and again. He angled the bow, testing the four different strings, and then, suddenly remembering his left hand, pressed down. The violin's voice leapt up a fraction of a tone, and Dima smiled. He was starting to understand its game.

Dima had never thought before about the limitations of the piano until he had a violin in his hands, grasping the appeal of an instrument that you could carry with you and play wherever you were. And more than that: an instrument that was the beating heart of an ensemble, an instrument that spoke to other instruments as equals. Dima lowered his arms, but when Arseny Grigorevich went to take the violin from his grasp he tightened his grip, unthinking, before forcing himself to relinquish it. Arseny Grigorevich sighed a little, and Dima braced himself for a scolding.

"Well, then. I suppose there's bound to be somewhere in this town where I can find one in your size."

Music was better than fighting. Dima told himself this as often as he could, and it was mostly true. When the keys were under his fingers, or the violin in his hands, even if he was just playing scales he had a sense of calm and control that he had never had before; when he had the chance to play actual music, the feeling was unparalleled. His whole body would knot with a boundless, inexpressible joy. His skin tingled and fizzed. He felt larger than himself, fathomless. At those moments, Dima wouldn't have swapped that feeling for anything in the world: not for his family, not for his sight. Nothing.

The difficulty was in holding onto that feeling the rest of the time. The reputation for fighting that Dima had built up during his first few months at school was not one he was allowed to step away from easily. Fighting was one of the few entertainments afforded the boys at the school, part of the reason they were separated so strictly from the girls – and they were unwilling to forgo it, resenting the implication that there might be something better than the simple release of flesh on flesh, resenting still more that Dima was setting himself apart. In the classroom he was safe, and at mealtimes, too, because there was no fun in a fight that the teachers stopped in seconds. The dormitory was a risk, but Dima had earned a reluctant respect from the boys his own age. His chief tormentors slept separately: Kirill, Fedya and Emil, two years older, who, before music, had been grooming Dima as a successor in their dynasty of petty violence. The yard was the one flashpoint where he couldn't avoid their attempts to drag him back.

Kulak bastard, they said. This troubled Dima little; it was hard to be insulted by something he didn't understand. *You and your family*, they went on: *kulak bastards. Bloodsuckers.* That was harder to ignore. Dima's feelings about his family were difficult; his chest felt rusty when he thought of them, as if he couldn't quite catch his breath. There was anger, still, rooted in the pit of his stomach, coiled in his knees and his shoulders and the small of his back, because they had sent him away and they hadn't brought him home over the summer and there were never any letters for the teachers to read to him and he had finally come to understand that it wasn't an oversight when, on visiting weekends, his name was never among those that were called. And he loved them, too, his love caught around his anger, twined together so tightly that he couldn't untangle the two feelings. An insult to himself was all right; in any case, he was fairly sure that he wasn't actually a kulak bastard. An insult to his family was something else…because what if they *were*? Dima balled his hands into fists and then, frightened by the surge of power he felt at that, forced himself to straighten his fingers, one by one. He would not rise. He would *not*.

It was surprising that it took the boys so long to realise that Piotr was Dima's weakness, the one thing that could always provoke a reaction. Dima resented it, denied it, but for Piotr he had come to feel a muddled protective urge, even as he was itching to punch Piotr himself. Piotr's was a voice that Dima would know anywhere, its aggrieved honk: "Stop it!

Stop it!" They were getting ready for bed, Dima hauling on his pyjamas as flimsy protection against the chill, and the cries were coming from somewhere near the door, where Piotr had obviously been ambushed on his way back from the bathroom; the loud breaths he took through his mouth made him instantly identifiable. Dima was heading towards the scuffle before he had allowed himself to think about it. "Let him go," he said. He was trembling with the fury that had flooded him, unasked for but searingly welcome.

"Why should we?" Kirill asked. His voice betrayed his pleasure in luring Dima out of his hard-won neutrality.

"Because it's cruel," Dima said. He said the words because they were true, not because he felt they would make any difference. These boys didn't care about cruelty, and Dima was unsure how much he cared himself, except that it was *Piotr*. He heard Kirill take a breath, he heard Piotr's squeak of fright as the grip of whoever was holding him tightened on his shoulders, he heard the unmistakable sound of a fist meeting flesh, he heard Piotr's wail. Dima sprang.

Afterwards, he could never remember the details, just a few minutes of confusion, arms and legs and fists and feet, the pleasing certainty of his body in motion, fleeting pain and elation – and then a firm hand on his shoulder, dragging him backwards, followed by shouting, as Vladimir Igorevich delivered a variation on the same lecture that Dima had heard at least a dozen times, barely audible over the hot pump of his pulse in his ears. Around him, boys gasped and panted, catching their breaths. Piotr whimpered, a dull mosquito whine. "Is anybody hurt?" Vladimir Igorevich demanded. The possibility hadn't even occurred to Dima; it never did. His whole body tingled with energy. "Kirill, your eye is bleeding." Dima allowed himself a brief, grim smile at that news. "Dmitri, are you – what happened to your hand?"

As soon as Vladimir Igorevich said it, the pain surged in – pain and panic. His left hand felt disassembled, twice its normal size and throbbing. Dima tried to curl it into a fist and couldn't. The fear made him dizzy. Vladimir Igorevich lifted it to get a better look, and it was all that Dima could do not to shout. "It looks like somebody trod on it," Vladimir Igorevich said, his tone matter-of-fact. To him, it was only a hand, and a left hand at that. "Come along to the nurse. You too, Kirill."

The nurse was a brisk, unsympathetic woman, inured to the innumerable plights of the blind children she had seen over the years. She had a sureness of touch that Dima found easier to bear than gentleness as she examined his hand, decided that nothing was broken, only cut and badly bruised: no point bandaging it. Dima couldn't speak, couldn't even take satisfaction in the sound of Kirill snuffling back tears as the cut above his eye was stitched. Disliking Dima's pallor and silence, the nurse put him to bed in the infirmary.

The night was sleepless. Hating himself, Dima played the fight over and over again in his mind, taking himself back to the point where he had entered the fray. At the time, it hadn't felt like a decision, as inevitable as gravity, but now he saw the other options clearly. He could have called a teacher. He could have walked away. He could have trusted Piotr to look after himself, despite knowing that he couldn't. He could have ignored the wild yell of his blood that sounded, unstoppable, at the possibility of violence. Every so often, his hand flat against the covers, he was overcome with a fit of terror and tried to move his fingers. At first there was nothing, as if his will got as far as his wrist before flickering out entirely. But shortly after the clock struck three, he was able to lift his index finger. The pain was so immense that nausea rose like a tide from his belly to his throat. Dima didn't care. He moved it again, and again. By the time the nurse came in to wake him, he could move all of his fingers, and the spear of pain that each movement sent up his arm as far as his shoulder was a consolation.

His piano lesson was at four that afternoon, and Dima spent the entire day in a coiled up state of anticipation and dread. The time came; Vladimir Igorevich led him to the studio in a way that Dima normally found irritating – as if he didn't know every inch of the building by now – but today it was welcome, a buffer between him and Arseny Grigorevich. When Arseny Grigorevich opened the door, Dima could tell from the muffled sound of his voice that Arseny Grigorevich's back was to him. "Good afternoon Dima, I hope you – "

He stopped.

"I'm afraid Dmitri has been fighting again," Vladimir Igorevich said, as much for Dima's sake as for Arseny Grigorevich's. His voice was laden with disapproval. "If you want to cancel the lesson…"

"No!" Dima said. For a moment, no one spoke.

"You can leave us," Arseny Grigorevich said, in crisp dismissal. The door creaked and clicked. Dima stood, quiescent and waiting, and sucked back a gasp as Arseny Grigorevich took Dima's left hand in his own. He said nothing, turning it back and forth in silence. He pressed a tender point on Dima's palm, and stroked each finger in turn, straightening them. Dima submitted in silence, although Arseny Grigorevich's manipulations made him feel slightly sick. Then Arseny Grigorevich took Dima by the shoulder and led him to the piano stool.

"Begin the preparatory exercises. Just the first ten, to start with. Two repetitions each."

It felt like a privilege. Dima placed both hands on the keyboard. The pain in his left surged with the certainty of a metronome, marking the beat. At first his fingers wouldn't obey, and he fell silent in a clatter of wrong notes. He took a breath and began again. His right hand moved with assured precision; his left stumbled in its wake. Each movement of each finger was a decision weighed against the hurt it would cause. By the third exercise, Dima could feel blood dripping down his wrist and soaking into the cuff of his shirt. Tears clogged his eyelashes, but he would not let them spill over. By the fifth exercise he had given up any pretensions of musicality; only dogged determination remained. *Get it right*, he chanted in time with the throbbing of his hand. *Get it right.* He got it right, not one note out of place as the final C faded and vanished. Dima lifted his hands off the keyboard, resisting the temptation to cradle his left in his right, and awaited judgement.

"Thank you," Arseny Grigorevich said. His tone was cool, but Dima could discern the subtle tremble in his voice that spelled anger.

"I'm sorry," Dima said quickly. He knew by now that an apology was no panacea, but it was always worth a try.

"You don't have to come here if you don't want to, Dmitri," Arseny Grigorevich said. He sounded utterly detached. Neither the words nor the tone could have been chosen more carefully to wound Dima. "No one is forcing you. *I* am certainly not forcing you. Heaven forbid that you should be coming here against your will."

A tear spilled over and streaked down Dima's cheek. He wished, violently, that Arseny Grigorevich was blind too; it seemed appallingly unfair that he could be seen. "I don't – " His chest hitched. He didn't know what he would have said, even if he had been able to say it.

"Perhaps I have not made things clear enough to you," Arseny Grigorevich said, as if Dima hadn't spoken. "You have talent. You have *enormous* talent. But that is nowhere near enough. The one thing I hate more than talentless clods pounding on a piano or sawing away at a violin is talented clods who are wasting their gifts." Dima said nothing. Arseny Grigorevich's anger was no longer disguised; the naked flame of it was a relief. "If you want to become a street-corner ruffian, I won't stop you. If you want to walk out of this room and never come back, you can. But if you want me to teach you, you have to develop some discipline, and you have to learn how to value what it is that you have – because if you don't value it yourself, I won't value it either, and neither will anyone else. Do you understand?"

Dima knew that if he opened his mouth all that would come out was a sob. He pressed his lips together as tightly as he could. *Yes*, he thought, as loudly as he could. *Yes, I understand.*

Arseny Grigorevich seemed to pick up on Dima's mute appeal. "All right," he said, sounding slightly kinder. He took Dima's hand again, and Dima felt the touch of cloth, as Arseny Grigorevich, very carefully, wiped off the fresh blood. "Take a week to let the hand recover, and I will see you next Wednesday. Keep it moving as much as you can, but don't try and play anything in the meantime. And if you ever dare to come to me again in such a state, that will be the last lesson you ever get from me. Now go."

Dima pushed himself off the stool. "Thank you," he managed, his voice shaking only slightly.

"All right," said Arseny Grigorevich. For no more than a second, his hand came to rest on Dima's head. "All right."

~

It was always easy to find Piotr in the yard. By the fence were four trees that Dima recognised by touch and smell as birches, smooth-barked and straight, and Piotr was captivated by the feel of them, standing there as long as he was allowed, running his hands up and down the trunks with a fascination that Dima couldn't fathom. He had asked Piotr once what was so special about the trees, and Piotr, ablaze with enthusiasm, had reached for Dima's hands, placing them on the trunk with a certainty that Dima must understand what had so captivated Piotr. Dima didn't. It was just a tree.

The pain in Dima's hand had died down to a grinding ache. He was almost grateful for it: fitting punishment for his own carelessness, and as long as his hand hurt it meant that it was still there. As he crossed the yard, his fingers trailing along the fence, he caught the sound of Piotr whispering to himself, the way he always did when indulging in something he found pleasurable: *my tree, my tree.* Contempt rose up in Dima, and reluctant affection, all snarled up in each other.

"Piotr!"

"Dima?" Piotr always sounded uncertain, as if he couldn't quite trust his ears.

"Yes, it's me."

"They said you had to stay in the infirmary last night. Are you better now?"

"Mostly," Dima said. He couldn't muster the effort to explain, launching in directly instead. "Petya, you have to learn to fight for yourself."

There was a mutinous silence. "I *can* fight!" Piotr said at last, as Dima had known he would; it was Piotr's standard response to any implication that he couldn't do something, no matter how outlandish. He would have reacted the same way to being told he couldn't ride a unicycle, or walk all the way across the Soviet Union in a single day. "I *can*," Piotr insisted.

"So why don't you, then?" Dima asked.

Piotr said a very pointed nothing. Dima sighed, an irritated push of breath through teeth.

"It was all right, before. I didn't mind…you know, fighting the boys who were picking on you. But I can't do that any more."

"Why not?" Piotr's voice was small.

"Because…" *If you want to be a street-corner ruffian.* Dima could remember every nuance of Arseny Grigorevich's voice: the anger and the disappointment and the disdain. Just the memory of it made him feel hot and cold at once. "Just because," Dima said helplessly. "But you don't need me, anyway. I'm no bigger than you are. You can…"

"But they're *big boys*," Piotr said with an edge of panic.

"They're not so big. You're nine, aren't you? Kirill's the same, and the others are only ten."

"They *hurt* me."

"So you have to hurt them back, until they stop." Dima was frustrated. He remembered the way that Piotr was always harping on about his big brother Vasily, who – if you believed Piotr, which Dima mostly didn't – was the size of an ogre and impossibly tough and involved in all sorts of unlikely schemes. Dima felt again Alik's hands lifting his own arms, showing him how and where to punch, and thought that Vasily came off unfavourably in comparison – though, admittedly, at least Vasily wrote letters to Piotr, rather than the endless silence that was all Dima's family offered. "Didn't your brother ever teach you any of this?"

"No. He always – he did it for me."

"Well, he's not here, is he?" Dima said bluntly. He reached out for Piotr's shoulder and pushed him a little, gently, so that Piotr had to take his other hand from the tree he had been holding onto. It was the first time he had touched Piotr in a deliberate way, rather than just crashing into him in a fight, and he was surprised at the breadth of the boy. Dima moved his hand lower, curling his fingers around the improbable bulk of Piotr's upper arm. "You're strong!" he said, affronted. Dima had had the idea that they were around the same height – both tall for their age – because Piotr's voice always came to him at head-height, but he had assumed that Piotr was skinny and weaker than he was. The idea that he had been protecting a small hulk of a boy was both enraging and hilarious.

"Hold out your hand," he told Piotr. Piotr complied. His palm was sticky and a little grainy, and Dima winced; he had an odd squeamishness for certain textures, and a mild horror of not being clean. He bent

Piotr's fingers into a fist as Alik had done for him, curling the thumb around the outside. "This is how you do it," he explained. "You have to keep your thumb like that. Don't put it inside, or it'll hurt when you hit someone."

"But – "

"Shut up and listen." Dima stretched Piotr's arm out and bent it again, speculative. "Your reach isn't bad," he said. Alik had praised Dima's own reach; it made Dima feel good to echo his brother's words to someone else. "But all that really matters is that you hit hard enough. Move your arm from *here*," he squeezed Piotr's shoulder, "not from here," he bent his elbow.

"But how do I know where to hit them?"

"It doesn't matter so much. It's not..." Dima struggled to find the words to explain what he had always intuitively understood. "It doesn't matter whether or not you *win*. They go for you because they think you won't hit them back, and because you cry and you complain. You need to show them that...that you won't just let them do it. If you do that then they'll leave you alone." *I hope*, Dima added mentally. His own willingness to fight hadn't caused him to be left alone, but he had a sense that there was a mid-point between eagerness and cowardice that would cause the bullies to lose interest. "So just – just try and hit anything you can. Face is best. Stomach's also good. You can try kicking, too, especially if you have your boots on, but be careful not to fall over. Then you're really in trouble."

"What if I miss?"

"So what? You won't, anyway. You've never hit back before; they won't expect you to start now, will they? And it's easy. Listen to me, you can tell where my voice is coming from, can't you?"

"...yes."

"So that's where you try and aim. Look, just try it, listen and – "

The punch came without warning, connecting with Dima's jaw. He yelped in shock. "I didn't mean to *hit* me, idiot!" With uncanny accuracy, Piotr had managed to place his punch right on a day-old bruise. It smarted. "I just meant to *touch* my face, so you know where it is!"

"Sorry! Sorry, sorry!" Piotr was breathless with genuine apology. "I thought..."

"It's all right," Dima said, slightly wearily. He rubbed his jaw with his good, right hand, feeling the heat of the blood underneath his skin. "Good shot, anyway."

They practised for some time, Dima bending and straightening Piotr's arm, showing Piotr what Alik had shown him. Dima could feel the difference as Piotr's muscles seemed to catch on before Piotr's brain did, his movements getting stronger, more assured.

"See," he said, when Piotr had straightened his arm with such force that Dima, holding his wrist, nearly overbalanced. "You know it now. You'll be fine."

Piotr didn't answer. There was a slight puff as he sat down, and Dima sat down beside him. "Are you all right?"

"Yes," Piotr said uncertainly. "Just…I'll forget it all, when it happens. I'm not good at – at keeping things in my head. They get out, somehow."

This was the closest that Piotr had ever come to admitting a failing. Dima felt for him, suddenly, imagining for the first time what it must be like to be Piotr, never quite understanding why he seemed to be so universally despised. Awkward, Dima leant towards him, jostling Piotr's shoulder with his own in a way that he hoped would be read as friendly rather than aggressive.

"You won't forget. When it happens, your anger just takes over and you…" A thought struck him. "You do get angry, don't you? When the boys tease you, or hit you?"

"Not really," Piotr admitted. "Sorry."

"Don't be – but, then, how do you – ? What do you – " Dima couldn't imagine how it would be without the flare of anger to straighten his back.

"I just feel…sad. Sad that bad things are happening."

II: 18 April 1942

"So how did he do, when he had to fight?" Trofim asked. Dima's voice had dwindled into silence in a way that it rarely did: his stories had a tendency towards sharp, clean endings.

"Oh – he did all right. Ignored everything I'd said to him, of course, and just kicked like hell. Nearly took their legs out. They stopped bothering him after that – or not so much, in any case." He took a long, considering swallow of the ersatz coffee at his elbow before adding, casually, "He died a few years after that."

"He *died*?" Marina sounded outraged. The way Dima talked about his past, it was easy to forget that he was talking about real people that things could happen to, rather than characters for whom everything should end happily. Dima looked taken aback at her vehemence.

"Well, yes. It wasn't uncommon, at school. Epidemics, and a lot of the boys had poor health to start with. Piotr – he had a weak heart, apparently. Influenza finished him off."

"But that's – " *That's not fair*, Katya had been about to say, which was patently ridiculous. Dima seemed to intuit her meaning.

"It struck me that way, too. And Vasya said the same, the first time I met him."

"Vasya?"

"Yes – oh, didn't I say? Piotr was his brother."

III: 1931

"It's just not fair," Vasya said. His voice was rough and slightly unsteady. Dima said nothing, every nerve in his body stretched taut. Piotr had been dead for nearly a year, and Dima had filed his memory alongside a selection of others that were generally too difficult to think about, unless something conjured them up. Piotr had died in late autumn; wood-smoke, heavy frosts that hit your lungs like a punch, a clarity in the air making sounds louder and brighter: this bewildering confusion of sensations spoke to Dima of Piotr, and of grief. He mentioned him as little as possible, but for the past week the rest of the boys had spoken of almost nothing else: how Piotr's brother, Vasily, had come to visit for the first time in years, and had had to be told what had happened, and then manhandled out of the room in raging tears while the lucky few being visited listened in, agog. That Vasya had come back at all was astonishing; that he had asked to see Dima was inexplicable. Sitting opposite, uncomfortably aware of Vasya's bulk looming across the table, Dima wished now he had paid more attention to Piotr's stories of his fearsome big brother. The size of him was clear enough in the point from which his voice emanated, and the unwillingly deferential way the teachers spoke to him. Dima was fairly certain that the teachers wouldn't permit Vasya to kill him right there in front of everyone, but this knowledge proved a very meagre consolation.

"It's not fair," Vasya said again, his voice clearer. "I was going to come for him, you know? It was our parents who put him here, in this school, and I was going to take him out, take him to Leningrad. And for this to happen, just before – "

"It's not fair," Dima echoed. It wasn't. He had tried and failed to square it with himself, the fact that music had set Dima ablaze and he was burning his way out of the drab world in which he'd found himself, while for Piotr, eleven years of occasionally alleviated misery were all he was going to have of life.

"You know I was in Solovki," Vasya said. Dima started. He had known, or partly; he'd discounted the knowledge alongside most of the other nonsense Piotr had tended to come out with.

"Piotr said something about it."

"Stole some tools from the factory where I was working. Stupid. It's not like they were worth anything much, and as soon as I tried to sell them it was bloody obvious where they'd come from. So, I got sent off for sabotage. Five years on those fucking islands. Only got out a month ago. Parents didn't want to know, after that, but I wrote to Petya. He wrote back, now and again. Hardly more than once a year, at best. That was how I didn't know…I had a friend visit him once or twice, too. That was better. Couldn't say much in letters, of course, as someone was going to have to read them to Petya, and of course Petya, being how he was – well. It was better to have someone come to see him in person."

Perhaps, Dima thought, Vasya just wanted to talk. Dima allowed himself to relax a bit, only to tense up again when Vasya said: "You were the only one he mentioned in his letters."

"Mm?"

"Yes. Said you were his best friend."

Dima supposed that was one way of putting it, though he would never have said so himself. He had his group of friends, misfit boys, too rough and awkward to fit in with the teacher-pleasers who learned their lessons and repeated them verbatim, and not hopeless enough to fit in with the boys who fought and drank and ran away. Piotr's status in the group was uncertain, tolerated rather than welcomed. If Dima had been asked, he would have grudgingly admitted that he saw Piotr more as a brother than anything else; he understood brothers, from having so many of his own, and he had adopted a similar role with Piotr to that Alik had had with him: a distanced protectiveness. From the first moment Dima had launched himself into a fight on Piotr's behalf, he had claimed him for his responsibility, and he would not shirk it. He could hardly say that, though, not to Piotr's actual flesh-and-blood brother.

"He used to talk about you a lot, too," Dima said instead. "Even more than your parents."

A damp, tearing sound came from Vasya, as if he were fighting back tears. Sympathy flashed through Dima like lightning. He was sure Vasya wouldn't appreciate it if he were to offer it; he held his tongue and waited.

"We were close," Vasya said at last. "I hadn't seen him for years, and he used to drive me crazy when we were younger, but – we were close."

"Same here," Dima said. It was true, in its way. He realised, suddenly, surprisingly, that he liked Vasya. There was a powerful simplicity to him that reminded him of Alik, and a strange sort of goodness, too. If you stripped back all the things that had been wrong with Piotr, Vasya was probably what you would have had left.

"It's strange not to have a brother any more," Vasya said at last. "It was just the two of us, you see. Our mother was already getting on when she had him. I think that was – why he was like he was. You have any brothers, Dima?"

"Four," Dima said, "and three sisters."

"Fuck your mother." Vasya sounded both awed and congratulatory.

"I don't – " This was the thing that Dima didn't speak about, the one thing that could still provoke him to violence, though now he was vigilant to keep his hands tucked under his arms and use only his knees, his elbows, his feet and, when strictly necessary, his head. There were advantages in this: it meant his combatants never knew where the first blow was going to come from. "They don't come," Dima said at last.

"In that case," Vasya said, with a tentativeness that was strange to hear coming from someone so physically formidable, "in that case, I would like to."

Dima stiffened. *Don't feel sorry for me.* There was nothing he hated more than that. He stayed silent; Vasya rushed to explain.

"For me, I mean. I always imagined – I think I would miss Petya less, if I was still able to come here. Talk about him a bit."

Still silent, Dima examined Vasya's tone with a surgeon's precision, seeking out any faint trace of pity. He found none. When he allowed himself to consider it – a visitor, for *him* – he felt oddly inflamed.

"If you wanted to come," Dima said carefully, "it would be nice to – to speak to you. If you wanted."

"I would like that," Vasya said. He heard Vasya's chair scrape back, and pushed back his own chair likewise. Vasya took his hand, and Dima prepared his best manly handshake, but instead Vasya placed Dima's hand on his face.

"Petya used to do this when he first met people," he said gruffly. "He said it helped to feel people's faces, to get an idea of what they looked like."

"Thank you," Dima said. Touched, he was unwilling to explain to Vasya that it was something he rarely bothered with, having so little memory of sight that he couldn't translate what he felt into anything meaningful. Obligingly, he moved his fingers. Vasya's skin was surprisingly soft, slightly oily, under a layer of stubble. Dima ran a thumb over his lips, which were thin, while his index finger took in Vasya's nose – large and slightly bent – and eyes – deep-set. It felt strangely intimate.

"I'll try and come next week," Vasya said. Dima allowed himself a half-smile.

"Until then, I suppose."

CHAPTER NINE

I: 1 May 1942: Afternoon

Trofim's arms felt frail and watery, and his lungs like flattened paper bags. Around him, the rest of the brass section were packing up their instruments, with a variety of involuntary accompaniments: grunts and sighs and groans. Trofim couldn't move. It wasn't so much the weakness, though that didn't help – it was more the sense of unreality that assailed him sometimes when he played, and from which it took some time to recover. It had always been like this: he had a tendency to be engulfed by music, absorbed into it, to the extent that when he played with a band or an orchestra he had to fight to hold onto the line of his part with every scrap of his concentration. It was more difficult, now that he had so little energy to spare; his head span, and his skin seemed to shiver around his body. Trofim focused, rebuilding himself from the soles of his feet up.

"You coming, then?" A heavy hand landed on Trofim's shoulder. Vadim, a trombonist from one of the military bands, a colossus of a man with arms like girders – Trofim felt dwarfed by him, although he himself was by no means small. Behind Vadim stood the rest of the Crew, the musicians from the Front – mostly brass players, looking weary and wrung out. It was time to go. But sometimes, after rehearsal, Trofim found that he couldn't quite hoist his heart high enough to return to the Front right away. Sometimes it seemed too much to handle, this liminal state: the scraps of the war that travelled with him wherever he went, an invisible grime under his nails and in the seams of his clothes; and yet back at the Front, he stank of music. It rattled through his head, and he wanted to shake it, to dislodge it. Trofim hadn't moved; Vadim was still looking at him. He couldn't go back while he still felt so flimsy, tacked together; so insubstantial.

"I'll – I'm coming later," Trofim said at last. Vadim shrugged, unconcerned. It wasn't uncommon for one of them to stay behind a little, visiting family or friends or just basking in the novelty of being somewhere else. They had been issued passes to show to anyone who questioned their presence in the city, but mostly, no one asked.

The rehearsal hall emptied, and Trofim's head sang with silence. Staring at his knees, he thought that they might just about hold him, now. The world was starting to feel more solid. From the other side of the room came the faint sound of bickering, and Trofim smiled, without looking up. Dima and Daniil – they had their routine down pat, a barbed, uneasy friendship that seemed to be rooted in elemental disagreement. Today's subject appeared to be the influence of jazz on orchestral music, which Dima was enthusiastically defending, much to Daniil's feigned disgust. When Trofim raised his head it was only the four of them left: Daniil, Dima, Katya and Marina. They seemed to be waiting for him. Marina, smiling, raised a hand, and Trofim ducked his head again, but this time with bewildered pleasure.

It hadn't been deliberate, the way he had fallen into this little knot of people, and indeed the first few days of rehearsal he had stuck close to the rest of the Crew, feeling a low creep of guilty discomfort at the thought of getting too close to civilians. But then there had come a day where he had felt catastrophically, nauseatingly untogether – no good reason why any more so than other days, but it took him like that sometimes, even in peacetime – the noise from the table where the Crew were eating lunch made him flinch, and the nearest empty seat had been two down from Dima. For the first five minutes Trofim had been gripped by an anxiety as great as it was baseless, so that all he could do was hold onto the edges of his bowl of broth and breathe carefully until the world stopped slipping and colours started to trickle back in and he could hear people talking over the roaring in his ears – and when things finally started to steady themselves, Trofim found that Katya had poured him a glass of water and set it in front of him, no questions, no fuss, and when he looked up and caught her eye, she gave him a small, commiserating smile. After that, he sat with the four of them more often than not: Dima, with his utter disinterest in anything that was going on in the war, was refreshing company; Daniil, too, with his sarcasm and prickly dissatisfaction; the steady quiet of Katya, and her surprising, occasional slides into incisive humour; Marina, who seemed to smile more than anyone Trofim had ever met – in other circumstances he might have suspected her of mild idiocy, but now it was a comfort. Comforting, too, was the fact that he always seemed to be let off the hook conversationally, and that lack of expectation allowed him to talk more. It was the same with Sasha, he realised with some surprise – this sense that he didn't have to be anyone, that his unadorned self was, briefly, enough.

Outside, the sun shone bright and fierce, bringing tears to Trofim's eyes that he had to blink away. At first he only saw her in silhouette, the woman who was standing outside the Radio House, blotted into darkness, until she unpeeled herself from the wall on which she was leaning:

"*There* you are. I thought you were never coming out."

Beside Trofim, Katya started, and when he looked down he noticed her flushing.

"Lidiya – what are you doing here?"

She was coming into focus now, taking on shape and colour and solidity, a jawline like a pen-stroke, short pale hair in waves, an extreme prettiness that Trofim found almost alienating. "They asked me to come in and do a little work," she said, indicating the Radio House. "Reading some children's stories – first thing I've had to do in months, and I thought it was worth it for the sake of the rations, if nothing else." Trofim noticed her voice, then: not beautiful, but there was something in it, a taut-strung line, that made you want to keep listening. "I finished about half an hour ago, and thought I might as well wait for you."

"How was it?"

"Oh, fine. You know how it is these days – constant roll-call of who's dead, who's sick, who's evacuated. There are some people who just seem to *relish* telling you about it. If you listened to Zoya Vadimovna you'd think she'd spent the whole winter dragging people half-dead of dystrophy out of their apartments and to the feeding centres. God, if she'd come knocking on my door I'm not sure I wouldn't have preferred death." She looked at Trofim then, and at the rest of them in turn, head cocked, an intensity of interest that was nearly aggression. "Aren't you going to introduce us?"

"This is my friend, Lidiya," Katya said, flushing even pinker; Trofim wasn't sure why, but he had a particular fondness for Katya, his reluctant ally in awkwardness. Dima grinned, surging forward and holding out a hand for Lidiya to shake; Daniil and Marina, who promptly made their excuses, claiming they had a trolleybus to catch; then:

"Trofim," he said. For one horrible moment he was sure his tongue was going to snag on the first letter of his name, but it dropped out of his mouth neat and full-formed.

"Trofim's one of the army musicians I was telling you about," Katya explained. Lidiya looked him carefully up and down, taking in the uniform, the greatcoat and the trumpet case clutched in his right hand.

"That's evident." Her gaze was one of cool appraisal, lasting a little too long to be strictly polite. Trofim had a confounding lack of certainty as to whether her end judgement was negative or positive. Turning away, Lidiya tucked her arm into Katya's. "Come along, let's get home," she said, steering her in the direction of Nevsky Prospekt. Dima trailed them, looking a little put out, and Trofim followed – feeble as he felt, perhaps he could take a walk, just for ten or fifteen minutes, before boarding the trolleybus that would take him back to where he was supposed to be.

But Nevsky thrummed with a strange energy. It wasn't just that it was busier than usual; the people there seemed more concentrated, directed. There was a power behind them. Even Dima seemed to sense it.

"What's happening?"

"There's something going on – maybe a parade," Katya said. She sounded eager – anything different caught alight in the city these days, whipping excitement out of the monotony. She started pushing through the crowd, Dima in tow. Lidiya followed, while Trofim brought up the rear.

It was a parade of a sort, but the men who trudged before them were filthy, lousy, worn down to bone. Most of them kept their eyes down on the scarred road in front of them, but one or two raised their faces to look at the crowds that were lining the street. It took three full beats of his heart before Trofim realised that these men were German prisoners, guarded by a paltry phalanx of Russian soldiers. A quagmire of feelings bubbled up inside him: anger, as always, but below that, an insistent drag of kinship. These were the men he faced across the frontlines every day; these men – he knew in a moment that he had more in common with them than with the battered, ravaged mob surrounding him. There was nothing fearsome about the bedraggled soldiers with their lowered eyes, exuding an indefinable mix of pride and humility.

"We should go," Dima said. He looked anxious, unhappy. The confidence that he normally waved like a flag was missing: Katya, beside him, seemed to sense his tension and looked up into his face, concerned. This was something Trofim had noticed about Dima, the way he was often able to catch the mood of a person or a group before anyone else did; he had a finely tuned nose for danger. Almost on cue, anger snapped through the crowd like electricity: women, children and older men vibrating with it, as they seemed to understand, belatedly, what was going on, who the men were that were being marched in front of them. The shouts started, and when these had little enough effect on the men, the crowd started casting about for other things to throw. Trofim saw one of the prisoners stumble, and realised that the man had staggered to one side to avoid a brick that crumbled to powder on the road by his left foot. Trofim turned; the person who was withdrawing their arm, a look of satisfaction on their face, was a woman in her sixties, a woman who could have easily been Trofim's own grandmother. On his other side, a teenage boy bent, hunting for ammunition. Hungry, the crowds surged forward; Trofim looked around for Katya and Dima – his height should have made him easy to spot above the churning mass, but they were nowhere. He knew that they had been sensible, to withdraw before things turned ugly, but he felt a hot surge of resentment all the same, as by his elbow, her body pushed into his by the press of people, was Lidiya, her face fixed and still, and she had evidently become his responsibility now.

He had to say her name twice before she seemed to hear him, turning her face up to his. It held nothing of the careful unconcern or bravado that he would have expected to see there, but nor did she seem scared, or angry – just baffled, shocked. Trofim had the sense that he was seeing her for the first time, stripped bare, without artifice.

"Do you see Katya?"

Trofim shook his head. "She's gone, she and Dima both. Best thing they could have done, probably." The crowd heaved again, undeniably malign. The handle of his trumpet case was slippery in his hands. Trofim caught the eye of one of the police keeping the crowd back, and felt an instinctive cringe of shame, until he recognised the look in the man's eyes as one of respect: the greatcoat, the cap, the rest of it. It felt like nothing to do with Trofim, most of the time; *brave men* would always be *other men* to him. The crowd parted for a moment and Trofim caught a glimpse of one of the prisoners, on his knees and bleeding. The jeers and catcalls clanged in his head. Lidiya took a sharp, snatched breath, and he felt her pull away – by the time he turned she had nearly vanished from sight, burrowing through the crowd, away from the road. There followed a series of confused impressions: the press of too many bodies, the heavy smell of grime and bitterness, the mob heaving and swaying with an implacable, oceanic rhythm – and then they were out. Trofim filled his lungs with air as clean and sweet as spring water. Lidiya, ahead of him, slipped down a side street and Trofim, unthinking, followed her – it wasn't until he had nearly reached her that he realised that she was crying. It stopped him short.

"Lidiya – "

Lidiya raised a hand, warding him off. With her other arm she leaned on the wall, her face pressed into the soft underside of her arm. There was something about the pose that was helpless; it evoked in Trofim a violent desire to embrace her, to charm that defiant smile back onto her face. Instead he stood back, arm's length, watching as Lidiya stood very still, very silent, and then drew a long, shuddering breath, its meaning as clear as an announcement.

"Sorry," she said, gruff and ungracious. Pushing back off the wall she stood, looking anywhere but at Trofim, and delved into her pocket for a handkerchief, mopping up in a brisk, business-like manner. "I'm all right," she said, finally looking at Trofim directly. "You don't have to chaperone me, you know. I can make my own way home." Even as she said it he could see that she was shaking; her legs looked far too thin to support her.

"I'm in no rush," Trofim said carefully. "Why don't we stop for a bit, catch our breath?" He felt certain that if he suggested she needed to gather herself she would stalk off immediately, probably collapsing as soon as she was out of sight. Instead, Trofim sat on the edge of the road, his back to Lidiya, and after a few moments he heard her footsteps behind him.

She sat, too, beside him, her knees carefully together. Under the bright hem of her skirt they looked frighteningly fragile. "They brought them into the Radio House during the winter," she said quietly. "Two German prisoners of war. They wanted them to speak over the radio, to tell the city about – I don't even know what they wanted them to say. And they brought in a…a *picnic* for them. More food than I'd seen in weeks – months, even. It was like a mirage, for us. Nobody could even conceive of that amount of food. One of the men, he said the sorts of things that they wanted him to say, I suppose – about how we were stronger, about how people were surviving in Leningrad, despite the Fascists trying to starve us out, and how he'd realised their side would never be able to win. But the other man – he wouldn't play along. He told us that we were all going to die. They cut his microphone – probably put on that infernal metronome instead. And they packed up the picnic, all of that food – not a single crumb was unaccounted for. They took it all away. I have no idea what they did with those men." She closed her eyes. "It's not that I don't oppose them. It's not that I don't think our side is…*more* right, at least. I've heard about what the Fascists did in Kharkov, in Pochep and Diatlovo. My husband was Jewish. But they're still *people*. And it wasn't the Fascists who took my husband from me, after all. It makes me angry that our side have… have stolen my chance to hate them."

Trofim wished she wouldn't talk like this. It ran too close to the confused affinity he had felt while watching the prisoners march, and the vertiginous feeling he sometimes got, back at the Front, as if he was firing at himself. "It's easier when you can't see them properly," he said at last. He hadn't intended to say it out loud, but Lidiya turned to look at him, eyebrows canted.

"I expect it is," she said. "How did you end up in this, anyway? In the army, I mean. I don't know much about music – no ear for it at all – but the army…it seems a strange thing for a musician to do."

It was a question that Trofim hated, but it sounded different coming from Lidiya – as if she was genuinely asking, rather than doubting his credentials.

"My father fought in the Civil War. I'm the only son, so…"

"He wanted you to follow in his footsteps?"

Trofim laughed. "Quite the opposite, actually. He – and my mother, both of them – they wanted me to go to the Conservatoire. They both started off as musicians – my mother plays the flute, she still teaches. And my father played the trumpet, like me. He lost an arm in the war, so…" He shrugged. "That was the end of that. He was afraid that something similar would happen to me. I did a year at the Conservatoire, in Moscow, to keep them happy. But I couldn't – "

Trofim had never spoken about it, what had happened at the Conservatoire. He had never spoken about it because he didn't understand it, and that meant he couldn't even start to explain it. There had been a ball of anxiety lodged behind his ribs for as long as he could remember, but at the Conservatoire, with nothing to think of but music, it had grown and grown until he felt certain that it was going to consume him. He had stopped sleeping and eating; he had barely been able to speak to anyone. It had been as if something terrible and nameless was stalking him, mere inches behind him, choking him with fear.

And at the time, it had felt like the only thing he could do to stop himself from being afraid was to do something that proved he wasn't, that he couldn't be, no matter how he felt. When Trofim had been a boy, his mother had taken him to the May Day parade, to celebrate the anniversary of the Revolution. His sisters, older, had been in dresses so white they seemed to glow, and he had had a suit that was stiff with starch and uncomfortable, but which caused his mother to pinch his cheeks and tell him that he looked adorable. He had wondered why his father wasn't with them in the crowd of spectators, and it wasn't until he saw him marching with the other veterans that he realised what they had really come to see. The memory of that day still stung him into an uncomfortable tenderness, and it was something he always came back to, a shining beacon of *what mattered.* As a skinny and stammering boy, far more comfortable blowing into his trumpet than speaking, any idea of joining the army had seemed ludicrous. Then he had grown, and one day the person he saw when he looked in the mirror was the sort of person that you could imagine into a Red Army uniform. He had felt almost as if he had willed it into being. This other person that he could make himself into: it was someone who wouldn't be afraid all the time. He had been wrong about that, of course, but he'd always found tangible fear infinitely more manageable than the intangible.

"I couldn't think of anything else that would matter as much," he said at last. "I loved music, but the army was important. *Is* important. I joined as a musician, playing in one of the military bands. It seemed the easiest way. But when I first saw active service, during the Winter War, it started to seem – "

Even now, he was unsure about how much he should say about those few months, more than two years ago now: the white forests, the fear like a vice around his heart, the acid burn in the back of his throat. They had won, that was what you clung to, but before that there had been the rest of it, the sense of lumbering uselessness while the Finns had seemed to come from nowhere: the vicious crack of a bullet in an empty forest, the inaudible hum of freezing air, and the warm, cloying smell of fresh blood on fresh snow. He had been hit by a bullet once, a fact that still filled him with a faint sense of disbelief, and then afterwards there had been a field hospital, his shoulder singing with pain and the rest of him gripped by a brief, exultant certainty that he had done *enough.* Of course it hadn't lasted. And then this war; the early stages still held vast swathes of time he couldn't afford to think about, that he would push down, push back whenever the smell of damp, rotting leaves and wood smoke on cold air threatened to bring them back. But the pointlessness of music had been clear amid so much destruction, so much death.

"The band that I was playing with – they were wiped out, right at the start of the war. I was the only one to survive. And when I was reassigned to the Leningrad Front, I signed back on as a rifleman. The music – " He hadn't been able to bear to even listen to it for months – not until the Symphony. "It seemed so frivolous," he said, now, to Lidiya, and she nodded.

"And does it still feel that way now? You're playing again."

"Only until the Symphony. That's something different – it's something for the city."

"You're not enjoying it, then?"

"It's not that. I don't know if I ever would have bothered to present myself for the orchestra, but I have a friend. He – he insisted." Trofim had never been quite sure whether to take it as a compliment or an insult, Sasha's calm, assessing certainty as he'd told him that the orchestra needed him; *Leningrad* needed him. *More than we need you here*, that had been the unspoken addendum that Trofim had heard, whether or not Sasha had meant it – but Trofim had gone along with it. He hadn't argued. He had wanted it so terribly, so ferociously, and he had wanted not to have to make the decision. He had wanted it taken out of his hands.

"I used to think I would fight," Lidiya said slowly. It sounded as if the words were coming from a long way away. "If I got the chance. I've been trying to remember how that felt, to believe in something that much. I had a taste of it, once or twice, in the winter – we were holding on so tightly that what we were holding onto started to seem important again. And now – " she shook her head, a little helpless. "One of the women I work with at the Radio House, when war was first declared, she was rejoicing. All of a sudden, it was as if all of these things she had been holding back for years were pouring out of her mouth. She would have welcomed the Fascists into the city with open arms, because she couldn't believe it would be worse than anything she had already lived through. Two of her sons had been in the military, and in 1938 – well, you know what happened as much as anyone. The more she talked about it, the more sense it started to make. And now, again, I've started to see it. My god, think of the army we had a few years ago, think how easily they could have dealt with the Fascists if this country hadn't been hell-bent on destroying itself – its people – before they could ever get to us." She closed her mouth with a deliberate snap, as if it was the only way she could stop herself from talking. For a moment neither of them spoke – in the hush Trofim could feel his heart hammering; this manner of talk tended to bring about an entirely physical panic response in him – and then Lidiya laughed. "I suppose if nothing else comes out of this war, at least for a few moments we can say what we think."

II: January 1942

In January, a troupe of performers had come to the Front. The occasion had a ghoulish cast. For Trofim, the preceding weeks – months – had taken on the quality of a nightmare: the cold and the deprivation, the sense of profound futility and utterly crushing boredom. The performers had set up a stage on the frost-hardened ground, and the men had come to sit and watch because there wasn't anything else to do. The performers themselves had been skeletal, bone-pale: the songs they sang had a quality of breathlessness, and when they danced Trofim wondered, in a detached, half-dreaming way, how they could fail to judder to pieces with the effort. His exhaustion was such that he couldn't make sense of what he was supposed to be watching, as if it was in a foreign language, and the lack of response from the rest of the audience indicated that the other men felt likewise. Many of the men didn't look at the stage, studying their hands or their laps with a slack-bodied apathy. Some slept – when Trofim glanced at Sasha, nearby, he saw that he was leaning his forehead on the balls of his hands, eyes closed, an attitude of utter depletion. Next to him, Viktor was open-mouthed and snoring. But partway through, something had happened: a girl had come on stage, and when she opened her mouth, she hadn't sung any better than any of the other performers, but there was something about her that simply seemed more *alive*. More than that: it was contagious, leaping from performer to performer like fire, uncurling their backs and filling their lungs. It had affected the men in the audience, row by row; without meaning to, Trofim found himself sitting straighter, listening more closely. When there was a pause in the action, he understood at last that he was supposed to laugh, and surprised himself into doing so. The sounds from the stage strung themselves together into words, then sentences, a plot to be followed. When the performance came to a close, he found himself applauding with the rest of them; even Sasha had curved his mouth into a half-smile.

It was Sasha, not Trofim, who ensured that they ended up speaking to the performers afterwards, along with a little knot of appreciative and admiring soldiers. None of the troupe seemed in much of a rush to get back to the city, although it seemed impossible that the Front could be preferable. They didn't speak much about what was happening in Leningrad, and the soldiers didn't ask. It didn't surprise Trofim when Sasha left the mess hall with the singer who had woken them all up; his intent was clear enough, although Trofim couldn't imagine where Sasha had found the energy. And then, without willing it at all, Trofim found himself talking to one of the other women, trading banalities, and then standing together, each brushing invisible crumbs off their clothing and slipping out into the icy night air.

This happened every so often, and it never felt like something of Trofim's own volition. He had grown into his looks too late to acquire the habits of a handsome man, and his body, sometimes, felt like a weapon he had only the faintest idea of how to use. *You look like a fucking Red Army recruiting poster*, Sasha had said once, with lazy envy, and Trofim had noticed the other men looking at him from time to time with a sharper edge of jealousy, the way he never had to use coercion or force the way the rest of them did; the way it never occurred to him to try and barter food for sex with the frantic, desperate women who picked their way out from the city to the Front. Trofim supposed that he should be grateful, but more often than not he wished he could just skip the whole thing altogether.

He couldn't guess how old the woman was. She kept slipping in and out of focus: one face underneath the stage paint, and the face below was paler, wearier, but Trofim couldn't tell if it was an older woman made up to look younger or a younger woman made up to look older.

Their kisses were dry and mechanical, and when the woman – whose name Trofim had forgotten, if he'd ever known it – took Trofim's hand and placed it on her small, cold breast, he couldn't imagine what she could possibly be getting out of it. For Trofim, sex had never been anything but a plunge into cold water, eyes closed, nose blocked, something to be withstood until it was over. His body responded, as it always did, with all the enthusiasm of a well-trained animal, schooled into obedience, but his head felt miles away. Even the pleasure that finally came from it was tightly limited to the physical, but the rest of it – the closeness, the mess, the thunder of someone else's breath in his ear – filled him with a queasy sense of humiliation. When the woman drew back she was expressionless, quickly buttoning her blouse against the vicious chill, and Trofim found himself lost for words: was he supposed to offer money or food, thanks or praise? She didn't look as if she expected much, and Trofim had no idea how or what to give without feeling graceless or risking insult.

"I should get back," she said, as composed as if they'd done nothing more than share a cigarette. Outside the mess hall Sasha and his girl were waiting, both of whom, Trofim noted bitterly, seemed much happier than he and the woman were. Sasha was holding something in his hands, wrapped in brown paper, and he handed it to the girl, smiling a smile that Trofim never normally saw, utterly devoid of irony or mockery, seemingly genuine.

"There's some food in there, for your family. It's not much, but – " Looking up, he caught Trofim's eye, and in the uncanny mindreading that he occasionally managed to pull off, Sasha shifted his stance to encompass Trofim and the other woman. "You can share it, can't you?"

The girl with Sasha professed unconcern; the woman with Trofim gave the first expression of real excitement he had seen on her face as she seized the parcel. When Sasha leaned in to kiss his girl goodbye, Trofim did likewise with his own: frigid cheek against cheek. As they walked away, Sasha caught sight of Trofim's face and laughed, not unkindly, slapping him on the shoulder: "Trofim, my friend," he said consolingly, "you have got to get better at this."

III: 1 May 1942: Evening

There was something about Lidiya that snagged onto the memory, but she wasn't content to stay there, pacing the confines of Trofim's skull. That evening, back at the Front, Trofim framed sentences, discarded them, reassembled them, set them aside. There were moments he kept coming back to, like prodding a bruise: the precise angle of her head as she had straightened up after those unlikely tears; the vehemence with which she'd spoken; the frightening, pale vulnerability of the skin at her throat. Sasha watched him, half-frowning, with a mixture of concern and indulgence.

"Out with it," he demanded at last.

Trofim both did and didn't want to talk about it. Mentioning Lidiya to Sasha would bring her to life, crystallise her. It felt dangerous to want something. Those words chimed in his head, again, as they had been doing on and off for months: *Katiusha was walking, singing a song about her true love, whose letters she was keeping*. He let himself imagine, a rationed treat, how things might be different, how things might be *better* if there were someone he could tether himself to, someone that he could be doing all of this *for*.

"There's this girl," Trofim said experimentally.

Sasha snorted. "There always is, Trofim," he said, irritating and sagacious. "There always is."

CHAPTER TEN

I: 4 May 1942

"It's hard to muster much enthusiasm for a performance that we all know is going to be execrable," Daniil said sourly. Katya couldn't help but agree; even Dima looked daunted. Rehearsals were still composed more of rest periods than of anything else, and conversations in the cafeteria revolved more around food and bombing than music. They had not yet managed to play for more than an hour at a stretch; there was nothing to indicate that the evening's performance was to be anything more than a semi-comforting farce. "I'm almost relieved that my family aren't here any more," Daniil went on. "I'd be humiliated for them to hear me play like this."

"My sister's coming," Marina said. "Luckily she doesn't know enough about music to tell if we're awful."

"*If?*"

"What about you, Trofim?" Marina cut across Daniil's laugh. "You're from here – are your family – "

Trofim shook his head. "My parents left on the Ice Road in winter. They're with my sister in Moscow now."

"My friend Vasya's coming," Dima said. Pride struggled against embarrassment in his voice. "Says I've been going on about playing in a *real orchestra* for long enough, he has to see the finished product."

"My friend Lidiya is threatening to come," Katya said. The word *friend* sat strangely on her tongue; it didn't seem to describe Lidiya with any degree of accuracy. "She says it's an occasion, even though she hates most music. She has a terrible tin ear – can't tell Bach from Bartók."

Daniil smirked, humourless. "Well then, she'll love this."

~

The performance was to be at seven, in the Pushkin Drama Theatre, pending the repair of the Philharmonia after shelling. Katya arrived early; she always did. The cold of the auditorium still snatched her breath from her lips; the men wore padded jackets underneath their tailcoats, while the women, in a motley collection of dark garments, simply shivered. Outside the hall, the sky lit up with spheres of white fire: an artillery attack. Rumours kindled and spread: it was on Vasilievsky Island, Karl Ilych's home, and he wasn't going to be able to make it. Or no, it was to the south of the city, near the Kirov Works. Milling around with the rest of the Crew, Katya noticed that Trofim looked tense and guilty, as he always did when the war announced itself too boldly while he was busy with music. The rest of the orchestra trickled in, in ones and twos, most of them looking ill-assembled and half-panicked. Some were missing: one or two of the brass players, who hadn't been able to make it in from the Front; a red-faced elderly clarinettist, whose name Katya could never remember. Dima. Katya told herself she wouldn't worry; he could take care of himself. He always had before. She worried anyway.

A scant ten minutes before they were due to start, Dima hustled through the door in the company of a tall, thuggish-looking man whom Katya assumed to be Vasya. She blew out a breath, coasting on relief that was frighteningly intense. Dima's face was bright with excitement but unusually pale under that, and the hand that wasn't holding his violin was balled so tight that his knuckles were bloodless. Vasya seemed unwilling to hand him off to the orchestra, with a fretful over-concern that was at odds with his physique.

"You sure you're all right?"

"Stop fussing, I'm fine."

"What is it?" Marina demanded. She turned to Vasya. "Did you get caught in the bombardment?"

"Right underneath. We were stuck in the shelters near Ploshchad Vosstaniya." He looked more than a little shaky himself, Katya noticed.

"He always claims it doesn't bother him," Daniil said, indicating Dima. Vasya fixed him with a frown, under which Daniil quailed a little.

"So it doesn't, normally. But the first hit was just feet from us. The noise of it – "

"It was impossibly loud," Dima said. He grimaced. "My ears were ringing like my whole head was a struck bell. I still can't hear properly, not quite."

Of course. Katya had wondered, before, whether the raids were worse for Dima because he couldn't see. When the bombs fell or the shelling was severe, Katya herself always had the slightly ludicrous urge to open her eyes wider, letting in more light and more awareness, as if that could somehow help her. Once, just once, as an experiment she had closed her eyes during a raid, to try and imagine what Dima experienced, but immediately the ground began to buck and roll beneath her, living and malign – and the noise of it, hugely amplified: the creaks of the buildings as they sighed and settled around her, the violent hum of air against her ears, and from the radio, the metronome's tick like a death-watch. But of course, to Dima, the absence of sound would be infinitely more frightening than its presence. Katya tried to imagine: the dark, and the silence; Dima unmoored, floating, rudderless. It made her feel slightly sick.

No time to think about it. Karl Ilych arrived, stumbling out of the car of a Baltic Fleet commissioner – they had been right, he had been caught by the artillery attack and wouldn't have made it had he not been given a lift. His face pinched with exhaustion, he had to be helped to the rostrum. The singers stood in the wings, clouds of steam rising from their mouths as they warmed up. The audience looked like a flock of ghosts, and Katya wondered how the musicians looked to them, their worn clothes, gleaming instruments hefted by skeletal bodies. For a dizzying moment she couldn't remember what any of this was for. From the violas, Marina leaned forwards, smiling encouragement. In front, in the first violins, Daniil's poker-straight back telegraphed disapproval. Beside her, Dima's face was still strained. He worried his lower lip with his teeth. A memory came to Katya then, clear and whole as if it had been handed to her: her grandmother's work-toughened hands on Katya's violin as she played, feeling the music she couldn't hear. Dima's foot was inches from Katya's own, and she shifted, pressing her foot down on his toes, watching his expression lift with sudden understanding. Karl Ilych raised his arms, giving the preparatory beat, and Katya tapped her foot on Dima's, silent, her eyes on her conductor. His arms came down; they started to play.

II: 1917

Father was away. Father was always away, and Katya could not remember him outside the shape of her mother's words. Mother would refuse to mention him for weeks at a time, her lips knitting together into the tight white line that Katya, at five, was wise enough to recognise as a locked door. And then she would talk, suddenly, late at night as she was putting Katya to bed, or helping her on with her clothes, banks breaking in a ceaseless gush of words. It never seemed like she was talking to Katya; she was just talking. The father that Katya's mother spoke about was as mythical to Katya as the *domovoi*, and she hoarded the pieces of information like jewels, hiding them from sight, only taking them out to examine when she knew it was safe. Her father was tall. He was brave. He was fighting for what was right. He was trying to make Russia better.

Katya never said so aloud, because she knew that it was wrong, but she liked the way life was when it was just her and Mother. Mother could be strange some of the time, and she cried a lot, and sometimes she was silent even when Katya tried and tried to get her to speak. But when Mother was in a good mood, she and Katya were a team. They would go to the market together, and Katya would help her mother choose the best fruit and vegetables, the juiciest cuts of meat. At home, she would help her mother cook. Sometimes in the evenings they would read together; sometimes they would listen to music. Those were the best nights. The music would loosen something inside Mother: her body would unravel, her joints softening. Katya was sometimes allowed to climb into her lap and put her cheek against her mother's chest. Her skin smelled of a mixture of salt and sweet, make-up and oil. Katya's mother's heartbeat thundered in her chest like the hoof-beats of horses. It lulled Katya into a trance. She shut her eyes and watched the warm red of the inside of her head. Everything was still.

When Mother found out that Father was coming home, the whole apartment started to vibrate. Mother was constantly busy, but Katya couldn't see what was changing. Things were moved, and moved back. Pictures disappeared from the walls and came back the next day. Mother seemed desperate to do something, but uncertain what to do. When Katya tried to help she was snapped at, so she chose instead to stay prudently out of Mother's way, perched on one of the kitchen chairs with her feet tucked under her, watching Mother work, ready to be needed. Katya was becoming very good at staying still and quiet.

And when Father came home, it was like meeting a stranger. His height made him seem alien, more tree than human. Katya was small for her age, and couldn't take in his whole body at once: when she looked up at his face she forgot the rest of him. Katya had expected her mother to cling to him, weeping, like women did in stories when their husbands came home from the war, but instead Mother was restrained. She held back, embraced him, kissed his cheeks, and welcomed him home with words that sounded formal and rehearsed. Father bent down and picked Katya up in his arms. He hoisted her easily, and Katya waited to see what would happen next; she wasn't sure how fathers worked. Her father didn't seem certain either, and once she was at his eye level he didn't know what to do with her. His arms felt rigid around her, which made her stiffen in turn; he couldn't seem to cuddle her close, and he called her *Ekaterina*, which sounded like someone else, a grown-up. Katya studied his face without emotion. He was clean and scrubbed, smelling strongly of a chemical soap. His beard and moustache were neatly trimmed, and his hair slicked back so that Katya could count the tracks where the teeth of the comb had separated the strands and smoothed them down. Close up, Katya could see that Father wore his neatness and cleanliness as a mask. Below it, Father looked tired. He had a scar that ran down the length of one of his cheeks. It pulled at the corner of his mouth, vanished under his moustache, re-emerged and disappeared into his hair. His eyes shone strangely. They didn't seem to focus. When they looked at Katya, they wavered.

"Welcome home, Papa," Katya said. She leaned forward and kissed him on his cheek. It felt oddly cool underneath her lips.

~

Katya was happy that Father was home, and when she felt sad that she rarely got to see her mother now, or scared at how quickly everything had altered, that was only because she was being selfish. Now Father was home, everything was different, better, even though to Katya, the changes felt as deep and grinding as the end of the world. Father was rarely in the apartment, always somewhere else: *working for the Revolution*, Mother explained – but still he seeped into the house like smoke, his shoes by the door, his pipe in the ashtray. Mother was happy, but it was a reckless, careening happiness that cartwheeled abruptly into silence. The trips to the market continued, but Katya and Mother didn't feel like a team any more. Someone had switched sides. There were whispered conversations after Katya had gone to bed, and while Katya knew that this was better than the weeping she had heard through the walls *before*, she no longer had the excuse of comfort to creep into her mother's bed; she was suddenly on the outside of things. Her parents said things like *the walls have ears,* and Katya was old enough to know that they weren't talking about the walls, they were talking about Katya. Her pillow felt scratchy and too hot, both sides, and tears welled in the back of her throat. *Selfish*, she told herself. *Selfish*.

The Revolution was a quiet, stealthy presence in their apartment. Father used a lot of different words and collections of letters that Katya couldn't grasp, but when he spoke, Mother would look at him attentively and nod, and so Katya did the same. She didn't understand the Revolution, and she didn't understand how Russia was changing, because she only had the faintest idea of what Russia was. It was the sharp smell of snow and pine and the way that the cold air moulded itself around her body, but it was outside their apartment. There was home, and there was Russia, and Katya couldn't quite make the link between the two.

But it was easy enough for Katya to understand that she was bad. She tried hard to be good, but Father was always disappointed. Every time they ate, Father would frown. "It is so terrible," he would say, "that we are eating this food, this good meat and these potatoes, while so many people have nothing at all." At first, these declarations would make Katya afraid. It was terrible, she knew, and unfair that she should have more food than the mysterious poor children that her father invoked to reproach her with – but she liked her meat and her potatoes, and she didn't want her father to send them away. Father never did. He sighed and pronounced about the shamefulness of the food they had on their plates, but he always ate with gusto. He talked about the tragedy of overcrowding now that the cities were flooded with migrants from the countryside, but he did not suggest that they give up the spacious apartment that he had inherited from his own father and move into a communal apartment. Katya filed away this information, putting it with the other fragments she knew about her father. These pieces seemed contaminated, though. They tarnished everything else a little bit.

Father had ideas, too, about how Katya was supposed to grow up. It wasn't enough simply to be; she had to be *created.* She had always helped around the house and been glad of it, because it was a way of helping Mother, but now her chores were numbered and plotted on graphs. She was taken on visits to the poor, to orphanages, to hospitals for those who had been wounded in the Civil War, and Father said that it was so that she could develop a social conscience, but Katya didn't know what that was, only that the orphanages made her sad and the hospitals gave her nightmares. Tutors were engaged to teach her French and German, so that she would be proficient before she went to school. At six, Katya started on both piano and violin, but it was hard to connect the scales and exercises that made her wrists ache with the music she and her mother had listened to *before.* The sounds that she eked from both instruments didn't seem to please anyone overmuch, but that wasn't the point of them. The point was the person that Katya was expected to become.

III: 1918

Katya started school at the same time that Mother's pregnancy started to show. Katya didn't really know what it meant. She understood that she was going to have a small brother or sister, and she understood that her mother was getting bigger around the middle, but even when her mother took Katya's hand in a rare display of affection and pressed it to her belly, and Katya felt the drum beat inside there, as if her heart had shifted, she could not quite connect that small, bold movement with the sibling that was coming to her. Katya wished for it to be a girl, a sister, whom, Katya decided, would be called Svetlana. She would be strong and brave and plain, like Katya herself, and when she got older Katya would help her with her lessons, and they would tell each other secrets. Svetlana would be on her side, Katya decided bitterly, as the whispering from the kitchen crept under her door, taunting her with snatches of words she couldn't make out. Svetlana would redress the balance in the apartment, so Katya wouldn't be small and alone with two tall strangers who spoke in a language she didn't understand. She saw them both in the future, pale-faced and quiet, together in their solitude.

But some babies are designed to crack open the hearts of their parents the first time they lay eyes on them. Svetlana wasn't Svetlana: she was Yevgenia, Zhenya from birth, and Father never failed to pamper her with diminutives – Zhenka, Zhenushka – even though half the time he still hammered through every staccato syllable of *Ekaterina*, leaving Katya with a disconcerting impression of formality. It wasn't until much later that Katya was able to look back on childhood photographs of herself and her sister and see the difference between her own pinched, sallow face and her sister's round one, offering guileless smiles; at the time, Katya only understood that Zhenya was adored in a way that she was not. Six years old, she could not have explained it if she'd tried, but she knew that her parents' faces changed when they looked at Zhenya in her cot. There was a siren song in Zhenya's laugh, and even her cries were somehow endearing. It was impossible not to love her, although Katya tried her best. Like Katya, Zhenya wasn't given toys – Father wasn't so far gone as to compromise his principles entirely – but taking up permanent residence on Mother's hip, she had something better, rarer. On the evenings that Father was home, no matter how tired he was he would make the time to hold Zhenya on his knee, smiling as her small fingers stretched out and examined his face, pulling on his moustache, tracing his scar. Before Zhenya had been born, Mother had carefully explained to Katya that it was an important part of the Revolution that responsibility for children be shared, and it was likely that they wouldn't see much of the new baby, because she would stay in a communal nursery. As soon as Zhenya became a bewitching reality, all talk of nurseries was dropped.

~

Instead of Svetlana, Katya was given her grandmother. Katya's grandmother had a face like a walnut, eyes dark as earth. Her hands were hard, their skin tough. She was there one day when Katya came home from school, and Katya didn't know quite what to make of this old woman who seemed to have dragged the countryside into the middle of the city, still shaking soil off her skirts.

"You remember your grandmother, Katya," Father said. Katya didn't, but she nodded anyway. She had become adept at reading her father's tone of voice, and she found wariness there. It was natural to be wary of parents, Katya thought, but it seemed strange, in this case; Father's mother was so much smaller than he was, her arms as thin as wire. "She's come to stay with us, while the baby is so small," Father explained. In a flash, Katya understood: Mother and Father belonged to Zhenya now, and Grandmother was hers; small compensation. Katya resolved to hate her, as politely as she could.

Katya's room was her grandmother's too, now, and Grandmother's corner of the room was full of pictures of men and women with ancient, stern faces, leaved and winged in gold. Katya's mother hated them. Katya had heard her pleading with her grandmother to put them away, hide them. Sometimes, when Grandmother was out, Katya's mother would steal into the room, take the pictures and wrap them carefully in cloth, placing them in her own wardrobe, out of sight. It was never long before they reappeared in the room, and the lamps in front of them, their light as soft as butter. Curiosity was stronger than hatred, sometimes; Katya asked her grandmother what they were, these pictures, and why they were so important. She had to ask twice, her grandmother's face turned towards her, her old eyes on Katya's lips, but when she understood, Grandmother shook her head.

"No. Your parents would be angry if I explained these to you, Katya."

So it *was* something to be hidden, then; something wrong. Katya had learned about denunciation – it was a duty, a civil virtue. Her father had made Katya promise that if she knew someone was doing something that threatened the Revolution she would denounce them – even if it was a teacher, even if it was Mother or himself. Katya couldn't see how the golden pictures Grandmother had were hurting the Revolution, but despite her parents' whispers, Katya had been taught that things that had to be kept secret were usually wrong. It worried her that something dangerous was going on in her apartment, and she worried, too, because a little worm of something had slipped into her hatred for her grandmother and was gnawing it out from the inside. Katya wanted to ask her mother, but whenever she practised the words in her head – *should we denounce Grandmother?* – she imagined her mother angry, or laughing. She wasn't sure which would be worse. Instead, she said nothing to her mother, and she didn't ask her grandmother about the pictures again, but at night when the lights were out and the room glowed copper from the candles Katya watched through her eyelashes as her grandmother talked to the pictures. She seemed to talk more to them than she did to anyone else.

Grandmother looked after Zhenya during the day, when Mother and Father were at work, but when Zhenya got croup over the winter, her breath like sandpaper, Mother had insisted on staying home to nurse her. It made Katya wonder. A few weeks later, when Katya woke up in the morning, she thought: *I have a sore throat. I have a cough.* She produced the latter, clutching her throat and looking pitiful. Father had already left for the day – he normally went before Katya woke up – but Mother was still there, harried and distracted.

"I'm sick," Katya said, hopeful. "I think I should stay home from school."

Mother ran an agitated eye over her, pressing her hand to Katya's forehead for a scant second. "You don't feel hot – "

Katya coughed, pointedly; her mother sighed and relented.

"All right. Get back into bed."

Katya went, thrilled at her success, but five minutes later she heard the door of the apartment close, and it was her grandmother, rather than her mother, who brought in the bottle of foul-tasting medicine that Katya had decided was suitable penance for her untruthfulness. For a moment, Katya was so astonished by this substitution and its bitter injustice that she forgot to act, and Grandmother's eyes narrowed in something that was nearly a smile.

"I don't think you really need this, do you?"

Katya said nothing, but her red and shamefaced expression spoke volumes, and Grandmother laughed. It was the first time Katya had heard her do so, but it wasn't the witch's cackle she would have expected from a face as haggard as that: it was quieter, gentler.

"Well, I don't suppose it'll do you any harm to miss a day of school, will it?" Wary, Katya shook her head. Her grandmother twitched back the blankets. "Come on, then, unless you want to waste a day off lying in bed."

In the living room, Grandmother went to her sewing basket, and Katya's heart sank. Grandmother could spend hours there, darning, mending, covering the fabric with stitches that were so tiny they were nearly invisible; was Katya going to be made to sew hems in atonement? But instead, Grandmother drew out of the basket a selection of scraps, a pair of buttons, some ribbon. "We're going to make you a doll," she said.

IV: 1924

The year Katya turned twelve, Zhenya turned six. The age difference was such that they weren't expected to spend much time together, and Katya was glad: she didn't know what to do with the roaring rush of feelings her sister inspired in her, the helpless love that made her feel like she had been shucked out of her own skin, and the sickening envy as she watched the way Zhenya picked up the world and held it in her hands, turning it this way and that as if it were a bauble for her to admire. Katya understood now, at twelve, what she had only grasped at instinctively six years before; she could see that Zhenya was beautiful in a way that Katya could never be. Zhenya's hair was a glossy black, and her eyes were the exact colour of water under clouds. Her skin was smooth and flawless, and her features delicate without being doll-like and artificial. Everywhere they went, people would exclaim over her beauty, and Katya was used, now, to her mother's blushing demurrals.

"Oh no, I don't know where she gets it from. Not from me or from Yefim, of course! Yefim's mother was a very beautiful woman when she was young, I'm told. Zhenya has her colouring."

No one ever said anything, but during these conversations, or after them, people's eyes would always slide over Katya, and there would be pity in them. *Poor girl*, the eyes said, *always going to be in the shadow of her younger sister*. Sometimes Katya would overhear people talking; she had developed the habit of being overlooked, invisible. "You see the way that Yefim dotes on his second daughter," people would say, or "it's a shame that the older girl doesn't have the charm of the younger. She could never compete on looks, but if she had charm that would go some way to help her."

Katya had started to study herself in the mirror, and she knew that they were right. In their household, vanity was not encouraged. Austerity was part of the Revolution, and ostentation and decadence were reviled. When Katya visited the houses of her friends she would feel a mixture of revulsion and envy when she saw flowers in a vase, or a gaudy landscape on a wall. Their own apartment had been stripped down until it was little more than a series of cells. The only mirror in the house was a narrow, dim strip in the bathroom, fly-spotted with age, enough to ensure neatness and cleanliness, nothing more. Alone in the bathroom, Katya gazed into her own eyes and categorised her physical faults. Her hair was limp and a dull brown, a non-colour, absorbing rather than reflecting light. Her eyes were too small, too close together, and her nose too large. Her teeth – they were something, strong and white and even, but what were teeth, after all? No one paid attention to teeth. Her skin was smooth, and that was a blessing; she had seen her classmates blighted by pimples, and at least she had escaped that fate – but it was sallow and somehow sickly, indicating too much time spent indoors. She was too thin, her eyes were an insipid pale blue that made her look always on the brink of tears. Everything she had always been taught told her that appearance counted for nothing, and everything she had always seen had shown her the opposite.

Charm, too – that was the other thing they spoke about in relation to Zhenya, something that Zhenya had and that Katya lacked. Katya couldn't get a handle on it, what it meant and how it worked, though she saw clearly its results. Zhenya smiled, dimpled, cajoled, persuaded. When Katya tried to do these things, even in the privacy of the bathroom in front of the mirror, they felt laughably false, tools fumbled in the hands of someone who had never learned how to use them. There had to be something else in her workbox. Brains were no use; no matter how hard she worked, Katya remained resolutely in the middle of her class, neither brilliant nor a dunce. Pioneers helped: when she wore the red scarf Katya felt taller and braver, and she developed a group of friends, sober-faced girls who were Pioneers too – but the wall newspapers and the marches and the mock-trials sometimes felt hollow and meaningless. The idea of having nothing to fight welled up in Katya from time to time like an ache. She had been born too late to be part of the struggle; her mother and father had fought and worked and suffered to create the world anew, and Katya had the poor taste simply to expect to live in it. Zhenya – but Zhenya's existence was certain; it wasn't something that she had to justify.

And then there was music. Katya couldn't remember, now, the moment that it had fallen into place for her, when she had first translated the drills and the exercises and the hours of tedious practise into something entrancing. The longing that she felt when she thought of her violin had to be something improper, to want something that much, something that had no worth beyond the aesthetic, and yet she couldn't stop. When she got it right – it was rare, but when she *did*, the music seemed to melt her inside, a feeling like falling. It was something she couldn't stop chasing.

When Katya was twelve, she played in her first concert, organised by her teacher: Debussy's violin sonata, which she had been working on for months. From the wings, she watched the audience enter: her father, smart as ever in his military uniform; her mother, in the one decent dress she kept for the theatre; her grandmother – and Zhenya, too, white-frocked, beribboned, already engaged in stealing the hearts of all the adults around her. Katya felt herself flush with anger: why had they brought her? She wouldn't be able to sit still throughout the performance; she would talk and she would fidget and Mother would have to take her outside. Katya's hands shook; she felt disarrayed. But once she was standing on the stage, her violin in her hands, that fierce certainty overcame her, that this was going to be one of the good times, she was going to get it right. When she started to play she felt it, the iron that ran through her blood, making her movements certain, and the loosening of her body. Her smile hid, just behind her lips, and the applause, when it came, was the surge and crash of a wave.

Afterwards, her parents smiled and congratulated her, while Zhenya, well-behaved throughout, played around their feet. "Your teacher says that you have a good chance for the Conservatoire," her father said, sounding mild and pleased. Pleased, but not…not *enchanted*. Not *transported*. If her parents had felt, listening, any fraction of what Katya had felt while playing, surely it would show on their faces? She searched for it: nothing. Her father's face held distant pride; her mother's, distracted weariness. There was no point looking to her grandmother; you couldn't be moved by something you couldn't hear, and her face gave little away at the best of times. Yet it was her grandmother who caught her arm as she was packing up to leave.

"What's wrong? I thought it went well."

There could be something so warming in cruelty. Katya wanted to cover her mouth so her grandmother couldn't make out her words. She would not, and she felt her frustration drain out of her, replaced by something smaller, something colder.

"It did go well." She wanted, suddenly, to explain, to have someone understand it. "But it doesn't matter to them. They didn't – they don't *feel* it."

Her grandmother said nothing, weighing up her words. Katya prepared herself for a defence of her parents or an attack on her own ungratefulness, which she knew she deserved. "It's yours, then," her grandmother said instead, finally. Startled, Katya looked up from the sheet music she was packing away. Her grandmother nodded, decisive. "It's something you can keep for yourself."

V: May 1942

It wasn't terrible, the concert. Nor was it good, but there were a few points, no more than three or four, when the sounds wove together in a way that felt right to Katya, that tilted her a little off-centre with pleasure. Afterwards, Dima was unusually quiet, but when Marina came over, touched his arm and asked, "Well then, how did it feel, your first concert with a *proper orchestra*?" he smiled in a way that made Katya feel as if she had stumbled. "It felt…good," he said quietly. "It felt very good."

Three days later, when Katya left the Radio House, Dima by her side, Lidiya was waiting. Eyeing Dima with a frank curiosity that Katya didn't much like, Lidiya gave him the sketch of a greeting and handed Katya a paper bag.

"There you go."

"What is it?"

Lidiya rolled her eyes, and Katya looked inside, flushing instantly. "*Lidiya*…"

"What?" Lidiya demanded, faux-innocent. "You asked me to get them for you. I just picked them up, and as I was passing…"

"What is it?" Dima asked, curiosity piqued. Katya widened her eyes at Lidiya, jerked her head in Dima's direction, pantomiming fury; Lidiya shook her head in despair, whisking her hands in Dima's direction: *give them to him*, she mouthed.

Katya had never been comfortable with gifts, giving or receiving: they opened you up to wanting something too much, either something tangible, or the warm flood of appreciation, which could be just as intoxicating. Shooting Lidiya a look which Katya hoped transmitted her intention of swift and painful retribution, Katya turned to Dima, pressing the bag into his hands.

"They're for you. Lidiya – she knows someone who works in the metal works, and they use these to protect their ears from the noise. I thought – after what you said when you got caught in the raid – "

Dima unwrapped the headset, turning it over in his hands. His face was curiously blank.

"It's probably a stupid idea," Katya muttered. Still silent, Dima set his violin down on the ground, placed the headset on top of it, and straightened, swiping at Katya, nearly missing her, pulling her into an embrace.

"It's wonderful," he said into her ear. "Thank you."

Obscured as she was by Dima's shoulder, Katya could sense Lidiya's amusement. She put her forcefully out of her mind. Dima smelled of soap and rosin. Katya could feel the jut of his ribs against her own. There was a furious clamour inside her; she squeezed her eyes tightly closed, blocking out the light. "You're welcome," Katya said.

CHAPTER ELEVEN

I: 7 May 1942

Living in Leningrad her entire life, a city as familiar to her as her own body, Katya could be ambushed by the wounds the Blockade had inflicted upon the place. Sometimes it would be turning a corner to see a familiar building spilling its guts onto the street below, and sometimes it would be something she had seen a hundred times, but which, in a particular slant of light or a specific mood, still had the power to shock. It was like that with the Anichkov Bridge: she crossed it every day now, on her way to and from the Radio House, and most of the time she thought she was used to the loss of the horse statues, rearing up in terrifying splendour, a sight that used to thrill and half-frighten her as a child. And yet sometimes their absence was a blow, a painful object lesson of what was different. Katya remembered Tanya, little more than a baby, stretching her arms towards them, hands like stars; she remembered laughing as she lifted Tanya so that she could touch one of the hooves with her fingertips. Memories like this were gut-punches; it was all Katya could do not to fold under the force of them.

Dima must have heard her draw in her breath; he always heard more than Katya expected him to. "What's wrong?"

"Nothing," Katya said, her customary, instinctive response, and then: "It's the bridge. The horses. I keep thinking I'm used to them being gone, but sometimes it still catches me unawares."

"The horses," Dima echoed, musing.

It was so easy to forget that Dima couldn't see, and Katya was starting to feel less guilty for her lapses, because he never seemed to be bothered about them himself. Still, this one made her flush a little.

"Oh, of course, you wouldn't have seen – "

"I know about the horses, Katya," Dima said, chiding. "*Everyone* talks about the horses." He gave a swift grin that made Katya smile back, unaware. "Come on. I want to show you something." He quickened his pace, Katya trotting behind.

It was telling of how much the city had started to wake up in recent weeks that Dima, hunkered down on his heels by the railings of the bridge, drew some curious looks from passers-by – only a month or two before, you could sit down and die on that bridge without anyone paying much attention. Katya put on her best expression of disdain: *what, you've never seen a blind man feeling a bridge's railings before? How provincial.* She was so intent on repelling the stares of one particularly insistent woman that she'd almost forgotten what she was doing there when Dima took her hand, drawing her closer –

"Oh!" She caught her breath; a feeling ignited that could only be delight. Squatting down beside Dima, she put her hand next to his, on the ironwork wrought into the fabric of the bridge.

"See, horses," Dima said. His voice was mild, but his face was ablaze with smug triumph. Grinning back, unable to help herself, Katya traced the sculpted metal horses that formed part of the railings, face to face, their hooves like flowers.

"I can't believe I never noticed."

"People scarcely ever do. Of course, they're hardly your standard horses, as far as I can tell." Dima ran his hand along one of the horses' backs, where it seemed to dissolve into some strange sort of sea creature. "Certainly, none of the horses of my acquaintance have ever had scales on their hindquarters. Or a tail coming out of the middle of their back."

Katya laughed. "How extraordinary." Dima started to rise; reluctantly, she followed suit, one hand gripping his for balance. They began to walk, slower now, as Dima added:

"There's more, too. Fish, and – and mermaids, Vasya says."

"How did you find them?"

"Oh, Katya, they're right *there*!" Relenting, he went on: "I noticed them the first time I came to Leningrad, with my old music teacher – I was fifteen, and still at school. It struck me – " The smile dropped from his face, suddenly serious. "It struck me that someone had gone to all that trouble to turn something functional into something beautiful, even though most people were probably going to overlook it." He shrugged, looking slightly embarrassed. "I found that – I found it pleasing."

II: 21 March 1935

Dima couldn't even conceive of how Arseny Grigorevich had managed it. Ordinarily, pupils weren't allowed to leave school grounds unless accompanied by a family member or strictly supervised on the very rare school trip that was organised. What Arseny Grigorevich was proposing – travel to Leningrad, staying for two nights, an *orchestral performance* – was so unthinkable that Dima's brain shut it down almost before Arseny Grigorevich had finished speaking. It had been a few years now since the violin had eclipsed the piano in Dima's universe, won over by its intransigence, its prickly nature and the way it never let him get away with anything; a chance to see what it could really do – what *Dima* could do, if anyone let him – was seductive and impossible.

"They'd never allow it." *They*, to Dima, were to be considered separately from Arseny Grigorevich. Arseny Grigorevich was on Dima's own side, an ally.

"I *am* a teacher, you know, Dima," Arseny Grigorevich said with deceptive mildness.

"Yes, but – " *Not a real one*, he nearly said, stopping himself in time. Arseny Grigorevich waited just long enough for the blush to mount from Dima's neck to his hairline, and then said, airily:

"Well, I already have permission, in any case. Provided you want to go, of course."

Want didn't even begin to cover it. The moment the two of them passed through the school gates, everything felt different. The air was lighter, the breeze sharper, the sun like a flat-handed slap against Dima's back. Inside him, a balloon was tethered, and it rose, dizzily, up from his diaphragm to his throat, no matter how many times he tried to swallow it down. He folded his excitement inside himself as small as it could go. He had practised, the night before, the air of nonchalance he wanted to adopt, as a fifteen-year-old on his first significant trip out of school for years: "I'm going to Leningrad," he had said experimentally, to the small clutch of miserable, aggressive boys who, like him, had been left behind for the spring break, and who were plotting a raid on the girls' quarters. Something had been thrown at him – a shoe, perhaps – and he ducked instinctively. Kirill, probably. Fedya had drawn a deep sigh: "Yes, to go to a *classical music concert*," he had said, with such mocking venom that Dima had had to laugh. "A classical music concert," he said, musing, "…in *Leningrad*," and ducked in anticipation of the second shoe.

By the time they reached the train station, it was as much as Dima could do to hold onto himself amid the maelstrom of unfamiliar sounds and smells. People pushed past him. Noises made him start. School was never quiet, but Dima appreciated for the first time the muffling effect of being shut away from the world, and constantly around people who understood him. Arseny Grigorevich didn't talk much, which was a relief; the strain of having to maintain a conversation seemed overwhelming. In theory, Dima had welcomed the chance to spend time with Arseny Grigorevich outside of school, perhaps talk about things man-to-man (although Dima was rather hazy on what those things might be). But when it came to it, Arseny Grigorevich was safer as a cipher. As a normal, fallible man, he became dangerous, a risk.

At least the sound of wheels against train tracks was soothing in its repetitiveness. As Dima rested his head against the cool glass of the window, a memory tripped him, catching him unawares: the last time he'd been on a train, seven years old; his mother pressing him to her side; not understanding why she was trembling. It still felt like a cold space opening up inside him, to remember his family, and he carefully, deliberately sent his mind down another path, counting the beats of the train wheels clicking, setting a series of melodies in time. Opposite, paper slid across paper as Arseny Grigorevich read. Other people entered their carriage, talking; one, a man, tried to engage Dima in conversation but the words kept slipping away from him, he couldn't concentrate and in the end he took refuge in his best defence, closing his eyes and pretending to sleep.

The trip to Leningrad took over two hours, and by the time Dima got to his feet, his legs half-numb from disuse and his tongue thick in his mouth from silence, his head felt feeble and delicate, as if any sharp movement or loud noise would jolt it off his neck altogether.

"Are you all right?" Arseny Grigorevich asked. Concern didn't suit him; it made him snappish.

"I'm fine," Dima said.

"Are you sure? You look pale."

They stood on the platform, wreathed in smoke. The inside of Dima's mouth tasted of tar, and he felt covered over in grime. Anxious, he passed his handkerchief over his face. He needed to wash.

"I'm fine, honestly. I just need a bit of fresh air."

The air in Leningrad was not fresh, and they only walked for five minutes before Arseny Grigorevich took Dima's elbow with gentle clumsiness and drew him forward, into the roar of the street and onto a trolleybus. It was early evening, the trolley was full and the two of them stood and swayed together. Dima had never known such a press of people. The pain in his head pushed outwards, intensifying. By the time they were on the street again it took all his remaining effort to put one foot in front of the other, moving forward.

"Not far now," Arseny Grigorevich said. His solicitude made the back of Dima's neck prickle, but against his will he was comforted. They reached Arseny Grigorevich's friend's building, turned away from the street. Sounds started to recede. On the first floor, a door opened. Dima took what felt like the first deep breath he had taken in hours.

Arseny Grigorevich's friend, Olga Andreyevna, was small and friendly and cheerful, pushing Dima and Arseny Grigorevich into chairs as she rushed to get them something to eat. Dima's head throbbed, and he tried to uncurl his fingers from where they had been clinging onto the handle of his overnight case, a bulky old-fashioned monstrosity he had had to borrow from Arseny Grigorevich. His knuckles creaked.

"You must be famished!" Olga Andreyevna said. There came the click of a plate being put down in front of Dima. The dense, damp smell of cabbage rose from it, something Dima normally quite liked, but now nausea uncurled itself languorously from the pit of his stomach, stretching along his spine and down his arms until the tips of his fingers felt cold. *You will not be sick*, he commanded himself; obediently, the nausea retreated a little, enough to allow him to risk opening his mouth to speak.

"I'm very sorry," he said, with as much politeness as he could muster, "I've got a bit of a headache. Would you mind if I lay down for a little while?"

"Of course, of course!" Olga Andreyevna sounded anxious. Dima sensed her hands fluttering towards him and flinched involuntarily, hating himself, hoping she wouldn't notice. Under Dima's flattened palms, the table seemed to dip and sway alarmingly. He held on.

"Are you ill?" Arseny Grigorevich demanded, his voice low. He sounded half angry.

"No. Just, it's just…" His smile felt weak on his own lips. "It's just *a lot*, today. Everything. The train, and the city – it's a lot."

"The boy's exhausted," Olga Andreyevna said to Arseny Grigorevich with mild reproof, and then to Dima: "I'm afraid it's only the sofa, the apartment just has the two rooms…"

"It's fine, it's fine," Dima said, rising. He hadn't the energy to try to explain that this was the first time he'd been in a home for eight years; a bed, a sofa or a floor took second place to that basic fact. Olga Andreyevna took his hand with unexpected assurance and placed it on her shoulder, leading the way. Dima found a sofa, a pillow, a crisp sheet and a blanket worn soft. He still hadn't washed his face, but when confronted with the bedding, the quiet, and the promise of being horizontal, he found he didn't care. "I'm sorry to be so rude."

"Please don't apologise," Olga Andreyevna said warmly. She reached out to him again and this time Dima didn't move away as her palm brushed his forehead, pleasingly cool.

"No fever," she said.

"Honestly, I'm not ill."

"No. But everything's so new – it must be a bit overwhelming for you."

"Yes," Dima said, surprised.

"Rest now. Take as long as you want. The city will still be here when you wake up."

~

At school, time was divided by bells into neat segments. A bell woke them in the morning, bells announced the start and end of classes, bells summoned them to meals and told them that it was time to go to bed again. Dima's only real understanding of time was *now* and *not yet*, and so when he woke in Olga Andreyevna's apartment he had no sense of whether it was the middle of the night or close to morning. His waking was gentle and easy, and as he lay on the sofa taking account of himself he understood that yesterday's headache and nausea were gone; he felt emptied of them, emptied of everything, a hollow boy ready to receive whatever the city had to offer. It felt good. His skin trembled with energy. Not far from him he heard Arseny Grigorevich's breathing, stentorian and steady. Dima was used to the sounds of other people sleeping around him, but this was *Arseny Grigorevich* – it struck him as shockingly intimate. He still wasn't sure how to think of Arseny Grigorevich as human.

Dima got up. It was the first time he had woken in an unfamiliar room since his first day of school, and for a moment fear rushed in, the floor seemed to shift, he was abruptly, frighteningly aware that he had no idea how big the room was, whether a wall was inches from his nose or miles away, what myriad obstacles and traps there might be standing between him and the bathroom. Mentally, he shook himself: bravery was all very well at school, where he knew every wall and every step and every person in the place, but if he quailed in the face of the unfamiliar his courage was worthless. The fear receded as quickly as it had come. Dima felt for and found the sense of place and space he had learned to cultivate. Objects arranged themselves around him, their nearness and solidity: the sofa from which he had just risen, something that loomed at knee-height – probably a table – and beyond it the sound of Arseny Grigorevich's breathing, presumably on another sofa. Dima bent, reached for and found his bag, tucked neatly at the end of the sofa. He was still in yesterday's clothes, which felt suddenly unwelcome on his body, clotted with dirt. He shuddered.

Bag in one hand Dima walked, silent and careful, until he found a wall, and then, ghosting it with his fingers, a door. He knew this one: Olga Andreyevna had led him through it the night before, and therefore it must lead to the kitchen. No use. Beyond it, a corner, and then another door. This was where the risk came in: a two-room apartment, Olga Andreyevna had said last night, which meant that one door led to the bathroom, and another to her bedroom. The idea of surprising Olga Andreyevna asleep filled Dima with horror. The door was cool and smooth with paint and he pressed his ear against it, listening for a clue. For a long moment, nothing, and then the round sound of a drip from a tap. Dima grinned fiercely and foolishly at his own small triumph.

In the bathroom he used the toilet, stripped off, and using his washcloth cleaned up as well as he could, missing, unexpectedly, the industrial showers of school. Dima wasn't always aware of what he lacked in being blind, but he had come to realise that his extreme sensitivity to dirt was probably part of it, his drive to remain as clean as possible at all times for fear of leaving himself open to mockery. It did seem terribly unfair, on the rare occasions that he considered it, that he had to have a public face that other people could see when he not only could not see them, but could never even see himself.

Dressed in a clean set of clothes, he edged the door open, cautious of creaks. The apartment still lay silent, a heady quiet that was filled with sleep. In his head, Dima mapped the building, the direction from which they had entered, the turn on the stairs, the front door opening into the living room, the kitchen on the right...he deduced that the window in the kitchen must face onto the road outside. Making his way there, kneeling on one of the kitchen chairs so he could ease open the catch at the top of the window, he swung it open: cool air flooded in like water, displacing the stagnant weight of indoors and the filth and grit of the day before. Beneath him, on the street, there were footsteps, the sounds of doors opening and closing. Not far away came a whirr and a whoosh: a trolleybus. A man called out a greeting. A dog barked. Shivering a little with cold and elation, Dima listened to the city waking up around him.

By the time Arseny Grigorevich woke up, Dima had been sitting at the window so long that his legs were cramped and his skin icy.

"I should have known you'd be awake at the crack of dawn, given that you were unconscious before eight last night," he grumbled, not bothering with *good morning*. "Are you feeling better today?"

"Much."

Arseny Grigorevich grunted, a noise Dima had come to interpret as indicating grudging pleasure. "Well then. We've got the morning to ourselves, and then I've arranged to meet some old friends this afternoon. You're welcome to come along."

"It's all right, you don't need to do that. I can easily wait here if you'd rather."

For a moment Arseny Grigorevich said nothing, a silence that Dima groped to understand: shouldn't he stay here? Was he in the way? Should he have shown more willing and enthusiasm? Arseny Grigorevich cleared his throat.

"I'm sorry, Dima. What I meant to say was that I'd like you to meet my friends. I think it would be a constructive meeting, on both parts."

The corners of Dima's mouth twitched. Arseny Grigorevich sounded discomfited, but that was a compliment, surely? Dima decided to take it as such; he came by them so rarely.

That morning, they walked. Arseny Grigorevich did not question what a blind boy could get out of exploring a city, which Dima appreciated. Something in him had toughened up since yesterday, a scab or a scar, and the new sounds and smells, the sheer press of people and the weight of newness felt exhilarating rather than overwhelming. The broad smack of water against the wide shallow steps leading down to the river, and the rich smell of the Neva, smooth and cold. The scrape of stone against Dima's hands as he ran them along the edges of the buildings, the explosive certainty of space in Dvortsovaya Square, the ornament and decoration that seemed to blossom everywhere Dima could put his fingers. The solid, definite tap of a woman's high-heeled shoes against the pavement, and the way people spoke, garrulous and sure. Dima thrilled to it. Once he caught the edge of a voice that sounded like Vasya's, and that jolted him – it hadn't occurred to him that Vasya's Leningrad was the same as Arseny Grigorevich's. The two did not map onto one another at all; Vasya's Leningrad was a place of subterfuge and risk, peopled with crooked characters and all-night bars, while Arseny Grigorevich's could only be full of music.

Dima had expected the friends Arseny Grigorevich was taking him to meet would be musicians, but he was surprised when he introduced Yuliya Aleksandrovna and Maksim Sergyevich as members of the trio with whom he used to play. This was something Arseny Grigorevich had never mentioned, only telling Dima about his orchestral playing and his short-lived solo career. "The trio was never serious, we never performed much," Arseny Grigorevich explained, "we played more for our own enjoyment." Yuliya Aleksandrovna and Maksim Sergyevich lacked the eager friendliness of Olga Andreyevna; their greetings to Dima were laconic, and Dima was sure he picked up a twitch of amusement in Maksim Sergyevich's voice when he was introduced. It bothered him surprisingly little; he was accustomed to underestimation.

The conversation eddied around Dima while he sat in silence, playing the morning's adventures back to himself, ensuring that he had memorised the precise sound that the trolleybus made when swinging out into the street, and the feel of it, its insinuating push and pull. He didn't dare to let himself think about the plan for the evening lest his excitement come bubbling up from the pit of his stomach and out of his mouth. Arseny Grigorevich, Yuliya Aleksandrovna and Maksim Sergyevich discussed people Dima had never heard of, and it was evident even to him that their conversation avoided as much as it laid bare. Arseny Grigorevich had never told Dima why he had left Leningrad, and Dima had never thought to ask, but the reason was there, hiding in the chasms that opened up between sentences; Arseny Grigorevich seemed uncomfortable, chilled, and the room was foetid with the unacknowledged stench of unease. When the three had skidded into silence for the second time, Maksim Sergyevich cleared his throat: "Enough gossip. I'd like to hear your young prodigy, if I might."

Dima had never heard the word *prodigy* applied to him before. It was a shame that on Maksim Sergyevich's tongue it had to sound so much like a slight.

"Of course," Arseny Grigorevich said coolly. "Perhaps a duet?"

"But – " Dima hadn't brought his violin. He hadn't dared to, the terror of taking it out of the school and opening up the potential for theft and loss and breakage had been too much, and he hadn't thought he would have the chance to play.

"It's all right. Use mine. I assume you still have one, Yuliya, that I can borrow?"

The silence sounded taken aback, disconcerted. "Well…yes, of course," Yuliya Aleksandrovna said. Dima felt the case of the Guarneri under his hands. This was a rare treat he was being afforded; Arseny Grigorevich occasionally let him play his instrument, saying that he wanted Dima to develop an appreciation for the art of the luthier, but he had never thought that he would be permitted to play it in front of anyone else. Opening the case, the smell that came from the instrument was sacred.

They tuned up. Dima's heart seemed to be beating in his throat. He didn't know why, because he wasn't nervous. He *wasn't.* "The Telemann?" Arseny Grigorevich said. It sounded like a question, but Dima wouldn't have dared to gainsay him.

"All right."

He lifted the violin to his shoulder and took as deep a breath as he could, groping for his confidence and snagging a shred of it. *They may* know *more about music than I do*, he told himself, *but they couldn't possibly* feel *it more*. Arseny Grigorevich counted under his breath. Dima found a still, bright spot at his centre. Arseny Grigorevich began to play, Dima echoing the sharp, bright opening phrase, and there was no room in the apartment for anything else.

The final note seemed to hang in the air for longer than it ought. Dima fought with his urge to smile, certain that to show too much pleasure in what he had just played would seem obnoxious. He lost the battle conclusively. Arseny Grigorevich said nothing, but his presence was soft in a way that showed that he was pleased. For a moment Maksim

Sergyevich and Yuliya Aleksandrovna said nothing either. Their silence felt like a challenge.

"Why don't the three of us try something together?" Maksim Sergyevich asked at last. His voice was pushing something down, forcing it away, denying. "Me, and Yulya, and Dima, I mean."

"Excellent idea." The faux-casual tone of Arseny Grigorevich's voice told Dima that this was what he had intended all along.

"Fine with me," said Dima, overly flippant. His heart reared up again. Playing with Arseny Grigorevich was what he was used to; playing with other people – especially two other people – was a different matter altogether. This was the test, he understood. There was something liberating about people expecting him to fail; it meant it didn't matter if he did. Briefly but powerfully he wished that Arseny Grigorevich didn't have such high hopes for him, and also that he didn't hide them so well.

"How about the 'Ghost' trio? The allegro movement," Arseny Grigorevich suggested. He had been planning this for weeks, Dima realised, recalling the hours he had spent playing the violin part over and over to the accompaniment of a choked-sounding recording. He felt tricked and flattered, both at once. A piano stool scraped against the parquet floor, papers rustled as Maksim Sergyevich searched for music, and the clasps of Yuliya Aleksandrovna's cello case clicked open. Dima stood. He felt ready. It didn't matter, anyway. It *didn't.*

"What sort of tempo can you manage, Dima?" Maksim Sergyevich asked in a voice that pretended to be kind. Keeping his face carefully still, Dima tapped his foot on the floor, marking a speed that was fractionally faster than the one he had practised. It was idiotic, he knew, but that *can you manage* had stung.

"All right." All pretence gone, Dima heard Maksim Sergyevich lift his arms. His back straightened as if he had been yanked upright, and time slowed down so much that Dima felt he could catch it in his hands. Practising so often with Arseny Grigorevich, Dima had never been sure of the line between habit and intuition, the extent to which he was able to anticipate Arseny Grigorevich's playing and the extent to which he was just accustomed to it. When he heard the sound of Maksim Sergyevich lifting his arms, Yuliya Aleksandrovna raising her bow, everything seemed to fall into place at once with beautiful clarity. He could seize the exact moment when they would start to play. It floated in front of him: *there, now*. He was ready for it. When his bow hit the strings, it felt like a leap. The music was sure under his fingers, it sang in his head. He wasn't playing with Maksim Sergyevich and Yuliya Aleksandrovna any more, he was playing with the music itself, or it was playing him, his body the instrument, designed for nothing more or less than this. The melody hooked him, pulling him in, sure as a dance. It was a romp, a joy. As the music came to a close he heard, distinctly, the sound of Yuliya Aleksandrovna mouthing the word "...extraordinary."

Afterwards, Dima could never quite gather together the shards of memory of the next half hour; whatever was going on around him was secondary to the shout of exultation that echoed in his own head. Only one sentence pierced the din: Maksim Sergyevich, sounding peculiarly sincere: *come and see us if you ever find yourself in Leningrad.* Dima only came back to himself on the pavement outside Maksim Sergyevich and Yuliya Aleksandrovna's apartment, Arseny Grigorevich at his side, the door closing behind them and the cold on his cheeks like a slap.

"That seemed to go rather well," Arseny Grigorevich said, with careful understatement. Dima smiled, silent for once. That was just the overture, glorious as it had been; the biggest treat was still to come.

III: 7 May 1942

"I was supposed to be a chamber musician," Dima told Katya. They were standing outside the Vladimirskaya Church where their paths usually split, but Dima didn't seem to want to stop talking, and Katya certainly didn't want to stop listening. "Well, no, I wasn't supposed to be anything much at all. But when it started to seem possible that I might be a musician, Arseny Grigorevich wanted to steer me towards chamber music. A quartet, probably, or maybe a trio like he had played in. He thought it made the most sense – you're not as reliant on being able to see as you would have to be in an orchestra or as a soloist, especially if you've been playing with a group for long enough that your playing grows into each other. But the first time I heard an orchestra playing live I couldn't imagine anything I wanted to do more. It was an explosion, something so big and uncontained. Chamber music is so… careful. An orchestra is flamboyant. It fills you up. After that, anything else felt too thin to me. Too anaemic."

IV: 22 March 1935

The smell of the auditorium was something that Dima couldn't have imagined, a mixture of dirt and sweat, hundreds of women's perfumes mingling, shoe leather, wet wool, cigarette smoke. The room crackled with anticipation, laughter like gunshots. Dima sat as still as he could, as if his happiness were breakable if he dared to move. There was something dreamlike about the experience, splendid and impossible. Arseny Grigorevich offered him a sweet and he put all his energy into sucking on it until it was just a sugary sliver on his tongue.

The orchestra started to tune up, the strings squealing and growling, the woodwinds showing off with runs and trills that sparkled in the melange of sound. The noise around Dima diminished. The sense of tension and attention was physical; Dima was sure that if he moved his hand it would travel more slowly through the air, impeded by the leaden weight of eagerness surrounding him. Every muscle in his body tightened, every nerve strained to the extent that his heart bounded and started to hammer at the rainstorm of applause that greeted the conductor. He hoped Arseny Grigorevich hadn't noticed the way he had started.

And then the music.

V: 7 May 1942

"I had listened to so much recorded music. Arseny Grigorevich had always insisted on it as part of my training. He knew that I never heard any music otherwise, and he would say that all the practising in the world was useless if I didn't know how to *listen* properly. I thought I loved music, listening to records, but there was always a calculation there, working out how I would play the piece, taking something from it rather than just letting it be. And then I heard an orchestra for the first time in a concert hall, and I just…" Dima trailed off. He was smiling, but looked almost sad. "I wish I could explain how it felt. I wish I had the words. It was as if I was the music, and the music was everything. There was no space between us any more, no space between anything. It was…it was transcendent."

VI: 22 March 1935

When it was over, Dima found that he couldn't move. Arseny Grigorevich didn't push him, but sat quietly while people squeezed past them, climbed over their legs, clicking their tongues in irritation and disapproval. It was only when the auditorium was nearly empty that Arseny Grigorevich nudged Dima. "Come on. We can't stay here all night."

Dima had forgotten where his legs were, or that they existed at all. For years he hadn't bothered much with words, knowing that music was enough, but now he desperately wanted to explain to Arseny Grigorevich how it had been, the way that his ribs had cracked open with the power of the sound, his spine had liquefied, his body had disintegrated and disappeared. It was more than a metaphor, it was a fact: he had been engulfed, encompassed, consumed. As long as the orchestra was playing, he forgot that he was human. It took him until the corner of Olga Andreyevna's street to collect together enough syllables to speak. "It was *amazing*," was what he came out with.

Arseny Grigorevich chuckled. "Well, it was certainly *interesting*. I'm not quite sure about Popov, though; he's running the risk of – "

"*No*," Dima said sharply, and then flushed at his own rudeness. "I mean, I'm sorry. But please…"

"Don't spoil it?"

"No. Please don't." Dima thought for a moment, and then said, "It was everywhere. The music – it was *everywhere*."

Arseny Grigorevich did not reply for a moment, but his silence was one of consideration. "I'm trying to imagine what it must be like for you, to hear something like that for the first time," he said. "I can't. For one thing, I grew up with music. I can't remember a time before my father was taking me to concerts. And then, of course, I have my sight. I suspect that – that it dilutes things, a little."

"I forgot myself," Dima said. It was terribly important that he get this right, communicate to Arseny Grigorevich how it had felt, what a gift he had been given. "If you had asked me, I couldn't have told you my name. I couldn't have told you...*what* I was. It was – I've never felt anything like it. *Never*."

"I see."

"That's what I want to do. I want to play in an orchestra."

"Well, there's the Leningrad Orchestra for the Blind..." The reasonableness of Arseny Grigorevich's tone smarted. Dima wasn't used to being patronised, not by him.

"I want to play in a *real* orchestra. I'm sick of – I'm sick of *things for blind people*. School for the blind, orchestra for the blind – you know I'm good. You don't tell me much, but I know that you know. I heard what Yuliya Aleksandrovna said today." He hadn't meant to say that. "I want to be a proper musician. Not a...not a *novelty*. And I want to play in an orchestra." The petulance in his voice caught up with him, and he stopped, but anger still rode high in his chest. He was rarely angry at being blind these days, he had given that up when he had found music, but it was still there, ready to ensnare him, hiding behind his heart.

"What about following a conductor?" Arseny Grigorevich asked. Primed to spring, Dima scoured his tone for condescension, but found none. It was as if he was genuinely asking.

"I can't. But I can follow the person next to me." He remembered the sound of Maksim Sergyevich's arms lifting, the beautiful certainty when everything fell into place. "I followed Maksim Sergyevich and Yuliya Aleksandrovna today. I could tell what they were going to do before they did it. Before they even *knew* that they were going to do it. You saw that, they did too. I can train myself to get even better at it, to pick up on cues. When someone lifts a bow. When they sit up straighter. When they take a breath."

From the moment he had first placed his fingers on a keyboard in front of Arseny Grigorevich, the moment he had first taken a violin in his hands, from the first time he had played a scale, to the Bach partitas he was working on now, Dima had always wondered, in a detached, clinical sort of way, whether there was anything he could do, any door he could push on that would make Arseny Grigorevich say no: *no, too far, stop here, it's finished*. The silence lengthened between them; Dima's anxiety started to rise: was this it, the point at which Arseny Grigorevich was going to say that Dima had gone far enough, learned enough, taxed Arseny Grigorevich's resources enough? He would not open his mouth, he would not ask. Arseny Grigorevich's key was in the lock of Olga Andreyevna's door, his hand on the handle when he sighed, a near-soundless acquiescence.

"Well, then. It's good to know what we're working towards."

CHAPTER TWELVE

I: 11 May 1942

The war had made a study of fear, and Katya had learned a lot about the different ways people dealt with it. Some gave into it, a helpless surrender. Others swallowed it back. Lidiya turned hers into a particularly virulent sort of anger, precise and sharp as a knife blade. Dima wrestled with his, trying to take it down. And Katya – Katya's own fear worked on her body, sweeping through it like a hurricane, leaving everything in disorder. No sense, no rationality could act on it; fear turned her almost entirely animal, nerves and instinct to the fore, her brain dragged helplessly in their wake. This abandonment was nearly as hard to describe as it was to explain.

"It's funny, isn't it, how you can get used to anything?" Dima had asked her once, the morning after heavy shelling which he claimed he'd slept through, having to be shouted awake by Vasya to move to the hallway.

Katya had shaken her head. She'd just about stopped feeling strange about doing things like that in front of Dima – to start with, ridiculous as it'd seemed, she'd felt as if she was rubbing his nose in his own lack of sight. "I can't get used to it."

"It still scares you?"

"That doesn't feel like quite the right word." Katya had paused, thinking. "It's like…it's a very physical kind of fear. I tell myself – well, that the worst has already happened, and that there's nothing I can do about it in any case. But my body – " Her knees still went to water, her head roared like a thunderstorm, tears sprang to her eyes, and her skin felt alive, separate from her borrowed flesh. She had said none of this, leaving the details for Dima to imagine. His interpretation would make as much sense to him as hers – probably more. "It was almost easier when things were worse, over the winter. I cared less, then. But now, the power and the noise of it…I wait for it to end," she had said finally. "I just wait for it to end."

When it happened, right there in the Radio House, the building became Katya's ribcage; they shook in unison. Someone called *all right, let's get to the shelter*; someone else sighed, clicked their tongue in annoyance. Katya caught Marina's eye; Marina shrugged, rolling her eyes, putting her viola away. Katya's body moved, independent of herself. She fumbled with the clasps of her violin case, gathered together her music with hands that felt more like paws, bloodless, thick-fingered and clumsy. She stood; moving through a scratched and dusty film reel, there were the stairs, there was the shelter. She needed a wall at her back and at her side, something solid, albeit trembling. Her vision had narrowed so much that Dima seemed to come from nowhere, swimming out of the dark.

"Katiusha," he said, his voice low. No one had called her that since her childhood, since Zhenya. Every drop of moisture had vanished from her mouth; she could hardly assemble her tongue and her teeth to speak.

"You'll have to speak up," Dima said, smiling, pointing at his ears: the headset. Something in Katya softened, just a little: the ease of his smile, that anything could be easy in this place, under these conditions. He took her hands; her pulse pounded all over her body, swollen. Facing her, Dima held her left hand in his right, her right in his left.

"Left hand," he said, squeezing her right, "and here are the strings." He pressed the fingers of her left hand one by one, naming them: G, D, A, E. "Now guess what I'm playing." His fingers started to move.

At first her mind was too scattered, scrambled, to concentrate. She felt each breath that passed her lips, hot and dry. Something hit, close, outside; the building heaved like a sob; blue sky, metal, the smell of blood: Lychkovo. Katya stiffened.

"Katiusha," Dima said again. "Katiusha, Katiusha." His voice was almost a croon, the tone you'd use to a fractious baby. "Pay attention. I'll start again. Slowly."

She couldn't think. He was asking too much from her, to put her brain back in charge. It was impossible. Dima's breathing was steady and his hands were cool. With reckless desperation, Katya tried to match her breathing to his, counting his exhalations – her lungs hitched and stumbled. She tried again. There was something there, now, barely believable: a pool, cool and still, deep inside her, buried under layers of terrified flesh and blood and bone, but it was there. Dima's fingers moved on hers; she realised he was humming under his breath. Against the sound of the shelling Katya could only catch the barest shreds of sound, but it flashed through her all the same.

"It's – "

Her mouth was as parched as stone. Dima stopped, stilled, waiting. Katya swallowed against the boulder in her throat and tried again. "It's the Paganini. The first caprice, the one you played – "

He was already smiling, his face alight with it. Folding her hands inside his he lifted them, fisted, shaking them like she was a champion boxer having just delivered a knockout punch. Katya wondered at the gesture – had Alik done that for Dima, the first time he fought? Had he learned it from Vasya?

"Brilliant," Dima said. His voice was pitched low enough that no one but Katya could have heard. "Katiusha, you're a genius."

II: 1936

Dima didn't think much of the Paganini beyond its worth as a challenge. The shift to E minor and the descending scales in particular were what he both loathed and was obsessed by. He could not bear not being able to do something, and it was doubly enraging when that thing was music. Arseny Grigorevich showed him, showed him again, placed his fingers on the fingerboard and guided his arm. Slow, Dima could do it. Faster, the music ran away from him. Arseny Grigorevich was surprisingly patient. He showed him again. Dima played like he was racing. It was coming, he could feel it stretching ahead of him, he was there, and at the first descending scale his bow shuddered its way off the strings again.

"Fuck your mother nine times," Dima said without thinking, and as soon as he heard the words he shut his mouth as tightly as he could, as if that was a way of taking them back. If his hands hadn't been full with the violin and the bow, he would have clapped them over his mouth like a child. He had heard Vasya say that very thing the week before, and Dima had been struck, almost charmed by this colourful turn of phrase, repeating it to himself in quiet moments with a secret relish. It was never something that was meant to come out in front of Arseny Grigorevich, and Dima expected his punishment to be swift and just.

Arseny Grigorevich said nothing. It was as if he hadn't heard. He took the violin and bow from Dima's hands, and substituted his own instrument. Dima recognised it at once, the weight and heft of it, the warm butter softness of the wood; startled, he lifted his head. He had come to understand what a privilege this was.

"Try again," said Arseny Grigorevich quietly. Dima lifted the violin and tucked it under his chin, pausing a moment to breathe in its light, rich scent and to feel it quicken against his skin. "Slowly, this time," Arseny Grigorevich said. He clapped to mark the beat, speeding up almost imperceptibly as Dima started to play, stopping entirely as Dima got into his stride. *Sometimes you just know*, Dima thought; perhaps it was the magic of the Guarneri, or perhaps the gift of being entrusted with it – the music was a straight line ahead of him, beautiful and inevitable. The key changed; the descending scales were no obstacle. His fingers moved as surely as a heartbeat. It was over before he knew it; elated, he wanted to laugh. "Well done," said Arseny Grigorevich. It was the fourth time he had ever used those words to Dima, who had kept a reluctant tally.

"Your violin – "

"No. Your confidence."

"Perhaps," Dima conceded. He held out the instrument and the bow, but Arseny Grigorevich did not take them.

"It's yours now."

Dima went cold. Something was badly wrong here. He replayed the lesson in his head, looking for what he had barely noticed amid his frustration with his own playing – Arseny Grigorevich's unusual gentleness, the fact that he hadn't berated Dima for his outburst of foul language, the thin cord of tension that had held up his voice, audible even below the croak.

"I don't want it," Dima said. He was trembling as he held the violin out. "It's yours. Take it back."

"I want you to have it. A gift."

"It's yours! I don't want it!"

Arseny Grigorevich said nothing. Dima could hear his breathing, harsh and slightly uneven. He lowered his hands to his sides, still holding the violin and bow. "Are you ill?"

Arseny Grigorevich made a sound that was half cough, half laugh. "Not that I know of."

"Then what?"

"Maybe nothing." Still that maddeningly gentle tone.

"But maybe *what*?"

"I may have to go away, Dima."

Go away. Dima considered and discarded a number of interpretations, settling on the worst, the only one that made sense. He felt sick, suddenly, and wanted to sit, but he couldn't remember where the stool was, and with the Guarneri in his hands he couldn't feel for it. Stepping back, he felt through his shirt the cold wall of the studio, comfortingly solid against his shoulder blades.

"But why – ? Can't you – "

"Can't I *what*, Dima?" The sharp edge to Arseny Grigorevich's voice was back, perversely reassuring. "You're sixteen years old. You know by now how these things work. You must have guessed why I left Leningrad, why I'm here. And now – for someone with my beliefs, it doesn't seem possible to get far enough away any more."

For a moment neither of them said anything; then Arseny Grigorevich took the violin from Dima's hands. "This was my grandfather's," he told Dima. "He was a violinist, and my father too. Did I ever tell you that? My grandfather was given this violin by his teacher, when he was studying in Italy, a century ago. He passed it on to my father, and my father to me. I have never been sure if I have done it justice. I always felt that my grandfather was the better musician. My father, I think, I managed to surpass – but my grandfather…there was something in his tone, in his expression that can't be taught and can't be learned. If I had had a son – or a daughter, I suppose – a child who played, I would have passed it on to them. But instead I'm giving it to you."

"I'm not good enough," Dima said, with miserable certainty. "The Paganini – it took me forever to get it right. Even now if I tried it again I probably couldn't do it. And the Taneyev – I'm not good enough. I'm not."

"Perhaps not yet," Arseny Grigorevich agreed, "but you will be. I know how hard you work, how much this means to you. And you have what my grandfather had, and what I do not – that sensitivity, that feeling. You make the instrument speak – "

"Oh, *please* stop being so nice to me!" Dina said, wretched. Arseny Grigorevich laughed.

"If you insist. Your technique's still sloppy, you rely too much on emotion and not enough on precision, and speaking of emotion, I don't think you understand yet the difference between that and cheap sentiment. Not to mention your deplorable habit of…"

"Of dancing around while playing," Dima finished for him. He smiled with difficulty. "But even if I could be good enough, you've said yourself that you don't know what future I can have."

"True enough. I don't know if a blind musician can ever be seen as anything more than an oddity, not with a background like yours. And when I – *if* I go away, god knows what sort of second-rate musician they'll hire here to replace me. You will have to put in a lot of hard work alone from now on. But despite all that…well, no harm ever came from giving a good musician a good instrument."

Without warning, Dima felt Arseny Grigorevich's palm on the side of his face, his roughened thumb moving against the fine hair at Dima's temple. A flush rose to Dima's cheeks; he bit his lips in a frantic attempt to contain himself; presently, Arseny Grigorevich dropped his hand.

It was a Friday. Dima spent the whole weekend feeling queasy with anxiety. *Right now*, They could be coming to Arseny Grigorevich's apartment, rifling through his papers. *Right now*, Arseny Grigorevich could be in Their offices – and *now* he could be in a cell, or even already on a train. It was too easy to imagine, and at the same time impossible. He hated himself, too, for never asking after Arseny Grigorevich, only thinking of his own training: perhaps Arseny Grigorevich didn't think Dima cared at all beyond Arseny Grigorevich's usefulness to him. There were things he could have said, should have said, only Dima had never set much stock by words, and there hadn't seemed to be the space in his relationship with Arseny Grigorevich for the sorts of things Dima might have wanted to say.

On Monday, Dima barely spoke. He feared that opening his mouth would be inviting questions he couldn't answer, or information that he did not want to know. Lessons ended, and Dima made his way to the music studio, conjuring up Arseny Grigorevich as he did so, his wiry hands, the spicy scent of his tobacco, the reluctant laugh Dima was sometimes able to tease out of him. *I've been foolish*, he told himself, *and so has Arseny Grigorevich, these morbid imaginings…*

"Dmitri." The voice was Vladimir Igorevich's; as the teacher who had led Dima to Arseny Grigorevich in the first place, he had always taken a semi-proprietorial interest in Dima and his musical progress. Dima couldn't bring himself to answer. "I'm afraid that Arseny Grigorevich isn't able to come today."

"Is he ill?" Dima's voice sounded weak and breathless even to his own ears. "When will he be back?"

There was a silence. "He won't be back," Vladimir Igorevich said bluntly, at last. "We're doing our best to find a new music teacher, but it may be some time. In the meantime, you can use the studio for the next two hours to practise."

Vladimir Igorevich handed Dima his violin, always in safekeeping between lessons to protect it from the carelessness of boys. Dima wondered, half-hearted and uninterested, if Vladimir Igorevich had even noticed the substitution of the Guarneri for Dima's old and undistinguished instrument. The lock clicked, Dima entered, and the door was shut again behind him. He felt for the piano stool, laid the violin case on it and undid the clasps. The sharp smell of rosin rose into the air. Dima stroked a finger along the smooth lines of the Guarneri. He plucked the E string, and the note hung before him, pure and round. "I hate you," Dima said softly, but as he lifted the instrument out of his case he had never handled anything with such tenderness.

Dima stopped sleeping. On Monday night the loss of Arseny Grigorevich lodged itself somewhere deep in his lungs, making it difficult to breathe. Every time he started to doze off he awoke with a start, his heart hammering, choking on an indrawn breath. After hours of lying on his back, his side, his front, his other side, and his back again he gave up, propping himself up in bed as best he could, the limp institutional pillow at his back. His mind was unbearably distracted, leaping from one snatch of music to another in a horribly discordant way. Dima tried to fix his mind on a Bartók duet that he and Arseny Grigorevich had been working on, the delicious way that the two instruments slid over one another. His powers of concentration were usually intense, at least when it came to music; but now Dima could not bring the duet into focus. The music in his head swerved from the Bartók to Bach to Mendelssohn to the Paganini that he didn't even like, and which now brought a bitter taste to his mouth. When the morning bell rang to wake them at seven, Dima had still not slept. He hoped that it was a freak occurrence, but the maddening snatches of music continued throughout the day, and when he went back to bed in the evening, although his shoulders were heavy with exhaustion, the night was similarly sleepless.

By Thursday, Dima had started to feel as if he were disintegrating. He couldn't eat. Everything he put in his mouth was insufferably dry, and no matter how much he chewed, he couldn't bring himself to swallow. His skin felt thinner than normal, as if he was running a fever. Dizziness and nausea started to sweep over him in waves, coming upon him without warning, and he would have to pinch himself hard until they retreated. He still had difficulty catching his breath, and had started to suffer from inexplicable pains in strange places: his hips, the hinge of his jaw, between his shoulder blades. His mind was never silent, yet never harmonious. He wondered whether he was going mad. The only time that Dima felt like himself was when he was alone in the music studio, the violin in his hands or the piano under his fingers. Then, his chest would loosen, his mind would clear and he took full possession of himself again. Each time, when Vladimir Igorevich came to fetch him at the end of his three-hour practise slot, he desperately hoped that the peace he had found would remain. It never did.

By Friday, Vladimir Igorevich was concerned. Dima submitted to being marched off to the infirmary, and underwent a barrage of tests at the hands of the frighteningly competent nurse, although he could have told them from the start that they would find nothing wrong. His pulse was normal, and so was his blood pressure. When the nurse pressed the cold metal of the stethoscope against his ribs and back, she found his chest was clear, despite his breathlessness. He didn't have a fever.

"I told you I'm not ill," Dima said.

"Then what is it?" Vladimir Igorevich sounded anxious. He had marked Dima as a trouble-maker when he had first arrived, full of pent-up anger that he had seemed ready to vent on whatever target was closest, but since that first year, if Dima hadn't quite transformed himself into a model pupil, at least he hadn't been an active source of concern. The change in him over the past week had been visible and shocking, and Vladimir Igorevich had hoped that he was sickening for something that could easily be remedied.

"Can I practise more?" Dima burst out. It was the only thing he could think of.

"But you already have three hours a day, even at weekends, and two more hours on the days you used to have lessons…"

"Double it," Dima demanded. The urgency in his voice was such that Vladimir Igorevich didn't upbraid him for rudeness. It was clear that this was desperately important to him.

"Six hours a day? You'll be exhausted – "

"I won't. Please. I can keep up with the three hours between three and six, and then another three after supper? Or I could get up earlier in the morning and have another three hours before lessons start." Vladimir

Igorevich said nothing. "Please," said Dima. He didn't like the note of craven begging in his voice, but he couldn't help it. "*Please.*"

Vladimir Igorevich wouldn't agree to six hours, but offered four, and grudging agreed when Dima bargained him up to five. It helped a little; while Dima's malaise remained, it was easier to get through the day when he knew he would have five hours' respite from it. He started to snatch a few minutes of sleep in the studio, here and there: when he would finish a piece and find his limbs leaden with exhaustion, Dima would put the violin back in its case with obsessive care and sit on the floor, his back against the wall, his knees drawn up to his chest and his head pillowed on his arms. It wasn't much, but it was something.

Before long, though, different anxieties started. It struck Dima powerfully one day that without Arseny Grigorevich's guidance, he had no way of learning new music. There was no one to play records for him, no one to pick out a melody that he could copy, no one to go to the trouble of tracking down the braille music that Dima occasionally made use of for particularly complex or unpredictable pieces. The thought of it made his heart knock in his chest with such ferocity that it seemed to be trying to escape. No new music, and then the looming horror of losing what music he had. Dima's memory was exact and retentive, but he became frightened that the hundreds of pieces he knew would gradually be forgotten. The fear played havoc with his focus; he would break off in the middle of a Beethoven sonata because he had gone cold with terror that he couldn't quite recall the fingering on a Ysaÿe divertimento, and would have to play it through to reassure himself. Reality shifted and buckled under Dima's hands. It started to seem outlandishly unlikely that Arseny Grigorevich had ever been there in the first place. His memory, insubstantial as smoke, began to drift.

Vladimir Igorevich didn't have much of an ear for music, but he could tell what it meant to Dima, and he stepped up the school's efforts to find a replacement music teacher for him. Dima appreciated his enthusiasm, but knew with abject certainty that he would never be able to find anyone even half as good as Arseny Grigorevich had been. It had been an improbable stroke of luck that had brought a musician of his calibre to a regional school for the blind – luck for Dima, that was; ill-luck for Arseny Grigorevich, as Dima had come to understand. What was more, despite his outward lack of sentiment, Arseny Grigorevich had had an instinct for how to teach someone who couldn't see, and over the years had developed an intimate understanding of the way that Dima's mind worked. There could be no one, Dima was sure, who could ever match up to that. Two weeks after Arseny Grigorevich's departure, Dima was called to the studio after class to meet the new music teacher. Vladimir Igorevich sounded so pleased about the appointment, and Dima wanted to share in his excitement, but he could not. The woman, Galina Ivanovna, sounded fairly young, and her voice was kind when she asked Dima to play; half hating himself, he tuned the Guarneri with care and, taking a deep breath, launched into the Paganini caprice that had caused him so much trouble, which by now he had perfect. After he had finished, there was a moment of silence.

"Well," Galina Ivanovna said at last, "that was very impressive indeed." She sounded slightly stunned and Dima felt sorry for her, as if the Paganini had been a taunt. "This is beyond my level, I'm afraid," she said to Vladimir Igorevich. Dima liked her more for the straightforward way she admitted it. "The other pupils I'd be happy to take on. But you, Dmitri," her shoes squeaked on the boards as she turned back to face him, "I wouldn't be able to teach you anything."

It was four weeks after Arseny Grigorevich's disappearance before Vasya next came to visit. He usually tried to come every second Saturday at least, but would sometimes vanish on mysterious errands for weeks on end, about which he was clumsily and deliberately vague on his return. His visit was a small flame of gladness amid the storm of panic and despair in which Dima was floundering, but at least it was there. He couldn't remember when he had last spoken to anyone voluntarily. The anger that had beset him when he first came to school was back in force, and he didn't trust himself any more. It was frightening to discover that all the qualities he had come to like in himself over the past few years – his optimism, his friendliness, his easy humour – were utterly contingent on music; without it, he was the same mixture of frustration and misery and rage that he had been at seven years old, just a little taller.

"Fucking *hell*," Vasya said, when Dima sat down opposite him at their customary table. He sounded worried. "What the fuck has happened to you?"

"That bad?" Dima asked. He tried a smile, but like a half-forgotten melody, he couldn't quite remember how it went.

"That bad. Have you been ill?"

"Not exactly." The room felt oppressive. Dima's skin was too tight and the air was hot and heavy and full of other people's exhalations and he couldn't suck enough of it into his lungs. He was on his feet before he had thought about it, fumbling for the back of his chair to stop it from falling. He heard Vasya stand, too, and his anxiety stung like a blow.

"Dima – what – "

"Can we go outside?"

Vasya puffed out a doubtful breath. "Well. No harm in asking."

It wasn't usually done; the teachers liked to keep the students and their visitors where they could see them, to keep attempted breakouts and mutinies to a minimum – but Dima's inadvertently pathetic state had wrung a degree of bemused sympathy from some of the staff. The two of them were permitted to go into the yard. It was the end of October and the wind smelled sharply of the threat of snow. They had barely walked ten steps before Dima's head swam and his legs started to shake. He felt for the wall and leaned against it, half doubled over, as if in pain. Vasya stood beside him, baffled and uneasy. He put a hand on Dima's shoulder and squeezed. "Hey," he said gently, evidently not knowing what else to say. "Hey, hey."

"Sorry," Dima managed. His voice sounded tight. "I think I'm going crazy. Sorry."

"What the fuck has happened?"

Dima laughed breathlessly. He had missed Vasya's ability to slip an obscenity into any sentence. "My music teacher has gone," he told Vasya, conscious of how stupid it sounded. "He…had to leave. And since then I – I am going crazy. I can't sleep. I can't stop *thinking*. They can't find another teacher good enough. I'm practising five hours a day now, but it's not enough. I'm learning nothing, I'm standing still, and before long I'm going to start going backwards. I can't bear it." Tears came now, embarrassing and unbidden. Dima folded his arms over his chest and curled in on himself. He rocked back and forth a little, a mean attempt at self-comfort that he hadn't employed since he was a child. "It was the one thing, the one thing that I – I can't *bear* it."

Vasya took him into his arms with a complete lack of awkwardness. It was the first time anyone had done so in nine years. Dima breathed in the ammoniac smell of Vasya's sweat underneath the stale smoke of his cigarettes and the harsh, chemical soap with which he'd washed his shirt. There was solace in the warm bulk of him, and Dima couldn't help it: he sobbed once, twice against Vasya's shoulder. Vasya said nothing, but one of his hands rubbed Dima's back, unerringly finding that painful spot just between his shoulder blades. Another sob rose in Dima's throat and he bit his lips against it. It subsided. A leaden weariness settled in his joints. He was still shaking. For a moment he didn't move, his face pressed against the now-damp fabric of Vasya's shirt. He could hear Vasya's rough, regular breathing, and the clatter of wind in the dry leaves of the birch trees that had been Piotr's. Drawing in a deep breath, Dima pulled back. He found that he had been clinging onto one of Vasya's untucked shirt-tails and, with an effort, released it, smoothing the creases his fists had made.

"Fuck your mother nine times," he said shakily. To his relief, Vasya laughed.

"You can say that again."

"Sorry to be such a – " His voice faltered a little and he took a breath to steady it. "Sorry to be such a baby."

"Don't be. Fuck, you should have seen me when I got the news about Petya. I was a fucking mess. Sobbing on anyone and everyone who'd give me the time of day. Still do, sometimes, if you catch me at the bottom of a bottle of vodka."

Dima smiled. But the simple relief of telling someone what had happened was already starting to wear off. No matter how sympathetic Vasya was – and he was sympathetic, if a little perplexed by the intensity of Dima's feelings – it didn't change things. Dima was still in the same situation he had been in five minutes before.

"So what now?" Vasya asked.

Dima shook his head dismally. "Nothing. That's the worst of it. I'm completely powerless. They're being all right about it, the teachers, but there's no one here who can teach half as well as Arseny Grigorevich could. They brought a new teacher, but she wouldn't take me. She said she couldn't teach me anything, and she was right."

"Well, what about in Leningrad, then?" Vasya asked, ever practical. "There's bound to be good teachers there."

"Of course." *Come and see us if you ever find yourself in Leningrad*, Maksim Sergyevich had said. Had Arseny Grigorevich been anticipating something like this, even back then? "But they'd never let me go into Leningrad for lessons. It's over two hours each way, and then there's the expense – "

"So leave school," Vasya said, as if it was the most obvious thing in the world. "You're sixteen now, aren't you? You don't need to be here any longer. Fucking hell, I wasn't much older than you when they sent me off to Solovki. If I was old enough for that, you're old enough to leave here. Are you really learning anything so important?"

Dima cast his mind over his lessons. History and mathematics he quite enjoyed, but even they had no strong hold on him. "No. But – " He felt suddenly angry that Vasya could be so obtuse. "How can I leave school? I'm *blind*. I can't – do you know what people do when they leave this school, the ones like me with no families to take them back and help them? They go and live in one of the blind ghettos and work in a factory. That's all. So what, I move to fucking *Podolsk*? And then what? I'd be as badly off there as I would staying here."

"So kip with me in Leningrad," Vasya said. He employed a tone more commonly used when talking to an infuriatingly intractable child. "I've got a room to myself. Plenty of space for an extra bed. I could spot you some money until you find some sort of work. There's bound to be something you could do, playing in restaurants or something, isn't there? Then you'd be free to have the lessons you want."

For a moment the promise of this future life hung before Dima, something he could hitch his hopes to. He shook his head. "They'd never let me."

"Dima!" Vasya sounded genuinely annoyed now. He took Dima by the shoulders. "It's not up to them to fucking *let* you! You're sixteen. You want to leave school, you can do it."

Vasya's forcefulness was convincing in a way that persuasion wouldn't have been. Dima thought of his parents. He thought of his family, of his older sisters, Tamara, Irina and Zinaida, and his brothers, Gregor, Valentin and Stepan. He thought of Alik, of the bed they had shared, of the house where he was sure he could still remember the silent path through the creaking floorboards at night. He remembered the dull, damp scent of the dairy, the spring of the grass beneath his bare feet, the home that he had been holding up like a banner for the last nine years, no matter how hard he had tried to forget it. School had been the last place his family had left him, and if he moved away, he knew that he was probably letting go of any glimmer of hope that they would ever find him again.

And then he thought of the thrumming hush of the concert hall when Arseny Grigorevich had taken him to Leningrad, the trills and swoops of the orchestra tuning up. He remembered the sense of swooning as he had plunged into the music, sinking like a stone as his heart rose from his chest to his throat to his mouth, the itch in his fingers and his wrists that told him that this was what he wanted to do forever and ever. Abruptly, his head cleared. The shaking stopped. He felt stronger than he had in weeks.

"All right," he told Vasya. His voice was steady. "Yes. Yes."

CHAPTER THIRTEEN

I: 19 May 1942

"You're quiet today," Katya said, as they turned onto Nevsky Prospekt. It wouldn't have been true of anyone else, but normally Dima breathed in air and breathed out words; for him, any silence was to be filled, by music or by speech, his own or that he drew out of others. He smiled, tilting his head in acknowledgement.

"Can't talk *all* the time. Actually, I've got a bit of a headache." He made it sound like a confession. Katya noticed the slight crease between his brows, which she'd seen once or twice before. He looked tired. "It's your turn to talk, anyway. You're getting better at it, don't think I haven't noticed. It's only fair to give me a bit of a rest from rambling on all the time."

A year ago, even a month, something like this would have panicked Katya. Intimacy, physical or emotional, had always felt like intrusion, something being taken from her. It was different, though, if you offered it.

"What do you want me to talk about?"

Dima's smile broadened. "The Conservatoire," he said, sounding enraptured. "Tell me about the Conservatoire."

II: 1931

There was no god and to believe in him was rank superstition, and yet every time Katya entered the Conservatoire she could not help but offer up a fervent thanks to the constellation of musicians painted on the walls, even to the indolent, lyre-strumming angel painted on the ceiling. It seemed all right to worship them instead. The Conservatoire was what she had longed for since the age of twelve, partly for the simple fact of the music, but mainly for the imagined sense of camaraderie, a group of peers who all valued the same things, who spoke the same language. At home, Katya was loved, she knew that – by her sister, at least, and probably by her mother; she was less sure about her father – but she had a persistent sense of her own alien nature, lacking her father's dogmatic political certainty and her sister's charming frivolity and her mother's ability to make sheer endurance seem like a virtue. She didn't hope for anything outlandish like admiration; just a niche, only that, somewhere she could breathe more easily.

At the Conservatoire there were conversations about music, classes in composition and counterpoint, the occasional tantalising glimpse of one of the institution's stars – Dmitri Shostakovich, Nikolai Malko, Ivan Sollertinsky. Katya was not the best, but she had not expected to be; all she had wanted was not to be among the worst, and she found to her surprise and sweet, secret pleasure that she was certainly in the better half of her cohort. She was praised, sometimes, for her accuracy, the restraint of her playing, and her certainty of expression. She found she was sought after for duets, trios or chamber music, because she was said to play unselfishly. It didn't occur to her to do anything else.

Natasha was the first close friend Katya had ever had, and yet Katya had started off hating her. Natasha was not pretty; in fact, when Katya ranked her fellow female students in order of attractiveness – a habit that was so ingrained in her that she barely noticed herself doing it, and would have sworn that it was something that everyone did – Natasha was one of the women she placed closest to herself, with her figure that was little more than a series of balanced spheres, her hair that was dull and lank, cut straight across her forehead in a way that just accentuated the broadness of her face. But Natasha did not seem to accept her fate as an ugly woman. Natasha spoke loudly, laughed loudly, argued when she wanted to, talked to men, *flirted*. For weeks, Katya could not even look at Natasha without feeling her shoulders rise involuntarily, her whole body cringing away in half-acknowledged fear and anger. Sometimes Natasha's eyes settled on Katya in class, and they held a curiosity that Katya was certain was only one step removed from mockery.

Natasha played the cello, and Katya, vicious, thought the swell of it suited her, its thick body tucked between Natasha's thick knees. She wished for Natasha to be bad, although at the Conservatoire that was impossible, and she shuddered with a mixture of disappointment and pleasure when she first heard the velvet sounds that Natasha charmed out of her instrument. Natasha was one of those musicians who could provoke a physical response in a listener, raising the hairs, prickling the skin, softening the bones. She played with abandon, closing her eyes and swaying in a way that Katya wanted to dismiss as affected, but which, from Natasha, she couldn't help but believe.

When Natasha first spoke to Katya, Katya was amazed that Natasha even knew her name. It was halfway through Katya's second term, and Katya had established a circle of friendly acquaintances among the quieter members of her class. She would not have said they were dull. Nor would she have said they were less talented than the other students, but she couldn't stop her mouth from twisting when she watched other groups talking in the cafeteria, flamboyant and boisterous, the sorts of people she imagined musicians should be. It wasn't jealousy she felt so much as incomprehension: how to get from here to there?

"Katya, are you free this afternoon?" Natasha stood beside the table where Katya had been eating a solitary lunch, going over a score. Natasha's cello case was over her shoulder, her face was flushed and there was a fine sheen of sweat on her forehead. Katya could see damp rings on the fabric of her dress under her arms, darkening the gaudiness of the pattern. She felt revulsion, pity, admiration. Natasha was waiting for her to speak.

"Yes, I think so. After four, anyway. Why?"

"It's just that three of us – Ivan Petrovich and Daniil Aaronovich, you know the two of them, and me – we want to pull together a quartet.

Just for fun, really, and practise, but we want it to be good, still, of course. We're looking for a second violin. Would you be interested?"

Katya shrugged. She took sharp pleasure in her lack of grace. "Why are you asking me?"

Natasha frowned, as if she could genuinely not understand the question. "Well, because you're good, of course! We think your sound will blend well, and you're properly professional. Half the violinists here are too busy worrying about their future careers as soloists to be any use playing in an ensemble. Daniil's a bit that way himself, to be honest. But I heard you playing the Bach concerto with Anton Semyonovich the other day. You play…you play generously."

Katya wanted to say no. She wanted to show Natasha just how little she valued the invitation, how it was neither a gift nor a privilege to be asked to join her little coterie. The only problem was that it wasn't true.

"All right," Katya said, with as little enthusiasm as she could manage.

Natasha didn't seem to take her tone amiss. She smiled, so broadly that her cheeks rose and reddened and her eyes were squeezed shut. "Wonderful. We'll meet back here at half past four; Ivan's trying to secure a studio."

~

Natasha laughed when she made mistakes. It was a nervous habit that she was trying to break, and she always covered it with a storm of apologies, interspersed with giggles. Most people seemed to find it endearing, if unprofessional. It made Katya stiff-backed with irritation. But the quartet was good. Chamber music was Katya's treat, which she normally rationed as carefully as chocolate; it was too exposed to suit her as a career, too risky, and she had fastened her sights on a job as a rank and file violinist in a half-decent orchestra. Still, the idea of playing with a quartet regularly, three days a week, was indecently beguiling.

The first violin was Daniil Aaronovich, who was Jewish and bespectacled and lithe, full of a troubling, inward-focussed energy. He spoke too much and too quickly, and when he played his brows lowered like clouds over his eyes. He had a tendency to speed up while playing, and a shameful liking for virtuosic flourishes. Katya tethered him when they played together, hanging her notes off his like pendulums, and when she did so Natasha would smile, distracted and pleased. The viola player was Ivan, who was tall and fair and almost laughably handsome, so broad-shouldered that his viola looked more like a violin when he played. It was an unusual choice of instrument for someone who looked as he did – Katya would have expected something flashier and more given to solo performance, the violin or the piano or maybe a brass instrument. But Ivan was shy, quietly-spoken, and his viola was like the slow throb of a pulse. Every time they rehearsed, Katya felt her heart released, and every time the rehearsal ended she bound it back, unforgiving, telling herself she would not go again – it was too frivolous, too much fun, and it took time away from her studies and the occasional lessons she gave to contribute to her family's finances. These resolutions always failed, but she did her best to hold herself apart from the louche, joking atmosphere that surrounded the other three, orchestrated and conducted by Natasha.

"Come out dancing tonight," Natasha entreated. It was a Friday; they had been playing together for two weeks. The idea was almost entirely alien. Katya knew that people did that sort of thing – it was something that Zhenya was always talking about – but she had never thought to imagine herself into that world.

"I can't."

"Can't or won't?" Natasha asked, uncomfortably incisive. Katya smiled, just a little.

"Won't."

Natasha sighed. "I'm not going to ask why. But I'm going to keep inviting you. One day I'll wear you down enough that you say yes."

In the event, it didn't take as long as Katya would have expected. They were working on one of Haydn's later quartets, and there was something in the cello line that kept slipping from Natasha's fingers. They tried it once, twice, three times, and each time the melody faltered under Natasha's hands, normally so sure. Between giggles, she apologised, again and again. "I don't know what's wrong with me. I could manage this fine last night, I was practising it on my own."

Fourth time: slower, now, Katya reining Daniil in carefully. It was so close Katya could touch it, but again Natasha stumbled, letting out a gush of laughter before she could press her lips together and stop it. She shot a guilty glance at Katya. "Sorry, Katya. Sorry, sorry."

Looking up, Katya caught Natasha's eye: a tactical error. Natasha, red-faced and quivering, fighting to keep from laughing: there was something far funnier in this effort than there was in her customary abandon. The corner of Katya's mouth twitched upwards. She looked down, but it was too late: the laughter was already on its way up from the pit of her belly, refusing to be arrested at diaphragm, sternum or throat. Katya let it out; Natasha, her expression a mixture of relief and astonishment, did likewise. Daniil and Ivan were both grinning. Now she had started, Katya found that she couldn't stop, the laughter that she had held back for weeks gurgling out like champagne. She hunched over, her face in her hands, and felt Daniil's hand on her shaking back, friendly and matter-of-fact.

When she was finally able to lift her face, Katya found she had tears in her eyes. Natasha was looking at her with transparent glee. "Shall we try it again, then?"

Katya grinned back, half-savage; she hadn't known a smile like that was in her. "If you get it right this time, I'll come out dancing with you tonight," she said, recklessly brave. Natasha's eyebrows tilted, and she settled her cello between her knees, loose-limbed and easy.

"Now, that's a challenge I can't help but rise to."

It was a private party that night, a cavernous apartment off Volodarskogo Prospekt, musicians and hangers-on, blaring jazz and the rugs rolled back for dancing. From the first moment she entered, Katya was sure she was going to hate it, and then something came over her that felt like surrender. They didn't leave until past four, she and Natasha, and the sky outside was the delicate, breakable blue of a duck's egg. The wind caught the back of Katya's dress, which was damp with sweat. She shivered. There was an ache in her calves like something strung taut, and her arms were trembling slightly. She felt different, lighter.

Beside her, Natasha limped: "Blister," she explained. She had torn her stockings and taken them off, dancing most of the night with her feet bare inside her shoes. Her heels were streaked with blood. "Let's sit for a bit," she suggested, indicating a low wall by the Fontanka. They did so. Natasha eased off her shoes, rubbed her feet and sighed. Katya watched the metallic glimmer of light on the water and wished she never had to go home.

"You seemed to have a good time tonight," Natasha said at last, in careful understatement. Her lipstick was smudged and her smile was weary, but seemingly irrepressible. Katya considered a sarcastic reply, but her physical exhaustion and the lateness of the hour had laid her bare.

"I did. Thank you for nagging me."

"You dance well."

"Really? I've never done it before."

"I thought you'd be good. You're a musician to start with, and you move beautifully. I've noticed the way you walk, and the way you hold yourself."

Katya hated compliments. They always rang false, and she never knew what to do with them, embarrassed by the strength of her desire to believe them. Thankfully Natasha didn't seem to expect any response. She leaned back and lifted her arms, stretching expansively. Katya caught the scent of her sweat, wild and sharp.

"So are you going to be nicer now?" Natasha asked. Her tone was innocent, but her grin was sly when Katya looked at her.

"I haven't been…not nice, have I?"

"Maybe not *not nice*. But you're all tangled up. You make it hard to be around you. It goes away when you're playing, but as soon as you stop…" Natasha clapped her hands together in illustration. "Boom! The doors slam shut again. Until today, at least."

"I'm just…different from you. That's all."

"I suppose so." Natasha yawned. "What did you think of that boy you were dancing with? The dark-haired one?"

"What do you mean, what did I think of him? He was a good dancer – "

"Oh, come on!" Natasha scoffed. "You can't be that naïve. He liked you."

"He didn't."

"Katya, he *did*. Why didn't you do something about it?"

"What was I supposed to do?"

Natasha sighed in evident frustration. "Flirt with him! Talk to him! Smile at him, at least!"

"This is what I meant when I said I'm not like you! I don't know – how do you do it?"

"What do you mean?"

"You know what I mean."

"I think you mean, how do I manage to go out and have fun and live my life *while being ugly*?"

Mutinous, Katya pressed her lips together. Natasha had spoken quietly; Katya couldn't tell if she was angry or not. But then Natasha laughed, and something inside Katya eased, just a little. "It's so funny. It's always the other plain girls who resent me the most." She hauled herself onto her feet. "Come on, let's get going. My mother will be having kittens."

III: 1933

"How do you feel about Moscow?" Natasha asked idly.

Katya shrugged. "It's all right. My aunt lives there, we go and visit every so often. I'm not sure…" Suspicion dawned. "Why are you asking?"

"Ivan's thinking of going for a job with the Cinema Orchestra. He has a friend, says they need a viola player."

"Oh!" Katya was taken aback. She had known that it would happen at some point – the quartet was just for fun, they'd always said that, actual jobs had to take precedence. And yet the past two years had been so blissful, Katya had let herself nurture rose-tinted dreams that all four of them would manage to get work in Leningrad, so they could still play together from time to time.

"And I was thinking of going with him," Natasha added. Her voice was carefully casual, but she was darting glances at Katya out of the corners of her eyes, as if worried about her reaction.

"*Oh*," Katya said again. Natasha and Ivan never broadcast their involvement, but it was common knowledge nonetheless. Katya had never been able to work out quite how serious it was or wasn't – Natasha still flirted at every given opportunity, while Ivan, in his way, was quietly, steadily smitten. It surprised Katya every day, and she hated herself for being so surprised. "Are you going to look for work there, too?"

"Not straight away, no." Natasha took a deep breath. She still did not look straight at Katya. "I'm pregnant."

"*What?*"

"I'm pregnant." Natasha breathed out on a shaky laugh. "That's much easier to say the second time, actually. I'm pregnant, I'm pregnant, I'm pregnant. And before you ask, yes, it's Ivan's, and yes, he knows."

"Natasha, I – " Katya couldn't gather together the words she wanted to say. "Congratulations." That wasn't it. Katya's own happiness, barely two years old, was too new and too fragile for her to be able to spare any for someone else, even Natasha. Natasha looked flushed, shy, anxious and overjoyed all at once, and Katya knew she should be happy for her, she should be flinging her arms around her and asking her for all the details because that's what friends were supposed to do, that's what Zhenya would do if she were in the situation, and yet all Katya could say was *congratulations*, in a voice that sounded like it was limping.

"And so I was thinking – why don't you come? You were talking about staying at the Conservatoire for the musicology course, but why not do it in Moscow instead? And then the quartet – we could keep rehearsing, and maybe start taking it seriously. It's possible, look at the Komitas! Maybe even Daniil would come, but even if not – you could take over as first violin, we could find another second."

Katya was silent. There was something fizzing up within her: hope, or possibility, or something that was greater than the sum of both. Moscow. *Away*. Now that Natasha had mustered the courage to look straight at her, she seemed unwilling to shift her gaze, her expression fervent.

"Think about it, Katya. That's all I'm asking. Just think about it."

IV: 19 May 1942

"But you didn't go," Dima said. He half smiled. "I can't say I'm sorry, but – why not?"

Outside the Vladimirskaya Church; this time they had sat down, but it would still have been reasonable for Katya to declare the conversation finished: time for Dima to go his way and she hers. Instead, she bit her lips, thinking, slightly uncertain how they had got to this point. There were things you couldn't say. How could she explain to Dima the way she had thought back then, imagining herself in Moscow: a shared apartment with Ivan and Natasha and whatever it was between them, which hung like a fine mist in the air whenever they were together; music, the intoxicating surge of it; friendship, intoxicating too, in its way – and the sour taste in Katya's mouth whenever she caught a glimpse of Ivan looking at Natasha, as if she was something precious and rare, the only person to exist in the world: the weight against which everything else was found wanting. Even if she had wanted to, Katya could not have found the words to explain that to Dima.

"There was Yevgeny," Katya said instead.

V: 1933

Yevgeny was a friend of her father's – or no; fifteen years younger than Yefim, he was more of a protégé. A shadowy presence in the family apartment, often closeted with Katya's father; if Yevgeny seemed unusually courteous or attentive when he met Katya in the hall, she thought little of it: friends of her father were respectful men, and she was worthy of respect as her father's daughter, if nothing else.

Katya was twenty-two when Zhenya lost her virginity at sixteen to a handsome university student named Arkady. Zhenya and Katya's parents had spent years publically touting the values of free love, decrying the institution of marriage as bourgeois, but Zhenya was at least smart enough to know that their progressiveness did not extend to their younger daughter. Instead, she told Katya, whispering to her across the gap between the two single beds in the room they shared, the room Katya had shared with her grandmother before she died.

Katya tried her hardest not to listen, summoning up her grandmother as she sometimes did, her low murmur in the gold, flickering light, but Zhenya's words kept breaking through: *and then he…and we…and I couldn't help*. Zhenya's discussions of boys and men and their various merits had always been something Katya endured rather than enjoyed. Recitation finally finished, Zhenya lifted her arms above her head and gave a luxuriant stretch and wriggle.

"I should have started this *ages* ago," she whispered, a laugh at the back of her throat. "Katiusha, why didn't you tell me how nice it is?"

Katya froze. The air between them was very still. She didn't know if her sister had guessed the truth and was sounding her out, or whether she genuinely didn't know that Katya had never even kissed anyone. Despite all Natasha's coaching, eager and frustrated by turns, Katya still found it hard enough to talk to men; but then, she found it hard to talk to anyone on a level beyond the detached and impersonal. The other students at the Conservatoire made a game of flirting, and Katya had no idea how they did it. It wasn't that she was shy, exactly; she could talk easily enough about the subjects that interested her, and music, in particular, was something she was happy to discuss for hours. But as soon as the conversation turned to anything more personal, it became untenable. Katya started to dip her head and stumble over her words.

"You have, haven't you?" Zhenya pressed. "I've heard about the Conservatoire," she went on, with prurient satisfaction. "Everybody's doing it with everyone else."

"If only you had any sort of musical talent," Katya said tartly, but Zhenya only laughed.

"I don't need talent," she said. She wasn't being cruel, but it hurt all the same, the idea that talent was second-best, what you fell back on if you didn't have charm or beauty. It was a hierarchy that Katya accepted as reality. Still waiting for an answer, Zhenya propped herself up on one elbow. It was dark enough that Katya could only make out her shape, but she could sense the intensity with which her sister was peering at her.

"Of course I have," said Katya. The words sounded unconvincing even to her, and she could tell that even if Zhenya had been uncertain before, she didn't believe her now. Katya loved her sister, but she hated how well Zhenya knew her, and how quickly she could spring to judgement.

"Who with, then?"

"With Anton Semyonovich," Katya extemporised. This was a friend of hers whom Zhenya had met, a shy, gawky oboist who was unattractive enough to be believable.

"Really? I'm amazed he was bold enough."

His lack of boldness was partly what Katya liked about him. Anton was married, now, but he hadn't been a year ago, and in retrospect Katya could see, putting the pieces of information together with the objective interest of a scientist, that he might have been interested in her. They had played together once, a few years ago now, a Bach concerto for violin and oboe, and Katya had admired his playing, his light touch on the keys and the way he made it seem effortless; he didn't turn puce and sweaty like some woodwind players, but looked instead transformed, even beatific. In speaking, he stammered badly, and it would often take minutes for him to make out a sentence that should have taken seconds, but Katya was more patient with his stammer than most, and she never jumped in and tried to finish his sentences or guess at his words. She was happy to wait for him, because she had nothing better that she should have been doing. Anton Semyonovich was the sort of missed chance that Natasha was always berating her for; it was true that Katya felt little regret for having let Anton slip through her fingers, if he had ever been in her hands at all, but there was a sharp, bright fear, now, somewhere at the base of her spine, that Zhenya would beat her to the finish line in a race she hadn't realised she was running.

"So is Arkady – are you, is he – " *Is he your boyfriend now?* was what Katya wanted to ask, but it sounded so childish when she shaped the words in her head. Zhenya caught her meaning and laughed.

"Oh, no! No, no, no. God, Katya, I'm *sixteen*. The last thing I want to do is to tie myself to one man *now*." She squirmed her way back down under the covers, her voice half-muffled by her pillow. "I've got plenty of time for that."

Unlike you.

~

"You must be nearly finished at the Conservatoire," Yevgeny said, characteristically diffident. Katya would have been hard-pressed to pinpoint when this started, when they had slipped from brief pleasantries to actual conversation whenever they happened to meet. There had even been once or twice when Yevgeny had come to see her father and, on hearing he wasn't in, hadn't left immediately, staying instead to talk to Katya. She wouldn't have said she was comfortable with him, exactly, but the fact that he fell neither into the category of her father's contemporary, to whom she owed abject deference, nor her own, to whom she owed a bilious mixture of anxiety and resentment, made him a little easier to talk to.

"It's my last term," Katya said, nodding, "I'm thinking of staying on to do the musicology course, but…" *But I'm twenty-two*, Katya went on, silent, *and I can't be a music student forever, for lack of any better ideas*. She had always assumed that something would present itself when the time came, and perhaps, in the shape of Moscow, in the shape of the quartet, it had. Natasha was still waiting for an answer that Katya wasn't yet ready to give, but she was going to have to decide soon. "But I might move to Moscow instead," Katya told Yevgeny. His eyebrows jerked, sharp, and she started. Why had she told him that? She hadn't even mentioned it to her parents yet – not even to Zhenya; she had been clutching it close, the damp heat of possibility.

"*Moscow*? Why would you do that? Your family – "

"I haven't decided," Katya retreated swiftly. "Some of my friends, who I play with – they're moving there. They asked me – I haven't said anything to my parents yet," she added, half-pleading. "I might not go, anyway."

Yevgeny looked utterly wrong-footed in a way that Katya couldn't make sense of. As she watched, he seemed visibly to decide, hauling himself together. "This isn't the way I intended to do this," he said, sounding almost affronted. "But Katya, I rather thought we might get married."

I rather thought we might get married. As proposals went, it was hardly the height of romance. Katya didn't answer, didn't move, stilled to her core.

So this had been…courtship, then? This careful conversation, sat feet apart in the stultifying atmosphere of Katya's parents' home? They had never met outside the apartment; Yevgeny had never even *touched* her, beyond the dispassionate clasp of his warm, dry palm when they shook hands. It was so unlike all she had ever heard from Zhenya, half-secret assignations, trysts in dimly-lit cafés, the tumble of hands and lips and laughter, the delicious to and fro of it. Immediately Katya saw starkly, berating herself that she had not known this before, that what Zhenya had was not something she could ever access. Yet still she could not speak, could not move. In the face of her silence, Yevgeny's expression of patient enquiry faltered a little. "I've spoken to your father about it; he's given me his blessing. And I've just been allocated a three-roomed apartment, in a good building, not so far from here…" With an edge of entreaty, Yevgeny asked: "Katya – is the idea so strange to you?"

That loosened her tongue. "Not strange. I…it's just a surprise, that's all." *Why*, she wanted to ask, *why me*? She didn't think she could bear the answer. "Would you let me think about it?"

The only way that Katya could make it feel real was by telling someone. Not her mother, not yet; she needed at least a night to sleep on it first, to wake up and find it still true. Telling Natasha, while Katya was still uncertain – that was insupportable. The only option remaining was Zhenya. Katya waited throughout the evening, her throat tight with the news. Over dinner, her parents shot her looks of curious expectance, but thankfully forbore from asking outright. As Zhenya leant into her tiny hand mirror that night, taking off her make-up in broad, confident swipes, Katya rehearsed it in her head, trying out what she would say. She decided that she didn't have it in her to be coy.

"Yevgeny asked me to marry him this afternoon."

The drama of Zhenya's reaction was gratifying; her astonishment was not. Mirror abandoned, she flung down the cotton pad that she was holding, smeared with remnants of mascara and lipstick. Half her face still looked flawless, the other comically bare.

"What? Why didn't you tell me?"

"I'm telling you now!"

"Yevgeny..." Zhenya frowned. "Is he the one who plays the oboe? Or is he in your quartet?"

"He's not a musician," Katya said. She sighed at her sister's denseness. "You know Yevgeny." She hadn't wanted to phrase it like this, but she knew that it would make Zhenya understand. "*Papa's* Yevgeny."

Zhenya opened her mouth and closed it again, covering it with her hand. Her face creased, and for a moment Katya was horrified: she had made her sister cry. Then she understood that Zhenya was holding back a laugh.

"Papa's Yevgeny asked you to marry him? But – why would he do that?"

Katya flushed with embarrassed anger. This reaction was so typical of Zhenya; why had she expected anything else? "Is it so surprising to you that he should be interested in me?" she asked, her voice as quiet and cold as she could manage.

"No, Katya – "

Katya shook her head, looking away. Her smile was bitter. Zhenya crossed to her bed and knelt before her, grabbing her hands. "Katiusha, that's not what I meant! I meant it the other way round. Why would he think that *you* would be interested in *him*? You're twenty-two, you have your music, your career..."

"I'm going to say yes," Katya said. She didn't realise she had decided until the words were spoken: a long, slow drop, inevitable. There was a degree of sickening satisfaction in the shock on Zhenya's face.

"Katya. *No.*"

"Why not? He's a good man, he has a good job..."

"He's old enough to be your father!"

"Not *quite*, Zhenya." Katya used the cutting tone that was best designed to hurt her sister. Zhenya, who could never hide her feelings, duly flinched. "I know everyone must seem *terribly* old to you, but actually there's only sixteen years between us."

"But you don't love him!" Zhenya said, outraged. She was still crouched on the floor in front of Katya, leaning on Katya's knees. "You couldn't possibly."

"You're sixteen years old. You don't even know what love is."

"I know what it *isn't.*" She reached up and put her hand on Katya's cheek. "Look me in the eye and tell me you love him. If you can do that, I swear I'll never say another word about it again."

Zhenya knew well enough that Katya quailed in the face of a direct lie. Katya looked at her sister; she even opened her mouth to speak. In her head she heard herself saying the words: *I love Yevgeny*. They refused to be spoken. Instead she shook her head. "It's not about love, Zhenya. When you're older, you'll…"

"*No.*" Mindful of their parents sleeping in the next room, Zhenya kept her voice low, but it had the force of a shout. She stood and started to pace, possessed by an anger that Katya had never seen in her sister before. It awoke a degree of reluctant respect. "If I live until I'm eighty I'll never understand this. *No.*" She turned to Katya. "*It's not about love,*" Zhenya mimicked. "You're quite right about that! It's nothing to do with love, and I know exactly what it *is* to do with." She paused, inviting Katya to ask, but Katya didn't: another answer she didn't want to hear. Zhenya gave it to her anyway. "All my life I've watched you do this. I've watched you take the meanest, lowest portions and make the most miserable choices. You give everything away and then you feel short-changed because you have nothing left. Why do you do it? Is it all because of Papa? Or is it me? Is that why you're doing this – why you've been building a cage for yourself for as long as I can remember?" Zhenya sat down on the edge of her bed, as if abruptly exhausted. "I thought maybe things would be different for you at the Conservatoire. It's a world away from here, with people like you, who love the same things that you do – but now *this*? Have you told Natasha?" Not waiting for an answer, Zhenya shook her head, eyes narrow. "No, of course you haven't. You're too much of a coward."

Without warning, Katya started to cry. Only her sister could make her feel like this, so emotionally grotesque, all that love muddied with envy and resentment. "It's easy for you…"

"Oh, I'm glad you think so," Zhenya said coldly. Katya covered her face with her hands. "I know what you think. That it's all easy for me because of the way I look. But I'm the one who has to watch my sister – my *sister*, who I love most out of anyone in the world, burying herself alive because – "

"Don't say it."

" – because our parents love me better."

Neither of them had spoken the words out loud before. Katya had always been afraid of them, stepping around them, fearing the power that they had over them both. But her tears stopped, mid-sob. She took her face out of her hands. "Not just our parents," she said. Her voice didn't even shake.

"Maybe not. But not me, Katya. Never me."

Katya got up. She felt utterly emptied of emotion. With small, spare movements she undressed, not bothering to hide her body the way she normally did in front of her sister. She put on her nightgown, and brushed her hair, while Zhenya watched, unmoving. Ready for bed, Katya sat, smiled a little. "You really should finish taking off your make-up."

"Oh!" Zhenya touched her face. She picked up the mirror and the cotton pad again. Katya climbed under the covers and turned her back. Through half-closed eyes, she watched the shadow her sister cast on the wall, bobbing up and down as she undressed, hanging her clothes in the wardrobe they shared; if she blurred her vision, Katya could pretend that it was her grandmother, nodding in front of her icons, while Katya curled like a small, warm animal under the bedclothes. It offered a scrap of comfort. She smelled the traces of Zhenya's cold cream as she crossed to the switch by the door and turned off the light. Katya tried to close her eyes, but the lids wouldn't stay shut. They twitched. The mattress dipped as Zhenya sat down on the edge of Katya's bed. She put a hand on Katya's shoulder.

"Katiusha. I'm sorry I shouted." Katya said nothing. "I'm not sorry for what I said, but I'm sorry I shouted. I'm sorry I made you cry."

Katya lay stiff under her sister's hand. When it became clear that Zhenya wasn't going to go away until she had an answer, Katya muttered something deliberately indistinct, a humming mumble.

"Do you forgive me?" Zhenya asked. She sounded very young. Katya remembered, suddenly, the precise look on Zhenya's face when, ten years before, she had drawn over some of Katya's sheet music: the angle of her brows and the tremble of her lips, almost a parody of apologetic appeal.

"I forgive you," Katya said. She waited for Zhenya to get up, but Zhenya didn't move. The touch on her shoulder became a caress.

"Can I come in with you, Katiusha? Just for tonight?"

Surprised, Katya tipped her head back. Zhenya's face was hidden in the darkness. "Why?"

"Because I'm losing you," Zhenya said simply. Her voice was steady but thick. One tear fell on Katya's shoulder, then another. Zhenya did nothing to acknowledge them; she just sat, straight-backed, her hand on Katya's shoulder.

"All right." Katya wriggled closer to the wall. There was a cold blast against her back as Zhenya lifted the blankets, and then her warm weight settled against Katya, her arm around her, her forehead pressed against the base of Katya's skull. They hadn't slept like this for years, not since Zhenya was still prone to waking in the middle of the night, scared by the apartment's silence. The bed had seemed bigger then, the two of them so much smaller, but Zhenya had always insisted on curling up against Katya, and Katya, although she grumbled about Zhenya squirming and stealing all the blankets, had never really minded. But now there was something unsettling in the feel of Zhenya's body against hers, almost frightening. Katya didn't want to be reminded of the fact that she was corporeal, and that that corporeality could mean something to someone else. She couldn't relax in Zhenya's embrace. All that she could do was forget that she was there, fold in on herself, and try to become as small as possible.

First thing the next morning, muddled and unslept, Katya used her father's telephone to call Yevgeny and accept his proposal.

VI: 19 May 1942

"The strange thing is," Katya said to Dima, "my father was offered a job in Moscow a year or so later, so they moved, my parents and Zhenya. And Yevgeny took over my father's old job, so we stayed here. Funny how these things work out, isn't it?"

Dima didn't laugh. "And Natasha?"

"Oh, she and Ivan moved, just after Yevgeny and I married." Katya didn't like to think of the last time she'd seen Natasha before she'd moved: at Katya and Yevgeny's wedding, tearful, she had gripped Katya's hands and made her promise to write. *I worry about you*, she had said, *I want to know that you're all right*. "Ivan got the job in the Cinema Orchestra. Natasha – I don't think she plays much any more. The baby had poor health when he was born, and she had to spend all her time nursing him. You know how hard it can be, if you stop playing regularly..."

"You're still in touch?"

"We write." *Birthdays and new year*, Katya didn't say. "I sometimes see her when I go to visit my family." Dima said nothing. It was strange, Katya thought, how much easier she found it to talk to someone who couldn't see her – how she could just about pretend that she was talking only to herself. "I thought they would change things," she said at last. "First the Conservatoire, and then marriage. I thought they would change things, and they did, a little, but not – not how I wanted. I wanted – "

How to explain? There were things that Katya kept so deep inside her that she didn't know how to get them out any more. Her smile was a careful movement of lips and cheeks, and when she laughed, it sounded calculated and rehearsed, but she was sure she had had a different laugh, once, which came tumbling out of her like a fountain. In her head, Katya had an idea of the person she was: a little wild, a little adventurous, who laughed loudly and dressed boldly and had a circle of admiring friends who craved her acquaintance. This imaginary self flirted and sang and drank, she was careless with people and possessions, and was loved in spite of it. Katya was sure that this was the person she was meant to be; the person she appeared was an elaborate costume, crafted over a period of years, which she had forgotten how to get out of. She needed someone's help, someone who could look underneath and who cared enough to –

"I wanted an ally," Katya finished. Her face heated; she couldn't look at Dima. "I should go home," she said. She turned her back as he got to his feet.

INTERMISSION

CHAPTER FOURTEEN

I: 21 May 1942

That Dima was ill was less evident in his pallor and his breathlessness than in his silence. His arrival at rehearsal was always heralded by a stream of patter: jokes, pieces of news, queries after people's health, that of their families, the amount of disruption they'd suffered from the shelling the night before. But on Thursday, Dima didn't speak, outside the merest sketch of a greeting. He didn't move much, either, which was also unusual; Dima was rarely still.

"Are you all right?" Katya whispered as they sat.

"Of course," Dima said. He sounded irritable, far from his normal good humour. "I didn't sleep well last night. The shelling." *The shelling you can usually sleep through*, Katya thought, but kept quiet.

She was sure that no one else would have noticed, but Katya could tell that Dima's playing wasn't up to his normal standard. His bowing was less certain. There was a slight tremor to his hands. When they paused for Karl Ilych to run through something with the woodwind section, Dima gave a sigh that turned into a fit of coughing. It sounded so painful that the entire section froze, unwilling to move until it was over and Dima was wiping his eyes.

"Sorry about that."

"You sound awful," said Genya bluntly.

"It sounds worse than it is. I get something like this every winter, bit of a fever and a horrible cough for a few days. It passes. It always passes."

Genya looked unconvinced. "You can't take these things lightly. Even if you do get it every year, you're never normally as weak as you are now. Are you taking anything for it?"

Dima laughed. "What's to take? Any medicine in this city has long since been requisitioned or eaten as food."

It was the truth. Genya shrugged, uncertain. Dima flexed his hands, waiting for the shaking to stop.

On Friday, he didn't come at all. A froth of worry rose up inside Katya; she fought the urge to walk out, skip rehearsal, go in search of him; only the thought of losing her ration kept her in her seat. Marina caught her eye, leaned towards her, frowning, mouthed: *where's Dima?* If Katya had spoken she would have snapped; as it was, her shrug was more forceful than it needed to be. Rehearsal over, it felt wrong to be walking home without Dima beside her; at the Vladimirskaya Church she dithered: right for home, or left for Dima? Katya remembered Dima's cough, the racking strength of it, the way he'd curled in on himself to try and keep himself intact. She turned left.

She had only been to Dima's building once before, the first day they had met, when she'd inadvertently walked him home. The front door stood open; inside, the air was stale and still. Katya didn't know what floor he lived on, so she knocked on doors, a part of her aghast that she was doing this, even thinking of disturbing people. The fourth door was answered by a man, bearded and wild-eyed, but he listened to Katya's question – he didn't know Dima's name, but when Katya mentioned *the blind boy* he nodded, pointing upwards: "First floor, on the right." Katya's luck held; thrusting his hand into his pocket, he came out with a key. "Spare. Vasya left it with me for safekeeping. Bring it back when you're finished, all right?"

The apartment was dim, cold and institutional, a series of doors off a corridor; Katya tried them all until one opened onto a room that wasn't empty. Dima was sitting in a chair, swathed in blankets, his eyes closed. There was always so much life in him when he was talking, so much colour and movement that Katya had never noticed how thin he was. She had *seen* it, but she hadn't understood it. Now, his long body folded, covered, he looked painfully small. The room was dark and close, crowded with absence. Katya had thought that she was accustomed to death: a year ago she had never seen a corpse, and now the fact that the streets were clear of them seemed like a luxury. She had seen her husband's body, she had carried Elena wrapped in her bedspread shroud, she had helped dig under the snow and expose corpses damaged in ways that she still couldn't let herself think about too carefully – and yet Dima, silent and motionless, sent a wave of electricity through her, lifting the hairs on her body, head to toe. He couldn't be. It was impossible.

She spoke his name, and her relief when Dima turned his head towards her made her almost nauseated. Instinct made him open his eyes. "Is it Katya?" he asked. His voice was quiet and hoarse. The fact that he had known it was her filled her with a hectic pride. She knelt by the chair and lifted her hand to press it to his forehead, as if he were one of the girls, stopping just short. Even without touching him, heat radiated off his skin. His lips were dry and chapped. Katya could hear the breath whistling in and out of his lungs. "You're ill," she said unnecessarily. "You should be in bed."

The smile Dima raised was somehow ghastly. "It seemed…unwise."

Chilled, Katya decoded his meaning. It had become shorthand over the winter; Katya remembered Marina, just a few days ago, describing a friend of hers who hadn't survived: *he lay down in January*. The ones that lay down didn't get up again.

But both beds were unrumpled; the room gave off a sense of undisturbed stillness. "Where's Vasya?"

"He went out. Yesterday afternoon." Dima seemed only able to manage a few words on each breath. "After I came home from rehearsal. He hasn't come back."

"Do you know where he went?" Katya asked. She didn't know why it mattered.

"To visit a friend, near Moskovsky Station. He was going to collect our rations on the way back," Dima said. He closed his eyes again.

Moskovsky Station: Lidiya had been in that area the afternoon before, and when she had come home, delayed, impatient, she had told Katya about a direct hit on a nearby building, killing a number of people queuing for food below. Vasya wasn't coming back, and Dima knew it, though Katya couldn't bring herself to be the one to tell him.

"And you've been here on your own ever since?"

"I started feeling very bad when I got home yesterday. I think..." Dima's breath caught in his throat, and he coughed, a noise like tearing metal. Katya winced, glad that he couldn't see her. He struggled to sit upright, straightening his back, searching for fugitive breath. "I think I have a fever," he said at last, as if it weren't obvious, and then shook his head. "What – is it morning?"

"It's past three," Katya said.

"I've missed rehearsal?"

"That doesn't matter." She felt close to anger, with him and his dogged determination, with herself for waiting until after rehearsal to check that he was all right, with the wild-eyed man downstairs for doing nothing to help him, even with Vasya for going out and failing to come back. She didn't want to ask, but made herself. "Did Vasya take your ration cards?"

Dima nodded. To Katya's horror, his eyes filled with tears. It was clear, suddenly, how terribly young he was, and how vulnerable, beneath all the bravery and the bluster. "There's no food left here," he whispered. "I went through the kitchen last night – or this morning, I can't remember. I felt everywhere, in the cupboards and on the floor, underneath the table. I thought that I might find something that had fallen, but there was nothing."

"You must come home with me," Katya said, almost without thinking. Dima shook his head.

"I can't. What if Vasya..."

"Vasya is dead," said Katya. Dima's face didn't change, but Katya felt her heart contract into a fist all the same. "You can't survive if you stay here. If you come back with me, I can – we can help you. We have food, we can get more. I'm not going to leave you here." Dima was silent, and Katya repeated it, her voice rising. "I am *not* leaving you here."

For a moment, Dima did not move, and Katya began to muster a second line of attack, but then he started to edge himself forward, a prelude to trying to stand. "All right," he said, pushing back the blankets. Underneath, he was fully dressed. His hand swung below the chair, once, twice, his fingers groping for something. Katya took hold of his violin case, always within arm's reach. "I've got it," she said. The worried look on his face didn't change, and she took his hand and placed it on the rigid black surface. "It's here."

"I need – can you check that it's inside?" Dima asked. One side of his mouth quirked up into a half-embarrassed smile. "I've been having these dreams, waking dreams, I suppose. Birds coming through the window and taking it away."

Katya opened the violin case and placed it on Dima's knees. With both hands, he touched the dark red felt interior, ran his fingers along the length of the strings. "He wouldn't let me sell it," Dima said quietly. "Vasya. In the winter. I kept saying we could, for food. He wouldn't let me." Katya swallowed back her impatience, watched as Dima took the violin and attached the shoulder rest, tucking it under his chin. The bow, next, as he tightened the strings and added a swipe of rosin. A single chord was all he played, bold and brash, a burst of light in the dark apartment that seemed to last even after the sound had died away. Dima nodded, and packed the instrument away with unfussy care. "All right," he said again. "Let's go."

Dima's weakness was frightening, the suddenness with which it had claimed him and dragged him back, despite the increased strength that the spring had brought. In the street, Katya clutched a small bundle of Dima's clothes; Dima held his violin, reluctant to be parted from it. He leaned on Katya's arm, and even with his dangerous, bird-boned lightness she realised that she wouldn't have been able to help him two months ago; even a month ago she wouldn't have had the energy to spare, no matter how much she wanted to. And she could barely breathe herself for how much she wanted to help him, this boy she barely knew, whom she couldn't even have imagined three months before: how had she got here? The winter had shrunk her world; the spring had expanded it again, and so she took his arm, and she let him lean on her, and when he needed to sit and rest and catch his breath, she waited.

It took them nearly an hour. Dima could barely take twenty steps without going into paroxysms of coughing, and Katya felt her own strength ebbing as they stumbled along, a four-footed creature tottering its way through the streets. As they walked, she rehearsed her speech to Lidiya, whom she knew would be angry, bringing another person into their household, particularly one without ration cards, an extra mouth to feed, someone who couldn't help out in the same ways that the others could. As she ran through them in her head, Katya knew that her arguments were less than compelling. They came down to *but I wanted to help him* and *it seemed like the right thing to do* and something deeper and warmer that lay under that, which Katya couldn't, *wouldn't* put words to. And yet when they arrived at the apartment block, Lidiya met them at the door, coming from the opposite direction, a basket full of foraged leaves and grasses propped against her hip. Katya had prepared herself for rage, and yet Lidiya just looked at her, one eyebrow cocked.

"You remember Dima," Katya said, and Dima managed to raise his head and smile in Lidiya's approximate direction. "He's not well," Katya added, struggling for the right words to say, but Lidiya only shrugged.

"You'd better get him inside, then," she said blandly. "That wind's not going to do him much good."

The room looked smaller with Dima in it. Katya had known that having Dima to stay meant nursing him, and nursing him meant putting him in her bed, and yet the reality of it made her blush. The girls' beds had long since been broken up for firewood, but there were still plenty of blankets, and Katya would be perfectly comfortable on the table, she insisted, as Dima tried to protest even as she was drawing back the covers and pushing him down. He was asleep within minutes – asleep or unconscious; Katya couldn't tell. She watched him for a moment before going through to the kitchen; once there she couldn't think what she had come in for, and so sat, empty handed, at the kitchen table. Her thoughts felt violently disordered, as if someone had stampeded through her mind, knocking things carelessly to the floor. He was only a boy, she told herself, a sweet boy who played like an angel. She just wanted to help him. It was just what it was, no more and no less than what Lidiya had done for her or she for Lidiya or both of them for Ilya Nikolayevich, and yet Katya's eyes were drawn again and again to the photograph of Yevgeny that was nailed haphazardly to the kitchen wall. She had ignored the photograph as best she could since Lychkovo, feeling that to take it down would be more of an acknowledgement than just leaving it there. Yevgeny stared at the camera with an expression of slight disapproval. His eyes had been blue, but in the black and white print they took on an unearthly silvery grey. His expression had changed since he had died, which Katya knew to be both impossible and true: an almost negligible shift in the twist of his lips or the focus of his gaze. Katya looked at him, looked away, looked back. She was sensible enough to know that it was just a photograph, and the hairs that rose on the back of her neck as she met the gaze of her dead husband were more to do with her own internal disarray than with anything more sinister. Still. "Stop looking at me like that," she said at last. Feeling foolish, she got to her feet and took the photograph from the wall, laying it face down on the kitchen shelf. She paused for a moment, uncertain, and then took a dishcloth and covered it up, so that none of the frame was visible. *Ridiculous*, she told herself, and yet she could breathe a little easier, somehow.

It's the right thing to do, Katya had told herself as she was helping Dima from his apartment to hers, but that night, his fever spiralling higher and higher, she realised how stupid she'd been: she knew, suddenly, without any doubt in her mind that in moving him she had actually killed him. If he was going to die, she asked herself furiously, why had she brought him here for it, just so his surroundings would be unfamiliar, and so that she could have another death on her conscience? Katya had never been a natural nurse. She had difficulty with other people's bodies, even with her own; the only ones that she had ever managed to be free with had been those of her children. She understood, gradually and reluctantly, that she had taken Dima to be her own responsibility, and she both hated herself for making the decision, and resented him for his likeability that had unwittingly forced her into this position. On the occasions that Yevgeny had been ill enough to require nursing, Katya had felt a mixture of fear and disgust at the simple fleshy fact of his body. It was a reminder of the ways in which she was alien.

She could only guess at the height of Dima's fever, but heat cloaked his body and she knew that it was bad. *Cool cloths*, Katya thought. That was what you were supposed to do. In a cupboard she found some old pillowcases, which she tore into strips and dipped in water. She could only understand her actions if she broke them down into steps. *Take the cloth. Wet the cloth. Wipe the water on Dima's face.* She thought, suddenly, that she had a better instinctive understanding of how to work her instrument than of how to work her own body. Dima swam from delirium to lucidity and back again, his skin tight and fearsomely hot. He seemed unclear as to where he was, though Katya didn't know how much of that was to do with the fact that he couldn't see the room to recognise it. He could barely gather enough breath to speak, and when he did so, his words knocked into each other, making little sense: he spoke to Vasya, sometimes, in rough, conversational tones; to Piotr, too, and to other people, names that Katya didn't know. Snatches of conversation seemed to ring in his head, and his tone was friendly and plaintive and angry by turns. He complained about the smoke that was filling the room, although the air was as clear as Katya could make it. His breaths seemed to be getting shorter and shorter, snatched against his will, the spasms of coughing longer and more wrenching; Katya watched, feeling hope emptying out of her, helpless to the point of paralysis.

When Lidiya put her head around the door it was just after midnight. Lidiya normally went to bed with the children, Serezha finding it hard to settle when she wasn't there, and Katya had assumed that they were long asleep – indeed, Lidiya's face was creased, her make-up sketchily removed so that Katya could see the almost translucent luminosity of her skin underneath. She thought, incongruously, that Lida looked better when she wasn't trying to coax an impossible blush into her cheeks.

"How is he?" Lidiya asked. She rubbed a hand over her forehead, smoothing the lines from her brow in a gesture that Katya had come to recognise as unconscious and almost compulsive.

"Not good," Katya said. She was pleased that her voice didn't shake. Lidiya crossed to the bed and looked down at Dima, who lay silent, aside from the wheezing noises that came with each breath, noises that made Katya want to clutch her own chest in sympathy. "I'm worried that he might be dying."

She flung the word out there, as if saying it as starkly as she could would make her care less. "It's possible," said Lida. Her voice was dispassionate, but she bent over the bed to touch Dima's cheek, and instinct turned his face into her palm. *So that's how it's going to go*, Katya thought. The realisation came as easily as if she had always known it, without bitterness or rancour. But Lidiya turned back to Katya, and Katya did not see what she was expecting to see in Lidiya's face.

"He should sit up a little," Lidiya said. "Help me lift him." Katya didn't move, and Lidiya sighed. "All right then, I'll lift him, and you build up the pillows behind him."

Lidiya slipped her arm around Dima's shoulders and held him upright while Katya obeyed, trying to beat some life into the tired pillows on the bed. As Lidiya settled him back, Katya understood that what she envied most about Lidiya was not her beauty, but her ease of movement. Lidiya inhabited her body as if she felt she deserved to be in the world, while Katya's every movement was an apology. Lidiya offered her touch as a gift, while Katya assumed that hers was an intrusion.

"I've been trying to bring down the fever with cool cloths, but it doesn't seem to be doing any good."

"No wonder, if you're just using them on his face." Lidiya leaned forward and unbuttoned Dima's shirt in a series of deft, certain movements. It was more of Dima's body than Katya had ever seen before, the skin of his chest so pale that it was almost pearlescent, and the soft downy hair. It made him seem terribly vulnerable. Katya swallowed and heard her throat click. Lidiya dipped one of the rags in the bowl of cool water that Katya had prepared, wrung it out, and with assured gentleness, drew it down one of Dima's arms, and then the other. Katya watched, unable to step forward to help, or backwards to leave. Lidiya half turned.

"Boil some water," she commanded. Katya wondered if she should resent the casual way in which Lidiya had taken charge, but instead found herself profoundly grateful for it. She went to the kitchen and placed a pot on the stove without even considering why she was doing it. Back in the bedroom, Lidiya took the pot, setting it on the bedside table and bending Dima's face over it. "The steam," she explained, "it's good for his lungs," and then finally, frowning: "Didn't you ever have to do this for the girls when they were sick?"

Of course Katya had. She remembered now the winters when Tanya or Nadya or both had been barking with bronchitis, how she'd always prepared steam inhalations for them, a towel over their small and obedient heads. Katya could recall every fibre of the experience, the hot damp of the steam and the peculiar whistle that Nadya's breath had made one year when her cough had been particularly bad, and yet she had found herself completely unable to apply that knowledge to Dima. She stared at Lidiya, baffled and speechless, and Lidiya's face softened slightly.

"It's all right. We'll sort him out."

It was past four when they finally trusted themselves to sleep. Dima's fever was still high, but it no longer seemed to be rising. The steam had done some good, too, and his chest sounded less raw. Most importantly from Katya's point of view, he seemed calmer, more present. He didn't speak much – he didn't have the breath for it – and gave little indication that he knew where he was or who the two women fussing over him were, but neither did he speak to people who weren't there. It was an uneasy compromise, but, for now, the best they could hope for. "Well," said Lidiya, at last. Her pale face gleamed with sweat, though she had never broken her mask of impassivity. "He seems a little more comfortable, at any rate. There's not much more we can do at this point."

"Lida," Katya said. She didn't know how to continue, and could sense Lidiya's exasperation.

"Katya, people – "

"Don't say it," Katya snapped. She had never thought that she would talk to Lidiya like that, but the words came out, heartfelt and unconsidered. "Don't say that people die every day. Don't try to pretend that you're inured to it."

Lidiya sat back on her heels. She looked more tired than Katya had ever seen her, but there was a flicker of something that could have been pleasure on her face. "I never thought *you'd* be telling *me* that."

"I just – " Katya didn't know. It was almost more effort than she could manage to string words together into a sentence. She felt weary from her scalp to the soles of her feet. She was shaking. "I don't want him to die," she said.

"Well, perhaps he won't," said Lidiya. Her words were not comforting, but her tone was gentle. She got to her feet. "We should get some sleep."

"Yes. Yes." Katya looked around, disconcerted. She suddenly, strongly, did not want Lidiya to leave.

"I can share the table with you," Lidiya said. She was looking at Katya again in that same way, curious and appraising, as if Katya were a problem that she was struggling to solve.

"You don't need – the children – "

"Don't be ridiculous. The children were fast asleep when I left – they'll be fine for the next few hours, and we're well within shouting distance if they're not." She hoisted the pile of blankets that Katya had flung onto the table earlier, and with swift, military precision, laid them out to form a bed. There was something terrifying in Lidiya's efficiency, the effortless way that she could take control of any situation. "Get in," Lidiya ordered, whipping back the corner of a blanket. Katya obeyed, lying against the rough blankets and trying to arrange her body in such a way that the jagged edges of her bones rubbed as little as possible against the hard lines of the planks below. There was a swish and a creak, and Katya felt Lidiya climb up behind her onto the makeshift bed. Instantly she stiffened, hating herself for it. The only way that her body knew how to respond to proximity was to try and make itself as small as possible. Behind her, Lidiya sighed. Her exhalation stirred the fine hairs at the nape of Katya's neck.

"Relax," Lidiya said. Katya didn't move. She barely knew what the word meant, and even if she had, she was powerless over her body at that moment. She closed her eyes tightly against the vision of Dima in her bed, flushed and gasping, and Lidiya at her back. A weight landed on her side: Lidiya's arm. It pulled her closer. Katya felt Lidiya's breasts against her back, Lida's bony knees nudging the underside of her own.

When Lidiya spoke, Katya felt her lips move, almost close enough to touch. "I *said*, relax."

~

When Katya woke on an indrawn breath, morning was white-eyed at the gaps in the window. The light was the colour of milk. Lidiya was already upright and moving, hunting through the room for the shoes she had kicked off in the night; on the bed, Dima's eyes were closed, but after an initial, giddy moment of panic, Katya saw that his chest was rising and falling – too fast, too shallow, but breathing still. She propped herself up on her elbow, swallowing down her heart; Lidiya turned towards her, eyes squinting against exhaustion.

"It's not eight yet. You should go back to sleep – I'm only up to see to the children's breakfast."

"How is he?"

"No worse," Lidiya said, careful, judicious.

"No better?"

Lidiya shrugged. "No change."

It was no comfort. Katya swung her legs onto the floor, padded over to where Dima lay. Her heart was still leaping like a landed fish; all the deep breaths in the world couldn't slow it. She picked up the bucket, the rags, put them down again, picked up the pot, put it down. Her hands tightened into fists. She barely registered Lidiya's sigh of frustration, the prelude to an ambush: the next moment, Katya's coat had been wrapped around her shoulders and Lidiya was hustling her, not gently, towards the door.

"Lida, what are you doing?"

"Go out, if you won't sleep. Take a walk, burn off some of that nervous energy of yours."

"I can't! Dima – "

"Dima needs rest more than he needs anything else right now. I can keep an eye on him, and on the children, but not if I have to shepherd you as well." Cool, considering, Lidiya regarded her for a moment before plunging a hand into Katya's coat pocket, coming up with her keys. A grin lit up her face. "Aha, lucky guess. I'm confiscating these – you're not allowed back in under an hour. After that I'll leave them behind the drainpipe, down on the street." She took Katya's shoulder and began to steer; Katya, unable to think of anything better to do, acquiesced. "Go on. Go."

Outside, Katya felt bone-weary and brimful of furious energy, both at once. She walked, concentrating on nothing but her own footfalls, barely looking in front of her, let alone thinking about where she was going. It wasn't until she found herself crossing the Griboyedov Canal that she started to slow, dizzy and breathless; she had been walking the way she used to, before the war, an easy, strong-legged lope, and she had come, abruptly, to the tail end of her strength. She thought of the park in front of St Nicholas's Cathedral: she could sit there, gather herself; in half an hour she would be allowed to go home – but when she sat, she found herself looking up, arrested, at the cathedral itself.

It was hard to love the city without loving its churches, no matter how foolish or superstitious Katya had always believed them to be. The way that St Nicholas's stood on a bend of the canal made it seem like it was waiting to be admired. Its grounds were dug up for vegetables now, and the trees that framed it were almost picked clean by people searching for food; as Katya passed, she plucked a new lime bud off a branch, unthinking, and put it in her mouth, sticky and sweet. Before her, the building held together its tattered dignity. Katya thought of the Metropolitan, his icons in hand, circling the cathedral daily through the first winter of the Blockade. There was bravery in that, she thought. There was...there was grace.

Katya had never been inside. She had always considered herself and the church engaged in an uneasy truce, but she was better than it was, harder and wiser. As she stepped through the door, she was immediately conscious of the way her shoes looked against the gleaming floor, tattered and tired and old. The weariness she carried aligned itself across her shoulders. She felt yoked. For a brief, brittle moment, memory surged: December, the snow, sitting down on her way home, not getting back up. She longed for surrender.

Her feet kept moving. The inside of the church smelled of honey and milk, the soft sweetness of wax. The candles were points of indescribable brightness in the gloom. Katya's shoes scuffed and slapped against the ground and she felt huge, gawky, as if she was about to bring shame and mockery upon herself. She didn't know how to behave here, but nor did she know how to behave anywhere else. She had been shackled her whole life, and was only now starting to realise that she had donned the shackles herself, mistaking them for armour. Knots of people stood nodding, bowing, but no one turned to look at her. All Katya could see were backs. She took a sharp pleasure in her own irrelevance.

This is the place you come when you want to ask for something, she realised. She had never needed a church as a place to give thanks, but she had come to it today as a place to plead, and a place to offer. The room was crowded with the dead. Katya could feel them watching her, the girls and Yevgeny; her grandmother, whose icon-kissing Katya had disdained, once she was old enough to understand it; the thousands upon thousands of people who had died in the city. They pressed themselves into the church, watching, smug in their incorporeality. Staring at the floor, Katya saw it buck and heave. She was more tired than she had thought possible, more weak, more desperate. From the walls, generations of the city's sailors looked down. In front of her, an old woman, three inches of pure white against the dyed red of her hair, spoke in an undertone. Her eyes were closed. Her lined face was a map.

Katya saw the icons now. They were neither decoration nor ostentation; they were people. The Madonnas with their babies in their arms, blackened faces peering out of the gilt: those were to be avoided. Instead, she found herself standing in front of St Nicholas, the miracle worker. She remembered her grandmother's hands then, soft and hard at once. Katya had forgotten deliberately, cut her grandmother out of her life and her memory because she couldn't make sense of her. Now she remembered, suddenly, the rasp of her voice, her wide, flat vowels and the powder smell of her skin. She remembered, too, the stories that she used to tell, late at night, when they'd both pretended Katya was asleep: about St Nicholas, about the dowries that he had provided for the impoverished maidens, the demons that he had driven out of the shrines, and the way that he was so close to god that he could see whenever anyone was in trouble and come to them. There had been times when Katya had managed to forget that her grandmother was someone from the old way of life, someone to be disregarded. The cloth of her grandmother's skirts, and the sharp scent of the vinegar she used to pickle. The way that she had been the only person who ever preferred Katya to Zhenya.

Katya recognised St Nicholas's face. It wasn't friendly or inviting or kind. It was stern and forbidding and perhaps that was why she felt at home standing in front of him. The hand he held up was less a sign of peace than an admonishment, barring the way. It wouldn't do to ask something of someone who might grant it too easily. St Nicholas reminded Katya of her father, immoveable as a force of nature, impossibly powerful. Katya had thrown love at him uselessly, as feeble as waves battering a shore. She knew how to ask things of someone as unyielding as St Nicholas seemed.

No one had ever taught Katya how to pray, not even her grandmother, and she didn't know if there was a special formula for it, words that she should utilise or avoid. Instead, she looked into St Nicholas's painted eyes. *I need you to let Dima be all right*, she said, clear as a bell inside her own head. *I know how silly this must seem, I know how many people must have asked you for this same thing, for so many other people in this city. I know that the air in here is thick with prayers.* As soon as she thought it she felt it, the weight of wishes against her throat. She swallowed it down. *I know that you don't do what people ask, and I know that you know that I don't even believe in you.* Katya allowed herself a small smile at that. She imagined that St Nicholas might, too. *But I've never asked you for anything, and I never railed against you when you took my girls. I never* – her mind skipped a little as she realised: she had never been angry about the girls. She had never felt their loss as anything less than she deserved. And she was angry now, instantly, her skin alive with it. *Let him live*, she told St Nicholas. It wasn't a request, it was a demand. Although Katya did not speak aloud, her teeth clenched behind her lips, and her hands balled into fists again. *Let him live. Let him live. Let him live.*

It was two hours before she came home. The keys were where Lidiya said they'd be, and Katya let herself in, hauling herself up the stairs, too emptied of everything to move any faster. All sense of urgency was gone, now: one way or another, what would happen would happen. In her apartment, she was surprised by the children, curled on the floor, pencils in their fists, drawing. As Katya entered, Masha raised her head, frowning, her finger to her lips.

"Auntie Katya, we have to be quiet, Auntie Lida says. Someone's sick."

Lidiya herself was lying on the sofa, her face pressed into the cushion, her hands curled in front of her. Dropping a quick pat onto Serezha's head as she passed, Katya squatted by the sofa, squeezing Lidiya's shoulder.

"Lida."

"Ah, you're back," Lidiya said. Her voice was muffled. She didn't open her eyes.

"Is he – Dima, is he – "

"He woke up an hour or so ago. Ate a bit of bread, drank a bit of water. His fever's still higher than I'd like, but he seems to be back with us, for now, at least." Wriggling, Lidiya pushed her face further into the cushion. "Now go in and see him, and leave me alone."

In the bedroom, Katya was numb with something that seemed to go far deeper than relief. Crossing to the bed, quieter than she thought she could move; his eyes were half open, impossible to tell whether he was asleep or awake.

Katya recalled Lidiya's gesture of the night before, her palm against Dima's cheek, the way he turned towards it. Daring, Katya reached her hand towards the face on the pillow, her courage failing her just before she touched him. He turned anyway, and then her palm was cupping his cheek, the rest of her body frozen. She couldn't bring herself to breathe. As if her hand belonged to another person, Katya watched as her thumb moved, smoothing the hot, dry skin along Dima's cheekbone.

"Dima," she said, just to say it, without expecting an answer, but his expression changed and his lips parted, and an instant, certain spark flared through Katya, so intense as to almost be thrilling. She had spent half the night trying to call upon all her maternal instincts, and yet now: *don't say Mother*, she thought, bitter and brutal. *If you mistake me for your mother, I will walk out of here right now, and I don't know where I'll go, but I won't come back.*

"Katya," Dima said. She could have wept. On her knees, suddenly, beside him, with no recollection of how she had got there, Katya pushed his damp hair back from his forehead with her left hand, taking his own hand in her right. *So you just decide to do it,* she thought, *and then you do it, and it's done.*

"Are you feeling better?" she asked. He was silent for so long that she wasn't certain that he'd heard; only the movement of his hand, fingers tapping out compulsive rhythms against her palm, betrayed that he was awake at all.

"A little," Dima said at last. "Lidiya was here, before. She said I'm in your apartment?"

"Yes."

"I've been having the strangest dreams," he said. "Or not dreams. People kept coming and standing by the bed. They were shouting at me. I knew that they weren't there, not really, but they wouldn't let me ignore them. I thought I must be dying."

"You're not dying," Katya said, more forcefully than she'd intended. Dima smiled.

"I hope not." Closing his eyes, he yawned, lengthily and prodigiously. "God, but I'm tired. I feel like I could sleep for weeks." He pushed himself down in the bed, further under the blankets. "You'll stay, now, won't you?" he asked, his tone light, as if he were asking nothing at all. For a moment Katya couldn't trust herself to speak.

"I'll stay."

CHAPTER FIFTEEN

I: 25 May 1942

There was luck in it, that Dima had fallen ill at the end of the week. He slept for much of the weekend, waking at intervals to take water and a little food – *not enough*, Katya thought, torn between urging him to eat more and being grateful to have a little more remaining to go around. Eight days until the end of the month, and the issuing of new ration cards: she counted the days, counted them again, but no matter how many times she counted, the time got no shorter. Seven days to go: by Sunday evening there was no doubt that Dima was better than he had been, but nowhere near well: the delirium had passed, but his cough was enough to make even Lidiya flinch, and his fever, although lower, still spiked from time to time.

Monday: Katya sliced her morning's bread into careful, conclusive halves. It would be so easy to give him less, she thought; how would he ever know? She would not do it. All the honour she had left was imbued in those two halves of bread. She wondered whether Vasya had ever done anything like that, taken advantage of Dima's blindness. It was a shock, sometimes, to remember how dependent Dima was on other people's goodwill, despite his veneer of independence. It was a good thing he was so likeable.

"Did you tell me that Vasya was dead?" Dima asked when she brought the bread into the bedroom. His tone was almost conversational, as if he was asking about the weather or the price of potatoes in the market, but it was the question that Katya had been dreading, and she had been thankful every hour it had not come. She wanted to equivocate, to delay; she wouldn't.

"I don't know for sure, of course," she said, "but you told me that he'd gone to see someone near Moskovsky Station. Lidiya said that in the middle of the afternoon there was very heavy shelling around there, and a lot of the people queuing nearby were killed. Given that he didn't come back, it seems likely…"

"Yes," said Dima. His voice was steady, and there was no change in his expression. Katya handed him the saucer containing his bread – Lidiya's cunning illusion would make no difference to him, but it was habit by now – and he laid it in his lap, breaking the bread apart into tiny, sodden nuggets. He lifted one to his mouth, chewing slowly, his throat working as he swallowed. Katya wondered whether this was the end of the conversation. She had a horror of other people's grief, but Dima's complete lack of affect was disquieting.

"I don't feel anything," Dima said at last. "About Vasya, I mean. I keep saying it to myself: *he's dead, Vasya is dead*. Nothing. Why shouldn't he be dead?"

"So many people…" Katya began, echoing Lidiya, but Dima gave a sharp shake of his head.

"No. He was the first person who's died since this all began, the first person who I…who I *loved*." He emphasised the last word with reckless bravery. Katya guessed that it would have taken a gun to his head to make him say that when Vasya was still alive. "Before the war, yes. My family, Arseny Grigorevich – I was used to the fact that people could just disappear with no notice. Swallowed up by…by…" he made a complicated gesture with his hands that Katya interpreted: *by everything*. "But Vasya helped me to feel unstoppable, and so I thought that he was, too. I thought that nothing could touch us, either of us." He paused for a moment, thinking. "You know, on Thursday evening, when he didn't come and didn't come and didn't come – I must have known what had happened. I *did* know; it's happened often enough to others. And yet all I could think was, *that bastard, he's got my ration card. He's got my ration card.*"

There was nothing Katya could say. Dima fell silent, finished his bread, licking the tip of his finger to gather up the final crumbs. "Help me up, will you?" he asked at last, in the same casual tone. "We should get going soon; it's bound to take me twice as long to walk to the Radio House today. I wish I had time to wash properly, but I suppose I'll have to make do with a change of clothes."

"What do you – you're not coming to rehearsal?" Half an hour before, Katya had been going to suggest it herself. Now, coming from Dima, the idea was clearly absurd. Dima smiled a little.

"What else? It's still a week until June. If I don't go to rehearsal I'll lose my ration, and I can't keep sharing yours. Don't pretend you can spare it."

Katya couldn't. Her stomach had set up a clamour, protesting its reduction in supplies; it wouldn't have surprised Katya if Dima could hear it. He was already struggling upright, shifting closer to the edge of the bed. It was futile to fight him; Katya took his hand and helped him stand. "I'll wait in the kitchen, then. You're right, we should get going."

In the streets, Dima refused to lean on Katya as he had done three days before, when leaving his apartment for hers. His pride kept him straight-backed, but his face was pallid, smeared with fever colour along his cheekbones. They needed the extra time they had allowed for the walk: Dima stopped to catch his breath every block, and his breath was elusive. The sound of his labouring lungs was torment enough in the apartment, but out in the streets it took on a more frightening tenor for Katya, the outside world making things more real. Dima did not complain, nor did he talk. Instead, in uncomfortable parody of their normal walks to and from rehearsal, Katya kept up an unceasing monologue, mapping the city in a way that distracted them both. It was easier, now, so much easier, the words dropping from her mouth: she didn't think she could stop them if she tried. Memories came to her, disjointed: the café where she had gone, once, with Zhenya, playing bitter, unwilling chaperone; the apartment block where her first violin teacher had lived, its upper floor pockmarked now with shell damage, its roof slipping down rakishly over its window eyes. It was exhausting, the monologue, Katya had barely breath for it and yet she developed a superstitious fear, looking askance at Dima, silent and struggling, that something terrible and unnameable would happen if she stopped. She could not stop. Over the Fontanka, crossing the Anichkov Bridge: she could not help trailing her fingertips over one of Dima's horses, a hopeless talisman. New posters had been stuck to the wall and Katya read them aloud, without comment, the things that people were offering in exchange for food: gold cufflinks, a camera, a broken lamp. She described to Dima what she was seeing, the old women clutching bundles of firewood, the young men brazenly digging through a pile of debris for things that they could take or sell. At the corner of Proletkulta Ulitsa, Dima stopped, leaning against a wall, and Katya's skin lifted into goose bumps at the sight of his face. For a moment, his mask of determination slipped. He looked exhausted and ill and despairing. She had seen that look on the faces of the people who sat down in the snow and refused to move. But Dima moved. He pressed his palms flat against the building at his back and pitched forwards, but maintained his balance. His violin case was slung over his shoulder, secured there with a sash, as he couldn't trust his fingers to keep their grip on it. It knocked against his ribs, making a sound that was inhuman.

"Come on," he told Katya, the first words he had spoken since leaving the apartment. They walked on.

At the rehearsal, people were kind. The orchestra was used to weakness, and mostly intolerant of it. If someone was weak and ill, it was usually pointed out that everyone was weak and ill, and they could get on with it just as well. For Dima, though, his customary energy and humour seemed to have bought him more sympathy at the loss of them. Genya told him sternly that he should be resting. "And his ration?" Katya asked, irritable with worry. Genya shrugged.

"Of course, there is that." He turned back to Dima. "Don't play. Just sit and listen. Take in as much as you can. Eat, when it's time." He put his hands on either side of Dima's burning face and looked into it, seeming to forget that Dima couldn't look back. "You will be all right."

Throughout the rehearsal, Dima sat with his violin in his lap. His arms lacked the strength to lift it for any length of time, but his fingers moved on the fingerboard in time with the music. He coughed very little, but when he did the rest of the section seemed to wince in concert. Whenever she was not playing, Katya had an almost irresistible urge to reach out and touch him – his knee, his shoulder – just to reassure him that she was still there, and to reassure herself as well. She didn't.

When it was time for lunch, Dima ate in silence, and then curled up in one of the seats, wrapped in his coat. He was asleep almost immediately. Katya couldn't take her eyes off him, for fear that if she did he would disappear. The last days had made him terrifyingly insubstantial. She saw Trofim pass him, look again and then take off his own coat, laying it over Dima. The wave of fondness she felt for Trofim was unprecedented.

"Is he staying with you, then?" Trofim asked, sitting down next to Katya. He seemed to speak more easily when it was just the two of them, unobserved. Her face flamed.

"Yes. For now. It looks likely that Vasya was killed, and he has no one else, so I thought…"

Trofim nodded. "Of course. It's the right thing. I was worried about him on Friday too, when he didn't come, but I thought…" He shrugged. "No. I didn't think. You get so caught up in yourself…"

"He lives near me," Katya explained. "I didn't know if anyone else knew where. I worried that if I didn't go and check on him, no one would."

"It's amazing he lived through the winter, when you think about it," Trofim said. "What with the cold and the food and the shelling and… the rest of it," he finished. Katya knew what he meant. "Vasya must have been good to him."

"I suppose so." Katya was ashamed to realise she had never given Vasya much thought, other than having the vague idea that he was unfitting company for Dima, his boorish good-temper a strange foil for Dima's dizzying quickness of mind. It was too easy to see Dima as invulnerable, simply because he acted like he was. She offered a silent nod to Vasya, gone now, vanished into nothing like so many others: *thank you for keeping him safe.*

Despite the burden of his exhaustion, the rehearsal seemed to rekindle something in Dima. The walk home was easier, much easier than it had been that morning, and when they got back to the apartment, instead of subsiding into bed, as Katya had expected: "I need to wash," Dima said. Katya didn't like the idea. He was too weak, too ill, still; after the amount of energy he had expended, he should be resting, rather than stripping off in the bathroom, which was still nearly as icy as it had been in winter.

"Maybe tomorrow. You still have a fever – "

Dima shook his head. "No, Katya, please – I'm revolting. I'd feel a thousand times better if I were clean."

"Perhaps a bed bath…" Though she was far from certain she could cope with that herself.

Dima chuckled. "*Please*. Don't make me suffer the indignity. I'm not delirious any more."

He had always been fastidious about cleanliness, turning up at rehearsals scrubbed and pristine when half the orchestra couldn't be bothered to wipe the dust from their faces. Reluctant, Katya put some water on to heat, transferring it into the tub they had used through the winter. At least the taps were working again now that the pipes had finally thawed; that was a blessing. She mixed the water to a comfortable temperature, blood heat, the temperature she would use to bathe a baby, and went to fetch Dima. His muscles had stiffened after his walk, and it took him two tries to get to his feet; laughing at himself, he tottered like an old man. In the bathroom, Katya took his hand and placed it on the bath, the basin, the soap, the towel, the tub of warm water, until he said, with some asperity, "Thank you, Katya, but I have used a bathroom before."

"I'll leave you to it, then," Katya said, embarrassed. She closed the door behind her, but could not bring herself to step away. Through the door, she heard Dima sit. Water splashed. There was the sound of skin sliding against skin as he soaped himself. Water again. He sighed, once, which turned into a cough, and Katya flinched at the rough sound of it, imagining Dima bent forward, his fisted hand pressed against his ribs as if trying to keep himself contained. It seemed to go on for a very long time. Then silence again.

"Katya?" Dima's voice came softly through the door, and Katya froze. He had spoken so quietly that she wouldn't have heard had she not been right outside; to answer would be to expose herself. She said nothing, her heart juddering. "Katya?" Dima called again, a little louder, a little more urgently. For a moment, Katya hesitated, and then was overcome by a sudden burn of anger and self-disgust. *So what if he thinks it's strange that you're listening at the door! He needs you.*

"Yes, Dima?" She tapped a knuckle on the door, sketching a knock. "Do you want me to come in?"

"Would you mind?"

Katya opened the door. Dima was sat on the edge of the bath, the flimsy towel she had given him wrapped around his waist. He was so thin that Katya could see every rib, the shape of his shoulder joints. His collarbones framed deep, dark hollows. He turned towards her as she entered. "Sorry to bother you. It's just – " He held out his hands for a moment: they were shaking violently. "Think of the vibrato I could make with that," he said, smiling a little. "Would you mind terribly doing my hair for me? I can't seem to hold my arms up for long enough."

"Of course." Katya remembered the feel of his cheek against her palm two days before, the sudden ease of contact. She had been brave enough before; she could do it again. Sitting beside him, she reached out to touch his shoulder, moving him slightly so his head was over the bath. The smoothness of his skin was shocking. She put her hand on his hair, as soft as one of the girls'. "I'm going to pour the water on, now."

There was a jug on the edge of the bath. Katya filled it with water from the tub, tepid, fading to cool. It ran in rivulets down Dima's neck and back, and she combed her fingers through his hair, wetting it thoroughly. He shivered a little. Again, she filled and poured. Dima was quiet, his head bowed. Katya could feel the tremor in his legs as he fought to stay still.

"Now the soap." It was cheap soap from the market, with a heady, almost animal stink to it. Katya thought of the delicately scented soap that she had used to bathe the girls. She lathered it up between her hands, then rubbed it as gently as she could into Dima's hair, taking care not to let it drip onto his face, massaging it into his scalp. He made a noise, then, a humming sigh, and she stopped.

"Are you all right? Did I hurt you?"

"Not at all." He half laughed. "It just…it just feels nice, that's all."

Katya coloured. She bit her lips to stop a smile.

"I'm going to rinse, now. Tilt your head back."

Mindful of what he had said, she took her time over it, running her fingers through his damp hair. Experimentally, she brushed her nails against the fine skin of his scalp, and Dima smiled, his eyebrows rising in unconscious reaction. The third jug of water ran clear into the bath, and Katya couldn't draw it out any longer. The towel that she used for drying her own hair was resting on the side of the basin, and she pulled it towards her, wrapping it around Dima's head, tousling his hair dry.

"There. You're done."

"Thank you."

For a moment, neither of them moved. Katya waited for Dima to stand. He cleared his throat.

"Katya, I need to get dressed."

"Oh! Of course! I'm so sorry!" Katya leapt for the door, horrified. "I'll just…I'll just wait in the kitchen. You can shout if you need me for anything."

It was some minutes before he emerged, dressed, his hair dampening his collar. Katya took his arm and helped him back to the bed.

"Are you sure you're still all right sleeping on the table?"

"Perfectly." Katya shook up the pillows and arranged them as best she could, ensuring that they were at the angle that allowed him to breathe most easily. "Now lie back."

Dima did so. As Katya got up she heard again, in her mind, the sound that he'd made when she had been soaping his hair, that half-gasp, half-hum. "Do you think you feel things differently to other people, because you can't see? Physically, I mean?"

He didn't seem as surprised by the question as Katya was at herself for asking it. "Perhaps. I've thought about it a lot. My hearing's certainly different to most people's. I don't think it's better, necessarily, but I know I pick things up that other people can't, just because I have more need to. It would make sense that my other senses are more intense, too." He stopped for a moment, as if he was weighing up whether or not to continue. "And there's also the fact that from when I was seven until I was sixteen – all the time I was in school – I was rarely touched by anyone. None of us were. Certainly not with fondness. I suppose I still feel…starved for it, somehow."

Tanya had been seven. Katya tried to imagine sending her away: how long would it have taken for the brave heft of Tanya's shoulders to crumple? Tanya had always been self-possessed, but she had never failed to climb into her mother's lap for a kiss and a cuddle every evening, protecting her rights jealously against Nadya's attempted encroachments.

"Katya," Dima said, and then stopped. He looked diffident, an expression Katya had rarely seen on his face.

"What is it?"

"Katya – I don't remember anything much about the weekend, after you brought me here. Not until yesterday evening."

"Well, Dima, you were delirious."

"I know." He took a deep breath. "I didn't…I didn't say anything, did I? To you?"

"What do you mean?"

"I mean, I didn't say anything…strange? Anything that I shouldn't have?"

Katya was baffled. "You spoke a lot, but I didn't understand most of it. You were talking to people, to Vasya, and to Piotr, a little. Some other names I didn't recognise."

Dima's face relaxed. "So I didn't say anything to you at all?"

"I don't think you even knew I was there, most of the time." Katya decided not to mention Lidiya's role in the nursing; there was no need to compound Dima's evident embarrassment. "You kept complaining about the smoke," she added, remembering, "I suppose because you were having trouble breathing – " She stopped. Dima had stiffened as suddenly as if he'd been shot, a look on his face of extreme wariness. Her confusion turned to caution, mirroring his own: Katya sat down on the very edge of the bed, looking at him searchingly. "Was that what you were worried about?"

Dima laughed, but there was no joy in it. "No. No, that's…something else." He was silent for a moment, frowning, as if he were groping for words.

"You don't have to tell me," Katya said quickly. Other people's confidences still had the capacity to frighten her. Dima's frown did not lift.

"No, I'd like to. It's just – not something I talk about very much. It's hard to tell it right."

II: 1938

Two years in Leningrad, and Dima had its measure now, the shape and the weight of it. When he had first arrived, he had been struck uncharacteristically dumb: the city, the hot-cold push of it, its stench like a blanket, oil and too many bodies, the crisp clap of its air, the soul-deep, sole-deep rumble of the trolleybuses. For the first three weeks Dima had had a constant headache, lightning spears along his jaw, down his spine. His lungs clotted in the filthy air, and he sat up in the kitchen at nights so as not to keep Vasya awake with his coughing. Vasya, concerned, had told him to see a doctor, but Dima was certain, despite the whistle and rasp of his breath and the tender pain at the base of his skull, was certain that he'd never been happier or more well in his life. The city pushed down; he was gathering his strength and resources to push back, uncoiling himself little by little each day. He was hollowing out a space for himself, burrowing in.

Two years on, and he knew it now, he had mapped it in his head, he could find his way. He had a job, as an accompanist in a second-rate ballet school, and a teacher, on whom he spent most of his wages: one of Maksim Sergyevich's colleagues had agreed to teach him on Maksim's grudging recommendation. She was an older woman, whose playing was a crisp blossoming of sound, and as a teacher she was quietly, coldly incisive – it wasn't the same, could never be the same, but Dima felt his playing getting better, more precise, more refined, things drawn out of him that Arseny Grigorevich had never quite managed. He had fashioned a city for himself: not Vasya's, not Arseny Grigorevich's, but a little of both, and wholly his own.

Vasya took Dima to bars, and after the initial fear and shock of the noise and the clatter and the closeness faded, Dima started to love them for those very reasons. They had some of the same intense sensuality as an orchestral performance in a concert hall, layers of sounds and smells and touches and textures that Dima could bury himself in. It became clear that in the dim light and the press of drunken, unobservant people, Dima's blindness was not immediately obvious; if he should stumble on his way to the toilets, or not look directly at someone while he was talking to them, people would usually just assume that he had overdone it on the vodka. It became a game that he and Vasya both enjoyed, to see how long it would take people – particularly women – to notice. Vasya, with the help of the redoubtable Lyuba, his primary girlfriend, had taken Dima's love life in hand, evidently seeing his amorous adventures as an extension or reflection of his own; he had only been slightly put out when Dima's successes began to outstrip his.

Lyuba tried to explain it: "It's not just the way you look," she said, "Though that doesn't hurt. It's also because you don't look at women. If I'm out in a bar, I see a good-looking man who's ignoring me, it gets me interested. Most women like a challenge as much as men do."

"And then they come and talk to me…" Dima said, laughing.

"And they see how eager you really are!" Vasya concluded. Dima wondered whether any of the women he ended up talking to resented the contrast between the cool, aloof man they saw from afar and the overenthusiastic boy he turned into, but he hadn't had any complaints yet.

This woman, Dima could tell, was older. The scent of cigarettes and vodka clung to her, as they clung to everyone in the place, but Dima didn't mind that – underneath he could pick up the sweet scent of the face cream she wore, a lemon tang of perfume, and the deeper, feral smell of her skin and hair. When she had first come over to speak to Dima, Vasya had nudged him in the way he sometimes did to telegraph his disapproval. Vasya didn't like Dima sleeping with those women he deemed unattractive; he worried that it made Dima look foolish. Dima couldn't have cared less. Vasya had a self-declared love of variety, which explained why Lyuba was only one of a rotating set of girlfriends, albeit all buxom and blonde – blondes with tits, that was the way Vasya liked them, on which he expounded at numbing length – but Dima, always a quick study, had embraced Vasya's pro-variety stance with rather more vigour than Vasya himself would have wanted. Besides, abstract concepts such as appearance were irrelevant to Dima, as long as the woman gave him that languorous sensation of his blood running more slowly in his veins, rather than the sharp prickle of anxiety that raised the hair on his arms and put him immediately on his guard. One of his favourite experiences had been with a woman who was twenty years older than him and twice his breadth; the breathtaking sensual excess of her had made him speechless with delight, but when she had sobered up the next morning, she had seemed too shy and overwhelmed to agree to meet with him again.

There was a slight twist in the way this woman – Anna, perhaps, or Anastasia; Dima wasn't good with names – spoke, choosing her words with delicate care in an attempt to sound more sophisticated. Dima liked her – she had accepted his blindness with equanimity, not something that all women did – and so he found her tentative speech touching. He started listening out for when she slipped, and her real words came out. It was there in the roundness of her 'o's that he got it at last, a vivid memory of the house he'd been born in, the scent of fir trees and cold earth. "Are you from Vologda?" he asked, cutting across her detailed description of the last film she'd seen. Her voice stumbled to a halt and there was a brief, embarrassed silence. Dima was suddenly sorry that he had exposed the roots that she was trying to conceal.

The woman forced a laugh. "Yes, I am. I haven't lived there for years, though. I much prefer it here. It's so terribly backward, around there, I think. Full of superstition, and the *smells*…"

"I was born in a village not far from Vologda," Dima explained.

"Were you?" She sounded doubtful. "You don't sound…"

"I went away to boarding school when I was seven." It still cost Dima a little effort to say this – although he had long since accepted that school had brought him music and was therefore the best thing that could have happened, the memory of his early weeks away remained a chill stillness at the heart of him. "I haven't been back since."

"What village are you from, then?" the woman asked with unwilling curiosity.

"Hutor Dalniy."

"Really?" She laughed, still a little embarrassed. "I grew up in Ivanovo. It's only about ten miles away…"

"I remember," Dima said, smiling. His father had sometimes taken him there when he had gone to buy supplies. One of the old ladies in the market had once pressed an apple into his hand.

"What is your last name, anyway? I might know your family."

"Kaverin," Dima said. Reluctance stole over him even as he said it. "And my patronymic is Aleksandrovich."

The woman became very still. Dima knew, then. He felt nothing, but his head suddenly seemed as if it had a lot of space in it. "How old are you?" the woman asked carefully.

"Eighteen." It was something he normally lied about.

"And you went to school…"

"When I was seven," Dima said. He started to feel faintly sick. The woman took his hand and it was all he could do not to snatch it back. He had counted it out when they had arrived, six paces to the bar, and a further nine to the door: he could leave in seconds – but Vasya would worry. Vasya always worried.

"You know, don't you?" the woman asked gently. From the direction of the bar came a crash and the sound of quarrelling. Dima could discern Vasya's voice above the melee, but not what he was saying. Beside him, the woman jumped, but stayed seated. The dynamic between them had altered completely. Normally Dima resented it when women turned maternal in his presence; he didn't mind now.

"When I went to school," Dima said, half to himself, "when I went to school, they never wrote, they never visited. No one came to collect me for the holidays. I thought – at first I didn't know what to think. And then when I got older I started to hear about what had happened, what was happening. My father – the farm had been prosperous, at least in comparison to our neighbours. I guessed that they might have – they might have gone. But I thought maybe after five years, or after ten…"

She had seemed like a brash woman, and he never would have guessed at the care with which she chose her words as she told him, but it was a blow that was impossible to lighten. The family had been deemed kulaks; that much Dima had guessed. The Komsomol had agitated against them. His father's occasional carpentry work was denounced as capitalist. He was expelled from the village Soviet; his tools were confiscated. Dima's brothers and sisters were barred from the Pioneers. At school, they were persecuted, both by the other children and the teachers. One day, one of Dima's brothers – the woman didn't say which one, probably didn't know – had lost his temper and turned on his main tormentor. Dima recognised the name, recalling a vicious whip-crack of a boy, one of the crueller members of Volodya's gang. His brother had beaten him insensible. The boy's father had been a Komsomol member. That night, the house was torched.

"I only know what I heard," the woman said. She had dropped her voice so low that Dima had to strain to hear it over the brawling at the bar. "There were different versions of the same story. Some said that some of your brothers managed to get out of the house in time. But – "

His parents had not. "Yes," Dima said. His voice was calmer than he would have expected.

"I'm so sorry that you had to find out like this." The woman sounded near tears. Dima squeezed her hand.

"Don't be. I – I suppose it's better I know. At least now I won't be wondering." He thought for a moment. "When would this have been?"

"I'm not sure exactly. 1929, perhaps 1930."

Eight years. There was nothing else to say. They sat, and Dima listened with disinterest to the fight at the bar, the dull thumps of fists on flesh, Vasya's volleys of increasingly obscene insults. Then footsteps, and Vasya's voice, in high dudgeon:

"You won't believe what that fucker at the bar – " He stopped short. "Hold on, what the fuck's happened here?"

His hand landed on Dima's shoulder. Dima couldn't think of what to say; it all seemed too big for him to get a handle on.

"What – did you say something?" Vasya demanded of Anna, or Anastasia. His anger was palpable, and galvanic.

"Shut up, Vasya. It's not her fault."

"Then what?"

There was a tricky pause. The woman let go of Dima's hand. "I should go."

"No need. We're leaving," Vasya said tersely. He pulled Dima to his feet, and they walked. Dima counted six steps, then nine. The door opened to the cool air of the street. Now that they were walking, all of Vasya's questions seemed to have dried up.

"What happened, then?" Dima asked at last. He put on a fairly convincing imitation of Vasya's gravelly voice. "That fucker at the bar…"

Vasya didn't laugh. "Thought I touched his girlfriend's tits."

"Didn't you?" Dima asked, innocent. Vasya snorted a little at that.

"No. Well. Maybe. It was crowded!" He cuffed Dima on the shoulder. "Anyway, what happened with you? You and that woman seemed to be getting on well enough when I went to the bar. Though I knew she was trouble. Didn't I tell you – "

"You didn't *tell* me. You *nudged* me."

"And you know what that nudge means!"

"It was nothing she did," Dima said firmly. He felt quite protective of her, Anna, Anastasia, whoever she was, this unwitting emissary of his family. He suddenly, powerfully, didn't want to talk about it. "It doesn't matter, anyway."

"Something happened, Dima. I can always tell when you're upset – "

"*Everyone* can always tell when I'm upset. I'm emotionally incontinent, like you keep saying."

" – you were white as paper. And you were doing that thing with your hands. You know. Fists."

"Well, I'm not now, am I?" He extended his hands with a flourish, clowning a little, waggling his fingers. "I'm fine. I'm fine!"

"Hmm." Vasya sounded unconvinced, but he closed his mouth.

And Dima *was* fine. After the initial sick shock, the knowledge settled into him, a stone dropped onto a riverbed, sinking down so deep that it could barely be dredged up. Nothing had changed. His family was gone; they had always been gone. What he had feared the most – a return of the terrifying, nameless malaise he had suffered when Arseny Grigorevich disappeared – didn't come. He slept. He joked, he talked, he laughed. Perhaps that laugh had an edge to it, and he could feel Vasya's eyes on him from time to time, sharp and concerned. But he was fine.

It wasn't until a week later that he woke in the night, choked with tears, Vasya's arms around him.

"What – "

"You were shouting," Vasya whispered. He sounded young, almost frightened. Dima wanted to reassure him but couldn't. In his dream there had been the savage stink of smoke, and his mother's hands on his shoulders, pushing him away. He rested his face on his bent knees, not sobbing, but the tears wouldn't stop. Vasya held him steady. "I *knew* you weren't all right," he told Dima. There was a ferocious pride in his voice that made Dima smile. *Vasya.* He palmed the tears off his cheeks, and as clinically as he could, told Vasya what the woman had told him.

Vasya listened in silence. When Dima had finished, he blew out a long breath. He didn't say he was sorry, and Dima was glad of it. "Why do you think your school never told you?"

"Maybe they didn't know themselves. A lot of boys weren't visited; some of them didn't have families. It's a big country, and things change fast. It's not for them to keep track of people." Dima sighed. "I don't know why I'm so upset. I wasn't until now," he added, with an element of bumptiousness he didn't feel. "It's not a surprise. I knew I wouldn't meet them again. And it happened years ago now."

"They were your family," Vasya said.

"Yes. I hate – " He caught his breath. It was hard, sometimes, to shake off the shreds of dreams. Without vision to ground him, the real and the unreal had more of a tendency to blur together. "I hate the thought that they suffered. But then, if they hadn't died, they would have been sent to the Gulag, wouldn't they? And they would have suffered there, perhaps just as badly."

"They would," Vasya said with certainty. His time in Solovki wasn't something he talked about much, outside the usual boastful tales of bravery and stupidity, shared with others who had been there too. Dima never asked about it, but he knew, also, that Vasya didn't always sleep so soundly himself.

"Anyway, at least I know now why they never visited. Except…it was two or three years from when I left to when they, to when that – that happened."

"When did you go away to school, 1927? Things were already starting to look bad for kulaks by then, though you would have been too young to notice. Maybe they wanted to protect you. Maybe they thought it would be easier for you if they cut ties."

"Maybe." Again, Dima felt the press of his mother's hands on his shoulders, pushing him away as she had in the dream. His back was stiff and sore. Experimentally, he stretched, rolling his shoulders back and forth. If he had known what was happening, what had happened, how would things have been different? He didn't even know how to begin to think of it, and he deliberately shut it out. "Sorry I woke you."

"It's all right. Not like I have to get up for work in the morning, is it?"

"I suppose not." Vasya didn't move. "Anyway, I'm all right now," Dima prompted. "You can go back to bed."

He couldn't grieve for his family in daylight, but for a year afterwards, the nightmares continued. They seemed to happen more often when Dima was sleeping somewhere unfamiliar, and after the third time he had woken up, his heart hammering and his throat raw, in the bed of a woman he hardly knew, he stopped spending whole nights away from home. He would have died before admitting it aloud, but he needed Vasya at those times, the solid, straightforward strength of him. On the worst nights, when the dream would come back again and again in all its ferocity whenever he started to drift off, Vasya would lie down beside him, one arm flung over Dima's body. It didn't stop the nightmares completely, but it helped. Vasya never complained about being woken, and refused to accept any of Dima's apologies. After a while, Dima stopped offering them. Vasya was a sloppy and maudlin drunk, but Dima had never minded the nights he had spent keeping him company while Vasya wept and rambled about Piotr, painting him in such heroic terms that Dima barely recognised the awkward, lumpen boy that he had known. There was balance there, between the two of them.

III: 25 May 1942

"So," Dima said, conclusive. His face was carefully calm, but Katya saw his hands clenched, half-hidden by the blankets. Her body ached with tension; she had been unable to move during Dima's monologue, told with little of his normal animation. What do you say to a story like that? What *could* you say? Katya thought back to the comments that had been offered to her on speaking of her own loss, all the condolences and apologies, and couldn't think of one that hadn't felt like a kick to the heart, the fact of acknowledging what had happened serving to crystallise it, firm up its edges, make it more real. The only words that could comfort would be a lie: *no, you've got it wrong, they're safe, I know where they are*. Impossibly, as she watched, the edges of Dima's mouth started to curve upwards.

"That's one of the things I like about you, Katya," he said at last. "You know when to say nothing. You know when there's nothing to say."

CHAPTER SIXTEEN

26 May 1942

In the middle of the night, Katya woke disoriented. The table was hard beneath her and it was still cold enough to tease her breath into clouds whenever she exhaled. For a moment, she had no sense of where she was, or who she was, disembodied, floating in space. It was oddly peaceful. Dregs of dreams clung to her, and as she shook them off she realised: *dreams*. It was the first time she had dreamed since the start of the Blockade.

Below her, on the bed, Dima slept. His breathing sounded much better than it had two days ago, but it was ragged, torn around the edges, and as Katya listened, he started to cough. She winced; it still sounded painful. The mattress squealed as Dima pushed himself upright, bending forwards, trying to straighten out the tangle of breath within him. Feeling wide awake, surprisingly untired, lit from within, Katya slipped off the table and knelt beside the bed. She felt for the box of matches on the bedside table, struck one, and lit the long wick of the squat oil lamp. The light it cast was unsettling, and shadows leaped up the walls like startled ghosts. Dima had his hands pressed against his narrow chest, as if trying to force it into submission, and Katya hesitated for a moment, her palm an inch above his back. If he had been one of her children she would have had no qualms about stroking his back to soothe him; if he had been Yevgeny she would have done the same; even Lidiya, Ilya, Marina. Her wariness about touching him was ridiculous, but it felt different now, uninvited, now that he was himself again. Her flattened hand met the thin cotton of his shirt, the skin underneath radiating heat, his spine like a fence, each rib easily felt. There he was: solid, corporeal. It was strange comfort.

Dima caught his breath. For a moment he didn't move, his forehead resting on his knees. Katya's hand was still on his back: she was unsure whether it would seem stranger to leave it there or to snatch it away. Presently Dima reared upright. "I'm sorry," he said, his tone oddly courteous for someone in his nightshirt in the middle of the night. "Did I wake you?"

"I don't think so. No," Katya said. She added, wondering, "I was dreaming. I haven't dreamed since before the war." No, that wasn't right. The middle of the night invited confidences. "I mean, I haven't dreamed since my family died."

The heat of his skin told Katya that he was feverish again, but Dima's face was calm, present. He shuffled backwards a little, propping himself up against the wall. "You never talk about them," he said quietly. "Can you – will you tell me about what happened?"

And Katya found that she wanted to tell him, a gift for a gift. She had stored up her memories of the girls and her old life inside her, guarding them jealously, as if telling them would let the air in to spoil them – but shutting things up could spoil them just as easily. She closed her eyes: now neither of them could see the other, equal footing. "We were on the last children's evacuation train, in August," she began. "I didn't want to leave, I certainly didn't want the girls to leave without me, but Yevgeny, my husband, he worked for the Party, and he fixed it so that all of us could evacuate, not just our daughters. We had two girls, Tanya and Nadya." *The girls*: it was the first time she had spoken their names aloud since Lychkovo, and the first time that the very sound of them didn't fill her with a stomach-turning, vertiginous panic. Dima was silent and still, his hands in his lap. "Already, I should have known that things were bad, but I shut my eyes to them, I trusted Yevgeny to take charge and to know what was best. But then, who's to say that they would have survived the winter in the city, anyway, if we'd all stayed?" Katya paused, thinking. "We made it as far as Demyansk before things started to turn. The Fascists were coming towards Leningrad, cutting off the railway lines along the way. They were so fast, I found out afterwards. Faster than you could believe. My daughter Nadya saw the paratroopers coming. They floated so silently, it seemed peaceful. She thought that they were butterflies." As she spoke them, the words had the feeling of a chant, an incantation. Something inside her loosened a touch. Each breath she drew in felt deeper. "We couldn't stay in Demyansk, so they put us into trucks and cars and rushed us to Lychkovo. It was the last line that wasn't cut off yet. We could hear the planes coming, now. The children were so calm – not just Tanya and Nadya, but all of them. I don't know if they didn't understand what was happening, or they were so tired and hungry they didn't care – some of them had been travelling for days by this point. But it seemed like they just trusted us so much, they thought that they had nothing to be afraid of. At Lychkovo, the train was waiting for us. Tanya, my eldest daughter, was so attached to Yevgeny, and Nadya would follow her sister everywhere. On the platform it was chaos. There were so many infants, and not enough adults to load them into the trains, and so I told the girls to stay with Yevgeny, and I went to help with the smallest children. All the time the planes were overhead. But we thought – or perhaps just I thought, I was so naïve – that they weren't interested in us. Who cares about a load of children trying to get out of the city? The aeroplanes were so low that we could see the pilots' faces. They knew that we weren't soldiers, that we were no threat to them. I don't even remember when the bombs and bullets started to fall."

Katya dragged a hand across her face. There was a level of incredulity that came, still, from telling this story, reliving it. It seemed astonishing that it had happened, and equally astonishing that less than a year later, she was still alive, walking around, breathing and eating and talking and thinking and making music. The only thing worse than an unimaginable loss is realising that it's possible to go on, after all.

"I don't know if I lost consciousness, but when I…I woke up, my body was already moving. It was like my mind had skipped to another place. There wasn't any past or any future, there was just right then. The worst of the attack was over, but the destruction – I didn't react at the time, I don't think I even understood what I was seeing. When I played it back later in my head, it was like a film that I had seen. So many dead. The railway carriages tipped over, many of them on fire. Bodies of children, and…and parts of bodies. So many in the station, and in the fields around. They had shot them while they were running away. And at first, I didn't even think of Tanya and Nadya, let alone Yevgeny. They didn't enter into my mind. It was as if I could only react to what was right in front of me. Anything else, anything that I couldn't see was too abstract for me to make sense of. And then I remembered. Then I remembered."

She remembered now. As she had run, her shoes had slipped on blood. The air had been full of the stench of burning wood and burning flesh. Every glance had taken in new horrors. She had called Tanya and Nadya's names, calmly at first, because they were probably hiding and afraid and she didn't want to alarm them. When they hadn't come out, she had called louder. There had been a note in her voice that set her own bones trembling, and the faces that turned to hers seemed to hear it, too. Every few minutes she had caught a glimpse of a fair, floating curl, and her heart had seized up inside her. It had never been them, always some other child, prettier or plainer or younger or older. She had started to hate them, these living, breathing children. She had wanted to shake them, to hurt them, as if that could be the sympathetic magic needed to summon her daughters back. A straightforward exchange seemed logical. There were no words that she could think of to explain how it had been to Dima. Instead, she said, "I found Yevgeny's body, but not the girls'. For weeks, I waited for them to come back. Then I knew that they wouldn't."

Katya had never told the story in such detail, but she had told it before, in the early days, before everyone had their own tragedy. She had cast it in the briefest, starkest phrases that she could – *we were evacuated, Yevgeny was killed and the girls are gone* – and she had always hated it most for the expressions on people's faces when they heard her, unctuous pity or panicky, unconscious fear, that the listener would have to think of a way to respond. Dima's face held neither of these expressions. Perhaps it was because of his blindness – Katya had noticed before that his face didn't always react in the way that she would have expected – but for whatever reason, there was nothing to show that he pitied her, or that he was afraid of saying the wrong thing.

"Even now, sometimes sleep makes me forget what happened. Not every day, but often, most mornings even, when I wake up there's a second when I think of the girls, asleep in the next room, and how I should get up and start making their breakfast. And then I remember. Then I *really* wake up."

"Do you ever wish you hadn't?" Dima asked. His voice was impossibly gentle. Katya thought of the soft skin at the back of Nadya's neck, the smell of Tanya's hair.

"Most days," she said. It was a truth that left her feeling almost giddy for the telling of it. "Less so now, but that, itself – that's a different kind of pain."

Dima only nodded. "I'm sorry that happened to your family." The words sounded almost formal, and Katya laughed.

"Months ago, when this all started, Lidiya got angry with me, and she told me that I wasn't the only person who had lost someone," she told Dima. "That's almost the worst of it, I think. At any other time, losing my husband and my two children would be a tragedy. Now, it's normal. There's hardly a mother in this city who hasn't lost a child. When suffering is so widespread, so universal, it stops meaning anything. I don't know how to make sense of that."

Dima half-shrugged – a gesture that Katya had come to understand, in him, as signifying not dismissal or dispassion but simple uncertainty. "It's not the same, I know, but do you remember how I told you about how when I first went to school, I was so angry? Angry that my family had left me, and angry at…at god, maybe, or at the world for making me blind. I knew that if I had had my sight, I could have stayed with my family, and helped them, and I knew – or I thought I knew – that my life would have been so much easier." He smiled. "And what made me even angrier was that *everyone else was in the same situation*. How could I rail against my lot when I was no worse off than everyone around me? I wasn't even entitled to my anger and my misery. That seemed like the greatest injustice, at the time."

Silence stretched between them, thick like treacle. Companionable at first, it took on a life of its own, suddenly hard to break. The warm, flickering light made mountains out of Dima's cheekbones. His throat was a rope, his eyelashes fields of grass, his eyes unfathomable. In the half-light, Katya could almost pretend that he could see her. A sudden sense of vertigo struck her. A chasm yawned at her feet. "Would you like tea?" she asked, too quickly and too loudly, not knowing what she was going to say before she said it. Dima looked baffled by her abrupt change of subject, but, good-humoured, said that he would. Katya stood, stumbling into the kitchen. She had thought that her feet had got used to negotiating their way around the holes in the floor, where the boards had been gouged out in the winter for firewood, but this time she tripped over every one.

In the kitchen, Katya leaned over the sink and spoke to herself firmly. She was old and she was ugly and she was bereaved. Dima was young and blind and – and beautiful. Anything that she thought she felt was fabrication, and anything that could happen between them would be fraudulent manipulation. She was setting herself up to be a laughing stock, she was misunderstanding whatever weight had settled over them in that room, she had to protect herself from Dima and protect him from herself. Katya made the tea, filling the kettle, boiling it long enough that her hands stopped shaking. It was tea only in the loosest sense: hot water, flavoured with ground chicory, but it was hot and coloured and tasted of something other than water. Katya paused in consideration, and then carefully took down the bowl where she kept her sugar, adding a tiny pinch to each cup. Perfect.

In the bedroom, Dima turned when he heard Katya coming, and something about the look on his face made her stomach clench. "Here, tea!" she said, overly cheerful, as if she was talking to a child, hating herself as soon as the words came out of her mouth. Dima didn't speak as she put the cup into his hand. Blowing on it, he took a sip and then grimaced slightly. Katya was thankful for the small burst of anger that came then. "Well, of course it's not proper tea, but it's hot and sweet. I thought…"

"Katya, it's fine," Dima said. His calm only increased her internal disorder. He was eight years younger than her; she was supposed to be the one who was in control, he was supposed to be the one who was discomfited. She took a mutinous sip of her tea, and put the cup down on the bedside table with a little too much force. Dima was right; it really was revolting. Following her lead, he extended his arm, feeling for the table. Katya steeled herself not to help him, and sure enough, within moments he had found it, and his cup was next to hers, discarded. Katya took a deep breath.

"I could get you something else if you want, water, or..."

"Katya. I don't want anything else."

His meaning was unmistakable, even as Katya searched frantically for alternate explanations. Dima reached out for her, found her shoulder. Katya sat motionless as his fingers walked their way up her arm to her neck. His palm was flat against her throat, his fingers in her hair. She could not move. It was a challenge to remember to breathe. She tried to think of the last time that she had washed her hair, the last time she had brushed her teeth, and at the same time she berated herself for daring to think that way, because what she thought was happening could not be happening. Dima hooked his hand behind her head and started, gently, to pull. Katya could not fight it. She was falling towards him. Her lips met his.

Every thought in Katya's head broke apart, spun, crystallised and reformed, completely different. It was as if she had been walking blindfolded, her ears covered, and suddenly saw everything in sharp, clear focus, heard a breath from a room away. She was aware of the roaring of her blood through her veins, the papery brush of Dima's hand against her cheek. His skin was hotter than seemed possible: he was still feverish, he must be, and delirious, otherwise this wouldn't be happening. Couldn't be happening. Katya was suddenly very conscious of her hands, balled in her lap. It wasn't right for them to be lying there like cut flowers, not moving, while all this action went on above them, and yet she couldn't think what she was supposed to do with them. Move them? Take Dima's hand? Touch his face? Touch...any other part of him? When his fingers fastened around hers she was so taken aback that she started, her whole body stiffening. Dima laughed into her mouth, but the laugh was gentle, chiding. "Relax," he said.

"I am relaxed." Every syllable of every word vibrated with tension. Dima drew back.

"Do you want me to stop?"

She should say yes. She should get up and walk away and in the morning they would laugh about it or never talk about it and it would always be that thing that had almost happened, and she would never have to deal with his regret if they went on. It was wrong and inappropriate. She was a married woman, widowed, yes, but still she was married, she had been married, she was respectable, her husband had been a respectable man, she had had two children, she was thirty-one years old and had long given up any idea of this sort of thing. And yet she didn't want him to stop. The touch of his hand was the most warmth that she had felt in months. There was fire in her veins, a bright light at her centre where there'd been gloom before. She couldn't believe that he could possibly want her.

"I don't know," she said finally. Dima didn't move. Instead, they sat, foreheads nearly touching, saying nothing. Katya could feel Dima's breath on her lips. It was a stalemate: he wouldn't move forwards, and he wouldn't withdraw, either. Katya realised that he'd taken her 'I don't know' as literal, and was simply waiting for her to make up her mind.

She kissed him. Everything disappeared.

Katya woke to a scream in her mouth that was out before she could stop it. Something was terribly wrong, her body too hot and too damp, her head full. She was tangled in blankets, her face pressed into the pillow, cotton in her mouth and everything the wrong size, the wrong shape, the wrong place. She felt as if she were filled with howling open spaces. She didn't know where she was, but she knew she had to get away. Struggling and rolling, her hands touched flesh. The sensation was unbearable, and her screams battered against her own ears. Her heart leapt inside her chest, and her blood prickled. Her eyes were open, but nothing she could see made any sense; shapes, colours, nothing relating to anything else. Her only instincts left were to fight and to run.

The thumping noise was what brought her back to herself. It was as if she was putting on her body again, bones and flesh and skin. Suddenly conscious that the appalling noise that she heard was coming from her own mouth, Katya shut it abruptly. Her teeth clashed together. She forced herself to take a deep breath, and then another. Every part of her body was shaking, but her heart started to slow. She no longer felt like an arbitrary collection of limbs and organs; her hold on the world still felt frighteningly tenuous, but it was there. Deliberate, she tightened her grip.

The banging came again, and then shouting. A voice that Katya recognised, harsh with panic: Lidiya's voice. The door handle rattled but could not move against the chair that was propped underneath it, preventing entry. The chair: Katya remembered putting it there, her hands against its wooden back. She remembered smiling as she moved it. What had she been smiling about? Lidiya's voice was muffled through the door, but Katya could just about make out her words. "What the hell is going on in there? Katya? Is someone blocking the door? If you don't answer me right now I'm going to break this door down. I have the hatchet right here. I'm going to count to three…"

"Lidiya – "

Only when he spoke did Katya remember Dima. He was standing on the other side of the bed, breathless, his shirt opened and loose, a blanket hastily wrapped around his waist. He looked terrified, Katya realised, one hand clutching the blanket and the other reaching for the door.

"I don't care about you, Dima, I want to speak to Katya. Is she all right? Katya!"

"She's all right, wait…"

Dima was at the door now, fumbling with the chair, trying to remove it, swearing under his breath, catching at the blanket as it slipped. The chair shifted at last and Dima opened the door a crack. From where she was standing in the corner, her back pressed to the cold plaster of the wall, Katya couldn't see Lidiya's face, but she could imagine it. Lidiya always responded to fear with anger, and she was evidently spitting with rage, even as Dima tried to placate her. "It's fine, honestly Lidiya, please…"

"I don't believe you. I heard her screaming. Let me see her."

Lidiya's shoulder was through the door before Dima could stop her, and Katya was galvanised, understanding all at once that she was naked and freezing and frightened and she had no wish for Lidiya to see her like that. She dived for the bed, and she was in luck: the first thing that came to her hand was an old winter coat of Yevgeny's that she had taken to using as an extra blanket. She wrapped herself in it, aware of how ludicrous she must look, but better that than naked. Lidiya was in the room now, and the look on her face was exactly as Katya had pictured it. With a bubble of hysterical amusement, Katya saw that Lidiya really did have the hatchet in her hand.

"I'm fine, Lida." Katya's voice sounded strange to her, a thousand times calmer than she felt. It echoed along her bones.

"What happened? I heard you screaming, and I thought…" Lidiya stopped, shrugging. "I don't know what I thought. I was worried."

"I had a nightmare, that's all." As she said it, Katya realised that it was true. "I woke up shouting. I'm sorry I scared you, but I'm honestly all right." *More or less*. Every muscle in her body was still strained, and her heartbeats were so strong that they rocked her body. They felt almost like gunfire.

"You didn't *scare* me," Lidiya scoffed, and again Katya felt the urge to laugh. She had never seen Lidiya look more frightened, not even when she had had to take Masha to the feeding centre in February – there was something touching and childish about Lidiya's stubborn bravado. "I was just worried, that's all." She glared at Dima through narrowed eyes, and although Katya knew that he couldn't possibly have seen or even imagined the expression on Lidiya's face, he still seemed to quail slightly under the strength of her sudden disapproval. With Lidiya, alliances could bend and shift in a moment, and Dima had evidently crossed over to the wrong side, for now at least. Still staring at Dima, Lidiya asked, "Do you want him to leave?"

Katya both did and didn't. It was coming back to her now, Dima's lips on her own and his hands on her body and the sheer proximity of him; the calmer she got, the more certain she was that she had just made a colossal, gargantuan fool of herself. She both wanted never to be apart from him and never to see him again.

"No, Lida. He didn't do anything wrong. Just…it's all right, I promise. Look, I'm going back to bed now."

"If you're sure…" Lidiya looked anything but. With another suspicious glare at Dima, she started to back out of the room. "I'll leave you to it, then. First sound of any trouble, though, and I'll be back. And this time I will take the hatchet to the door – and to anything else that gets in the way."

The door closed. Alone again with Dima, Katya sat on the bed. She felt as if everything that had held her upright had vanished all at once, leaving her limp and useless. Dima made his way back towards her, and even in the circumstances Katya noted that he managed to skirt all the missing boards on the floor. She never failed to be amazed by his ability to remember a room or a route after traversing it only once. He sat on the very edge of the bed, careful not to touch her. In another context, Katya might have interpreted his wariness as revulsion; as it was, she felt that he was handling her the same way that he would handle an unexploded bomb, should he happen to find one of those in bed with him.

"I'm so sorry," he said formally, "if I did anything that you didn't want, anything that I shouldn't have – "

"No, it's not that," Katya said. Dima closed his mouth, waiting. Katya remembered the impossible fact of his hands on her back, his mouth at the tender hinge of her neck and shoulder, and smiled, despite herself. "It's absolutely not that. Not at all. In fact, I am the one who should be apologising to you."

"Please don't," Dima said quickly. He sounded pained. For a moment he didn't speak, and Katya could see his mind working on what he wanted to say, composing and discarding phrase after phrase, so unlike his usual easy flow of words. "I'm not accustomed to this," he said at last. "I mean, I'm not accustomed to women like you. Or rather women whom I…I am not accustomed to feeling the way I feel about you. Nothing has been as important as this, before." His voice was almost desperate. "I don't want to cause you pain, or distress you, or… or do anything wrong."

Katya heard his words, but she couldn't quite take them in. "It was nothing to do with you," she said absently. "I was dreaming. Or maybe it wasn't exactly that…" She couldn't remember anything of what had been in her head before she'd woken, her mouth full of panic. Just thinking back on that sensation, everything inexplicably wrong, made her guts lurch. An image rose out of nowhere: Lychkovo, Yevgeny, hardly any blood but the feel of his skin, death unmistakable, and the way that she had found herself prodding him, squeezing him, as if she was testing a plum in the market for ripeness. She hadn't realised that *flesh* had come to mean *death* to her. "It has been a long time since there was someone else with me in this bed," she said at last. It was the closest she could come to an explanation. "I think I have just become accustomed..."

She stopped. Her use of the word recalled Dima, groping for the right way to say what he meant: *I am not accustomed to feeling the way I feel about you.*

"What did you mean, what you said before? That you're not accustomed..."

Dima flushed. "Well, I'm not new to all of *this* – " he moved his hands, encompassing himself, the bed, Katya – "but mostly it has been...*casual.*"

"No, I mean, what you said about – about the way you feel about me." Katya hardly dared ask. She wouldn't have thought it possible, but Dima flushed even redder.

"You must know." Katya said nothing. Dima's expression changed, slowly, from mulish embarrassment to surprise. "But surely – surely it's obvious? The rest of the orchestra have been teasing me about it for weeks." He dared, then, to reach out to her. His hand landed unerringly on her arm, just above the elbow. He did not hold on to her, just rested his palm flat against the thick fabric of the coat that was still wrapped around her. "I'm crazy about you, Katya."

"No," was all that Katya could think to say in reply. For a moment Dima's face registered hurt, and then he relaxed, seeming to understand that her *no* was not refusal; it was incomprehension.

"You really didn't know? Did you think that this was just...just opportunism?"

"I didn't think *anything,*" Katya said, and then realised that that wasn't quite the case. "Or no, I thought that perhaps you were grateful. For me looking after you."

"*Grateful!*" Dima sounded disgusted. "If I slept with everyone I was *grateful* to...well, it'd be a very different list indeed. No, don't you see –

don't you see at all that this is the end point of a long and carefully fought campaign for me?"

Katya laughed, half in amusement and half in disbelief. "Since when?"

"Since the first day I met you. When we were walking along Nevsky, and I said – I don't even remember what I said, but you replied, *are you making fun of me?*"

"I only carry it around so that kind ladies will feel sorry for me and offer to walk me home," Katya said quietly.

"What?"

"That's what you said. *I only carry it around so that kind ladies will feel sorry for me and offer to walk me home.* You were talking about your stick. And I said, *are you making fun of me?*"

"Yes," Dima said. His voice had dropped to match hers. "That was when I started thinking…and I had no idea what you thought. None. I can't tell you how frustrating that was for me! Normally it's easy, I can tell within a few words whether – well, you know, whether someone's interested or not. But you – you were always so kind, and I could tell that you *liked* me, but anything beyond that, I just…didn't know."

"Because I never even considered it," Katya said, in instant realisation. "I never dreamed it would be possible. I wasn't thinking *yes* or *no* because I couldn't even imagine the question."

Dima shuffled closer. His hand was still on her arm. "What on earth are you wearing, by the way?"

"This? It's an old coat of Yevgeny's. I've been using it as an extra blanket, and it was the first thing that came to hand when Lidiya came bursting in here."

"Ah, yes." Dima had evidently forgotten Lidiya's precipitous entrance. He wrinkled his brow. "She is a fearsome woman. I've rarely been so petrified. Do you think she'll be able to forgive me, or will she be waiting outside the door with that hatchet to ambush me in the morning?"

"I'll talk to her," Katya promised. Dima may have been able to joke about it, but she felt terribly embarrassed. It was so unlike her to cause a fuss, and poor Dima, who barely knew Lidiya…

"It's all right. In fact, it's nice to see that she's willing to protect you so valiantly." He smiled. "But it's probably all right if you take the coat off now."

"Oh! Of course." And yet Katya felt shy. She knew that Dima couldn't see her, but he had removed her clothes for her, before; there was something brazen, she thought, about taking something off of her own volition. Telling herself not to be so silly, she shrugged the coat off her shoulders, and it fell halfway down her back. Catching the sound of the movement, Dima lifted his hand and moved it so that it fell on her bare shoulder.

"*Oh,*" he said involuntarily, and then laughed at his own transparency. He touched her collarbone, her neck, her throat, ghosting his hand back and forth. Katya stayed perfectly still. She felt bewitched by his long, slow movements. She thought, oddly, of the extravagant way that he used his bow.

"If I kiss you, do you promise not to start screaming again?" Dima asked. His tone was an attempt at lightness, but so laden with want that even Katya could not fail to hear it. *What would Lidiya say?* Katya asked herself.

"I'd be more likely to scream if you don't."

When Katya woke, the bed was empty, and it took her a moment to put her finger on quite why that was wrong – the peculiar way the sheets were tangled around her, when she was normally a still and silent sleeper, and the sense that the bedding held the shape of someone absent. Her body felt slightly bruised, swollen with tenderness. She sat up, remembering piecemeal. It all seemed so unlikely that she couldn't bring herself to believe it. From the kitchen came voices: Lidiya's forceful, Dima's good-humoured, the querulous buzz of the children. Mild panic suffused her: what could they be talking about in her absence? She gathered together a collection of clothes, dressed, gave herself a cursory once-over to check that she didn't look egregiously ridiculous, and, bracing herself for interrogation, opened the door to the kitchen.

Dima was sat at the table in an attitude Katya recognised as mid-flow: arms raised, palms outstretched. Lidiya sat opposite, her fingers laced around her tea, watching him in what seemed to be detached amusement. Masha, astonishingly, was leaning against Dima's knee, gazing up at him in rapt amazement, while Serezha stood diffidently behind his chair. While Dima was still terribly pale, his face blazed with life.

"Good morning," Katya said, as blandly as she could manage. The look of pure pleasure on Dima's face at the sound of her voice was overwhelming, but his greeting matched hers for understatement.

"Good morning, Katya."

"I was starting to think you were never going to get up," Lidiya said archly. "It's nearly nine."

"I didn't sleep well," Katya replied, giving Lidiya a hard stare.

"I should think not," Lidiya shot back, undaunted.

"As you can see, no one's hit anyone with a hatchet so far this morning," Dima said cheerfully, "although *this woman* has just been telling me that she can't bear Shostakovich – she said she thought his music was – what was it?"

"Tuneless melodrama," Lidiya said, taking a casual sip of her tea. Dima slapped the table and turned to Katya in furious appeal.

"You see? So things may come to blows yet."

"I did say I liked the Leningrad Symphony," Lidiya said mildly, "though probably I'd hate that too, if it hadn't been written for us." She looked at Dima and smirked a little.

"Auntie Katya, I'm sorry about the spider," Masha said. Katya, confused, looked to Lidiya.

"The spider that scared you last night," Lidiya said pointedly.

"Oh! Yes! Well, it was only a spider," Katya said, flustered. "It was nothing really to be scared of. I was silly to scream like that, Masha."

"Auntie Lidiya was silly to try and kill the spider with the hatchet," Dima murmured, as if to himself. Lidiya looked like she was trying not to laugh.

Breakfast – such as it was – continued in a similar vein. Dima and Lidiya seemed to be thoroughly enjoying one another's company, but Katya was intensely relieved to see that their interactions were purely combative. At one point Ilya Nikolayevich wandered in, and, seeing Dima sat at the table, extended a hand.

"You must be the boy who's been so ill."

"That's me," Dima said. "I'm Dmitri." For a moment Ilya's hand hung there, unshaken, until Ilya gave a start, seeming to take in Dima properly, and grasped Dima's hand in his own.

"I hope you're feeling better?"

"Much," Dima said robustly. Katya could barely believe the energy of him – only four days after she had been certain he was going to die and there he was, sitting up, arguing with Lidiya and telling Masha stories.

Ilya Nikolayevich eased himself down into a seat; Lidiya stood up. "Katya, help me clear, will you?" she demanded, peremptory. At the sink, Lidiya stared at her, cool and appraising, and Katya mustered the strength to stare back. As Lidiya's eyes settled on a point slightly south of Katya's face, Katya fought the impulse to twitch her collar over her collarbone, covering what she now remembered – painfully clearly – must be a small red mark in the shape of Dima's mouth.

"Don't think I'm going to apologise," Lidiya said at last. Her voice was low, but her chin was thrust out in a way that Katya recognised: stubborn, defiant. "You were screaming like you were being tortured. No matter what's happening between the two of you, I wasn't going to ignore you making that sort of noise, and I'd do it again. I'm not sorry."

"I never dreamed you were," Katya said, courteous and wry. Lidiya snorted, narrowing her eyes, a precursor to one of her rare, barbed smiles.

"He's staying, isn't he?"

"He's staying."

❧

III: ADAGIO

OUR COUNTRY'S WIDE SPACES

CHAPTER SEVENTEEN

7 June 1942

The sun was a coin beaten flat, against a sky the colour of milk. Lidiya walked. The grey, churning Neva was behind her now, and there was fierce, grim enjoyment in spending the strength she couldn't afford on movement. Of all the things she had missed during the winter, perhaps her body was what she had missed the most, although she couldn't have named it at the time: this sense that her whole self was crowded into her head, lurking just behind her eyes, and the rest of her an inconvenient appendage, even a liability. If the city of the winter had been populated by ghosts and ghouls, the summer city was not much less unearthly: the field of cabbages behind St Isaac's Cathedral, the stone facades pitted by shells, the blind gaze of the boarded up windows. Something about the sunshine made the horror more acute but also more distant. Women had started to pin small bouquets of flowers to their lapels, and Lidiya had followed suit with a sprig of lilac, the sweetness of its scent dizzying. It was a tiny flag, signifying a temporary victory.

After the trolleybuses had started running again – perhaps it had been April, perhaps May; time meant less, these days – Elena's sister Sonya had come knocking, looking for her sister, her nephew and niece. Her grief, on hearing of Elena's death, was muted: an eventuality she had clearly prepared herself for, shoring herself up inside. The children hadn't known quite what to make of her, this older facsimile of their vanished mother, someone they had known *before*, but their entire world had buckled and warped since then, and the places that had been kept for things could no longer hold them. Sonya had asked Lidiya to bring the children to visit her, maybe even to stay overnight, and Lidiya had been slightly sickened by her own reluctance. Semyon had visited only once since January, and for three months now there had been no word of him at all; even the children had stopped asking. She wouldn't have admitted it even to herself, but Lidiya had started to think of the children as *hers*. Sonya was a frightening complication, and there had been so many reasons to put it off: Masha developed a cold, then Serezha; two days of particularly severe shelling in Petrograd had allowed Lidiya to claim that the trip was too big a risk. She recognised what she was doing, even if Sonya and the children didn't, and so that morning she had forced herself to take them. During the trip across the city, the clatter of the trolleybus had been so loud it had brought Lidiya's heart into her throat, threatening to choke her. Her palms still itched where the children had been gripping her hands. There was a marrow-deep conviction that she was never going to see them again, and she bit it back, swallowed it down, knowing it irrational. Now she was trying to outpace it.

When Lidiya was a child, holidays had been spent at her grandfather's dacha, with a constantly circulating cast of cousins who were worshipful and envious and libidinous by turns. Despite her city upbringing, there was a specific hum of happiness that Lidiya always associated with the smell of warm earth, the hiss of wind in the trees and the clarity of air that made breathing feel like a treat. It was a make-believe future she had had with Lev, the unspecified point at which they would move out of the city, when Lidiya would evolve into a broad-hipped, red-faced matron, herding a brood of children, and Lev would…that part had always remained uncertain, a fantasy that had been far more hers than his, something he had humoured her in. She had known, even then, that it was never going to happen, but the fact of sharing it made it real, albeit dreamspun and insubstantial. The way that the countryside was now pushing its way into the city was something that Lidiya welcomed:

the grass in the pavement's cracks, the serried ranks of potatoes in the public parks.

When she thought of the winter, now, what she remembered most was the absence of any sensation that came from outside herself, no sound that wasn't her own tired pulse roaring in her ears, the cityscape of white and grey and black. Colour and sound had been things that she had longed for, but now they were too easily overwhelming. When the sky was cloudless, Lidiya found her eyes leaking so much that she had to look away. A bright red coat on an elderly lady made her lungs seize up so that she could barely breathe. Noise was worse – a too-loud laugh would make her jump as if at a gunshot, and the elemental bellow of the trolleybuses caused her to press her hands together to hide their trembling. She hated this in herself, this animal, instinctual fear of something she had longed for throughout the winter, but there was only so far she would push herself. She would take a trolley with the children, to save their strength on the journey across town, but on her own she would choose to walk, even when it filled her limbs with a treacly weariness that made her feel like she was dissolving. It didn't matter: she would rest, subsiding on street corners until the thundering of her heartbeat stopped shaking her body with its urgency, until her skin felt more like itself and less like an ill-fitting dress she had shrugged on in a hurry.

The year's shift towards light always took Lidiya a little by surprise, even in normal years – the sun was so high in the sky that it could have been any time from seven in the morning to nine at night, but her watch said it was nearly midday, closing in on lunchtime, and she should get herself and her bag of food home. On the edge of the Field of Mars, an old woman with a burnished copper samovar sold a murky liquid that she claimed was tea. Seeing Lidiya sitting, she came over, tin mug in her hand, and Lidiya sipped obediently, trying not to grimace at the bitterness.

"It'll give you strength," the woman said. Her voice whistled through gaps in her teeth: it was something you saw more often now, people having sold their gold for food over the winter.

"What's in it?"

The woman pursed her lips, narrowing her eyes conspiratorially. "It's my secret recipe," she said. Lidiya's own lips twitched; she guessed it was all right to laugh at an old woman who was laughing at herself. And unexpectedly, Lidiya found that the warmth of the liquid seemed to have pooled in her joints; her knees felt like they might be able to bear her again. Experimentally she pushed herself up onto her feet and found herself standing, relatively steady and disproportionately pleased. The woman gave her elbow a companionable squeeze, and Lidiya pushed a kopeck into her hand.

Ilya was fishing in the Moika. It was a habit that he had taken to, since the weather had improved, although Lidiya suspected that it was more of an excuse to sit outside and pretend to be doing something than anything that was likely to be productive. As Lidiya approached she could just about make him out, his silhouette dark against the beaten metal of the water, still and silent, his line in front of him.

"Ilya Nikolayevich!"

He turned. Lidiya had come to recognise the warmth that lay behind the slight softening of lips that passed for a smile.

"Lida. Where have you come from?"

"I dropped Serezha and Masha off with their aunt. She'll bring them home this evening." Her palms itched. She breathed back the anxiety that coiled up her throat like smoke. "I thought I'd walk back."

"You must be crazy," Ilya said easily. Lidiya joined him, easing her way down the damp steps to the path beside the canal. Ilya had brought with him a tattered old rug to sit on, and he motioned to the space next to him, inviting Lidiya to join him; she contemplated sitting, but couldn't have counted on her ability to get up again. Instead she leaned against the railings, wriggling a little to find the most comfortable lie of the metal against her bones.

"Catch anything?"

Ilya shook his head. "I'm not convinced there's anything alive in there. It's an exercise in futility – " He broke off. On the other side of the bank a man passed, raising one hand in a casual wave. In his other he held a bouquet of silver fish, glinting like sequins. Ilya huffed out a laugh. "Or perhaps I'm not trying hard enough."

"At least it saves the rest of us the agony of having to be polite enough to eat whatever you bring home." Lidiya offered it as a joke, but on some level she meant it. She couldn't have brought herself to turn down anything edible on offer, but at the same time she had a strong aversion to anything dragged out of those dark, shifting waters. The thought of it made her shudder, the idea of what could be down there.

"Are you on your way home now?"

"Mm," Lidiya said, half-hearted and noncommittal. It was easier to say these things when no one was looking at her, and she was looking at no one, her eyes instead fixed on the water. "It's not that I begrudge them at all. It's good to see something so – so hopeful."

"Ah, our young lovers?" Ilya's tone was wry, indulgent. Lidiya smiled.

"Of course. It's transforming Katya."

"And Dima is certainly an engaging young man."

"It's just – " Lidiya stopped, closing her eyes. Behind her eyelids she saw Dima's hand reach out, his palm flat against the side of Katya's throat, Katya turning into the caress. It was a tiny movement, almost nothing – they probably thought they were being discreet – and yet there was so much wrought into it. Lidiya could just about remember how it felt, the plain fact of a man's warm hand on her skin and then the meaning behind it, a gesture as shorthand communication. With Lev, it had been his fingers on the back of her hand, the tips stroking the dips between her knuckles, and it had taken on different meanings over the years, anything from *pipe down, I'll tell you later* to *wait till I get you home*, but it had always been something she understood. It wasn't jealousy, what Lidiya felt when she caught sight of Katya and Dima in the moments they thought themselves unobserved – or not exactly. Lidiya's heart was a dropped anchor: Lev had been gone for four years, and if she had had it in her to waver, she would have done so before now. "It's just that sometimes, when I look at them, I feel like I may as well be a hundred years old."

When she opened her eyes Ilya was looking at her, sidelong, chiding. "Lidiya. You can't be more than thirty."

"Twenty-eight," she said too quickly, stung. Ilya smiled.

"I apologise."

Lidiya flapped a hand, waving him off. "Don't be foolish. I know the winter didn't do me any favours."

"I always liked Lev, you know," Ilya said. His eyes were back on the water.

"I didn't know you two knew each other."

"Not well, of course. Hardly at all. But we'd talk, sometimes, when we met on the stairs. He had a good sense of humour." Lidiya knew what was coming next, as sure as the next verse of a familiar song: "But it's been five years now."

"Four."

"Four, then. And you haven't heard anything in that time?"

"At first – but nothing for three years."

"You could meet someone else. Marry again."

She had known he was going to say it, but the words still made her jerk, drawing in her breath in a half gasp. It was a conversation she'd had so many times over the past few years; it wearied her. "He might still be alive."

"I suppose so." Ilya's doubt was clear in every word, but Lidiya couldn't bring herself to be annoyed – it wasn't as if she believed it herself any more.

"And even if not…" She had never worked out a way to explain this, the fact that she wasn't hanging on due to some tedious understanding of loyalty, but because she genuinely had no idea how to do anything else. "It's *Lev*," she said at last. "It's not something I'm choosing. And you, Ilya, you're not one to criticise; you never remarried yourself."

"Ah," Ilya said, sighing. "I was much older than you when my wife passed away. She had had the best part of my life; what did I have left to give to someone else?"

"It's no different," Lidiya said. She sounded mulish, even to herself, but it was true: Lev had had the best of her; all that was left was an uneasy mix of prettiness, bitterness and too-sharp humour. "Sometimes… sometimes it's not something that you choose." She pushed herself forward off the railings. "I should go."

"I haven't offended you, talking about this?"

"Of course not. I'm tired, that's all. You're not coming home for lunch?"

Ilya laughed. "Not while there's still a chance for me to bag a sturgeon. Anyway, I have some bread in my pocket. That should keep me going."

Whatever strength the foul-tasting tea had given Lidiya had long since gone; before she had even climbed the steps back to the road there was a hot thread of pain running from her neck down her back and into her hips. She was accustomed to it now, but that didn't mean she had to *like* feeling like an old woman, and she liked still less the idea of looking like one. She wouldn't stop again, she *wouldn't*. She was concentrating so sharply on willing herself on that she didn't notice that the young man with the unusual, fluid gait approaching her was Dima until he was nearly on top of her.

"Dima!"

"Hello, Lida." He smiled, stopping, and put out a hand to lightly touch her shoulder. Lidiya noticed that he looked slightly disarranged, distracted, no coat, no scarf, and despite the sunshine the wind had changed in the past hour, whipping in cold and unforgiving from the north. Even in June, a wind like this could cut through clothes, worm its way under the skin and settle itself in the tender places where bones met.

"For god's sake, you're in Leningrad, not Yalta. You'll freeze if you go out like that, even at this time of year."

"I suppose it *has* got colder. I've been out a couple of hours now, it was quite warm when I left."

"Where are you off to?"

He shrugged. "Nowhere in particular. Just walking. It still feels like a bit of a novelty. I thought I might try and find Ilya, but it looks like I've found you instead." He crooked his arm and held it out to her, clowning a little. "Allow me to walk you home?"

"How unusually gentlemanly of you." Lidiya folded her arm into Dima's, tucking herself close to his side. He formed a reasonably effective windbreak. "Oh, and you can take this if you want, while you're being chivalrous." She passed him the string bag she'd had looped over her arm as they started to walk.

"What have you got us this time?"

"What makes you think I've got *you* anything?"

"Lida, I know you well enough by now to be aware how gloriously smug it makes you to produce some bizarre foodstuff with a flourish, and bask in our applause."

She couldn't help laughing. "See for yourself, if you want."

As careful as if he were handling china, Dima slipped a hand into the bag, drawing out a small and lumpy potato with evident joy.

"Where did you get this?"

"Someone I used to work with at the radio – she's set up a vegetable plot in the Field of Mars. Lots of people have, but she's been tending it like you'd tend a baby. She lives near the children's aunt, and she swapped me a couple of these for a bit of buckwheat – "

"And where did you get the buckwheat from?"

"Sonya gave it to me, to thank me for bringing the children over to visit." Lidiya never would have thought of herself as a trader, but she was surprised at the sharp, bright nugget of enjoyment that she got from these chains of deals, brokering exchanges, leveraging what little she had – it felt, sometimes, like almost as much of a miracle as if she'd waved her hands and created a potato out of thin air. Dima's hand plunged into the bag again, bolder this time, and came out clutching a bunch of greenery.

"And this?"

"Grasses. Goose grass, sorrel, a few dandelions – there are some nettles in there too, you'll want to be careful." Dima withdrew his hand as if he'd been bitten, and Lidiya fought back a smirk before remembering she didn't need to. Dima was smiling too.

"More delicious grass soup?"

"Don't sound so ungrateful! Full of vitamin C. Strength-giving. You'll be glad of it, stop you from getting scurvy."

"I expect so." Tentative, he lowered his face into the handful of grass, sniffing deeply. "God, that's good. That smell. I didn't realise how much I'd missed things like that. In the winter, everything was so dead – " He grimaced at the word. "I don't mean – "

"I know what you mean. I was just thinking about that, actually, about how things – sounds, and smells, and colours – sometimes they even feel like too much now, after all that silence. All that white. Like – "

she huffed out a half laugh. "Like gorging yourself after you've been starving."

"Not that we'd know what *that* feels like." Dima nodded, thoughtful. "The silence – I think that was what got to me the most. You know, that's why I love weather like this – the wind, I mean. It's cold, but it draws sounds out of everything. Rain's good, too – I can nearly make out the shapes of things, when I can hear the way the rain's falling. But snow – it covers everything, it deadens everything. And without the shops open, the smells of the bakeries or the sounds of the trolleybuses – I know this city so well, I had to learn it when I moved here. But the winter took away all of that. I was terrified I'd get lost, and wouldn't be able to find my way home."

"Everything became so small," Lidiya said. It was odd, the enjoyment people seemed to get now from talking about the winter, going over it again and again in obsessive detail. She supposed it was a celebration of their own survival. "I didn't care about anything outside our building. Katya, and Ilya, and Elena and the children. The rest of the city could go hang for all I cared, as long as we made it through."

Dima nodded. "It was like that with me and Vasya, too. Most of the time, anyway. Sometimes – we went to the library, once. Did you ever?"

"Once or twice. I was looking up how to make candles, I think."

"Vasya said he wanted to look something up too – I can't even remember what, now – but I think he mostly just wanted to get warm. So did I. They always had the stoves going. When we got there – at first I couldn't bear the smell of it, all those people, sweat and unwashed clothes, smoke and soot – "

"I remember." Even the memory of it closed her throat.

" – but then something seemed to flip over, and suddenly I was glad of it. It was as if I'd forgotten that there were other people in the world, and I needed to be reminded. It made me feel safer, somehow, as if I couldn't die with other people looking on. Although of course people did all the time."

"There was one night – " Lidiya stopped. She wasn't sure if she wanted to tell this story, even now. "There was one night when I was sure I was going to die," she said at last. There was no need to give the details; the memory was more dreamlike than factual. It had been the end of January, perhaps the start of February, and although she had felt no hungrier and no weaker than she'd felt for weeks, a physical certainty had lodged itself under her skin, in the balls of her thumbs and the base of her spine: if she lay down she would die. The closeness of death was impossible to ignore – it filled the apartment, but the panic that she should have felt was dulled, muted, and that was even more frightening. She had wanted to wake someone, Katya or Ilya or even Masha or Serezha, with the childish idea that company could chase death away, but at the same time she was convinced that someone seeing her weakness would only fix it into being. The clock had struck midnight, then one. Weariness dragged at her, threatening to close her eyes. In the end, she had taken up some paper and an old, bitten stump of a pencil, and she had written her way through the night. She had described herself, in minute detail, described the state of the apartment, described her fellow residents. It was the letter to Lev that she had been holding back for nearly six months; since the start of the Blockade she hadn't been able to bring herself to write, although before it had been her habit to write once a week, even knowing that the letters would never be read. Her hands were so weak that it was hard to form the words, but she wrote as small as she could, covering the paper, and when she had run out of room she turned the paper sideways and wrote across the lines she had already written. Three times she had to take a knife from the kitchen to sharpen the pencil. By the time the sky at the window started to lighten to the rich purple of a bruise, the paper in front of her was black with words, illegible, and the stump of the pencil was curled so tightly into her chilled fist that it took minutes for her to loosen her fingers enough to relinquish it – but it was morning, and she had written herself back into existence. When the children awoke, she was able to haul herself into the kitchen, boil up some water, serve them their breakfast. That night had been a marker, a point from which things couldn't worsen, from which everything else could be dated. Out of the corner of her eye, she saw Dima nod.

"There was one day too, with me and Vasya. We'd gone to the Haymarket to try and get some food, and we met a man who offered to trade with us, back at his apartment. And when we got there, we thought – " He closed his mouth, shrugging. "What we thought at the time seems impossible now. And you hear so many other stories like it, you can't help wondering what we were thinking, why we were so sure. There can't have been that many. So much of what happened back then seems so unreal, you can never be sure how much you just… dreamed into existence."

In silence, they rounded the corner into their own street; Lidiya pushed open the door to the building, and they started to climb the stairs. That was another thing that was dreamlike, she thought: that day when she and Katya had returned from the river, carrying water, and the stairs to Katya's apartment had seemed as insurmountable as the dome of St Isaac's. It gave her a rush of satisfaction – walking around the city only served to highlight how much weaker she was since the start of the Blockade, but these little triumphs – perhaps she should concentrate on them more. Things were getting better.

But Dima was hanging back; by the time they reached the door he was three steps below her. "Are you not coming in?" she demanded.

His smile, this time, looked strained. "I might just take another turn around the block."

"Don't be silly. That wind's getting bitter, and it's nearly lunchtime." She frowned. "Is something wrong?"

"Katya – I wanted to give her a bit of space. I think she needed – " As Lidiya watched, Dima's hands flexed, clenched and flexed again – the last a visible effort. "I don't know what she needed." As if all the energy had been drained out of him, he subsided onto the top step. With reluctant sympathy, Lidiya prodded him gently with the toe of her shoe, then sat down beside him.

"Did she say something?"

"No, nothing like that. Just sometimes she…withdraws. I can't get close to her. I know it's hard for her, a lot of the time. She doesn't – she can't – "

"She can't be happy when it's delivered right to her, neatly wrapped and tied with a bow," Lidiya said sharply.

"Lida, that's not fair." Dima was speaking so quietly that she wasn't even sure she was meant to hear, and she had to strain to catch his words. "It's hard for her. There's so much she can barely bring herself to talk about. What happened with her girls, and also…also her husband. I know the facts of it, of course, but beyond that – and it's not just the war, it's older than just that." He took a breath, as if bracing himself. "Did you know Yevgeny?"

"Barely. Just to say hello to."

"And was he – "

"He was vile," Lidiya said, with a venom that shocked her. There were some things that time and death couldn't touch. Dima looked taken aback.

"Do you mean he was vile to her?"

"Not particularly, not that I'm aware of." He was clearly waiting for her to expand, and Lidiya gave a terse laugh. "Perhaps I'll tell you more about him one day. But he didn't beat her, if that's what you're getting at. And I never overheard screaming rows through the ceiling." She paused, considering. "It was as if there was nothing between them," she said finally. "They always seemed to get on all right, but if you saw them together in the street, you'd think that they were two strangers who'd met on the trolleybus and just happened to be going in the same direction. Nothing more than that."

Dima nodded, his lips pressed together. Lidiya had never seen him so tense; it made him seem unusually concentrated, almost combustible. Thrusting a hand into his pocket, he pulled out a pouch of tobacco, some ragged scraps of *Pravda*, and started to roll. Lidiya had seen him do this for Ilya, from time to time; she understood better now Dima's powerful need to occupy his hands.

"Was it – " Dima paused, clearly weighing his words. "You and your husband. Was it – was it – "

"Was I in love with him, do you mean?" Lidiya asked. People always assumed she didn't want to talk about Lev, dancing around the subject as if mentioning it had the power to worsen a wound that was already mortal. It was as much about other people's discomfort as her own, which was why Lidiya never bothered trying to explain. But she had noticed the transfixed expression on Katya's face when someone mentioned the girls, how welcome was some extra indication that they had once been real, and Lidiya wondered why Katya had never bothered to apply the principle of that pleasure to Lida, and to Lev. Sometimes all you wanted was some evidence you hadn't imagined it, invented it wholesale, a happiness that was no less intense for the extent to which it had been taken for granted. "Of course I was in love with him," Lidiya said. She had meant to sound brusque, but the words came out soft-edged, tame. "Do you think I'm the sort of person to shackle myself to someone else if my heart isn't in it? My god, it's so much easier to be on your own, I don't know why anyone would tie themselves to another person if they could help it."

Dima's mouth quirked a little. "Ah. Well, my circumstances are somewhat different, but I do see your point. How did you and Lev meet?"

Lidiya snorted. "We were in the same Pioneers group, if you can believe something that clichéd. He was…he was almost comically ugly. Short, thick-necked, eyebrows like caterpillars. But he had – perhaps it was confidence. He never seemed to doubt himself. It made him seem… more *there* than other people. More present."

Dima nodded, as if that made perfect sense. "Vasya was a bit like that."

"We hated each other at first, me and Lev. I thought he was boringly serious, and he thought I was frivolous and…and unnecessarily unpleasant. But then after a while I realised that his seriousness made him more interesting, and I think he realised that my unnecessary unpleasantness was…"

"Necessary unpleasantness?" Dima asked, deceptively innocent. Lidiya punched him in the arm, not gently, but couldn't hold back a grudging laugh. Dima winced, and raised his eyebrows: *see what I mean?*

"I prefer *forthrightness*."

"Of course you do." A little of the tension seemed to have gone out of him; his smile was easier. Lidiya leaned into him a little, her shoulder against his, confiding.

"And you and Katya?"

He was silent for so long that Lidiya had given up on getting an answer. "She doesn't believe in it," Dima said quietly, at last. "Even when – when she's not like she is today. She thinks that I'm deceived, that it's something to do with the war, the Blockade, that at some point I'm going to…to wake up, and laugh, and leave." He shook his head. "I know I talk a lot, but I never know how to say the right things, the real ones. I feel like I'm just trying to say all the words I can think of, hoping that she'll be able to pick the right ones out of the whole mess of them. Ever since I met her, it's as if I've become bigger. Inside. I want more, I want to *be* more, but for her, not for me. I can't get close enough to her, sometimes. It probably gets annoying."

"And Katya?"

"Most of the time – she's not very good at saying things, either, but I've got a better idea, now, what she's thinking, or what she's feeling. It helps. And then there are days like today." Dima reached out, gripped Lidiya's arm. She had noticed this habit of his, holding onto someone when there was something he wanted to make clear to them. "All I want is to make things better for her. Lighter. Most of the time I think I'm doing that. And then days like today, I feel like I'm crucifying her, just by existing, just by being here when her girls aren't. I can't work out which one weighs more, *most of the time* or *now*."

In the dim light of the stairwell, Lidiya felt suddenly crowded by ghosts. Katya's girls, Lev, Elena, even Vasya, whom she hadn't known. The air felt oppressive, muffling her voice; she spoke so softly that Dima had to ask her to repeat herself.

"Who here hasn't lost someone?"

Dima winced. "But it's different, with children, it's different – "

"*And you go on*," Lidiya said. She didn't speak loudly but Dima reared back all the same. Lidiya could feel the weight of her words, dropping like liquid lead. She closed her eyes. "You go on. She doesn't realise, she doesn't see her own strength. She's survived. I told her once – it would have been easy enough to die, if that was what she'd wanted. Enough people did, willingly and unwillingly. But she's still alive, and the least she owes the rest of them is to be grateful about it, and to hold onto whatever happiness she's offered with both hands." Her eyes were still closed: she conjured Lev, as she sometimes did – less often than before, unwilling to invite him into the shape of her new life, with its cold and its dark and its roughened edges. He had had a twist to his smile, a way of lifting one corner of his mouth that was often mistaken for sarcasm, but which Lidiya had come to read as delight, all the more delightful for the secret of it, a physical code that only she knew.

"You're right," Dima said. Lidiya opened her eyes. In his lap, Dima's fingers tapped, one by one, numbering the dead. "You're right," he said again, softer now. "I just don't know what I can do about it."

"You're doing enough," Lidiya said shortly. She stood, feeling the click and slide of her joints, and took Dima's hand in hers, hauling him upright. "You'd better come in. It's nearly time for lunch."

CHAPTER EIGHTEEN

I: 28 May 1942

And so this was the fall: a long, slow dive, heart-first, the rest of her body drawn behind it, the flaming tail of a comet. Katya had heard it called that before; Zhenya's breathless, whispered accounts had made much use of such metaphors, love or attraction or infatuation as a physical malady, giddiness and vertigo and a constant, internal tumble. Still, Katya hadn't expected it to be so literal: sitting on her hard chair in the chilly Philharmonia, her eyes carefully trained on her music but ineluctably aware of Dima's presence in the seat beside her, catching the edge of his movements out of the corners of her eyes, she was simultaneously aware of an inner swooning, an unstoppable plunge. She could not look at him, but when Dima reached down for the cloth he used to wipe his strings, Katya became transfixed by his hands: the length of his fingers, and the faint smell of rosin that was as much a part of him as his fingerprints; the scent of it had risen when he had run his fingertips along the planes of her face and the curve of her lips. Could that really have happened? And yet her body remembered, even as the rest of her doubted, drawing itself into a hot, cramping tension that mingled discomfort with pleasure. She wanted to put Dima's hands into her mouth, make them part of her. What was it, this desire to consume the things that tugged at her core? When the girls had been babies, pale as cream and soft and smooth as if they had been carved, whole, from marble, Katya had felt the same primal urge to devour their tiny limbs, to nibble on their cheeks and bellies. There had been a moment, the night before, or perhaps that morning, when Dima had cupped her face in his hands and Katya, pure instinct by this point, had shifted, opened her mouth and caught the flesh at the base of his thumb between her teeth, not biting, just holding him there. He had laughed, soft and low in his throat; she hadn't wanted to let go.

"When you're *quite* ready, Katya," Genya said. His voice was clipped. Katya looked up; the rest of her section were poised, instruments raised, eyes on their scores. Dima dipped his head a little, clearing his throat. From the violas, Katya caught sight of Marina, her eyebrows raised and her lips drawn down into a comical grin. Katya lifted her instrument, mouthing an apology to Genya, willing herself not to blush.

"We probably shouldn't tell the others in the orchestra about this," Katya had said that morning, as they were leaving the apartment. Dima looked taken aback.

"Really? Why not? I mean, I don't want to make an announcement or anything…" A grin crept across his face, irresistible. "Well, actually that's just what I want to do, but I doubt Karl Ilych would approve – "

"Stop it." Katya swatted him on the arm. Even this little physical intimacy was a small spark of pleasure. "I just – I want to keep it separate." She couldn't imagine what they would think if they knew. The very thought of it made her cringe, certain she was making herself ridiculous – but that wasn't the sort of reason that Dima would understand. Instead, she said: "Some of the other musicians – they knew Yevgeny. It doesn't feel right, to…"

At the mention of Yevgeny, Dima's face became serious. "All right. I won't say anything. But Katya – " He looked anxious. "I'm *terrible* at keeping secrets. It's not that I'll tell anyone, but Vasya used to say that he knew exactly what I was thinking just by looking at me. I don't – " Even as she watched, that grin started to sneak its way back onto his face again, and he pointed at himself, half laughing. "You see? If I'm happy, I can't not *look* happy." He pulled a mournful face. "It's one of the tragedies of my affliction."

He had managed, though; for all of Dima's much-vaunted emotional incontinence, it had been Katya who had blushed, whose words had stumbled over one another, who had been unable to concentrate on what anyone else was saying to her because her mind was crowded with the events of the past twenty-four hours. Her playing had been shaky and uncertain; twice she had failed to come in on time, and once, even worse, too anxious to prove she was paying attention, she had anticipated, breaking the silence with a squeal of strings and then a muttered cascade of apologies. As they were leaving, Genya shook his head at her: "I know you're tired, Katya, but we're going to start rehearsing the Shostakovich in earnest any day now – you need to be at your best." Katya nodded, bending her face into an expression that she hoped transmitted sincerity and commitment, and beside her, Dima clapped Genya on the shoulder: "Don't you worry," he said blandly, "I'll whip her back into shape."

He was still laughing when they turned onto Nevsky Prospekt, minutes later, and much as Katya wanted to be annoyed, her face kept falling into a smile. She wanted to tuck her arm into Dima's – she felt she could never have enough of the touch of him – but she couldn't be sure they were unobserved. His pace was still slower than usual, following his illness, and Katya matched her footsteps to his instead.

"Remember the first time we walked this way together?" Dima asked, as they approached the hunch of the Anichkov Bridge. "It was about here that I decided to set you in my sights."

The mixture of sentimentality and bravado in his voice, with its tentative undercurrent, made Katya ache.

"Of course I remember." He was always so straightforward that it made it easier for her to be, too. "What was it about me that made you…" She cast about for the words she wanted, but was still too embarrassed to use the ones that were the most accurate. "You know. That made you…like me? That first day we met."

"*Are you making fun of me?*" Dima mocked. She elbowed him, hard, in the ribs, and he yelped.

"I know what I said. But anyone could have said something like that. So what was it that made you interested?"

Dima said nothing. His free hand was curled into a loose fist, his fingers tapping against his palm. Katya sighed a little. She knew by now that Dima had a habit of getting lost in the music in his head, which meant she was probably never going to get a straight answer.

"It was your voice," Dima said. Katya glanced over at him sharply; his face was creased with concentration, the effort of summoning up the moment. "You have such a beautiful voice. Has anyone ever told you that?"

Katya gave a half laugh, looking away; compliments still made her squirm. But Dima took her by the wrist, halting her. He turned to face her, laying the flat of his hand against her throat. "Say something."

"What should I say?" She felt her words vibrate against his hand. Dima laughed, quiet and charmed; on the other side of the bridge, a young woman shot them a curious look.

"There you go. That's it. Not deep enough to be a cello. More like a viola. Glinka's viola sonata in D minor." Starting to walk again, Dima dropped his hand; Katya felt the shadow-shape of it like a brand. "But it's not just that. Not just the sound of it, I mean. There's so much of *you* in your voice – when you let it in, that is. When you said that, when you asked if I was making fun of you, it was like…" He paused, thinking. "You know sometimes when a piece of music is so beautiful that you almost can't stand it? As if – as if you're being squeezed out of yourself. As if your…your soul is bigger than your body, somehow."

"Mm." Katya knew.

"Like in Mozart's Requiem. The Tuba Mirum. You have the trombone echoing the bass, that wonderful floating melody – " he sang it, completely unselfconscious. "And then the same phrase, rising, three times…" Dima shivered in remembered bliss. "It's as if he's pushing right to the limits of what the listener can bear. My god, the first time I heard that – it was some dreadful old recording of Arseny Grigorevich's, you could barely make out the melody under the hiss of the gramophone, but it practically floored me."

"Bach's Concerto for Two Violins in D minor is like that for me," Katya said, shy. She was accustomed to talking about music, but not the effect it had on her. "Right at the start of the Largo, that falling melody – and then when it's echoed by the second violin, an octave higher…" She hummed the melody, rather more self-consciously.

"Or even in Shostakovich Seven," Dima said eagerly. "At the start of the third movement, after the whole orchestra has played those first chords together, and then the strings come in on their own." He drew in a breath and sighed happily. "It's so…brave, somehow. Brave and bright."

Katya could barely remember it. Neither of them had heard it since its broadcast in March, but Dima's memory had a retentiveness – from necessity – that Katya's lacked.

"Or the Tchaikovsky serenade for strings, that descending opening line…"

"*Decadent*," Dima intoned sepulchrally. Katya laughed. She had always been a little ashamed of her secret fondness for Tchaikovsky's more sentimental excesses, but she didn't mind being teased by Dima.

They fell silent again. "Anyway…" Katya prodded at last. She knew by now how easily distractible Dima was.

"Anyway what? Oh, yes. You're still waiting for your compliment, aren't you?" He touched her cheek. "*Anyway*. When you said that, when you asked if I was making fun of you the first day we met – I got that exact same feeling. I'd never had it from anything but music before. It was…startling. And after that, I couldn't get you out of my head."

"I see," said Katya, acutely pleased. It was such an idiosyncratically Dima-like explanation, its careful accuracy, and that made it better than anything else he could have said. She carried it with her for the rest of the day, whenever she spoke, a burr of satisfaction.

In bed that night, darkness as thick as a curtain around them: "You never said what it was about *me* that you liked." Dima's voice was muffled, his face pressed into the curve of Katya's shoulder. She smiled.

"You? You don't need compliments! You're one of the most confident people I've ever met."

"About some things," Dima said. There was something that Katya couldn't quite identify in his tone. "Thanks for not saying 'arrogant'."

"It was a close-run thing."

He was quiet for so long that Katya started to think he had fallen asleep. Finally, he said, lightly: "So, was it just a case of right place, right time for me, then?"

"What do you mean?"

"I mean, could I have been anybody?"

His words were ambiguous but his meaning was clear enough. Katya half sat up in her surprise. "What? You don't – of course not. Of *course* not." There were a thousand things she could have said, about his humour or his easy charm or the eerie beauty of his playing or the precise angle of his jaw. "It was the light of you," she said at last. The words felt so true on her tongue that she hoped he would forgive her for using such a visual metaphor. Bending closer to Dima's face, Katya spoke softly. "You were so bright that at first I could hardly bear to look at you. And now…and now, I can hardly bear to look away."

II: 7 June 1942

When she concentrated on the small things, Katya could catch the very edge of belief, allow herself to trust it. The trick was one of focus: when Katya took Dima's hands in her own there was something inside her, caged behind her ribs, not her heart but near her heart, which swelled and loosened, and if she was careful, if she kept her mind out of it and limited her world to herself and to Dima, the raft of their bed adrift and unmoored, she could hold onto this feeling that wasn't happiness but something rarer, a sense of overwhelming absorption. Holding onto that feeling the rest of the time was more of a challenge.

You are so beautiful, she said to him, eleven mornings in, long enough that Katya had started to understand that he would be there when she woke up, even before she opened her eyes. She had thought he was still asleep when she spoke the words, under her breath, mouthing them with her lips against the soft hairs at the nape of his neck, but he laughed, sleepy, and turned towards her, bundling her into his arms. Katya's face found, without seeking it, the smooth hollow between Dima's throat and his shoulder, the skin fine and stretched tight over the bone. His body had a spare, mechanical elegance: she had thought, once, weeks ago, watching Dima move, that he handled his body with a casual arrogance that spoke of unquestioning possession, and that ease now extended to her body, something to be arranged, manhandled, used for pleasure. She was shocked at how much she liked it.

"*You're* beautiful," he said, drowsily insistent. Katya stiffened, involuntarily. There it was, that jolt, that flipped switch, shifting everything imperceptibly sideways, just enough for it to feel wrong. She rolled away from him, towards the edge of the bed, her feet on the floor before she realised that she'd decided to move.

"Don't be ridiculous. You don't even know what that word means."

Behind her, Dima coiled his arm around her waist, a prelude to pulling her back into bed. "What, because I can't see?"

"Of course."

"Now *you're* being ridiculous. You've never called a piece of music beautiful? Or – a perfume, or the smell of a really well-cooked meal?"

"That's…not the same thing at all." Katya stood, taking a perverse pleasure in seeing the teasing look drop from Dima's face, replaced by consternation. "It's past seven, anyway. I should get up, help Lidiya with the children's breakfast." This was a duty that Lidiya was quite happy to manage alone, as Dima was well aware.

"But it's Sunday – no rehearsal today. Couldn't we…"

"The children still need to be fed, whether we're rehearsing or not," Katya said tartly. "I'll let you know when I'm out of the bathroom."

By the time they were sitting down to breakfast, the first sting had passed. Katya wanted to reach and touch Dima's cheek, push her fingers through his hair, a simple, physical rapprochement that would go deeper than words of apology. But for Katya, once withdrawn, it was always a struggle to find her way back. Lidiya, distracted by readying the children to visit their aunt, didn't seem to notice anything amiss in the crushing atmosphere that had descended over the table. All the things that Katya wanted to say were arrested somewhere just behind her teeth: *forgive me, I don't know how to do this right; some days I can't separate out the happiness from the guilt*. Instead, she poured Dima's tea, put his plate in front of him with a deliberate click, emitted an ill-tempered sigh when his arm knocked against her own cup, causing a bare quarter-inch of liquid to slosh into the saucer. Lidiya and the children left in an explosion of barked commands and reminders, Lidiya's palpable anxiety trailing through the kitchen like fog; Ilya slipped out quietly just behind them, pail in one hand and fishing line in the other. The silence they left behind was oppressive. The ticks of the clock seemed to stretch and slow. Dima got to his feet.

"I think I'll go out for a while. Have a walk."

"Suit yourself." Katya could have cut her own tongue out at the clipped, peevish tone of her voice, but Dima only gave an oddly formal nod. She didn't look up from the table as he left, and only noticed after he'd gone that he'd forgotten his coat.

By the time Katya heard the front door slam again, she had been sat by the bedroom window for close to four hours. She did not move. Sometimes misery was paralysing, and sometimes it was impossible to resist the temptation to luxuriate in it. Stiff, still, she waited for the sound of the bedroom door, but it didn't come; instead, she heard the low murmur of voices in the kitchen: Dima, Lidiya. The bash and clang of pots; Lidiya was an expansive cook, scattering equipment far and wide, leaving the clear-up to Katya. Well, not this time. Still she didn't move. The clatter stopped, and then came the drag of chairs being pulled out around the small kitchen table. Silence again. There was a lead weight in Katya's stomach that blocked out hunger; they were welcome to whatever they were eating. But shortly afterwards the bedroom door opened. Katya didn't turn: it wasn't Dima's light, quick footsteps, but Lidiya's firmer, heavier tread.

"I brought you some lunch. Nettle soup, and a bit of bread."

"You can leave it on the table." With some effort she drew out the word: "Thanks." It wasn't Lida that she was angry with, after all. She heard Lidiya put down the bowl and waited for her to leave, but Lidiya didn't move: Katya could feel Lidiya standing behind her, by the table, expectant.

"I don't want to talk, Lida," Katya said, warning. Lidiya ignored her, as Katya had known she would. She approached, settling her narrow backside onto the wooden arm of Katya's chair, her own arm slung around Katya's shoulder in every pretence of easy conviviality, which Katya knew it was not.

"If you push that boy away out of guilt or shame or a sense that you don't deserve good things," Lidiya said, her tone conversational, "I will beat you within an inch of your life. I will beat you within an inch of your life, and then I will carefully, gently, lovingly nurse you back to health, just so that I can beat you within an inch of your life again."

If Katya had had a smile within her to be raised, that would have raised it. She didn't. "It isn't that."

"Oh, yes it is, Katya. What is it, if not that?" Lidiya leaned down towards her, and Katya tried to suppress her instinctive flinch, uncertain whether Lidiya was going to slap her or whisper in her ear – knowing Lidiya, either seemed equally likely. Instead, Lidiya pressed her lips – cool, smooth – to Katya's temple. Katya held her breath, while Lidiya rocked back, stood and left the room.

Evening insinuated itself with a lengthening of shadows. Katya's stomach growled, furious – she had left the soup too long; unpalatable enough when warm, it was completely inedible cold, and the bread had been little more than a mouthful. Katya had moved to the bed, where she lay, sprawled, her head to one side. From the sheets she could catch a faint suggestion of Dima's smell. She had begun to seem ridiculous to herself, but felt too feeble to struggle free of the snarl in which she had found herself. It had always been like this; a row with Zhenya would have her crawling into herself, staying there and licking her wounds for days. From across the hallway, she could hear Dima practising in Elena's old apartment, a stultifying series of scales and arpeggios, unleavened by even an occasional detour into melody. Katya still marvelled at how assiduous he was in such a tedious task; it filled her with an unwanted tenderness.

Sound erupted in the building, slamming doors, rustling clothing and voices: the children were back. Across the hallway, the scales cut off abruptly, and moments later Katya could hear the hum of Dima's voice in the living room, interspersed with the shriller patter of Masha and Serezha. The door to the bedroom opened again, slow and tentative, and Masha regarded Katya sideways, owlish and eager.

"Auntie Katya, Auntie Sonya gave us puppets! We're going to do a play. You have to come and watch."

There were people whom Katya could say no to; Masha wasn't one of them. She let herself be led into the living room; its boarded up windows gave it an all-day gloom, which meant that it was rarely used, abandoned in favour of the kitchen, which looked onto the courtyard. In one of the stiff old chairs that Yevgeny had favoured, Dima sat, Serezha squeezed in beside him, at ease in the semi-darkness. Officious, Masha installed Katya in the next chair, as Lidiya poked her head around the door, giving Katya a long look.

"Finish getting ready, Masha. Uncle Ilya and I'll be in in a few minutes."

Clearly the play was Masha's brain-child rather than Serezha's; she went to tend to the somewhat frightening pair of marionettes at the front of the room, a pile of wooden limbs at impossible angles. Catching Katya's eye, Lidiya mouthed the word *terrifying*, and withdrew into the kitchen. To Katya's right, Serezha was much more interested in Dima than in the play; she seemed to have come in on a conversation that had been going on for some time.

"...so if you can't see any of this, what *can* your eyes see?"

Dima looked nonplussed. "Well, nothing, Serezha! That's what blindness is."

"But it *can't* be nothing! When I close my eyes – " Serezha did so, helpfully demonstrative – "I can see *black*, and sometimes bits of other colours, too. Can you see that?"

"Ah," Dima sounded regretful. "I don't know. I don't really understand about colours."

To Serezha, this was clearly preposterous. "*How* can you not know? You *must* understand!"

"Well, think about it for a moment. If you closed your eyes and I handed something to you, and you didn't know what it was, you'd be able to touch it and feel whether it was big or small, what it was made of, whether it was hot or cold, all those things, wouldn't you? But you wouldn't be able to tell what colour it is. That's what it's like for me – except I've *never* seen colours. I don't even know what they mean." Serezha had his eyes screwed shut, clearly trying to imagine. Dima ruffled his hair. "It's probably the one thing I'd like to see the most."

"I see colours when I hear music," Katya said. She hadn't meant to say anything. Dima turned to her, his face shadowed, inscrutable.

"I've heard other people say that."

"I suppose it's something I've always taken for granted. I can't even imagine how I'd play something if I didn't have a – a kind of picture of it in my head."

Dima nodded. "I feel music when I hear it, or when I play it. Certain notes are in certain parts of the body. There are…sensations; I don't think I could ever explain them." Nonetheless, he reached across the space between the chairs, his hand hovering over Katya's sternum. "C is here," he said, touching her gently with an index finger. "It vibrates just so. It's how I always know where to find it."

From behind a makeshift curtain, Masha called for Serezha, directorial. Sliding off Dima's knee, he ran to join her. In the half-light, Katya held herself still, overwhelmingly conscious of the press of Dima's finger against her breastbone. Her breathing felt jumbled and uncertain.

"Are we friends again, then?" Dima asked. His voice was so low as to be unreadable. He moved his hand to her shoulder, sliding it down her arm as far as her wrist, until he was encircling it like a bracelet.

"Yes," Katya said. This was how it happened; things shifted again, suddenly all right. She let out a lungful of air in profound relief. "Dima, I'm sorry – "

"Hush," he said. Katya still couldn't see his face, but she could tell by his voice that he was smiling. He enveloped her hand in his own. "The play's about to start."

III: 11 June 1942

"I bet that's the face he has in the bedroom," Marina murmured to Katya. Katya ducked her head, smiling. The problem was that Marina was right: the expression Dima wore when tackling a particularly challenging piece of music – as he was doing now, demonstrating a Bach partita for Daniil – was basically identical to the expression of fierce concentration mingled with delight that he wore in bed.

Katya couldn't say exactly when things had become common knowledge in the orchestra, although of course Marina had been one of the first to catch on: it had been clear from the start that she was fond of Dima, and she had also claimed Katya as a friend, though Katya had never precisely considered her as such, merely part of Natasha's wider circle from the Conservatoire. There had been no announcement, no dramatic unveiling, just the fact that a few days before, during a break in rehearsal, Dima had clearly forgotten the need for secrecy and leaned into Katya's shoulder, complaining of a headache – and after a quick, breathless glance around to see that no one was looking either mocking or scandalised, Katya had put her arm around him and pushed her splayed fingers into his hair.

Break, again: Marina and Katya sat, wrung out and shaky, watching Dima and Daniil, powered by high spirits and competitiveness respectively, play snatches of tunes at one another.

"I'm glad you finally gave in to Dima, by the way," Marina said. "It was tragic, the way he was moping around before, like a kicked puppy." This description was so inappropriate for Dima that Katya couldn't keep from smiling, and once the smile had risen to her lips she found she couldn't push it down or bite it back; it bobbed up again as irrepressibly as bubbles in champagne.

"He's – " Katya stopped, uncertain of what she wanted to say, only that she wanted to talk about it, the cessation of secrecy feeling like a sudden privilege. She felt that Dima was an impossibility, a near miracle, and yet there was no way she could explain that to Marina without sounding half mad. "I'm...very fond of him."

"Of course you are." Marina grinned, indulgent. "He's adorable. In fact, I don't mind telling you now that if he hadn't been crazy about you from the very first moment, I might've had a crack at him myself."

"Really?" The idea that she, Katya, might have something worthy of envy was very new and rather pleasing.

"Really. Or, perhaps. Back then I didn't really have the energy. Now, though..."

"Marina, you've been in love, haven't you?" Katya rushed the words out before she had the chance to think about and regret them. She had to ask, and she couldn't bear the ridicule, real or implied, that was bound to come from Lidiya at such a question.

"Darling, back in the day I used to fall in love every week," Marina drawled. "These days, I try to keep it down to once a month. The sacrifices of wartime, you know."

"Is it always so…so uncomfortable?"

The bantering light faded from Marina's face. She touched Katya's arm. "What do you mean?"

"I mean – it's almost like anxiety, when I think of him. My stomach churns. I'm doing the most stupid things. I don't understand my behaviour, half of the time." She didn't mention the way that the world had sprung into technicolour, much as it had in the first days after having the girls: the way that the stars seemed bigger, and the scent of the leaves and the grass had changed.

Marina's face softened. "But Katya, you were married. Surely you know – "

Katya shook her head, vehement. "No. Yevgeny – he was a good husband, a good father. But it wasn't like this. It was *nothing* like this."

~

In bed, in the dark, Katya found it easier to loosen her tongue. No wonder Dima was such a talker – it was simple when you didn't have to look at people while telling them something, or have them look at you.

"When you call me beautiful, it makes me anxious."

Her eyes were closed, but she felt the bed shift as Dima rolled to face her, propping himself up on one elbow. "What? What do you mean?"

Katya said it again, cracking open one eye to look at Dima, who was frowning in bafflement.

"I'd got the impression you didn't like it very much. But anxious? Why anxious?"

"Because it feels like you're making fun of me. Oh, I know you're not," she spoke over his indignant protest, "but I'm not beautiful, you see, Dima, and when – well, the first time someone calls me that, why does it have to be someone who can't see me? Do you – can you – understand why I feel the way I do?"

Dima didn't answer, but the expression on his face showed that his mind was working furiously. "Light the lamp," he said at last.

"What? Why?"

"You heard me."

Huffing a little in frustration, Katya heaved herself up, reached for the lamp on the bedside table, struck a match. The room was lit up in a shaky, jaundiced light.

"Now I want you to look at yourself," Dima said. Katya laughed.

"What?"

"There's a mirror in the room, isn't there? Over by the door. I've felt it. I want you to bring it over here and look at yourself, and tell me what you can see."

"Dima…" Katya's reluctance hung heavy on her shoulders. She cast about for an excuse. "It won't mean anything to you. You keep saying…"

"Perhaps not. I still want to hear it. Indulge me." He smiled. "You can start with me, if you want."

"What do you mean?"

"Tell me what I look like." He nudged her. "Go on, bring the mirror over to the bed."

"It's cold! You can go and get it, if you're so certain about where it is."

"All right." Dima disentangled himself from the blankets and padded over to the door. He paused for a moment, as he sometimes did, consulting his mental library: he had told her once that he disliked having to grope for things, resenting those gestures that most marked him out as blind. Reaching out, he put his hand on the mirror, and smiled in triumph.

"Well done," Katya said, fondly, grudgingly. "It's hanging on a nail in the wall. Careful not to cut yourself."

"I'm blind, not clumsy," Dima said. Katya had heard that before.

"Either way. It would be most inconvenient if you were to get tetanus."

Back in the bed, Dima handed the mirror to Katya, who wondered if she could get away with dropping it. "Now, hold it so that you can see both of us in it."

Katya propped it up against her knees, angling it so that Dima's face took up most of it. Dima stretched out his hand, checking that the mirror really was facing the right way.

"Promise me you can see yourself in it," he told Katya sternly.

"I promise." It was mostly true: at least a third of her face was visible.

"You wouldn't fool a blind man, would you?"

"Of course not!"

"Because that would be *cruel.*" Dima's tone was doleful. Feeling slightly guilty, Katya adjusted the mirror minutely: half of her face, then. She fought a powerful urge to avert her eyes. Most of the time she was almost able to trick herself into believing she was barely corporeal – just a pair of hands to hold her violin, and, now, whichever part of her body Dima was touching at any one time. Evidence to the contrary was unwelcome.

"So. Me first."

"You…" Katya was so used to looking at Dima's face directly that it felt strange to look at in the mirror, one step removed. "You're beautiful," she said sincerely.

Dima snorted. "Well, that's helpful. Be objective, Katya!"

"I am!"

"You're not. Not everyone thinks I'm *beautiful.*" He pronounced the word with mild distaste.

"Who doesn't?"

"Lida, for one. She said I was – what was it? *Strange* looking, I think. Too nervy and sensitive, like an overbred horse." He laughed. "She has a gift for description, Lida. Even I was able to make some sense of that."

"Lida – she's so nasty, sometimes!" Katya was outraged, but Dima was still grinning.

"No, no – it was funny. It was when she wanted me to help her with something. She told me to stop sitting around, imagining I was being decorative."

"Don't you – didn't you mind her saying that?"

"Of course not! Partly because it doesn't make any sense to me. Mostly because – well, what does it matter what Lida thinks about how I look? I'm not trying to get into bed with *her.*" He gave Katya's upper arm a gentle pinch. "Happily, some women seem to appreciate the overbred horse type. Anyway, tell me about my horsey face."

"You don't – you're nothing like – "

Dima was laughing again. "All right, all right. My *beautiful* face." The quotation marks were clear in his voice. "What colour are my eyes?"

"Do you really not know?"

"No one ever mentioned it. I never thought to ask."

"Well – they're brown. A pale brown. Like weak tea." It didn't sound like a very flattering description, but Dima smiled.

"Weak tea, got it. Hair?"

"Dark. Almost black."

"Interesting. I thought women were supposed to go for blond men."

"Maybe some. I never have. They look too – unformed, somehow. Not properly developed, like babies born too soon. Especially when their eyebrows and eyelashes are blond, too." Katya remembered that Vasya had been fair. "Did Vasya tell you that about blond men?"

"I expect so. He always had too high an opinion of his looks. I take it I don't have blond eyebrows and eyelashes, then?"

Katya laughed. "No, of course not! Though how would you know – no. People's eyebrows and eyelashes are usually darker than the hair on their heads." She peered more closely into the mirror. Its distancing effect allowed her to be more objective. "You have a big mouth."

Dima snorted. "So they keep telling me!"

"Physically, I mean! It's – it's nice. Your nose is quite big too. I suppose that's where Lida got that overbred horse thing from." She clicked her tongue at Lidiya's foolishness. "It works well with your face, though. And I bet it would work even better if you weren't so thin."

"Hm," said Dima, musing. He shook his head. "No, still means nothing to me. Now you."

"If it means nothing to you, why bother?"

"Indulge me," Dima said again. "Come on."

Katya leaned in. She stared at herself, automatically enumerating the things that she hated about her appearance: the insipid colour of her eyes, the sallow cast to her skin, the way that none of her features seemed to relate to each other. "It's just a face," she said at last, half to herself.

Dima's hand was resting on her lower back. He stroked her, lightly, with the calloused pads of his fingers.

"What colour are your eyes?"

"Blue."

"Oh! Like the sky?"

"Not really. They're too pale. Kind of…" Katya remembered, suddenly, the misty blue of the sky in midwinter, when the air felt too thin to breathe. "Well. Perhaps a bit like the sky."

"And your hair?"

"Mousy."

"What does that mean?"

"It means no colour at all." She turned to him, flushing. "Dima, do I have to do this? It's horrible."

Dima was silent for a moment. "Do you know what I think is beautiful about you? *Here*." He splayed his fingers against the small of her back, where he had been stroking moments before. "It's the shape of it, the way your spine makes a dent all the way down your back – " he said, drawing it with a finger, " – and then spreads out at the bottom into this little dip. And the skin here, it's so fine. Almost like touching nothing at all." He stroked it again, momentarily lost for words. "Now you go. Tell me something you like."

"I have good teeth," Katya said quickly, before she could trip herself up. Looking into the mirror she bared them experimentally, drawing back her lips. "They're white and straight. Of course my lips are much too thin…"

"Too thin for what?" Dima asked innocently. "Anyhow, that's cheating. You're not allowed to say anything bad. My turn." He ran the back of a finger down Katya's jawline. "I love the shape of your face. Your chin, your cheekbones – it's so neat. Balanced. It fits very well in my hands."

Katya thought of her chin. She had always considered it too weak. "But – "

"No! Not allowed!" He dropped a kiss on her shoulder. "Your turn."

"How many do I have to do?"

"Let's say three. It sounds pathetically small, but consider this me letting you off lightly."

Katya looked in the mirror again. "I like my eyebrows," she said, surprised. "Lida said once that she was envious of my eyebrows. She's so fair she has to draw hers on. I thought she was just being kind – eyebrows, you know, it's what you compliment when you can't think of anything else. But she was right. They have a nice shape to them, and they're good and dark."

"Well done," Dima said approvingly. "You have wonderful hands. I love the way that when I hold them I can feel all the muscles in them, at the base of your thumb, along your wrists – all those things that make you play so well."

"You're better," Katya said. Dima gave a quiet moan of mock despair.

"*Katya*. I'm good, I know I am. But sometimes when I hear you play, it makes me think that I'm all flourish and bombast. You have such restraint, such subtlety. Arseny Grigorevich used to say that I couldn't tell the difference between emotion and sentiment. It's when you play that I really understand what he meant. It's like the way you speak – quietly, no histrionics, but people listen. People always listen. And with me, they tune out at least half of what I say." He laughed. "Not that I blame them. At least two-thirds of what comes out of my mouth is out-and-out nonsense. Your turn. Number three."

Did she dare? She decided she might. "I like my breasts," she said. Colour mounted in her face, but she continued. "The size and the shape of them. They're the only thing I've ever been vain about. When I had Tanya, I was worried that they'd change, and they did, a little, but they're still good." She laughed suddenly, remembering. "Lida said so too, once. When we went to the baths together this spring. She sounded almost outraged."

Dima took a deep breath. She felt him exhale against her shoulder as his hands stole up from her waist. He buried his face in the crook of her neck. "If you were trying to distract me, you've succeeded," he said, his voice muffled and slightly unsteady. "You're terribly calculating, you know."

"It wasn't deliberate!"

Dima gave a disbelieving hum. Reaching for the mirror, he set it on the ground, and with unmistakable intent, gathered Katya to him.

Katya was half asleep when Dima spoke again, much later, after an appreciable pause.

"If I'm not allowed to call you beautiful," he said, "I need another word that I can use instead."

"I suppose that's only fair," Katya said. Her voice sounded distant, almost slurred, thick with sleep and pleasure. "What do you suggest?"

"Delightful," Dima said quietly. She could feel him smiling. "*Magnificent.*"

"I like magnificent," Katya said, a little surprised to find that she did. It didn't feel like a word that fitted her, not yet, but she thought that she might be able to wriggle into it, over time.

"Magnificent it is, then," Dima said. He squeezed her hand once, as if shaking on a business agreement. "Magnificent it is."

❧

CHAPTER NINETEEN

I: 17 June 1942

Trolleybus Number Nine ran to the Front. This never ceased to strike Trofim as strange, the war so close to the city that the two could be bridged by public transport. The red of the trolleybus was an obscure comfort, immediately erased by the machine gun mounted on its front. As a child growing up in Leningrad and even as a young man, Trofim had always had to hide his glee at the trolleybuses' effortless glide through the streets. The rattle and shake of them recalled horses with bridles, tossing their heads, stopping only when they chose to do so. It wasn't like that any more: the trolleybuses started and stopped, started and stopped, dodging shelling and shrapnel and the occasional dazed, starveling pedestrian who lurched without warning into their path. Among the passengers, Trofim could pick out a handful that he recognised, soldiers heading back to the Front: a young, gape-mouthed boy he'd seen a couple of times before, whose default expression was one of mild terror; an older man, bearded and loose-limbed, swaddled in a padded cotton Red Army jacket and with creases spreading from the edges of his eyes like whiskers. He had an air of preternatural ease that reminded Trofim of Sasha. As the trolleybus jerked its way forward, the older man caught Trofim's eye, inclined his head to encompass Lidiya swaying at Trofim's side, and raised his eyebrows in a way that clearly telegraphed a mixture of surprise and respect. It made Trofim gasp a little, as if his breath had been punched out of him, pride and pleasure so intense that it was uncomfortable.

This was the fifth conversation Trofim had had with Lidiya; he had counted. The first had been the day of the parade, when her frank, direct gaze had caused his soul to seize up with something that felt like recognition. Twice after that she had come to meet Katya – and now Dima – after rehearsal and walk home with them; both times, while exchanging pleasantries, Trofim's tongue had felt heavy with the words he wanted to say, but even if he had brought himself to say them, they would have been nonsense: you couldn't take a girl out for lunch in a ruined city. The fourth time had been by chance: he had glimpsed her out of the window of a trolleybus coming into the city, and before he knew it he had leaped off three stops too early, resigning himself to a longer walk and a scolding from Karl Ilych for lateness just so that he could feign a chance meeting. This time, she had been waiting after rehearsal again, and Trofim had felt that now-familiar sense of sharp joy intertwined with exquisite humiliation, prepared himself for the sort of brief, excruciating exchange that he knew would leave him berating himself for hours. But instead of smiling at him and vanishing with Katya and Dima, it was Trofim whom she approached. "People have been saying that there's still food growing in the farms just behind the Front. I thought I'd go and have a look."

Katya looked dubious. "Lida, are you sure that's…"

"Safe?" Lidiya asked, eyebrows raised.

Katya half-smiled, shrugging. "You know what I mean. There's no point taking unnecessary risks – "

"Rather than necessary ones?" Lidiya grinned. "Don't worry. You'll be happy enough when I come home with a bag full of cabbages. Besides," she tucked her arm into Trofim's and he felt, awfully, a blush creep out from under his collar, "Trofim will look after me."

With a surgical precision, Trofim was coming to understand the anatomy of his feelings. There had been girls before, most of whom Trofim didn't much like to think about: girls at the Conservatoire, who had overlooked Trofim's blushing and ducking and made their own agenda perfectly clear; girls since the army, to whom Trofim had never had anything much to say. Had it been up to him he would have eschewed the whole business entirely: there was something about girls – about women – that seemed to expose how little substance he had, how weak he was, how flimsy. But Lidiya had gravity. Lidiya had a slow, certain depth to her. Lidiya brought Trofim into focus, brightly coloured and sharp-edged.

"It must be strange for you," Lidiya said. She had barely spoken since getting onto the trolley; her voice was rough and considered. "This change, I mean. Coming from the Front to the city every day."

"You get used to it," Trofim said. It was true. These days, he had the idea that there was Trofim the Soldier, whom he waved off every morning and who waited for him at the Front every day, and there was Trofim the Musician, who was packed away for the evening somewhere in the vaults of the Radio House, to be dusted off for rehearsals. This In-Between Trofim was something else, something that was, perhaps, starting to feel a little more comfortable.

"It's easier now it's every day," Trofim added. It was easier, too, to talk to Lidiya like this, side by side rather than face to face. "When I was first reassigned to the Leningrad Front, at the start of the winter, they were still giving us day passes into the city, those of us who had family here. This was before my parents left over the Ice Road. The first time I came into the city after the start of the Blockade – it shocked me. It felt very…very wrong."

II: 21 November 1941

Perhaps the changes in the city weren't as noticeable for those who lived there every day, but for Trofim it was alive with absences. The horses wrenched off the Anichkov Bridge. The Bronze Horseman encased in planks. The spires of the Admiralty and the dome of St Isaac's painted grey; Smolny swaddled in lumpen camouflage. On a day like this, late November, clouds scurrying in from the north and the sky so close you could touch it, the fierce bright gold of the Admiralty should have been a finger of light reaching up from the colourless river. Now the city was painted in shades of the same: the shrouded buildings, the hungering sky, the brisk cold metal of the Neva, the barrage balloons overhead.

The time *in between* was important; after leaving his parents Trofim needed to walk, pounding out onto the streets some measure of the frustration and anger that had pooled in his knees and ankles from enforced inaction. There needed to be this buffer between home and the Front; the two could not coexist. The others thought he was lucky, Trofim knew, to have family close enough to visit, to see them in the flesh and not to have to speculate. Still, Trofim envied, sometimes, those men whose families were distant, even those who had no families at all – remembered, suddenly, Sasha's cool face lit up by the flash of a shell, his cheeks hollowing as he sucked on his ever-present Belomor. Trofim had thought it often enough before, but that time he'd heard himself saying it aloud, the words borne up on a tide of trembling that rose from his belly to his throat. *Aren't you ever scared?* he had asked Sasha, and Sasha had paused for a moment, the smoke coiling upwards into the darkness, as if he were seriously considering the answer to Trofim's question. *It's not that I want to die*, he had said at last, as if that had been what Trofim had asked, *but I can't see as how it would matter too much, either way*.

That was the problem with Trofim. It mattered. It mattered too much, it always had, and it weighed on him. There was a practised insouciance to a career soldier that Trofim could never quite pull off with aplomb; it was as if, sometimes, there was something lurking inside of him that repeated, insistent, the words his mother was careful to never actually say: *this is temporary. You've had your fun, playing soldier. Now get out while you still can.* He was certain that the others saw it too, or some of them, at least – it was reflected back at him in Sasha's silent, appraising gaze, or in the egregious stupidity that Viktor sometimes displayed, which could feel like a weapon artfully designed to fillet out those things that set Trofim apart.

The street seemed to be full of women, wrapped up tight and dark, string bags clutched to them. They were thin, already, even though Badaev had only burned a matter of weeks ago. It touched off in Trofim a mild vertigo, the same sickness that he felt when shaking his father's hand and feeling the click and slide of the bones in his wrist, loose under his skin, or the taut coldness of his mother's cheek as he kissed her in greeting. "Come and stretch your fingers," she always said, a slightly affected nod to tradition, insisting on giving him tea and even sugar even though Trofim knew it meant that they would go hungry later. He had tried to refuse, but his mother insisted, she always insisted. When he took a sip, it was hot and sweet but something else too, dank and heavy. He said nothing, but his mother must have seen his face twist, and laughed. "Ah, you can taste the difference, can you?"

"No, it's good, it tastes – "

She waved a hand, stopping him. "Let me show you what they're selling on the market."

A jar of earth: Trofim's mother handled it as if it was something precious, and presented it to Trofim with baffled pride at her own resourcefulness. "I thought they were mad when I first heard people talking about it in the bread queues. Wasting their money on dirt, even if it is the stuff they've been scraping out from under Badaev! But then I tried it, and, darling, smell – "

Trofim sniffed the jar that his mother held out to him. The dense, damp odour of earth, but below that a suggestion, redolent with sugar and fat. It made his mouth water ever so slightly, and his mother laughed again.

"That was exactly my reaction! It was all I could do to stop myself from cramming handfuls of it into my mouth. Just look at it – doesn't it look edible? Like you could just stuff your face with it without having to do anything? But your father tried that and got terrible stomach cramps after only a little. You have to boil it up and then strain it, and then you have something that tastes like sugar. It has a bit of an earthy undertone, but…" She shrugged, smiling. "That adds something to it, almost, I think."

"It's good," Trofim said, not quite lying. "And you shouldn't be wasting it on me. You know, at the Front, they feed us – "

She shook her head. "Don't be foolish. You are our son, you are fighting for the city! If we can't even give you tea, what sorts of parents are we?"

This was it: it came again, that tap at the back of his head, that squirm of discomfort. It wasn't that he wanted to be a hero. That had never been why, not exactly, and during the Winter War, the endless fucking forests and the sweet stink of pine against the fresh snow, the startling sharpness of blood against the white, so wide and blank that it had torn the breath from his throat – he had understood, then, about heroism and how little it meant when stacked against fear and cold and loneliness. But there was something else, too, something about the sensation of food, hot and safe, in his belly, and the comfort of flesh on his ribs – Trofim hadn't joined the army so that he could be *safer*; that was it, that was what he was trying to put into words. You want –

"You want to believe that you're doing it for something, or for someone," Trofim had said, once, to Sasha. Sasha sat, impassive as ever, his eyes on the red ember of his cigarette. His silence had a tendency to shut people up, but Trofim had come to understand that he didn't mean it that way. Or perhaps that was just what Trofim wanted to believe; there was no joy in talking to someone unless you could imagine that on some level they wanted to listen. "You know, that we're suffering so that they don't have to. Or not as much." There it was: he hated the guilt of it, and the uselessness. He wanted to feel –

"You want to feel noble?" Sasha asked. "Like a martyr? Is that it?" He smiled, his voice mild, as if he was doing nothing but asking a simple question, rather than making an accusation.

"No, not that! Not – it's just – " *Just that they shouldn't be thin.* It sounded too foolish to say out loud, but that was it. Every face in the city that looked hungry, every shattered window, every rubbled building was a reproach; the women on fire watch and the children digging trenches a dropped gauntlet that the army kept fumbling.

"It's just a job, Trofim," Sasha said. He had an irritating trick of saying something reasonable as if he was barely managing to hold back a laugh. "Don't ever think it's anything more than that. We're no more and no less than the men in the factories or the fields."

It's only a job. That was the problem; that was always the problem. When Trofim had thought of the army, when he was a child and then a teenager and then in that breathless, jagged year at the Conservatoire, he had thought of it as a way to become something else, someone else. The army allowed no shirking; the army stripped you back until you could only be who you were. But that wasn't the way it had turned out. The army still felt like a costume to Trofim, one that could be stripped away to expose the feeble, wriggling person underneath.

III: 17 June 1942

The trolleybus crawled through a tangle of wire and wooden fences. Past the Kirov Works the passengers thinned, leaving only the soldiers holding on to the bitter end, until they were ordered off at the Kotlyarov Barns and left to navigate the blasted heath that formed the barrier between the city and the frontlines: trucks and tanks, fortifications and then the shell-pocked trenches – and now the women, coming to search for food. Mostly Trofim ignored them, mostly all the soldiers did; there was a palpable sense of discomfort at the idea of women so close to the Front, both the fact of their presence and what it implied, the soldiers' imperfect role as protectors. But Lidiya watched their fellow passengers with a hawkish intensity: a scrawny girl, fifteen at most, her body knotted into itself with a vicious resilience, and next to her, hand tucked under the girl's arm, an old woman, thin white hair knotted at her neck, her eyes half-closed, her face shuttered. The girl clutched a pair of begrimed baskets with mulish stubbornness. Trofim watched her, and then saw the gape-mouthed boy was watching her too, frowning, leaning forward as if gathering the courage to speak. The older man – was he with the boy? He had the air of a reluctant, unwilling protector – seemed to blow out a sigh, half-turning away. The boy spoke.

"Trying to join the army, are you?"

Trofim winced for him. He could hear the tone that the boy was reaching for – cheerful, jocose, the sort of tease that could tip over into a gentle, flirting back-and-forth. Instead, it came out plaintive, almost a whine. The girl, young as she was, flicked her eyes in his direction, set her lips, did not speak. The boy persisted – more strength in his voice this time, goaded by the girl's unmistakable air of reproof.

"You know this is the way to the Front, don't you? What do you want out there? You should be moving in the other direction, staying safe."

The girl choked out a single syllable of a laugh. Still she said nothing, but the old woman at her side turned, her face a collection of wrinkles, set into a hard stare.

"What's *safe*? You want to talk about *safe*? Two doors down from us, they were killed four nights ago. A direct hit, blew off half the building.

The street was full of their furniture, bits of chairs and tables. They found Vera on the other side of the street, her clothes half torn off her by the force of the blast. It's *safe* back there, then, is it?"

"I'd rather get hit by a bullet at the Front than starve, anyhow," the girl said. Her voice was clipped and sharp. "There are farms out there. They were cleared out pretty well over the winter, but now things are growing again. Have you seen the parks in the city, how every tree's been picked over? We don't get the rations that *you* get."

The boy flushed. The fearful expression had dropped from his face, and Trofim wondered whether this had been what he'd wanted after all, not a flirt but a fight, something that would galvanise him, something easy to win. "What do you mean by that? We don't deserve a little bit of food, when we're the ones fighting for – "

"For *what*?" the girl spat. The older woman tightened her grip on the girl's arm, perhaps to restrain her – but no, she was only drawing strength for an assault of her own.

"Yes, for *what*? After the winter we've had, we'd all have been better off if you'd put down your guns and let the Fascists walk into the city. What good's this war doing any of us?"

Lidiya leaned forward in her seat. Trofim didn't turn to look at her, but he could picture her face as clearly as if she'd been in front of him: the narrowed eyes, the mouth pursed, ready with invective. He knew so little of her, he couldn't even guess which side of the row she was preparing to launch herself into. The older man in the padded jacket turned back, putting his hand on the boy's shoulder: "Now," he said, warningly; the boy shook off his hand with a comical twitch. Without intending it, Trofim was on his feet, two steps and he was between the soldiers and the women. "*Enough*," he said. The word came out perfectly, low and powerful, not a trace of a stammer. It trailed its own strength, burning up through Trofim's belly to his chest. As the boy took a confused half-step back Trofim noticed, distantly, how small the boy was, how skinny, how easily bested. The older man offered Trofim a ghost of a smile, while the boy scowled, looking down, radiating defeat. Trofim sat back down, heart lurching, a tremble just under the surface of his skin; Lidiya turned to him, grinning, and stagily, out of the corner of her mouth, muttered, "Well done."

IV: 21 November 1941

By the time he got back, night had flooded over the Front with an alarming suddenness, amplifying sounds and making the uneven ground even more treacherous than usual. Trofim picked his way through, breath half held in concentration, jumping at small sounds: the snap of a twig underfoot, a barbed burst of laughter, the heavy-throated choke of machine gun fire – *miles away*, Trofim told himself soothingly, *miles away*. When he reached them, the thick smell of the dugouts reminded Trofim of the jar of sugared earth in his mother's kitchen. A room to himself, albeit scratched out of the chilled earth, was a privilege of the rank Trofim had only stumbled into – the unimaginable number of deaths had at least helped his promotion prospects – but Trofim couldn't bear the idea of being alone now, not while his thoughts were rising up around him, near-corporeal and impossible to ignore. Sasha's dugout, instead: it was always pristine, the floor swept, the bed made to a level of precision that Trofim suspected was unnatural, but next to the grime and the stench of thousands of men living in uncomfortable proximity, it was a small haven. There had been a time, when Trofim was eleven or twelve, skinny and pale with a tongue that had just started to trip him, when he'd been bullied mercilessly by a group of older boys who lived on his street, and even now that he was tall and broad-shouldered and not too bad looking (he thought, sometimes, making critical inventory of his thick fair hair and the sturdy line of his jaw), even though the words came out all right most of the time, even though he was in the bloody *army*, still that bullied boy's heart hammered inside him, expecting a taunt or a kick or a blow. Whenever he called in on Sasha, no matter how many times and how firmly he told himself that Sasha liked him, Trofim remembered that part of him, creeping and cowed – and the fact was that it didn't make sense. Someone as reserved as Sasha, who seemed to observe the war and everyone in it with a disconcertingly detached irony – why would he want to be friendly with someone like Trofim, who was clumsy and who stammered when he was anxious and for whom sometimes, shamefully (and he was certain that Sasha had witnessed this, at least once) the unutterable noise of a bombardment at close range would make his eyes fill with uninvited tears that threatened to roll down his cheeks if he wasn't vigilant enough to blink them back? And yet Sasha was always pleased to see him – or at the very least, never told him to go away.

"Ah, there you are." Sasha, book in hand, sat on the edge of his bunk. "Made it back safely, then?"

"Fine. Hardly any hits on Vasilievsky today. Or not close enough to be a problem."

"How are the family?"

"They – " Trofim ground to a halt. Something rose up in the back of his throat, clamping his teeth together; he knew that if he took the trouble to pry them apart the words would jerk out, disassembled. It was better not to speak. *Why do you do this to yourself?* The demand was savage and insistent. He didn't have to be there. He had chosen this world that he moved in with so little ease, so little grace. Sasha, lighting a cigarette, his face bowed low over the flame, turned towards Trofim wearing an expression of polite enquiry; seeing the look on Trofim's own face, and the terse shake of his head, he tossed the pack of Belomors in his direction. Trofim reached out a hand to grab them, seeing in his mind's eye the way he would gracefully pluck them out of the air, and succeeded only in batting them to the floor, scrambling immediately after them. Behind him, he heard from Sasha a sound that could have been a hastily suppressed snort of laughter. By the time he had collected the pack and sat up again, Sasha had arranged his face, leaning towards him with a lit match.

Trofim still hated smoking, the stink and the burn of it, and could never shake off the residual guilt from years of being careful of his lungpower, but Sasha was right in his silent offering: cigarettes steadied him, tied him to the earth, cleared his sight and his thinking. He closed his eyes as the first breath of acrid smoke hit, sucking it down, willing himself not to cough. In the darkness, the room heaved and steadied itself. Trofim's tongue loosened. *Magic.*

"My mother has bought a jar of earth," he said, eyes still closed. The words came out whole and perfect, coins dropped in a pool. He opened his eyes; Sasha watched him, eyes narrowed, eyebrows raised. "From Badaev. They're selling it on the market, apparently. You can refine it somehow – my mother knew all the tricks – and get the sugar out, the sugar that melted into the ground when the warehouses burned. She made me have sugar in my tea. *Insisted.*"

"And how was it?" Sasha asked blandly. Trofim blew out a breath, laced with smoke, and mustered the sharp edge of a smile.

"As you'd expect. Burnt-tasting. Earthy. Sweet, though. It does the job."

"I can tell what you're thinking," Sasha said. The half-smile on his face mirrored Trofim's own. "You've got that stupid martyr expression again. That look that makes me think you're going to run out and lie in front of the nearest enemy tank, or hang yourself up on barbed wire, just so you can feel like you're doing something useful."

Trofim laughed. He could never help it when Sasha spoke like this, an explosion of words shaken out of his normal silence. Sasha grinned, shrugged a shoulder, didn't stop. "Remember what I said. You don't get to be a hero – "

" – it's just a job," Trofim finished with him. "Sometimes I wonder if I'd feel more useful in a factory, though, than I do out here."

"Perhaps. But there's no need to get sentimental about it."

A call came from outside, long and drawn out: *Sashaaaaaa!* Sasha rolled his eyes. "They've got some vodka. Keep calling for me to bring the accordion out. Want to have a sing-along, see if they can get Fritz joining in like last time."

Trofim's throat felt raw from the smoke; the slippery salve of vodka sounded like it might be just the thing. And music, rough-hearted music that could only make him feel better, not worse. Nothing refined in it, just breath and guts and feeling.

"Why not? No point staying here, you're just going to lecture me."

"True. And this – " Sasha waved the slim book he was holding, more of a pamphlet really, and Trofim spotted the grotesque caricature on the cover, a hairy, bare-arsed Hitler. "This is fucking awful. Viktor lent it to me, said it was the funniest thing he's ever read. That boy could have half his head blown off tomorrow and none of us'd notice any difference in his intellect." Trofim bit his lips, stifling a grin. Viktor was goodhearted enough, but not much in the way of brains. "Still, I might hang onto it – good for wiping my arse on, if nothing else." Sasha scooped up the accordion, looping it over his shoulders, and squeezed out a plaintive bleat. Outside, a drunken roar of pleasure answered. "You coming, then?"

In the dark, in the press of men, voices and half-light, that was when it was easiest, when the men stopped being men and became only a collective; when the important thing wasn't who they were but where they were and what they were doing. That was part of what had drawn Trofim in, not the desire to be part of the group, but just to be welcomed by it; not to have to shoulder his way in, but to be seen as a part of it by design rather than by accident. Sasha, blank-faced in the firelight, worked his accordion, not singing – to Trofim's right, Viktor peppered the lyrics with obscenities, the filth and creativity of which made even Trofim smile from time to time. Other men sang, eyes closed, chins lifted, throats open with abandon; Trofim wondered whether they were conjuring up their own Katiushas, or Nastyas, or Anyas wandering through the flower-studded steppes; but Timofei, whose face was sprinkled with pimples and whose chin seemed to melt into his neck, or Kostya, who was casual with his violence and as liable to knock someone's teeth out as to wish them good morning – it seemed unlikely that boys like these had sweethearts back home who were pining for them and wishing them back, rather than being bitterly grateful for their absence, if they existed at all. It wasn't what they were singing about, though; it was the singing itself. *Stop thinking.* Trofim roughened his voice, sang as badly and as loudly as he could. Someone flung an arm over his shoulder and pulled him into a half embrace. Someone else passed a flask; Trofim drank and savoured the burn, cheap vodka and companionship. From beyond the lines, faint voices sounded, and a shout went up from the men: *Fritz, Fritz!* Trofim shouted too.

He didn't feel drunk, just warm and leaden with tiredness but then suddenly there he was in the middle of a conversation with Sasha, tongue thick but fluent, his voice echoing in his ears, fading in and out of clarity.

"…sweetening their tea with earth," he heard himself say. "Can't get sugar, can't get meat – it's just. They just – "

"You told me this already," Sasha said, factual but not ungentle.

"…and then I think I'm fighting for them, or for people like that, but my mother, she still wishes I'd just been a musician. She'd rather – she'd rather – and then I'd be in Tashkent, wouldn't I, with the Conservatoire, or in Novosibirsk with the Philharmonia. And I couldn't. I should be here, shouldn't I?"

"I'm not the right person to ask," Sasha said. He took a breath. "That's it, enough. You're going round in circles. Get to bed. You're going to feel like hell tomorrow."

Sasha stood, offering Trofim his hand. The ground was very comfortable, and the next moment very far away, at the end of feeble threads of limbs. Trofim still didn't feel drunk, not exactly, but he wasn't convinced that his legs would hold him up for long. Sasha edged and nudged and shouldered him in the right direction and then Trofim was waking up in the unforgiving morning, entangled in blankets, dry-mouthed and brittle, words rattling around in his head with the flat relentlessness of gunfire, Sasha's voice, though he couldn't remember him saying it: *you need to stop caring so much, Trofim. That's the only way you're going to get through this.*

V: 17 June 1942

The odd thing was that it still felt like the countryside, more or less: the rich smell of grass and earth, undercut with the sharp reek of gunpowder. Stepping down from the trolleybus, Lidiya stumbled on the pitted ground; Trofim took her elbow, righting her. He couldn't bring himself to meet her eyes, his gaze settling instead on the smooth expanse of her forehead, the curve of her mouth, the firm line of her jaw.

"Will you be all right from here?"

"Oh, yes." Lidiya cut her eyes to the side: the girl and the elderly lady were shuffling past, the girl settling her baskets more comfortably in her arms. "I'd better get on. Otherwise those two will grab all the best nettles."

Trofim smiled. More than her beauty or her poise, it was Lidiya's toughness that squeezed the air out of him and set his hands trembling. Something had shifted in her, perhaps, after that moment on the trolleybus when Trofim had stood and spoken and turned back towards her – perhaps he was imagining it, probably he was, but he had a sense of her gaze landing on him in a different way, something that excited and terrified him equally. He could feel it in his throat, the certainty that the words wouldn't come out right even if he tried to force them – all Trofim could do was to smile at Lidiya, smile and breathe and smile some more. Unexpectedly, Lidiya raised her hand, touched his cheek. Her fingertips were as rough as bark.

"I'll see you," Lidiya said, and turned, heading away from the Front. Trofim couldn't move – wouldn't move – until she was out of sight, her small, upright figure swallowed up by greenery. At the very limits of his vision she seemed to stop, reaching out a tiny, pale hand to touch a lilac bush, swagged heavy with blossoms. Trofim could imagine the gorgeous violence of its scent, could picture Lidiya lifting the flowers to her face, closing her eyes, breathing them in. And then a memory, overlaid on the scene as surely as one transparency placed over another, a slippage of time. October 1941, shortly after they had been reassigned to the Leningrad Front, the one time that he and Sasha had gone into the city together, Trofim to see his family and Sasha on some arcane errand of his own, neither spoken of nor asked after through mutual, silent agreement. They had found themselves on the same trolleybus going back, jumping off at the barns and picking their way back to the Front, the same ruined ground where Trofim now stood, but then the autumn air had been thick enough to drink, fog and smoke and dew. Close to dusk, for a moment the sun broke through the clouds, low and slanting, and everything shone, bright and golden, the clouds uplit pink. Trofim had had to stop, heart heavy and full. The moment was gone in a breath; he walked on, Sasha a step or two behind. And then out of the corner of his eye, he saw Sasha reach out his hand and pluck a leaf from a tattered birch tree they were passing, raising it to his face before slipping it into his pocket. Trofim said nothing, but the image would come back to him at unexpected times, surprising him with its plangent sweetness, and leaving him with something trembling on his tongue and his lips, leaden and unsayable. That the sky remained, no matter what it watched over: the trenches; the birch tree; the lilac.

CHAPTER TWENTY

28 June 1942

Pavel's hand felt just the way Dima remembered it: dry and tough, more like badly cured leather than like skin. As usual, he gripped too hard in his handshake – an older man's attempt to show his strength – and pulled Dima in to kiss his cheek. It had been months since they'd met, but Dima's body obligingly remembered exactly how far he had to bend to press his face against Pavel's. Pavel had a couple of inches of wiry beard growth; he smelled strongly of cigarettes, laced with an edge of vodka.

"Dmitri, my boy. Good of you to come to see me." He didn't seem immediately surprised that Dima had come alone, though Dima had always before visited with Vasya – at Vasya's insistence, if Dima were honest. Pavel had always been Vasya's friend and, since the Blockade, Vasya's project, something that Dima had resented bitterly at times throughout the winter, Vasya's insistence that every scrap of extra food that came their way had to have a sliver saved for Pavel. Dima wondered, now, how many other young men around the city had carried out the same task of painstaking scrimping and saving, lavishing Pavel with pathetically small gifts. Certainly Pavel spoke with a vigour that a half-starved man well into his fifties shouldn't have had.

"I brought you some vodka," Dima said, holding up the bottle, half-apologetic. Little thought had gone into this offering; in truth, he'd barely thought of Pavel in weeks. Dima had learned young that the secret to a good life was locking things away. He could see it in Katya, the messy way that her grief bled into her happiness, tainting it, and he wished he could teach her how to do otherwise. He had shut away his family when he had found music, tamping them down so that their absence couldn't scuff the bright shine of it; Leningrad had allowed him to close off the loss of Arseny Grigorevich; and now Katya and the orchestra let him ignore the ravening snarl of his still-empty belly, the creeping certainty that they were sliding inexorably towards another winter of the Blockade…the lack of Vasya. But Vasya had always been a slippery character, and he wouldn't stay hidden, rising out of the dark at the sound of a rough-edged voice like his, the thud of a heavy footstep, a clap on the shoulder like he used to offer. Sleep had always been the time when Dima's defences were most dangerously lowered, and when he had awoken in tears that morning, the fact that he couldn't recall his dream didn't change the dissoluble certainty of Vasya's absence, announcing itself with the same unapologetic fanfare with which Vasya had once announced his presence. Dima had managed to hide his tears from Katya, an arm flung hastily across his face, and within moments he had gathered himself together. But Vasya had stayed with him, and by the time Dima was dressed, a whole blank Sunday stretching before him, Katya occupied with the children, he had the powerful urge to spend the day doing something Vasya would have wanted him to do. It wouldn't do to visit Pavel empty-handed, however, and so the vodka had been procured through a hastily brokered exchange with Ilya, Dima recklessly promising him his tobacco ration for next month in return. Such arrangements were largely meaningless within the building where assets were generally considered communal, and Dima had been planning to hand his tobacco over to Ilya anyway, but it struck Dima as somehow unethical not to even pretend to bother.

Now, in his apartment, Pavel was sloshing the vodka into a couple of glasses. Dima forced himself not to wonder how clean they were or weren't. "And where is Vasily?" Pavel demanded, his tone querulous. "I haven't seen him in weeks. I expect he's dead, isn't he?"

Dima choked a little at Pavel's matter-of-fact tone. He had thought carefully about how to break the news to Pavel, and now all his delicate phraseology had been for nothing. "I – I'm afraid – "

"Well, don't pussyfoot around it, boy. It happens often enough, especially these days. I shall miss him, though. He was good company, was Vasily." Pavel pressed a glass into Dima's hand. "Sit down, Dmitri, and drink up. The least we can do is have a toast to his memory."

With his free hand Dima felt for the sofa, which seemed to be strewn with detritus and sticky with grime. Clearing a space he sat, surreptitiously wiping his palm on the side of his trousers, then hoisted his glass with grim resolution. The clean, chemical smell of vodka always reminded Dima of his father. He disliked drinking most of the time, but Pavel wasn't a person you could say no to. Despite the careful schooling of his face not to grimace at the vodka's slick burn, Pavel burst into raucous laughter at Dima's first, prim sip.

"Of course, you were never much of a drinker, were you? Despite Vasily's best efforts." He cackled again. "I'll always remember that night, the first night Vasily brought you out to a bar. And you – "

Dima remembered. His arrival in Leningrad, sixteen years old, filled with a combustible mixture of terror and excitement, had been precipitous. Vasya had met him at the station with exaggerated, anxious bonhomie, and brought him back to the single room they were now to share. Introduced to the communal bathroom and kitchen – the latter of which Vasya never used, and Dima had every intention of following suit – and to the one or two fellow residents that happened to be around (one an aging prostitute, Vasya explained in an undertone, the other a middle-aged man who was evidently so dull as to require no explanation), Dima had subsided onto the bed that was to be his, a narrow cot that reminded him of school. The mattress was lumpy and held the faint suggestion of damp; Dima could already tell that the springs were the type to squeal in protest at any movement more ambitious than an indrawn breath, and that his feet would stick out through the iron frame, ensuring that he would always wake up slightly chilled. The air in the room felt heavy and thick, and Dima had the sudden apprehension that both of them were wondering, inevitably too late, quite what he was doing there. Vasya, typically, broke the silence first:

"Come on," he said. "Let's go and get a drink."

That had been Dima's first night in a bar, the first time he met the formidable Lyuba, and the first time he met Pavel. They knew each other from Solovki, Vasya explained, and slightly later, drunk and expansive: "He's like a father to me." It had struck Dima as sad, the way that Vasya had surrounded himself with an ersatz family: Pavel in place of his father, and he, Dima, standing in for Piotr, but seconds later it occurred to him that he was barely any better, with his helpless love for Arseny Grigorevich – it was easier to admit it now that he was gone, but that didn't stop the sharp kick of pain at the memory. Vasya had pressed vodka on him, a glass, two...Dima lost count, as they all took turns to pour and Dima had no sooner thrown back one glass than another was pushed into his hand. It had been fine at first: Dima had quite enjoyed the way that his limbs warmed and turned to rubber, the delicious laziness that crept into every part of his body. Then the floor shifted and cold panic crawled through him. He had learned to hide fear well, and certainly none of the others gave any sign of noticing anything amiss; Dima bunched his hands into fists and forced himself to keep as still as possible, gulping down great draughts of the smoky air to keep his growing nausea at bay. This turned out to be a mistake. He was concentrating so hard on not falling off his stool that he barely registered Lyuba's hand on his shoulder, and her urgent whisper of Vasya's name; Vasya's *oh, shit* made a little more of an impression, as he took Dima firmly by the elbow and hustled him outside into the street, bending him over and pointing him at the gutter.

"*There* we go," Vasya murmured soothingly, as Dima was neatly, comprehensively sick; he rubbed Dima's back with unfussy solicitude, and passed him a handkerchief when he appeared to be done. The handkerchief smelled of motor oil and Dima suspected it was none too clean, but all things being equal, he didn't feel he was in much of a position to criticise.

"Sorry about that," he said thickly. Unpleasant as the experience was, at least the street felt steadier beneath his feet now.

"No, I'm sorry. I should have remembered you're not used to it. I suppose you never got much of a chance at school, did you?"

"Sometimes one of the boys'd get a bottle, but it always had to be shared between so many of us it never had much of an effect." Dima straightened, and carried out a quick internal inventory: stomach uncertain but seemingly under control, at least for the time being; a faint buzzing in his head, but his thoughts felt sharper-edged, less like they were coming from far away, relayed through a radio bristling with static. Lyuba was outside now, too, making him sip from a glass of water, and Dima was conscious of the saturnine presence of Pavel, a few feet off, watching the drama.

"Let's get you home, then," Vasya said. Dima heard him speaking to Pavel in a quick, apologetic mumble, while Lyuba stroked his damp hair off his forehead, clucking a little under her breath: it was the sort of quasi-maternal gesture that usually made Dima bridle, but Lyuba's fingers were unexpectedly cool and calming. Home was only a few minutes' walk away, and Dima was aware of Vasya marching sturdily at his shoulder, though he didn't turn out to need his support.

"I don't think I should make a habit of drinking," Dima said, as Vasya fiddled with the key to their room. He expected a degree of ridicule, or at the very least an attempt at persuasion, but Vasya just grunted.

"You're one sense down already, I suppose," he said. "Maybe you shouldn't mess around with the ones you've got left."

Dima's feelings for Pavel were about as mixed as they could be, but at least he always made it easy to be around him. As the day slid into afternoon the dusty warmth of the apartment descended on Dima like a blanket, and he felt his body settling into the topography of the old velvet sofa. They talked little; there was little enough to say. Presently Pavel asked: "Well, will you play?"

Dima was on his feet before Pavel had even finished the question. The piano was where he remembered it, but for once Dima didn't have to clear a flotilla of vodka glasses, coffee cups and ashtrays off the lid: could Pavel actually have been playing it himself? He felt for a chair and sat. Fifteen years since he had first sat down in front of a piano, and yet this moment still ignited something inside him, when he first set his fingers on the keys: he felt boundless, limitless, as if he held the world in his arms and all the music he could ever want to play was unravelling before him with crisp, bright certainty. "Any requests?"

Pavel hummed a little to himself. "Perhaps something from *The Well-Tempered Clavier*?"

Dima's laugh was half swallowed by the first warm, cracked notes; he started to play.

It had always been like this. For days after Dima's first meeting with Pavel and its ignominious end, the mere mention of Pavel's name brought about in Dima a cringe of embarrassed recollection; the promise of a piano was the only thing that had lent Dima the reluctant willingness to put himself in Pavel's company again. There wasn't much that he missed about school – dormitories, communal showers, indigestible institutional food were all things he continued to rejoice at escaping, in those early days – but lack of access to a piano made him twitchy. Ever since he had chosen the violin as his primary instrument the piano had become a tool of relaxation for Dima, and the idea of having keys under his fingers again made his palms tingle.

Even so, the first time he entered Pavel's apartment, he trailed after Vasya and Lyuba with the sullen, slope-shouldered slump of an unwilling child accompanying his parents on a tedious duty visit. Pavel lived in a single room, as did Dima and Vasya, but at home Dima was conscious of the low ceiling like the palm of a hand held just above his head, while in Vasya's room space blossomed above him. Vasya had explained that before the Revolution the whole floor of the building had belonged to Pavel's family, and gradually over time Pavel had been herded back into what had once been a master bedroom. That accounted for its spaciousness, and the cold flags of air that flapped in through the tall windows, open to the shudder and shout of the street beneath.

Vodka was poured, and a glass was pushed towards Dima, but he demurred. "Yes, probably best you steer clear," Pavel said, with clanking implication, and Dima raised a wan smile: he had rather suspected that Pavel was one of those people who would never let you away with anything. Around him, the conversation eddied, gossipy talk about people Dima didn't know, and he started to wish that he hadn't come, invented a prior engagement with friends Vasya knew he didn't have. Dima had never thought of himself as shy, particularly, but he was coming to understand that his utter inability to feign interest in anything he didn't care about shut him out of conversations just as surely as would an inability to string together a sentence.

"Vasya tells me you're musical," Pavel said to Dima at last. Dima had never known how to respond to such statements without sounding either coy or boastful, and usually ended up certain he was sounding both.

"I…I do like to play."

"Well, then." There came a series of groans and huffs as Pavel got to his feet; Dima was unsure which noises came from the furniture and which from Pavel himself. Taking this as his cue, Dima followed him into a musty-smelling corner, and Pavel pressed a pile of slightly damp papers into his hands. "It's got rather buried over the years. Put those down on the table, will you?"

Dima had only the vaguest idea where the table was; warily, he piled the papers by his feet. Pavel didn't seem to mind.

"Now, then."

Pavel didn't take Dima's hand, or make any move to lead him to the piano; Dima led himself. Reaching out he found the curve of the cover, slightly tacky with drink rings and scabbed with what seemed to be candlewax; as he lifted it, it emitted a roaring squeal that was as familiar as Dima's own heartbeat. He couldn't suppress a smile.

"I got rid of the stool years ago, but there's a chair here you can use," Pavel said. He remembered this time to place Dima's hand on the back of it. Dima sat, spreading his fingers over the keys. He had never played in front of Vasya before, not even the violin; it felt too much like showing off, and besides, sound seeped through the walls of their communal apartment in a way that would have made any performance semi-public. Tentative, he played a C major chord. The notes rang out: furred from disuse, slightly out of tune, and the E above middle C stuck alarmingly, but beneath it all the sound was mellow and buttery, a dim candle flame.

"This is a good piano," Dima said, impressed.

"It used to be my mother's," Pavel said shortly. "Come on then, Dmitri, give us a tune."

Dima thought for a moment, and then, with the sketch of a bow to where he imagined Vasya and Lyuba were sat on the sofa, launched into "Such a lot of nice girls" from Lyuba's current favourite film. From the sofa, he heard her soft, drawn-out *oh* of appreciation. Pavel, however, cut him off irritably.

"No, no, no – none of that modern nonsense. Play something *proper*."

Startled, Dima paused, wondering what counted as *proper* for a man like Pavel. Nothing romantic; he could guess that the pedalling wouldn't be up to it, and at least to start with he wanted to play something he could be proud of. You couldn't go wrong with a bit of Bach: as a little joke to himself, Dima started to play the C sharp minor fugue from *The Well-Tempered Clavier*, half-laughing and half-wincing at the chiming E that lasted twice as long as any other note.

When he had finished, Lyuba started to applaud, much to his embarrassment. "Very funny," Pavel said drily, surprising Dima again; he'd thought the joke was his alone. And then, rather tentatively: "I don't suppose you know any Schubert lieder?"

Dima frowned. He had taught himself one or two a few years ago, simply because he'd heard them on Arseny Grigorevich's gramophone and liked them, but they'd been rather unsatisfying to play against nothing but his own breathless humming. "I could probably remember 'Der Lindenbaum', from *Winterreise*?"

"That'll do."

In Dima's head, the first few bars unspooled; his fingers started to chase them. He was beginning to relax into the new instrument, working out how it wanted to be treated, but even so he nearly leaped out of his skin when Pavel began to sing. His voice was a little cracked, a little hoarse thanks to years of drinking and smoking, but it had a powerful vein of sweetness running through it, clearly trained; he sang the words caressingly, with affectionate familiarity. "Fuck *me*," Dima heard Vasya say, distinctly, from the sofa; other than that the room was silent. Dima had never accompanied a singer before but he'd played along with Arseny Grigorevich's violin enough, and he instinctively started to curl his accompaniment around Pavel's voice, burrowing underneath, bolstering it up: a prop rather than a centrepiece. At the end of the song Pavel's voice fell away, and the final notes from the piano dropped into the silence with the certainty of stones into still water.

"Fucking hell," Vasya said, clearly impressed. "Where did that come from?"

"All part of my shadowy past," Pavel said. He sounded smug and sprightly, as if the very act of springing a surprise had perked him right up.

"Where did you study singing?" Dima asked.

"I was a student very briefly at the Moscow Conservatoire, back in the day," Pavel said. "Until they threw me out."

"What for?" Vasya demanded.

"Oh, I can barely even remember these days. I was never going to be much good, anyhow – too lazy, and far too fond of vodka and cigarettes." He settled a hand on Dima's shoulder. "You play well, though, boy. Will you play a bit more? Vasily and I have some business we need to discuss, but background music is always appreciated."

"I'd love to," Dima said truthfully. It had been so long since he'd played that a queue of pieces was forming inside him, jostling at his wrists, keen for an airing.

This became the pattern of visits to Pavel's apartment: Vasya and Pavel, sometimes alone, sometimes with Lyuba and sometimes with a few anonymous associates, would be locked in tense and muttered conversation on the sofa, while Dima would play. Even after he'd secured a job as an accompanist that allowed him access to a piano and time and space to play, Dima found that he valued the chance to play in front of an audience, even one as irritating and capricious as Pavel. Sometimes, playing Pavel's piano, Dima had free rein; sometimes Pavel would bark commands at him from the sofa: "Play some Chopin! One of the early etudes," or "Tchaikovsky, ballet music!" or just "Liszt!" as if Dima was some sort of human gramophone. Dima found he didn't mind this – instead he rather took to the challenge of it, racking his brains to make sure he had enough pieces in his repertoire to satisfy Pavel's dictatorial commands. Only occasionally did he stumble; when he did, Pavel would call out "never mind", sounding mildly put out, and suggest something else instead. Once or twice he stomped over to his rarely-used gramophone to play Dima a piece that he felt Dima definitely *should* know; more often, either to test or to tease, he would call out a name Dima had never heard of. The first time Dima admitted ignorance Pavel just chuckled to himself and demanded Rachmaninoff instead; the next time, Dima, acting on instinct, called back, "I think you just made that up, Pavel," which Pavel seemed to find delightfully amusing. The next time Pavel tried it on, Dima said nothing at all, but began to play a piece of his own devising, a stormy and discordant thing perhaps overly influenced by Bartók's earlier string quartets. "What is that god-awful racket?" Pavel demanded; "Kaverin," Dima responded demurely.

Before coming to Leningrad, Dima had had only the most tangled, partial idea of Vasya's life there; he had expected that things would become clearer once he was there, too, but he found instead that what Vasya vaguely referred to as 'business' remained resolutely closed to him. Dima understood that what Vasya did involved vast networks of people who had to be kept sweet, and acts of very dubious legality, but beyond that it was a mystery. "You don't get involved," Vasya said brusquely, whenever Dima asked a question, no matter how innocent he had dressed it up to seem. "Dima doesn't get involved," he told everyone else, which was generally enough to stop a conversation dead in its tracks. It was frustrating, and did little to quench Dima's fierce curiosity, but Dima couldn't fault Vasya for his protectiveness.

But Vasya's mistake was to assume that Dima couldn't listen and play at the same time. It was true that when Dima was learning a piece his concentration was thunderous and complete, blocking out everything else, and that when Dima played something he really loved he would wallow in it to the exclusion of the outside world – but when he played at Pavel's it was purely for entertainment, which always allowed him to keep at least half an ear on the conversation. Much of it was so coded to be of little interest: places, people, vague references to products. Dima liked best to listen in when someone else was there, another associate or two, when Dima would follow the curves and twists of Vasya and

Pavel's voices to try and work out the intricate hierarchy of relations, an anodyne sort of spying.

This boy was young, perhaps not much older than Dima himself, and it was clear from the conversation that Vasya and Pavel had not met him before. His voice telegraphed a nervy deference. When the door closed behind him there came the rustling hiss of Pavel leaning back in his chair, and the snick and flare of Vasya lighting a cigarette.

"He seemed all right, didn't he? Knows the right sorts of people."

"I suppose so. He's got the connections we need."

"But he was lying," Dima said. He'd forgotten to pretend he wasn't listening; the surprise had jolted the words out of him, Pavel and Vasya's ignorance of something that had seemed to Dima staggeringly obvious. He was three chords away from the end of a Chopin prelude, and he stroked the keys with a careful, sensual gentleness.

"Dima – " Vasya said warningly.

"I know, I don't get involved." He played the last chord with illustrative vigour – but Pavel interrupted.

"Vasily. Let's hear what he has to say." To Dima, he asked: "Why do you think he was lying?"

"You could hear it in the way he spoke." It had been clear as a bell to Dima, clearer even than the words the man had spoken. "Couldn't you tell? There was…a sort of tremble in his voice, when he mentioned his contacts. He sounded like he could barely believe what he was saying himself, let alone expect you to."

There was a crowded pause. Then Vasya said: "But no – I'm sure he's all right. Yuri vouched for him."

"He did," Pavel said, contemplative. Dima thought he could detect a thread of doubt in his voice. "Ah, we might as well give him a try. If we have to explain to Yuri – "

"And you shouldn't be listening, anyway," Vasya added to Dima. Dima shrugged.

"Suit yourself." The opening notes of Dvořák's first Slavonic Dance suggested themselves; he attacked them with gusto, grinning a little when Pavel joined in the most bombastic parts with a percussive vocal accompaniment.

Dima was right: the boy didn't have the contacts he claimed to have, the deal – whatever it had been – fell through, and the first Dima knew of it was when Vasya came home, growling and spitting and making empty threats of violent revenge. Dima was inveigled into joining him and Pavel for a drink, which turned into several; as much as Pavel and Vasya tried to avoid the subject for Dima's sake, the drunker they got the more it started to slip into conversation, until Pavel rounded on Dima: "And you were bloody right. How the hell did you know?"

Dima shook his head, helpless. "I just…did. It was clear from his voice, from the way he spoke."

"Fucking sorcery," Vasya mumbled. Dima couldn't tell whether or not he was joking.

"It's really not. Honestly, either of you could tell the same things, if you listened closely enough."

Pavel slammed his palm down on the table, and Dima could hear the wet smack where it hit a viscous pool of spilled vodka. "That's it, then. From now on we run anyone new past you."

Dima couldn't play for long these days. In under an hour his arms were shaking and he was starting to feel insubstantial, lightheaded and a little breathless. When he lifted his hands off the keyboard they felt limp and drained.

"Better than last time, Dmitri," Pavel said from the sofa. Dima smiled: Pavel was one of the only people who accorded Dima the full three syllables of his name, and so Dima returned the favour by insisting on Pavel, never Pasha. *Last time* – had it been January, or early February? He had played no music for weeks, even months; in his weakened state he had become too scared to even try and lift the Guarneri in case he dropped it. In Pavel's apartment the piano keys had been covered in a thin lace of ice; Dima had played Debussy and almost wept as the notes showered through the frozen air like sparks. He hadn't been able to finish.

"It's coming back, now. The orchestra helps."

Pavel didn't ask about the orchestra. There was something between them now, Dima could feel it, something paper-thin but fibrous, unbreakable. This was what he had come to Leningrad for: for music, for the orchestra, but for one powerful moment Dima wished he could forget the orchestra, turn around, go back. There had been these other things, unlooked for but no less valuable, in what he had always thought of as the side-lines, the crevices, the dim spaces between one music lesson and the next: there had been all-night parties, the clatter of dancing on bare board floors while Dima played jazz on unfamiliar pianos till the sweat dripped down his back; there had been a parade of girls, once he had got the hang of it, sweet and bitter and sharp and soft and all wholly enchanting; there had been Lyuba, her unsettling mix of prurience and motherliness; there had been the searing excitement of being on the margins of whatever ill-judged schemes Vasya and Pavel were caught up in, the pride that they trusted his judgement, that Pavel was true to his word of letting Dima have his say on anyone new. It hadn't been the *point* of anything, not for Dima, and it had felt like a shadowy half-life at the time, a scramble and a struggle, a way-station – but he felt the weight of it and the worth of it now, cast suddenly in the light of having got what he had always wanted, the awareness of what he had put aside along the way.

"I don't suppose you've heard anything from Lyuba?" Dima asked.

"Not a thing. I can't imagine that she'd write to me."

Dima hated the fact that Lyuba didn't know about Vasya; whenever he allowed himself to think about it, which was as rarely as he could get away with, the idea sickened him that Lyuba was miles away, in some wholly imaginary rural idyll that her parents had packed her off to, almost as soon as war was declared, living her life and imagining that she would come back to Vasya after the war. The responsibility for letting her know of Vasya's death weighed heavily on Dima, but he couldn't imagine how he would manage it: he couldn't remember the name of the village where she was supposed to be living with an aunt, and he wasn't even certain of Lyuba's last name. These were just some of the things that he had thought were safely stored under the thick dome of Vasya's skull, because he hadn't ever been able to believe that anything would happen to Vasya.

"Vasya always said he was going to marry her," Dima said.

"Vasily said a lot of things," Pavel said, dismissive. And perhaps Pavel was right: it had always come up when it was just the two of them, Vasya in the state of piercing intensity that was the penultimate stage of drunkenness for him, threatening to tip at any moment into sloppy sentimentality. *I'm going to fucking marry Lyuba*, he would say, and Dima would slap him on the back with mock congratulations, humouring him, knowing that the next morning, if asked about the planned proposal, Vasya would laugh uneasily and change the subject.

The chair where Pavel had been sitting groaned as he got to his feet, crossing the room to Dima's place at the piano. Pavel's hand landed on the back of Dima's neck. For the first second or two it could have been taken as nothing more than a friendly pat; it then became more insinuating. Dima sighed. This had been part of his reluctance to visit without Vasya as a buffer: this old dance, its familiarity making it no less awkward to negotiate.

"Can we not, Pavel?" he asked wearily.

"Ah, Dmitri. You break an old man's heart." Pavel did not sound particularly heartbroken. Nor did he remove his hand. "I take it you've got a girlfriend these days?"

"I have, as it happens."

"Please tell me it's not one of those second-rate little ballerinas from your ballet school."

"She's a musician, actually. She plays in the orchestra." He felt, with a sudden thinning of breath, that he didn't want to say Katya's name in front of Pavel. These were worlds that should be kept separate, and he had a superstitious notion that saying her name would somehow summon her into this grubby apartment, redolent with the slippery and the marginal. When Dima thought of Katya he thought of the supple cool of water, or the bright smack of a fresh, chill breeze: clear things, open things. She didn't talk in ellipses and elisions.

Pavel snorted, tetchily disapproving. "That never stopped Vasily."

"Well, I'm not Vasya."

Pavel grunted. "*That* is abundantly clear."

It had only happened once, with Pavel, years ago. Vasya had been involved; it had been after a party where Dima had played until dawn, sleeves rolled up, with an ever-changing ensemble of drummers and brass players, and he'd been a little drunk and a little carried away, and it had seemed like, if not quite a *good* idea, then at least not a regrettably awful one. Lyuba had been – well, Lyuba had been elsewhere; she had always had a good sense of when to absent herself. The problem was that Pavel seemed to hold out hopes for a repeat, while for Dima –

"It was only ever Vasya," Dima said at last. Sadness settled in his chest as he spoke: it had been hardly ever, particularly in the last year or two, but that had only ever been the edge of what was between them, anyway, something that had grown out of the rest of it.

"You must…miss him," Pavel said, as if groping for words. He sounded awkward, uncertain.

"Yes," Dima said simply. Very gently he played an E minor chord, a key that had always evoked a special kind of desolation for him. "And I wish you wouldn't pretend that you don't."

He remembered the first time, a few months after he had come to Leningrad, shortly after Dima had started to discover girls and all they implied. It had seemed like a normal evening for the two of them, desultory conversation between the two single beds, but when Dima had got up to shuck off his shirt for sleeping, Vasya had got to his feet, too, standing just behind Dima, a little too close. It didn't bother Dima exactly, accustomed as he was to the press of boys at school, squeezing himself into the smallest possible space, but he was conscious of Vasya's presence down the length of his body. He half turned, and Vasya didn't step back.

"*Oh*," said Dima, suddenly understanding. He didn't step back either.

Vasya cleared his throat. "I don't suppose – you don't have to."

"I'm hardly one of your blondes with tits," Dima said, smiling. Vasya said nothing. His embarrassment was almost tangible, mixed with the sort of stubbornness that meant that now he had started this, he would see it through to its conclusion.

"No. But you're…" Vasya cleared his throat again. "I'm not…you know. But sometimes it's nice to…"

"Were you planning on finishing a sentence at any point this evening?" Dima asked courteously. Vasya coughed out a laugh.

"Shut up, you little fucker. I just…" He reached out and drew a finger down Dima's arm, stopping just above his wrist. "Just, sometimes this is nice, too."

For a moment, Dima considered. "All right," he said.

Vasya had explained, afterwards, a little defensive and a little awkward: it wasn't something he did very often, he wasn't like Pavel – and that had surprised Dima all over again, someone like *Pavel*… "It's Solovki," Vasya explained. "No women for years – it affects some men like that." Between the two of them, it had only ever been one item in a vast repertoire of friendship, an occasional indulgence, and remarkably easy to keep separate from everything else.

Pavel was still at his back. *I wish you'd stop pretending you don't miss him.* There would be such respite in it, just to know it was shared. The hand lifted from his neck, but Pavel didn't step back; instead he wrapped his arms around Dima's shoulders, his chest pressed against Dima's back. Dima was tall, and Pavel compact; Pavel's cheek rested on the top of Dima's head. After a moment, Dima understood: this was as close as he was going to get to comfort, to admission, from someone like Pavel.

It didn't last long. Pavel withdrew, clearing his throat as if embarrassed, and Dima got to his feet. He felt wrung out, attenuated. "I should probably get going," he said. "Katya will worry if I'm much later." Her name was both an effort and a relief. He said goodbye to Pavel at the door of the apartment, and made a promise he wasn't sure he meant, to come again in a week or two; when the door closed behind him Dima felt as if he'd staged an escape. He took the stairs two at a time with energy he could ill-afford; the street promised welcome anonymity, and he had nearly reached the corner when he heard Pavel calling.

"Dmitri!"

His voice came from high up: he must have watched Dima leave, and was calling from a window.

"What is it?"

"Get me a ticket for the Symphony, you hear?"

Something caught Dima by the throat; he didn't quite trust himself to speak. He raised a hand in acknowledgement; over the rattle of a trolleybus he heard Pavel's window close.

CHAPTER TWENTY-ONE

30 June 1942

There were dreams from which Lidiya still woke, gasping. They had gone away during the winter, with the dank, heavy sleep of exhaustion, but light and warmth and a stomach that roared slightly less loudly had called them back. The way the dreams started was the worst of it: Lidiya would dream herself in her bed, dreaming; she would wake to the low growl of a vehicle outside, the creak of the building's front door, and then footsteps in the corridor, firm and certain. In the dream her heart would seize: she would watch the ceiling, the stretch and warp of shadows, her breath caught in her throat, and she would count the steps: one, two, three – surely they were outside her apartment, now – four, five – and the shocking flood of relief that they had passed. But no: the knock on the door came like a pistol shot; that was what would wake her every time, a gasp in her mouth that was the edge of a cry, and she could only ever convince herself that she was really awake this time by reminding herself that in the dream Lev had been slumbering, warm and solid, at her side; in the waking world, the real world, she was alone.

There was little point trying to go back to sleep after a dream like that; besides, these days, high summer, light inveigled its way into the apartment almost all the time, making four in the morning seem as reasonable a time to get up as seven or eight. Lidiya slipped out of bed. The silence was a soft blanket. In the bed on the other side of the room, Masha and Serezha slept deep and sound, Serezha turned towards the wall and Masha curled around his back, her eyes screwed tightly shut. Lidiya paused for a moment, her hand hovering over the covers, tempted to touch and smooth and comfort. On cue, Masha shifted, turning her head so that her cheek rested against Serezha's back, a small, fretful noise in the back of her throat. Lidiya reached down, stroked the hair back off her face, baby fine and slightly damp. This was something so new to her, this cramped and secret pleasure that sometimes surged up so strongly that she had to close her eyes and clench her fists until it passed. She couldn't imagine it would feel much different if they had been her own children.

Upstairs, in Katya's kitchen, there was a tiny packet of real tea, proper tea, which Ilya had been given by an old student; if ever a time called for it, Lidiya thought, it was now: the dry, gritty horror of the small hours. As she crept past Katya and Dima's bedroom Lidiya paused again, listening and hating herself for it, but inside there was nothing but silence. In the kitchen she put water on to heat, and as she waited for it to boil she rested her arms on the table and her head on her arms. For a moment, staring into the dark behind her eyelids, she thought she might just be able to doze off. Exhaustion came down thick and swift and dark like feathers, the border between waking and sleeping the fine, soft edge of a brushstroke. Lidiya took a deliberate breath; she felt Lev behind her, his hand an inch away from the skin that prickled at the back of her neck. She breathed, settling into the dream she had invited: he walked to the stove, his footsteps silent; he picked up the kettle; he poured water into two cups. He would sit down at the table, then, opposite her, and they would sip their tea and make inconsequential, drowsy conversation as morning stole into the kitchen. Lidiya sat up, her eyes carefully closed. "I miss you," she said, barely even a whisper, her lips sketching the shape of the words.

This was something she did rarely these days. Before the Blockade, Lidiya hadn't realised that imagination was a luxury, one of a million tiny things sloughed off when the body pared itself back to necessities. In January and February she had barely been able to keep a thought in her head for more than a few seconds, let alone conjure up a whole interior world – and she was glad, now, because the world she had swum through in the winter wasn't one that she would have willingly invited Lev into. It wasn't the danger or the discomfort, but the size of it, tight and tough and circumscribed. There had barely been room enough for her in it. In the long exhalation of the summer there was more space for ghosts.

The problem, as Lidiya had found before, was that it was easier to invoke something than to banish it. In the early days after Lev's arrest and her own, following quickly on its heels, that had been welcome: she had had nothing better to do than to summon up Lev's memory and play with it for hours. Now, though, there were things that had to be done: children to dress and to feed, rations to collect, clothes to wash; there might have been space, but there wasn't time for the past to slink, low-bellied, into the present. Forgetting took effort, to deny and to push away, to swallow down and to hold back. By the middle of the afternoon tension had drawn a fine, crimson line of pain down Lidiya's temple, her jaw, the stem of her spine. Lights were too bright, loud noises made her flinch, and her skin felt highly charged and sensitive, a hint of fever. Lidiya was dressing the children for bed after their bath when Katya and Dima came home from rehearsal, and their high spirits felt like they could bruise. When the wind caught the bathroom door and slammed it behind her, Lidiya jumped as if she'd been scalded, and Katya looked up from where she was sitting at the kitchen table, hands intertwined with Dima's, sharp and concerned.

"Are you all right?" she demanded.

Lidiya shrugged. "Fine. Tired. I didn't sleep well." Finding herself compulsively smoothing the crease between her eyebrows, she forced her hands to her sides. Katya looked unconvinced.

"If you want us to take care of the children, while you get an early night – "

"What I *really* want," Lidiya said, too loudly, cutting across Katya, "what I *really* want is a drink."

Lidiya rarely drank alcohol: it had always been the sort of thing that other people did, and when she'd pushed some goosefoot grass into a bottle of vodka to steep, a few weeks ago, she'd had the idea that she was saving it for a gift, or a special occasion. But then the idea had struck her a couple of hours before: surely the perfect way to switch her brain off? Katya looked disconcerted, uncertain whether Lidiya was serious, but when Lidiya reached into the high cupboard and pulled out the bottle, brandishing it like a trophy, Katya gave a smile that was half resignation, half collusion.

"Join me for a glass or two?" Lidiya asked, surprising herself. She had thought that she wanted to be alone; all day she had longed for solitude, but now it felt less like a balm than a burden.

Dima grinned, shaking his head, rising to his feet. "Not me," he said amiably. "You know I don't like it much. I'll put the children to bed, though – leave you two to it." He scooped Masha up from where she was curled on the sofa, herding Serezha towards the door; his ease with them made Lidiya want to smile. When the door closed behind them the whole apartment seemed to settle into a fragile state of calm.

"All things considered, I'd prefer a decent brandy," Lidiya said to Katya, "but you've got to take what you can get."

"Quite," Katya said, tucking her chair closer to the table. Her forehead was furrowed with worry, and she was regarding Lidiya with minute care, as if she were something to be handled.

"For god's sake, stop *fretting*," Lidiya said irritably. She poured herself a glass, lifted it to her lips and knocked it back: it had the fresh, green flavour of the outdoors, cutting through the silky sweetness of the alcohol, and it went down surprisingly easily; the liquid burn streaked down her gullet, setting her aflame. She grinned at Katya, baring her teeth, and slid the bottle across the table like a challenge. Katya, to her credit, didn't hesitate: she poured her own glass, looking only slightly dubious at its murky contents, and tipped it back.

"You want to get drunk?" she asked. There was no judgement in her tone, only curiosity.

"I suppose I do."

They talked little, which suited Lidiya fine. Of the many things for which she had little patience, small talk was one, and she had come to appreciate Katya's own respect for silence. The evening was warm; Lidiya kicked off her shoes and drew her knees up to her chest, wrapping her arms around them. The febrile heat of her skin soaked through the thin fabric of her skirt. From downstairs came the occasional burst of laughter: Dima must be telling the children a story, or playing a game. Lidiya thought, vaguely, that perhaps she ought to step in, make sure he wasn't exciting them too much just before bed – but one night wouldn't hurt. The vodka lit her up from the inside. A series of candles flickered at her knees and elbows, her wrists and ankles. Her spine was liquid but her mind felt clear. The table's edges were sharp, and Lidiya ran her thumb along one of them, confirming its solidity. She realised that this was what she had been seeking in the alcohol, not oblivion, but a sense of the ground firm beneath her feet again.

When Dima came back upstairs his shirt was untucked and his hair disarrayed, evidence of some game too rough for bedtime.

"Are they asleep?" Lidiya asked.

"Masha is. Serezha's reading, he says, but he should be out soon. We were playing the Cat and the Mice – I thought it might wear them out. I always have to blindfold them, though – they're terrible little cheats otherwise." He stretched, raising his arms above his head, waggling his fingers. "I'm going to go across the hall and practise for a bit." Walking to the table, Dima reached for Katya's head and dropped a kiss on the crown of it – then, unexpectedly, did the same to Lidiya, before slipping out the front door. Looking over at Katya, Lidiya found her mouth tilted into a reluctant half-smile.

"He's a delight, that boy," Lidiya said, eyeing Katya narrowly. "If you ever tell him I said that, I will kill you. And it doesn't mean that I don't spend a lot of time wanting to slap him. But still, he's a joy. He lightens everything."

Katya laughed, and pressed her hand to her mouth to hide it. Lidiya wished she wouldn't do that. "Who would have thought," Katya said, her voice low, "a year ago, that we'd be living like this? You and me, Ilya, the children. Dima."

"Peculiar, isn't it? The people I care about most now are the woman who used to stare daggers at me whenever I passed her on the stairs, and two children whose main role in my life was to knock on my door and then run away." Lidiya ran her hand through her hair. "Mind you, your girls weren't like that. Terribly well behaved. Charming, really."

Katya looked up sharply. There was an expression on her face that was almost avid, the idea that someone other than herself had memories of her children. Lidiya felt a tug of empathy: she remembered, shortly after Lev's arrest, trailing after friends of his that she'd barely tolerated when he'd still been around, just for the chance to hear his name mentioned, a reminder that he had been real, once. She filled her glass again, drank it down with grim determination.

"I never thought that I'd be friends with you," she told Katya. The words slid around her mouth, slippery and sweet, the sort of sentimental nonsense Lidiya usually decried. It hadn't been what she'd meant to say; she hadn't meant to say anything at all. Katya raised her eyebrows.

"Is that what we are?"

"I suppose so. What else?"

"I suppose so," Katya echoed. Her expression was unreadable. "I wondered – well, not at the time. At the time I didn't wonder much about anything. But you worked so hard to keep me alive through the winter, when we'd barely said three sentences to each other before that. It wasn't even that I wanted it. Half of the time, I would have been glad not to wake up in the morning. I would have been glad to – to just *lie down*. You wouldn't let me."

"It's complicated," Lidiya said. It had been: a bilious mix of motivations and emotions that she could only now start to untangle. Lidiya had always had a need to win, and that had been a big part of it, the need to beat the Blockade, drag Katya through the winter with her. There had been fear, too, particularly after Elena's death: the emptiness of the building, the weighty responsibility of the children. And there had been that other thing, something that she had never wanted to admit to herself, but it came clearly now, a memory dredged up from early on, perhaps October, perhaps November: Katya's face, shattered with loss, a look of dumb incomprehension in her eyes, and somewhere in Lidiya's guts an icy flame of vindictiveness: *you live through this*, she had thought. *You learn what it's like, after*.

"I used to hate you," she said. Just saying the words filled her with a fizzing, sickish excitement. Katya reared back from the table; she hadn't seemed drunk before, but Lidiya had never seen so clearly the interplay of emotions on Katya's face, shock giving way to a wash of indulgent affection.

"What was there of me to hate?" she asked. The question was so *Katya* that Lidiya's skin blazed with irritation. She set it aside.

"You know, don't you?" Lidiya demanded. She had told herself a thousand times that she was never going to ask Katya this – the whole subject was dangerously off-limits, fenced off behind barbed wire and armed guards and mined ground. The vodka had flattened that, all at once. It seemed desperately urgent now to ask, to know for certain. She stared at Katya with fearsome concentration, watching for the giveaway moment when Katya realised what Lidiya was talking about. It didn't come.

"Know what?"

"About Lev. About what happened to Liova." That was another thing she had sworn she would never do, irrational as she knew it was – she had never spoken his name to Katya, never *since*.

"Of course I know," Katya said, sounding confused. "It was – it was horrible, but it wasn't unusual. So many people – two of my cousins, in fact. A number of my old colleagues."

That wasn't the point. It was impossible that Katya could be so dense. "And Yevgeny?" she asked.

"What *about* Yevgeny?" Katya sounded annoyed now, as if she was being drawn into a game she didn't know the rules of. Lidiya's gaze was locked on her face; she wouldn't say anything further: let Katya work it out. And *there* it was, that spark of knowledge catching light into sudden awareness. Katya's mouth fell open. Even amid the satisfaction of the moment, Lidiya felt an unwelcome twist of realisation herself: Katya really hadn't known.

"How can you know it was Yevgeny?" Katya asked. Her voice had sunk to a whisper, and Lidiya knew that it wasn't just for fear of waking the children: you couldn't talk about these things in full voice. "So many people were – how can you be sure?"

"Because Lev was so careful," Lidiya said. "He was – when we first met, when we were teenagers, he was the devoted Party man. And even when he started to have…doubts, he still knew how to give that impression. At work, he knew how to play the game. But at home, you want to think that you're safe. Even though you know – as you say, there were so many people, and how many of those were informed on by their neighbours, even their families? But Lev – he wanted to believe in it so much, that there was at least one place where he could say what he thought. And believing that was more important to him than – than ensuring he was safe. That *we* were safe."

Katya said nothing. She seemed to be waiting for Lidiya to go on. There was a distasteful good-badness in talking about it, like cutting into a wound to let out the infection. "Just a few weeks before, Lev had had some friends round to the apartment for dinner, some friends who had the same views as he did. They talked – my god, I was frantic for them to be quiet, to talk about anything else. And then as they were leaving – we were at the door to the hallway, saying goodbye – Yevgeny came down the stairs. The way he looked at us – " It had shrivelled Lidiya's heart in her chest. She had known, then, that it had stopped being a question of *if* and become a question of *when*. The day she had come home to find the apartment empty, Lev's papers strewn around, and Lev himself gone, the fact that it had finally actually happened hit her like relief. It had been a long time before she had stopped feeling guilty about that. "They were all arrested at the same time, everyone who had been at our apartment that night. It seemed – " she said, flexing her fingers in illustration, " – *obvious*."

"And you?" Katya asked. Her hands were pressed onto the table, as if she was forcing them into submission; her voice was very still, very flat, stripped of emotion. "I remember afterwards, you were gone for a few days, and I thought – "

"They took me in for questioning," Lidiya said. "And then they let me go. At the time, I didn't understand why. You know how it is – the husband's arrested, and nine times out of ten the wife's deemed to be complicit too. I was *desperate* for them to take me. Even though I knew I wouldn't end up in the same place as Lev, just being in the same *sort* of place would have helped. So I thought. It turned out, afterwards, that one of the NKVD men had been at school with Lev. They'd been friends. He came to see me, months later. Seems he thought he was doing me a favour, persuading the others to let me go. Perhaps it was a favour to Lev. It wasn't a favour to *me*."

Outside, the light had finally started to shimmer and dim. A mosquito whined. Katya struck a match and lit the squat oil lamp on the table. Lidiya wished she hadn't: the conversation had been easier to bear when their faces had been in shadow.

"Did you – did you ever hear from him, afterwards?"

"Two official letters, a month after he was taken, and then a couple of months after that. They were scraps, cut to pieces by the censors. I could barely make anything of either of them. No clue about where he was, of course. The only parts they left in could have been written by anyone, they were so generic. *I am well, I hope you are well.*" She still had the letters, locked away in a case beside her bed, though she rarely touched them any more: with the cheap paper and the holes, she had the sense that they were just a few careless handlings away from crumbling altogether. "And another letter almost a year after he had gone, which he got someone to smuggle out for him. It hadn't gone through the censors, but that was almost worse. His handwriting – it was terrible, shaky and spidery, as if he could barely hold the pen. He said that he'd been ill – typhus, there were epidemics all the time. He – it didn't sound like him, in the letter. As if his mind was wandering." It sickened her to think of it. That letter she kept with her, despite the risk: folded into a square, just so that she could touch something that he had once touched. "And since then, nothing. I kept writing to him – up until the war, anyway. Every week, through the camp authorities. Even if – I know the letters don't reach him."

"Do you think he's dead?" Katya asked.

For a second, Lidiya felt her teeth clench behind her lips; the anger burned out as quickly as it had come. "I don't know. That's the likelihood, of course, whether illness or the firing squad. It doesn't make much of a difference, either way, to be honest. I know I won't see him again, and at the same time, it's not as if his death – or knowing about his death – would *release* me from anything. He's still here." She tapped her head, knowing how crazy it sounded, and knowing, too, that if anyone would understand it would be Katya, the woman who had raced through the burning streets to chase after two girls months dead. "I used to talk to him, too, before the Blockade. Sometimes I could believe in him hard enough that it nearly made it real."

Katya nodded. They regarded one another for a long moment, in the shivering light of the lamp. "Do you want me to say I'm sorry?" Katya asked. From anyone else it would have felt like impertinence; from Katya, Lidiya understood it to be a genuine question.

"I don't know what difference it would make," she said. "Does it help, when people say they're sorry about your girls? Would it help, even if Hitler himself came to apologise?"

"No," Katya said. "But all the same. I didn't know because – because I turned my back on it, on everything outside my own family. And even if I had known, it couldn't have made a difference. But all the same."

"I don't know how I don't still hate you," Lidiya said, wonderingly. "I should. Even if you didn't know, even then, you were still his wife, and you knew what sort of a man he was. I worry, sometimes, that my friendship with you is a betrayal of Lev. It probably is. But I don't know what else I can do, now."

"Perhaps it will be different afterwards," Katya suggested, and Lidiya grinned, swift and sharp.

"You mean, perhaps everything will go back to normal and we'll be able to hate each other again?"

They laughed until Lidiya felt sick. Gasping back her breath, a hand pressed to her chest, she looked at Katya; flushed and damp-eyed, Katya looked back, studying Lidiya's face.

"You know, I used to be so envious of you," she said. The evening felt confessional. As Katya said it, Lidiya felt the truth in every word. *Used to be.*

"I guessed as much," Lidiya said. She sighed. "I've always had trouble with other women. Sometimes for good reason – I know I'm not easy company. But I could never understand – the way I look, it's not something I *do*. If I could change it – "

Katya snorted, disbelieving, and Lidiya inclined her head, conceding the point. "Well, maybe you're right. But did you ever wonder why I went into radio rather than film, or the stage?"

"That just annoyed me even more, back in the day. Looking like you do, and you didn't even have the decency to *flaunt* it?" She smiled. "I have a younger sister, Zhenya, in Moscow. She's always been the beautiful one. The two of you – you look nothing alike, really; Zhenya's dark, and her features are more delicate than yours. But you both – you *wear* your looks like a mantle. Something between you and the rest of the world. It was always so clear to me, from when I was a child, the difference it makes in how the world treats you. And Zhenya – she was always disingenuous. Always denying her own beauty, pretending that I'd been equally blessed. *Oh, Katya, I'm no better looking than you are!*" Katya adopted a high whine in mimicry, then looked ashamed. "She's got a lovely voice, actually. That sounded nothing like her. But it was her pretence – it made me angrier than anything else that she could have done. We ugly women know that we're ugly. To try and convince us otherwise, it's just insulting."

"I don't think you're ugly," Lidiya said. The words felt jolted out of her, neither glib nor patronising, but genuinely considered. "I mean, you're no beauty, that's for sure, and you don't help yourself out, either. Your clothes are terrible, and your hair is even worse – and I'm not just talking about now, when you've got an excuse. Even before the Blockade – would it have killed you to curl your hair up occasionally, or to match your hat to your dress?" Lidiya caught herself; Katya was gazing at her as if she was trying to decide whether to laugh or to slap her. "But you're still not ugly. When you're being yourself, when you're comfortable, then something of you comes out in your face. It's not beautiful, but it makes people want to look at you for longer. I used to see it sometimes when you were playing with your girls in the courtyard, when you didn't think anyone else was watching. And I see it now, with Dima."

"Lucky for me that I managed to find myself a blind man," Katya said, flippant. She tipped her head back and swallowed another mouthful of vodka. Lidiya looked into her glass, clogged with sodden greenery. The bottle was drained to the dregs, though she upended the bottle hopefully over her glass, garnering a trickle.

"Maybe so. But whatever happens with you and him, after the war…"

"He'll find someone else," said Katya. Her words were slightly slurred. Lidiya's own tongue was starting to feel too big for her mouth.

"Perhaps he will. But even if he does, I hope you won't forget the way you are now, the person you are now. It's not him that's made you like this, it's just…brought out something that was already there. And if you stay like this, if this is the person that you are now, no matter what, I might not have to go back to hating you once all this is over."

Katya laughed, but Lidiya shook her head. "Shut up, I'm serious. You – you're good company. And you make me laugh. And no matter what, over the winter, you kept on getting up. Even though you had much less to live for than Elena, you didn't just lie down. Dima's lucky, you know." As she said it, she found that she believed it.

"Lev was lucky, too," Katya said stoutly. She reached over the table to grip Lidiya's hand, and Lidiya, unsure quite how she had got there, found that she was crying, just a little, without feeling like she had much to do with it. Annoyed, she swiped at the tears with the palm of her hand, drew in a breath, flung on her broadest, stagiest grin.

"Luckier than either of us are, at least," she said.

❧

CHAPTER TWENTY-TWO

I: 2 July 1942

In the grounds of the Pioneer Palace, a jazz band was playing. The sound of it was tossed by the summer breeze across the Fontanka: Katya caught the bold blare of horns and the patter of drumbeats, capering on the air. She had always been slightly embarrassed by her fondness for jazz: it was chaotic and raucous and lacked subtlety, and yet there was a pomp and a power to it which she found intoxicating. Dima unabashedly loved it.

"Let's go in!"

Katya was tired. The rehearsal had been a difficult one; after a week of coasting while Karl Ilyich concentrated on the brass section, that day he had focused on the strings, and Katya's arms were trembling with strain. But Dima was hard to resist in the grip of one of his enthusiasms: to start with, Katya had thought that she was humouring him, but gradually she had come to realise that his enjoyment was infectious; she came to feel it, too.

The band comprised a drummer, a double bass, two trumpets and a saxophone. It was unnerving to see so much energy coming from people who looked so thin. The double bass player appeared to be leaning on his instrument rather than holding it upright, yet his hands were in constant motion; one of the trumpeters bent double, his hands on his knees, whenever he wasn't playing, but as unlikely as it seemed, he always straightened up and raised his instrument to his lips again. People stood and watched: young women in summer dresses that hung from their bodies like sails, Red Army soldiers whose smiles covered tired and worn faces, older couples, one or two children; all seemed to regard the band with wonder, as if they were a visitation from another world.

"Dance with me," Dima said, smiling.

"No one else is dancing," Katya said automatically, although she knew by now that arguments of this type never worked with Dima. Besides, it wasn't quite true – on the other side of the small crowd she could see flashes of colour and movement where two of the bolder Red Army soldiers had detached themselves from their fellows and asked two of the girls in the gaudiest dresses to dance.

"Then they'll appreciate it all the more if we put on a show," Dima declared. He handed her his violin. "Put them where you can keep an eye on them." Katya did so, leaving both violin cases near a middle-aged couple, who agreed with a nod to mind them. Dima took her hands.

For a few moments they stumbled, before settling into each other's pace. Dima had a light touch. He danced the same way he did everything involving music: with easy certainty and evident, lavish enjoyment. Katya shouldn't have been surprised, but she was.

"How did you learn to dance?"

"Lyuba taught me. Vasya's girlfriend, you know – or his main girlfriend, at any rate. Vasya was a terrible dancer, she said, and she wanted someone to dance with when we went out, so she made me learn." Experimentally, he extended his arm, and Katya, her body remembering before her mind did, twirled obediently. Feeling her movement, Dima laughed and Katya, a little breathless, joined in.

"I haven't danced since the Conservatoire. Yevgeny wasn't interested." She had forgotten how much she enjoyed it, the rare chance to concentrate more on what her body could do than on what it looked like. A memory hit her like a wave, intense in its physicality: nights out with Natasha and Ivan, drenched in sweat, her feet drumming, the dip and sway of her body, the way she had felt like she contained an entire orchestra. In the sure movements of her feet and the swing of her hips, she had been able to believe that she was good at it. "It was one of the few times that I could…forget myself."

"I was terrified at first," Dima said, "when Lyuba first made me dance in public. I thought I was sure to knock someone over and start a fight. But people mostly get out of your way." He spun Katya again, and, in neat demonstration, a woman nearby snatched her small daughter out of their path. Katya called out an apology, but both the woman and her child were laughing.

They danced through three songs before the band announced that they were taking a break. Katya's whole body felt like it was dissolving; she was amazed that her legs could support her. Dima, too, was shaking. "I couldn't have kept that up for much longer," he said. "It's so easy to forget how we are now, how we can't – " He stopped himself. "After all this is over, we'll go out dancing until dawn."

Katya bit back a smile. It still gave her a small surge of pleasure whenever Dima referred to *after*.

"It's a shame the violin's useless for jazz," Dima went on, musing. "The piano's all very well, but you can't take it with you to a party." His face brightened. "I should learn the trumpet. It's bound to be easy, isn't it?"

"Don't let Trofim hear you say that."

Dima grinned. "There you go. If *Trofim* can manage it…"

They were collecting their instruments when someone called Dima's name: one of the brightly dressed girls was pushing her way through the crowd, towards them.

"Dima! I thought it was you."

"Nina?" Dima sounded uncertain. When the girl took his hand, he smiled with such evident pleasure that Katya drew in a sharp breath. "My god, Ninochka?"

"It's me!" The girl – Nina – laughed. From a distance, Katya had taken her to be just another emaciated casualty of the Blockade; closer, it was clear that her thinness had a seam of strength running through it. The set of her head on her shoulders, the way she held her arms marked her out as a dancer. She was pretty in a sombre way: pale, dark-haired, large-eyed.

"So you're still here," Dima said. "I thought you would have got out before this started, gone to your family."

"No – the ballet school stayed open through the winter, so I thought… well, I don't know. One morning I woke up and I seemed to have stayed, without ever having made a decision about it. We could have used you," she added, slightly accusatory. "The accompanist they brought in to replace you was killed in one of the early raids. We've been dancing to records ever since."

"It never even occurred to me that the school was still open." Dima lifted his arms illustratively: they shook. "Still, I don't know how much use I would have been to you back in December or January."

"We weren't much use ourselves. But you know what Kamilla's like – wouldn't let us stop for anything. We put on some concerts at the Leningrad Front – god knows what the soldiers made of us. We could barely get through two minutes without someone hitting the boards. We told ourselves that it was worth it for the extra rations, but I'm sure we lost more strength than we gained. I was in the feeding centre in the Astoria for two weeks, around the start of February." She carried her thinness well, though, Katya noted, as if she was bred to it – she didn't have that bundled together look of someone who should be heavier than they were, as did Katya herself. "And what about you?" Nina glanced at the violin at Dima's feet. "I see you're playing."

"Ah, yes," Dima said, with a mixture of pride and bashfulness. "I'm playing with the orchestra."

Nina looked thrilled. "Really? The Philharmonic?"

"Not exactly – they're all off enjoying themselves in Novosibirsk, of course. It's the remnants of the Radio Committee Orchestra, and a collection of chancers like myself. But we're rehearsing in the Philharmonic, and…"

"And you'll be playing the Symphony! I bought a ticket a couple of days ago." She had a slightly wicked grin, which transformed her face from its natural solemnity. "That's wonderful. What you always wanted."

Dima nodded. "Yes. Funny how the war seems to have brought that about. Oh!" He coloured a little, reaching for Katya's arm and drawing her forward. "I'm sorry, I should introduce you. Nina, this is Katya – she also plays in the orchestra. I knew Nina before the Blockade…"

"In another life!" Nina said, laughing. She took Katya's hand, giving her a look of friendly curiosity. "I was a student at the ballet school where Dima used to play, before he moved on to better things…"

"A slightly larger ballet school, in this case," Dima finished. "Who *did* all flee the city at the first sign of trouble, leaving me and Vasya to fend for ourselves."

"Oh, and how is Vasya?" Nina turned back to Dima. "Is he – " *Is he alive?* was her obvious meaning, but she seemed reluctant to say it baldly.

"He was killed a couple of months ago. Or I assume he was – he was near Moskovsky Station when it was very heavily shelled. There's been no sign since."

"I'm sorry." Nina looked no more than mildly regretful; it was the sort of news that people had received so often these days that it had lost a great deal of its impact. "And Lyuba?"

"Her parents sent her off to her aunt near Vladimir when the war started. As far as I know she's still there."

"That's Egorka on drums, by the way. I don't know if you…"

"Yes, I thought I recognised his thumping. Give him my best, will you?"

"He'll be done in another half hour or so, if you want to wait?"

Dima shook his head, smiling; his hand was still on Katya's arm, and he squeezed it a little. "We should be getting back. You know how it is – I dance three songs now and I need a nap."

"I'll be seeing you, then. And Katya, good to meet you." She gave Katya a quick smile before turning to slip back through the crowd.

The walk home from the Pioneer Palace was not long; Katya spent it playing and replaying the details of the encounter in her head, examining the way that Nina had looked at her, had looked at Dima, picking it over for nuance and inference. She had a sickish, sinking feeling in the pit of her gut that was depressingly familiar. At her elbow, Dima was silent; only when they were turning into their street did he open his mouth:

"Are you going to tell me what's wrong, or do I have to guess?" His voice was oddly clipped.

"Nothing's wrong," Katya said, aware that her mechanical tone telegraphed the exact opposite.

"All right," Dima said, decisive. Pushing open the door to the building he began to mount the stairs, two at a time; Katya had to hurry to keep up. By the time she reached the landing he was already letting himself into the apartment, and she trailed him into the kitchen, where Masha was helping Lidiya to cook; Lidiya took one look at Dima, then at Katya, and took Masha firmly by the shoulder: "Time for a walk, I think. Let's fetch your brother."

The door closed, and Dima leaned against the edge of the table, arms folded. "Out with it," he said. There was something in his voice that Katya hadn't heard before, a fine edge of anger. She felt obscurely cheated: this wasn't the way it was supposed to go. He should be cajoling, reassuring, and after a while the acid burn in her stomach would cease, she would find she could take a deep breath again, and the storm would blow over. This new stance of his, combative, just made her clam up further.

"I told you nothing's wrong."

"Katya," Dima said dangerously. He looked properly angry now. She said nothing, and neither did he, silent and unmoving. Katya had rarely come into direct contact with the force of Dima's will, but she knew it to be every bit as unbending as Lidiya's, a steel cord of determination that underlay all his customary good humour. It was easier, in the long run, just to submit. She saw again, in her mind's eye, the slightly possessive way that Nina had taken Dima's hand, their ease with one another, the way they had finished each other's sentences, the half-hint of shorthand in the way that they spoke.

"You and Nina. Were you – " She couldn't say the word; Dima had no such compunction.

"Lovers? Yes. A long time ago now, just after I came to Leningrad." He gripped the edge of the table, his knuckles whitening. "For god's sake, Katya, I didn't spring into being just to meet you. Things happened before we knew each other. I have a past, you have to – "

"It's not that!" Katya found that it wasn't. She was still feeling her way, tracing her distress back to its root. She groped for words. "It's that you didn't – you didn't tell her about us."

Dima gave a short, humourless laugh. "You're angry because I didn't tell Nina that we're together?" He sounded disbelieving. "Do you really think it needed to be said? That it's not absolutely staggeringly obvious in – in the way that I touch you, and the way that I behave with you, and in…in *everything*?"

"But the way that she looked at me – " That careful up-and-down, that frank appraisal.

Dima sighed. "Katya. Back when Nina and I knew each other – I used to go to bars, a lot, with Vasya. Parties, too. There were…a lot of women. Nina, too, she had a boyfriend who wasn't supposed to know about me – that drummer, Egorka – and I was – I don't know, I was younger, and I had been at school for so long, and I'd only just discovered that side of life. It still seemed astonishing that any women were interested, that I could – " He passed a hand over his face in evident frustration. "It would be a surprise for Nina to see me with anyone in daylight, especially someone who's obviously more…more *lasting*. And a musician, too – Nina always knew how much that mattered to me." There was a pause, as if Dima was waiting for a reply. Katya wanted to say something, but couldn't even start to think of what. He sighed again. "Did you think that I was embarrassed? Is that it?"

"Yes," Katya said. She couldn't look at him. For a moment Dima said nothing, and Katya kept her head bowed, expecting anger.

"Why are you always so eager to think badly of me?" Dima asked. He sounded pained. When Katya looked up she saw nothing but hurt in his face.

"I'm not!"

"You are. You really thought that I was embarrassed by you, that I would – that I would *deny* you. I don't understand it. I try and make it clear in everything I do, and in everything I say, what you are to me. The way I feel for you – " he said, sketching something in the air with his hands, a globe, a sphere, " – it's so big. It's *everywhere*. I don't understand how you can't see it."

All the anger seemed to have dropped out of him. It was what Katya had thought she wanted – even as a child, scolded by her parents, she had babbled promises and appeals, anything to make them stop being cross with her. But now, this sudden cessation of combat, this softening just made her feel worse, a wrenching tightness in her belly. Her breath hitched, but as Dima reached out to touch her she stepped back, an unconscious flinch. "Stop – " She didn't know what she wanted to say until she said it. "Stop *forgiving me*."

Dima froze, and Katya wrapped her arms around herself. She wanted to double over, she wanted to wail. This was the rotten core of it; this was why, some days, the sun's brightness was a sharp blow to the heart, and all Katya could see when she looked at Dima was what she had lost. "I don't *want* this. I would – I would exchange you for them." She was sobbing now, barely able to get the words out. "I didn't ask for this! I don't *want* to be happy, I don't want them to be gone. *I didn't agree to this*." Her legs felt too feeble to hold her and she sat, abruptly, on the kitchen floor, drawn into a tight knot, hugging her knees. The noises that came out of her sounded inhuman: gulps and howls, a child's tantrum. There was so much of it that an abstracted panic descended upon her: perhaps she would never be able to stop crying; this was how people ended up in mental hospitals. But finally there came a sob that was not immediately followed by another; she collected her breath; a light-headed calm bloomed, which felt in itself like a sort of betrayal. Katya felt faintly nauseated and dangerously weak.

When she lifted her head from her knees she found Dima sitting on the floor a few feet away. There was an expression on his face that looked like relief.

"Sorry," Katya said. She had a sudden urge to laugh: the word seemed very small recompense for what had just happened.

"It's quite all right."

"You should have me carted off to an insane asylum."

"Oh no," Dima said seriously. He seemed unwilling to dismiss this with a joke. "That was necessary, I think. I seem to…I understand a bit better, now."

Katya nodded. It didn't matter that he couldn't see her. "I don't know how to put together then and now," she said, her voice carefully quiet, carefully still. "You and me, it's the thing that I wanted the most when I was younger, before I was married, before Yevgeny. And I only have it, now, with you, because of what – what I lost. And so when I find myself happy, sometimes I feel like I somehow…wished it into being."

"But that's not how it works, Katiusha," Dima said. "You can't bring your girls back by pushing me away. It's not an exchange."

"I know."

"I want you to be happy, Katya," Dima said fervently. "I want it more than I've ever wanted anything. Even music. And when you're happy, my god, you are a joy to be with. You are – you are an *explosion*." Katya laughed, damply. "And I think I make you happy more than I don't."

It wasn't a question, but Katya felt like it needed an answer anyway. "You do."

Dima nodded. "It could have happened another way, you know. You could have divorced Yevgeny. Perhaps he got a big promotion, went off to live in Moscow, and you stayed in Leningrad with the girls. Perhaps the war never happened, and then one day, perhaps, you bumped into me in the street, and I persuaded you I needed you to walk me home." He smiled a little. "It didn't need to be this way."

"But it is."

"It is." Dima inched closer to Katya across the floor, stopping short of actually touching her. "But can we try doing it this way? Can we try to just…start from where we are?"

We meant *her*, Katya knew. She drew a shaky breath, a muddle of gratefulness and resentment. "Why are you so nice to me?" she asked. For once, she found she wanted to know the answer.

"Because when you let yourself – or when you forget yourself, I'm not sure which – there's nobody in the world that's better company than you. I'm sorry that your parents never knew it, and that Yevgeny never bothered to find out. But that's not now, Katiusha. It's not me. And you need to stop turning something that happened to you into something you do. You need to stop tearing open everything good to look for the part that's going to hurt you."

"I don't know if I know how," Katya said. Her voice was very small and very thin. "I've been like this for so long."

Dima leant over and kissed her, gently, on each cheek. It was a chaste, almost old-fashioned gesture. "I don't know either. But I think we can work it out."

II: 5 July 1942

Sometimes a moment came in cupped hands, like a gift. Sunday morning, the air quiet and still, the city like a ghost town, half blanketed in early mist, and the apartment suddenly too small to hold them. Dima was drowsy but pliant, willing to be led – it was an idea that Katya had had a few days before, passing the wrecked building on the corner of the street. Its upper storey was open to the sky, offering a secret opportunity to be outside, without the people that thronged the parks these days, digging their patches of earth, turning spaces that had once been ornamental into places of use. Katya held Dima's hand as they made their way up the shattered steps: she was still training herself to accept that she was allowed to touch him, afforded privileges that others were refused. She worried, briefly, as they climbed, whether the building would hold them, or whether it would make an abrupt, groaning shift and come crashing down, leaving them entombed. But the building held fast. Dima's fingers brushed the walls, feeling for gaps in the crumbled brick and stone, and Katya tried to stop herself from peering into the abandoned apartments. It felt almost indecent, whenever her eyes landed on a curl of wallpaper or part of a fractured table, like spying on someone in their underclothes.

Above them, the sun looked like something that could be plucked out of the sky and eaten, an exotic fruit; its heat was liquid. The view from the roof was fragmented, patchwork squares of concrete and brick. When they sat, Dima's leg was warm against her own, and the morning's heat seeped up through the stone beneath them. Katya looked down at her feet, the scuffed, ill-fitting shoes, the skinny ankles and the frigid white skin below her skirt. The pattern of her dress was bizarrely gaudy, and she couldn't think where it had come from; a present or a cast-off, she never would have bought anything so lurid, and yet somehow it had stayed in her wardrobe over the winter, while more favoured clothes had been sold for whatever scraps of food they could garner, because Katya had liked the colours. It seemed appropriate to wear it, now, a silent announcement.

Dima tilted his head back and rolled his shoulders in a gesture of exaggerated contentment. Katya loved him for his physical freedom, and the way that he had never learned to rein in his body for fear of people making fun. "This is a treat," he said.

"Almost like a holiday," said Katya. That was how it felt. Dima grinned suddenly, fiercely, and an idea unspooled across his face.

"Close your eyes," he commanded.

Katya did so. The day was too pleasant to argue. She could feel the warmth soaking into her, layer by layer, touching skin and sinew and organs and bones that had been chilled for months. The air was like cool, clear water on her lips.

"The dacha is beautiful at this time of year," Dima said softly. There was something tentative in his tone, hoping that Katya would catch on. When she did, she felt that she smiled with her whole body. She kept her eyes closed.

"It's perfect weather for it," she said.

"Tell me what it looks like."

The house rose up in the centre of Katya's mind, pushing its way out of the weed-strangled ground. "It's…it's a little overgrown, because we haven't visited for a while. The brambles are terrible, and the trees in the garden need cutting back. But the house looks sound. The shutters are painted blue, and the paint has flaked off a bit over the winter, but the colour is still strong. It looks cheerful against the wood."

"What's growing in the garden?" Dima asked.

"The sunflowers are up. They look wonderful. They're – the centres are like dark brown velvet." With daring inspiration, Katya took Dima's hand and brushed his thumb gently along the soft skin on her inner thigh. His eyebrows jerked in involuntary surprise. "As soft as that," Katya whispered, her voice humming with laughter. "And their petals are a proud, bright yellow. Soon we'll be able to take the seeds and crack them between our teeth." Just the thought of it made her mouth water. Things had been so much better lately – the increased rations of the orchestra, the food that people were growing in the city – that she barely associated the gnawing in her guts with hunger, so different was it from the vicious demon of starvation that had stalked alongside her throughout the winter, its bony hands wrapped around her heart. Dima's throat clicked as he swallowed, and Katya went on: "There are tomatoes too, and potatoes in the ground. Carrots and…and apples in the trees overhead." It was a fantasy, after all; she could mix the seasons as she wished. "As much food as we could possibly want. We'll stuff our faces with it, and then when we've eaten ourselves sick, we'll pick as much as we can and bring it back to the city with us." Most of the time, they avoided the subject of food as much as possible, but the sunlight gave Katya enough strength to indulge in some delicious torture. "We'll give some to our friends, and I'll pickle the rest. Beetroot, cucumbers, radishes. We'll have enough to eat over the winter."

"Stop," Dima said. He sounded both pained and pleased. "I'm not tough enough for this sort of talk yet. Tell me, what's the weather like at the dacha?"

It's a beautiful, clear day. The words made it as far as Katya's throat and stuck there. She saw again a limitless blue sky and in it, the icy gleam of an aeroplane. Perfect weather would always mean Lychkovo. She pushed the thought away, and instead conjured up clouds. "It's one of those days where the sky's freckled with clouds. Hundreds of small, puffy ones, and a few of those long ones, the ones that look like veils. But the sun can work out a path between them. It's dodging them, so we're always warm, we never have that horrible moment of disappointment when the heat gets sucked out of us because the sun's disappeared. It's perfect." Dima was silent. Katya sneaked an eye open, feeling foolishly as if she were cheating. The vision of the dacha had been so clear in her mind that it was a small shock to see the stone expanse in front of her. Dima was smiling, and she asked, half shy: "Do you see it, when I describe it? In your head?"

"There is something," Dima said. "I don't know if I'm seeing the same thing as you're seeing. I don't even know if it's *seeing*, really, but it's something. Something…good."

"I wish I could see what you do." It was strange to be reminded that she was somehow shut out of his head. It made her wistful.

"It doesn't matter though, does it? The words are what matters, the words and the ideas. It's like…it's like mind reading, isn't it? You have an idea in your head, and you transfer it to me, and I'll never know if it's the same thing that you're thinking of, and you'll never know either, but it's enough. The words are more than enough. They're a gift, as much as if you wrapped them in paper and handed them to me." He leaned a little way towards her, until their heads touched. "What'll we do after we've finished picking all the vegetables and fruit, anyway?"

"Oh!" Katya thought, and invented a lake. She didn't know if she was describing somewhere she'd seen or read about, or making it up wholesale. It didn't matter. "We'll swim. You can swim, can't you?"

Dima nodded, looking offended. "Of course I can! My brothers made sure of that, before I went away to school."

"Good, good. The dacha backs onto the lake, and it's overgrown enough that no one will see us. It's quiet. Only the birds, and the splash of the fish. And the girls…" The words were out before she had thought about them. Katya held her breath, waiting for the pain. Dima's grip tightened on her hand. But when it came, it wasn't the sharp, nauseating jab to the heart that it usually was when the girls slipped into her thoughts unawares. It was something softer, a gentle ache, tugging at her like a tide. She could bear it, a little, just for now. She allowed herself to think about them: the girls as they had been alive, not the fearsome ghosts that had stalked the wrecked city in the winter. "The girls are swimming," Katya said, her voice quieter. She spoke half-dreaming, mesmerised. "They're splashing each other. Tanya's trying to be grown up, but she can't help herself against Nadya. Their hair is all slick down their backs, dark with the water. They look like *rusalki*." She could see them so clearly, the jut of Nadya's jaw as she determined to make Tanya laugh, and the shudder that ran along Tanya's lips as she tried not to succumb.

"Thank you," Dima said quietly. Katya knew what he meant: he was thanking her for allowing him into her family, even if it was only in a story about an imaginary dacha and a scene that had never happened and never would. She thanked him silently in turn, for giving her the space to think about them. Her throat was heavy with tears, but for once she didn't feel as if they were going to tear her apart. It wasn't recovery; it would never be that, but it was a treat unlooked for to be able to think of the girls without despair. Katya hoped she would remember that it had happened, and that it was possible. It was the very least that the girls deserved, to be something that could be remembered with joy.

❧

LYCHKOVO

18 August 1941, late morning: Rybatskoe

The girls were opposite Katya in the carriage. Tanya's back was straight and her heels together as she sat as quietly as she could, her breathing measured, as if she were counting each inhalation, her eyes on the book she held, heavy, in her lap. Nadya was by the window, trying sporadically to emulate her sister's careful posture, but more often distracted by the cascades of colour and movement outside the train window. It was a rare opportunity to examine her daughters' faces unobserved, and Katya noticed the broad bones of Tanya's face starting to come through her childish roundness, a mirror of Katya's own. She wondered what it would have been like to have had a beautiful daughter, whether it would have made her pleased and proud, or simply envious. It didn't matter. Tanya was clever and kind and well-behaved, and beauty was immaterial. It was a fact that Katya could be certain of in the case of her daughter, if not in her own.

At Rybatskoe, the station was teeming with children, behaving more like miniaturised adults than boys and girls of six or eight. Katya couldn't understand where they had all come from; next to her, Yevgeny's expression was so stern that she didn't dare to ask. On the platform, Tanya struck up conversation with a small boy about her own age, perhaps a year or so younger, in rumpled black trousers and a shirt that had once been white but was now begrimed with soot. The two spoke for a moment, their heads bent together, and then Tanya approached her mother, her expression worried.

"Gleb says he's been waiting here for two days. His mama gave him some food for the journey, but he thought it would only take a day, so he finished it all. He hasn't had anything since yesterday. Can I give him one of my apples?"

Katya had packed well, bread and cheese, fruit and pickles, enough for a few days even though Yevgeny had laughed at her for thinking they'd need so much. They could easily spare an apple for Gleb, but what about the other children that surrounded them, their bellies surely taut with hunger? Katya opened the case where she had packed the food, careful not to let them see: some bread, a little cold chicken, a pickled cucumber and an apple; she wrapped them in newspaper and passed the package to Tanya.

"Give this to Gleb, but tell him not to eat it in front of the others. We don't have enough for all of them." Katya waited for Yevgeny to object to her profligacy, but he was silent, and Katya ventured a question: "Is it true, that some of these children have been waiting for days? What's happened?"

"There was such a push to get them out of the city, there haven't been enough trains available to get them further than here. The organisation has been lacking." Taking her by the shoulder, he gave her a brisk shake, smiling. "Don't worry. The trains are coming now – all of these children will be safe in billets by the end of the day."

Yevgeny had a way of speaking with such authority that it seemed impossible that he could be wrong: as if he had created them wholesale, the trains arrived, the children boarded. In the crush, Katya lost sight of Gleb, his wide eyes and his freckled face; Tanya called his name once as he was swallowed into the crowd, but he didn't answer. He would be taken care of, Katya assured Tanya, and hoped it was true, but she couldn't afford to fret about one boy out of thousands: her own children held the monopoly on her love and concern; she had little room for anyone else.

And when the train slid into Demyansk, it looked as if it was going to be all right after all. The train station was mobbed with people wanting to welcome the Leningrad children. Katya had rarely had the chance to see her husband at work, and she felt a sharp throb of pride as he strode down the platform, his limp barely noticeable, to speak to a representative from the local *kolkhoz*. It was a good feeling after the nagging shame that had dogged her for the past few days, telling her that she was a coward for leaving the city. Katya wallowed in it.

"Mama, are we getting off?" Tanya asked. She had got to her feet, clutching the leather hold-all that had been entrusted to her. To keep Tanya happy, all you had to do was give her some responsibility. Nadya's face was pressed against the window, watching her father; Katya, gentle, tugged her back so that her cheek wasn't right against the grimy pane.

"Stay here for now," Katya told Tanya. Nadya looked engrossed in what she was watching, her hand splayed against the glass. "Look, Mama!" she said, her voice breathless with excitement. "Look at all the butterflies!"

Smiling, Katya crossed the carriage to look; the world shifted and resettled. They *did* look like butterflies, and for a split second Katya told herself that her daughter was right and she was wrong, because what she thought she was seeing had to be impossible. "Mama," Tanya said, alarmed and insistent, and Katya knew that Tanya had understood: the parachutes came down, silent and slow, their danger ungraspable. As they watched, a ball of white light rolled through the sky, the sound of it chasing behind: the anti-aircraft guns were firing. Children flooded onto the platform below, the older looking after the younger, their bags flung to the ground with frightening haste. At the sounds of the guns Nadya stiffened, looking over to her mother: "What is it?" she asked. "Is it fireworks?"

"That's exactly what it is," Katya answered, too swift to be believable; although Nadya seemed mollified, Tanya looked at her sharply.

"Mama, you shouldn't lie to her."

Distracted, Katya reached out and ran a hand through her elder daughter's hair, scanning the platform for Yevgeny. When he appeared, his face pushed close to the glass, his expression was as calm and bland as always.

"It's our anti-aircraft guns," Yevgeny said to Tanya, half an eye on Katya. He believed in treating Tanya like the adult she wanted to be, while Katya often made the mistake of treating Tanya like the child Katya wished she was. "They're special guns, designed for shooting down planes. Our army is so strong, you know that all this will be over soon. You don't have anything to be afraid of."

"I'm not afraid," Tanya said, bristling. She sat up straighter, and beside her, without even looking at her sister, Nadya sucked in a breath and straightened her back in unconscious mimicry. The girls taken care of, Yevgeny turned to Katya, lowering his voice: "We can't stay here. The Fascists have cut off the train line. Trucks are coming to take us to Lychkovo, and we'll get out that way." He smiled at her. "It'll be all right, you'll see. They may be fast, but we're faster."

But as he moved away from the train window, Katya made the mistake of watching, and she saw the smile slide from Yevgeny's face, wiping it clean, replaced by an expression Katya didn't think she'd ever seen on her husband's face before. It couldn't be, it was impossible – but if Yevgeny had been anyone else, Katya would have thought that the expression was fear.

IV: ALLEGRO NON TROPPO

VICTORY

CHAPTER TWENTY-THREE

I: 14 July 1942

It's midnight," Katya said. Her voice came soft as a breath, her lips close enough to tickle the fine skin behind Dima's ear. "Happy birthday."

"Twenty-three," Dima said wonderingly, and Katya clicked her tongue.

"Please don't remind me how ridiculously young you are. It's ungentlemanly."

The night was warm, the air at blood heat. A few days before Katya had taken the plywood down and they had moved the bed under the window, to gulp down the breeze that stirred the sheets. Dima found the touch of the soft night air almost unbearably pleasurable. He wriggled a little.

"Imagine living somewhere where the weather was like this all the time. Perhaps we should move to Yalta when this is all over."

There was a pause; Dima waited. Moments like this could sometimes still be tricky for Katya, the implications of *after*. This time she just hummed a little in the back of her throat and moved fractionally closer. "A year ago I would have said I'd miss proper Leningrad winters. Now, I feel like I'd gladly never suffer through another one." She sighed.

"What is it?"

"I wish you could have a proper birthday. With gifts, and a feast…"

For Ilya's birthday in late June, Katya had hoarded her sugar grain by grain, Lidiya had saved microscopic slivers of bread, and Dima had bartered half of his monthly salt ration with a contact of Pavel's to obtain the unlikely gift of a small, stale cake. The feast had been less than half the size of a normal meal a year before, but Ilya had declared himself replete. Dima's own birthday came up too quickly afterwards for them to be able to recoup any surplus in the interim. He found he didn't much care.

"A feast'd be wasted on me. All I really want…" he laughed. "All I really want is to feel *full*. Without that, a little extra sugar or oil doesn't make much difference." He found, now, that he could barely remember how it felt to be really, properly sated, heavy and addled with food. It was the sort of memory from before the Blockade that now seemed so unlikely as to be otherworldly: a time when he hadn't been able to fit his fist under his ribcage; a time when he had left food on his plate because he'd already had *enough*.

"Still," Katya said fretfully. "It was always my favourite thing, with the girls, planning their birthdays." Her voice took on a particular tenor when she spoke of the girls: fine and rare. Their mention was a privilege so recently accorded to Dima that he felt the need to hold his breath.

"When were their birthdays?"

"Tanya's was March, and Nadya's November." She caught her breath. "I was going to buy her a new sled."

Dima didn't move. He had said it himself: sometimes it's best to say nothing. And now Katya didn't draw back, which in itself was progress. He had developed his own ideas of the girls, child-wraiths, illusory and composite, cobbled together from what little Katya told him. In silence, he added an imaginary sled.

Tentative, Katya broke the silence, perhaps realising that Dima was unwilling to do so. "What about when you were a boy, before you went to school? What did your mother do for your birthday?"

Dima snorted. "Oh, next to nothing. There were eight of us, after all – birthdays almost every week, or that's what it felt like." A smile uncurled across his face. "My brothers, though – " It was one of his last good memories before school, before the grinding crunch of the whole world shifting; he'd held it close, buffed it regularly to keep the shine on it. Turning towards Katya, he felt his body move through the heavy air as if it were water. He put his mouth close to her ear. "My brothers knew how to make a birthday special."

II: 14 July 1926

The day that Dima turned seven, his brothers gave him a present. For the length of the summer they had been leaving him behind, and although Dima had only the vaguest idea of what they could be getting up to all day, when they came home they were always tired and sweaty and laughing, often cut and bruised, and Dima was glumly certain that they had been having the most marvellous adventures without him. It had been the same the previous summer, but then he hadn't minded so much staying home with his mother and his sisters, all of whom seemed to regard him as a mingled pleasure and nuisance, to be cuffed and then cuddled in a most bewildering way. This summer, his brothers' abandonment felt like the keenest insult imaginable, and so he couldn't have imagined a better gift on the morning of his seventh birthday than Alik jostling his shoulder, rough and friendly: "Hurry up, put on your boots. You're coming with us."

Dima knew the woods by their smell, sweet and heavy, and the spongy give of the ground under his feet. There were four of them: Grisha, Valya, Alik and himself, trailing at the back of the pack, trying to keep up but too easily distracted by the tantalising noises that crept out of the undergrowth, snagging at him like hooks. Dima had started to insist, a few months before, that he was much too big now to hold Alik's hand when they were out together; as a compromise, he gripped onto Alik's tattered shirt-tail where it straggled out of the back of his trousers, helping him find his way. When space flowered before him out of the dense nest of the trees Dima knew that they had come to the pond: this wasn't new to him, he'd been there once or twice before with one or other of his sisters, tagging along while they pretended to be collecting berries, although such outings always seemed to involve a great deal of giggling and the hum of low male voices and Dima being instructed to sit a certain distance away and *not go anywhere*, they'd be right back. Through the presence of his brothers the pond was transformed: the cool smell of the water and the whispery sound of it tumbling the pebbles on the shore. From the water's edge a cluster of voices greeted Grisha by name, and Dima picked out the threads of two of Grisha's schoolmates, older boys who had never treated Dima with anything other than superior disinterest. He was painfully thankful that Volodya's voice wasn't among them.

"Come on," Alik said. His grubby hand pushed its way into Dima's fist, pulling him along and upwards, and Dima suffered it, just this once. The toes of his boots knocked on something: steps, soft wood, up and up and up and then ahead, smooth and creaking under his weight. The sounds of his footfalls were light and hollow, and the breeze snapped at him more sharply. It lightened the heat of the day, which rose thick off the water and tangled at Dima's ankles.

"Where are we?" Dima asked, his voice low. He was sure he hadn't been to this particular place before.

"It's the jetty, where people tie up their boats for fishing."

Fishing. Perhaps that was what they were going to do: his brothers did sometimes come back in the evenings with fish, smothered all over with a bright, oily smell, soft and smoky on his tongue when their mother fried them up for their evening meal.

"Dima, stop – we're at the end," Grisha warned. Dima froze: he had been well-trained enough by his family to stop stock still when ordered to do so. From around him came the slithery noise of clothes being removed, and then a whoop and a splash: Valya.

"Now you take your clothes off," Alik said.

"Why?"

"Because we're going swimming." Alik took Dima's hand and pushed it against his own bare chest in demonstration. "See, we're all doing it."

"But I don't know how to swim," Dima said, his voice a little small. He was fairly uncertain as to what swimming actually was, but he knew that it involved a great deal of water, and he wasn't sure he liked the idea of it – he certainly didn't enjoy it when his mother tipped buckets of water over his head to wash his hair, how it smuggled its way into his nose and his ears and deadened the outside world.

"That's why we're here," Alik explained, with exaggerated patience, "so that you can learn."

"Get a move on," Valya called from somewhere below. He sounded bored and fractious.

"At least take your boots off, Dima," Alik entreated. Dima shut his mouth, mulish. He was so easily won over by inclusion, but sometimes he wished he did a better job of remembering that his brothers' surprises rarely ended well: a request for him to hold out his hands as often as not resulted in something slimy or scratchy or angrily alive being placed into them, his brothers laughing as he yelped.

"Right then," Grisha said, decisive. The next thing Dima knew there were hands under his arms, another set of hands under his knees, lifting him. Knowing from bitter experience that there was no use in struggling Dima did so anyway, silent and squirming like an eel, but the battle was short-lived as he was swung once, twice and then let go – a second or two of impossible freedom, cushioned on all sides by air, and then water exploded around him.

It was like being thrust into another world. Things like *up* and *down* didn't mean anything any more; his limbs may as well have been detached and reassembled in an utterly different order. When he opened his mouth his shout escaped in a bubble; his clothes swirled around him; for a brief, blissful moment his head broke the surface and the sun smacked down on his wet hair, he heard the bark of one of his brothers yelling and then he was under again before his brain had processed what he had heard Grisha say: *kick*. Dima kicked. His boots were heavy on the end of his legs but he found himself propelled upwards, forwards, his face out of the water again and he was prepared enough this time to catch some air in his mouth before going under. He moved his arms now, thrashing them as if trying to dig through the water around him and his body moved too, awkward and jerky but affording him another gulped breath. His brothers' voices came to him now, stretched and distorted by the hiss and growl of the water: thrusting his arms above his head Dima felt a violent surge of joy and relief when hands gripped his wrists, pulling him up and out, and then he was back in the air again, choking on its luxuriant availability.

"Reach with your feet," Alik said. "It's shallow here, you can stand."

Dima found that Alik was right. Wet stones slipped and clicked beneath the soles of his boots as he stumbled after his brother out of the water, up to the shore. Subsiding onto the damp grass, he couldn't stop coughing, and then his belly heaved as he vomited a cool stream of pond water, while Alik on one side and Grisha on the other made noises of good-humoured disgust.

"Look at the state of his boots," Grisha said resignedly. "Mama's going to kill us." He didn't sound overly worried at the prospect.

Dima spat. His mouth tasted horrible, and his chest was making an upsetting bubbly, dragging sound, but he managed to gather enough breath to speak, his voice coming out scratchy and muted. "Was that swimming, then?"

Grisha laughed. "Well. Sort of."

"Sorry we had to chuck you in like that," Alik said, transparently unrepentant, "but that's how you learn. Grisha did it to me – "

"And Valya did it to me, and I suppose Stepan did it to him," Grisha concluded.

It was the tragedy of being the youngest, Dima understood, that he would never get the chance to fling an unsuspecting younger brother into a pond, half drowning him in the process. Perhaps that was why people had children of their own.

"I did it though, didn't I?" he asked. "A bit, anyway." His body remembered, as it sometimes did, the way it had felt, pushing upwards through the water towards the air, the way the water had thinned and warmed, and the sudden possibility of moving in a different way.

"You know, people can't see well underwater," Alik said casually.

"Really?"

"No. Some people can't even open their eyes underwater, but even if you can, you can't see much."

Dima contemplated this. His shirt was cold, plastered against his back, and he started to undo the buttons. "I suppose there's not much to smack into underwater, is there?"

"Not much," Alik agreed. Dima bent to tug at his sodden laces.

"Let me try again."

~

Grisha was right: all four of them went to bed that evening with the backs of their legs smarting from the birch rod their mother used when she was particularly angry; even Grisha's insistence that Dima's boots would be perfectly all right if they were left in the sun for a day did little to mollify her. Dima's skin felt tissue-thin under the rough blanket, and he couldn't stop running his fingers over the hot welts on the back of his thighs. Next to him Alik shifted, managing unerringly, as he always did, to jostle all the tenderest parts of Dima's body with all the sharpest and boniest parts of his own. Dima made a noise, half whine, half grumble, under his breath, enough to telegraph his annoyance to Alik without risking waking anyone else.

"Your hair smells like pond mud," Alik whispered. Dima failed to muster much by way of indignation – the unfamiliar sensations from swimming were still too new to him, his body glutted with them: the ease of it, the way that the water had parted to let him through it. He hoped their mother wouldn't still be so angry that she would stop them from going back to the pond the next day.

"I was a pretty good swimmer by the end there, wasn't I?" Dima whispered.

"You weren't bad." Alik shifted again, shrugging an arm over Dima in a casual sort of hug. "Good birthday, then?"

"Good birthday," Dima agreed. "Thanks."

III: 14 July 1942

They were done, now, the summer concerts, and all that remained in front of them was the Symphony, nearly four weeks away, a prize and a goad at once.

"Now the hard work really starts," Daniil said gloomily. They had all begun copying out their parts by hand, the civilians offering to take on the work for the Crew – all but Dima, who would be reliant on memory, learning his part from Katya as she practised. He had promised that he could do it, back in March, and in the ensuing months he had the sense that the rest of them had stopped doubting him, which meant that this was certainly no time to start doubting himself.

Daniil had been right about hard work; Dima had thought that it had been tough before but there was another side to Karl Ilych now and to Genya, and to all of them, a bitter determination that they would get this right. By the end of the rehearsal Dima's arms were shaking more than they had since the spring, and he felt liquid with physical exhaustion.

"What a birthday present for you," Marina said ruefully, but she didn't understand: this work, hard as it was, had a keen edge of pleasure that Dima couldn't ignore. Katya had told them all that it was his birthday, which gave him a kind of pleasure stippled with embarrassment. Circumstances aside, he could hardly have designed a day better. He had slept late, waking from a dream of music so rich and lush that his body had felt dense with it, sodden. At breakfast, when Lidiya had passed him his morning portion of bread he had been certain that it was slightly larger than usual, and Masha had even managed a present, pressing a piece of paper into his hand: "It's a drawing of you and me and Serezha and everyone." Serezha, standing behind Dima's chair, had leaned in to whisper in his ear: "She doesn't understand that you can't see it," he said confidentially, as Dima thanked Masha with grave enthusiasm; he had developed a particular soft spot for Serezha now, a nervy, awkward boy, lacking Masha's ingenuous charm and therefore more of a challenge to love. Outside, the day was full of the clean smell of sunshine, seagulls calling to the breeze, and throughout it all the still, cool presence of Katya beside him, a gift so unlooked for it seemed almost magical. When he had told her, last night, about his seventh birthday, swimming and his brothers and the chill clasp of the pond, she had listened in silence, but as he spoke his half-whisper into the dark her face was so close to Dima's own that he could feel her smiling. At moments like that it felt like the bitterest injustice that they hadn't always known each other, that there had been nearly twenty-three years in his case, and thirty-one in hers, that they had missed of each other's lives.

"If I had met you when I was seventeen…" he said, foolish and unthinking, and Katya put her hand over his mouth.

"When you were seventeen, I had a two year old and a baby," she said. It was nearly a misstep, but somehow, impossibly, it wasn't. "It could only be like this now."

IV: 14 July 1936

"You must grow your hair," Lyuba said. Dima felt her fingers, the tips calloused, her nails sharp as glass, thread their way into his hair, scratching his scalp. He shuddered a little with reluctant pleasure. "You look like you're just out of prison. You're a good-looking boy, but with that hair you just look – too thin."

"Semi-criminal," Vasya suggested.

"You'd know," Dima quipped.

Vasya's laugh was soft-edged, lazy. He gave no indication that he minded his girlfriend handling Dima in this over-intimate manner. Dima wasn't sure whether he should be relieved or insulted that Vasya evidently didn't see him as any kind of a threat.

Vasya had never tried to hide the fact that he liked women. He had a library of opinions on the smell and the shape and the taste of them, which he would expound to Dima in the evenings when he was feeling voluble and expansive. Dima himself had no strong views on the matter, and was indeed mildly alarmed to find that he had no strong views on women at all. The girls at school had been kept strictly separate from the boys; it was the most they could hope for to sometimes hear the girls' voices over the yard fence, when the wind was blowing the right way, and although Dima had been happy enough to join in the obligatory bawdy talk, he had always suspected that the other boys were just as inexperienced as he was, and their boasts as much fantasy as his own. Sex Dima understood: he knew the mechanics of it, as unlikely as they seemed, and he was certainly no stranger to sexual desire. Many of the boys at school had come to pragmatic arrangements for dealing with matters, nocturnal fumblings or misplaced hands in the shower, and Dima hadn't stood aloof from that – but these excursions had been nothing more than scratching an itch or yawning when tired, a practical response to a physical need. Women were something different. He knew that he was supposed to desire them, but he didn't know how. When he had been seven years old, his mother had hugged him goodbye when he started school, and aside from occasional, perfunctory contacts with teachers and nurses, that had been the last time he had been close to a woman before he came to Leningrad. But now there was Lyuba, who was always adjusting his collar or smoothing his hair or kissing his cheek in greeting, trailing the scent of hot skin and cigarettes. There was the ballet school where he worked, the breathless heaves and grunts of the women as they launched themselves into complicated series of movements he couldn't begin to imagine, the heavy tap of their shoes on the floor, and the slide of fabric on skin as they shrugged on cardigans, pulled on shoes, tugged up stockings. There was the smell of the room when Dima came back to it after Vasya had been there alone with Lyuba (or Oksana, or Anya, or any number of other women whose names Dima had forgotten), the sweet-tartness of perfectly ripe fruit. It unsettled and disconcerted him.

Alone that night, Lyuba gone, Dima found himself rattled, discomfited, almost angry with Vasya and Lyuba, although he knew he had no real reason to be. Vasya, in turn, was unusually quiet, and the air felt somehow thunderous with expectation that Dima wanted to shrug off.

"Dima…" Vasya said at last. He sounded hesitant, bordering on shy. Dima had rarely heard Vasya use this tone of voice before, and it made him even more uneasy.

"What?"

"Have you ever fucked a girl?"

Dima sighed. This was the question he had been dodging ever since he moved in with Vasya. He considered a lie, and then reluctantly abandoned it, certain it would never stand up to Vasya's merciless scrutiny in one of the few areas in which he considered himself an expert.

"No, I haven't."

"Why not?"

"I haven't really had much opportunity, have I? Until a couple of months ago I was stuck in a school with hundreds of other boys all year. The only women I've been near since I was a kid have been teachers and nurses, and before you ask, no, I never thought about trying it on with any of them."

Vasya was silent. Dima could practically hear him thinking. Vasya wasn't a particularly clever man, but he had a peculiarly enviable straightness of thought and logic.

"Would you like to, though?"

"Of course I would!" Dima snapped. At least, he thought he would. He wasn't quite sure, and he had no idea how he could make something like that come about, anyway.

"Because one of the ballet dancers at the school where you work – she's friendly with Lyuba."

Oh. Dima hadn't realised that this conversation had been anything more than idle speculation and a possible precursor to mockery. "What does that have to do with anything?" Dima asked, although he knew quite well.

"This girl – Nina, I think her name is – she likes you. Thinks you're handsome. She was asking Lyuba about you, whether she thought you'd be…interested."

"And she knows about…?" Dima waved a hand illustratively in front of his face.

"Of course she does, idiot. She sees you every day at the ballet school. Doesn't care, apparently."

Dima was still struggling to unravel it. He hadn't realised until just this moment the extent to which he'd accepted the disability of his blindness, assuming that it cut him off from all sorts of things that others accepted as their due. The idea that this might not be so was a little frightening.

"Is she…" He wasn't sure that this was a question he should ask, but forced himself to ask anyway. "Is she pretty?"

Vasya barked with laughter. "What do you care?"

"I don't, not really. But it's the principle of the thing."

"Well…yes, I suppose she is. Not my type, you know I like blondes and tits, but she's not bad looking, Nina. Dark hair. Nice face. Slim."

Dima had no idea what that meant, but Vasya's approval counted for something.

"So I thought maybe we could ask Nina along when we go out for your birthday" – it was a celebration that Dima hadn't asked for, but which seemed compulsory: a bar, vodka, the usual – " and afterwards

I could go back to stay at Lyuba's. Her roommate's going to be away. You and Nina could have the place to yourselves, and…" Vasya's voice trailed off in insinuation. Dima's skin was crawling a little: there was something essentially humiliating about Vasya and Lyuba arranging this tryst with the mysterious Nina, and Dima had a vision, suddenly, of laughing in Vasya's face, telling him that he hardly needed his help to find a woman. And yet he undoubtedly did.

"I suppose…"

"Don't sound too enthusiastic!" Vasya's voice had an edge of sharpness. He evidently felt that he was doing Dima a favour, possibly in lieu of a birthday gift, and that Dima was showing insufficient gratitude. Anger flared inside Dima, and was almost instantly extinguished. He wished fervently that he didn't owe Vasya as much as he did, and he wished, too, that Vasya wouldn't keep being so unfailingly decent about it.

Every nerve in Dima's body was taut and tingling. He told himself he had no need to be nervous, Nina was just a girl. But she was *a girl*, and he was alone with her, and Dima was certain that he was about to make a terrible, crashing fool of himself, and his only recourse would be escape: the apartment was only on the first floor, he could probably make it out of the window if he had to. He had drunk as little as he could get away with, in order to be on the best form possible, but was starting to regret it: drunker, he might perform less well, but at least he'd *care* less.

Nina was making tea. Dima had offered, but she had said she'd do it, and Dima's nerves were too jangled to insist, the way that he normally would when he thought someone was babying him. He sat quietly, listening to the domestic sounds of spoon on cup, the scraping of the sugar, the flare and whorl of the flames from the gas ring licking the bottom of the kettle.

"Here," Nina said. Her voice was a little countrified, her accent rural and somehow familiar. Dima remembered that Kirill from school had spoken in a similar way, and he wondered if Nina was from Kharkov, too.

He considered asking, and then thought better of it. Polite conversation had no place there.

Nina placed the cup in his hand, and Dima thanked her. Unthinking, he took a sip and swore as he burned his lip. *Idiot,* he told himself silently, *you are the biggest idiot who has ever lived.* Leaning down to place the cup at his feet, Dima expected Nina to laugh at his clumsiness, turn on her heel and walk out. She didn't. Instead, she placed one of her fingers on his lip, where he'd burned himself. Dima stopped breathing.

She was close enough that he could smell the warm animal scent of her hair. It was somehow galvanic, and Dima understood, in a rush, what Vasya had been fumbling to find the words to explain. Her fingertip on his lip was soft. He could feel every loop and curl of her fingerprint. "Did you hurt yourself?" she whispered.

Dima couldn't speak. He made a noise that was half cough, half whine, and the very sound of it brought blood and heat rushing to his face. He was starting to understand that this whole experience was going to be balanced on a knife-edge between crushing embarrassment and impossible excitement. Nina laughed, but it was a gentle, friendly sound. There was no mockery in it.

"Are you feeling shy?"

Dima's tongue abruptly loosened. "I'm sorry, you must think I'm a complete dolt, it's just that…" *That what?* Although he knew that Nina knew that he had never done this before – he had considered asking Lyuba to invent a whole romantic history for him, but had thought better of it – the idea of actually opening his mouth and saying that in so many words was inconceivable. Nina only increased the pressure of her finger against his lips.

"Hush," she said. Dima sensed that she meant to sound seductive, and ended up sounding motherly instead. It didn't matter: Dima hushed. She moved her finger along his lip, tracing the lines of it, moving up along his cheek and then down his jawbone. "You're so beautiful," she said softly. "I knew the first time I saw you. I said to Lyuba, *he's the one that I want.* I don't care that you can't see. I can see you."

Nina's fingers moved to his chest, freeing button from buttonhole, *pop, pop, pop,* from his collar to his belt. Dima's shirt hung open, and Nina pushed her hands below his vest, her palms flat against his stomach. For a moment she didn't move. Dima could feel nothing but the warmth of her body pouring into his through the flat pads of her hands, the splay of her fingers. When she moved back, Dima felt such an acute sense of loss that he could have wept, but she didn't move far. He heard the hiss and rustle of fabric as she lifted her dress over her head, like dry leaves falling. He smelled the perfume that she had dabbed between her breasts, cheap synthetic violets, and more intoxicating than that, the smell that came from under her arms and between her legs, hot metal and grass combined. He had never felt like this before, a desperation that was beyond excitement, nearly painful. He had never felt so conscious of the great length of him, too tall and too thin, his cock hard in his trousers, his hands quiescent by his sides. The music in his head had stilled for the first time Dima could remember. The silence that replaced it was exquisite.

He could feel her on the air, the way that it changed its shape when her shadow fell over him. The mattress heaved and rocked as she climbed onto the bed, her thighs straddling his. The weight of her pressed down upon him. Dima closed his mouth on an involuntary groan, and it whistled through his teeth. Nina rocked herself back and forth against him, gently, as if she were rocking a child. She hummed something low, under her breath and tuneless. Her hands fell on either side of his chest, and her hair trailed against his belly. Dima was sure he had never felt anything so soft. When she kissed him, he opened his mouth to her instinctively, a man drowning, and she laughed again, the same warm sound flooding into his mouth and down his throat. She ran her tongue against his lips, top and bottom, and barely knowing what he was doing, Dima caught her lower lip between his teeth, holding it firmly for a moment before her squeak of pleased surprise made him let go.

"So, it's like that, is it?" She sounded gratifyingly breathless as she sat back, taking Dima's hands in hers. "Touch me," Nina demanded. His hands fell on her waist, his fingers moving downwards and then upwards, explorative. Her skin was so fine it barely felt like skin at all. It was like running his hands through water. She was the shape of a violin, and Dima was determined, suddenly, to coax music out of her.

~

Nina was long gone by the time Vasya came home the next morning, scrubbed and cheerful after a night at Lyuba's. Dima could hear the grin that he knew must be plastered all over Vasya's face.

"So? How was it?"

"Mmph," Dima replied. It wasn't something he could put into words, or at least not the sort of words that Vasya would appreciate. Every inch of his body was still vibrating with the golden, glittering certainty of a perfect major fifth. He couldn't stop thinking of what Nina had done, what *he* had done, and how it had all felt – a heady tumble into sensation, intoxicating as vodka, but joyous rather than frightening. As Nina had touched his body he had been filled with a series of unlikely memories: cool water over his hands as he dipped them in the stream by his parents' house; the curiously clean smell of new snow; the sound of his name in his mother's mouth. Dima couldn't imagine how to parcel all of that up into a few feeble words and hand them over to Vasya. "*Mmmph,*" he said again, with some emphasis. Vasya laughed, catching his meaning.

"That good?"

"That good."

"How many…?"

Dima raised four languid fingers in Vasya's approximate direction.

"Four times! Good going."

"Well…" Dima felt he owed it to Vasya to be scrupulously honest, recalling his somewhat abortive first attempt. "The first one didn't really count." He felt his face flush, which seemed terribly unjust. He hated it when his face did that; it wasn't like he needed to be on a still less even footing when it came to knowing what other people were thinking. Vasya snorted, not without sympathy.

"It happens to the best of us, Dima." His hand came down heavily onto Dima's shoulder, somewhere between a slap and a caress. "Happy birthday."

V: 14 July 1942

The rest of the household had gone to bed when Katya took his hand in the soft, warm darkness. "I have a birthday present for you," she said.

Dima had caught the edge of it all evening, her tentative excitement, the sense of something suppressed. He didn't know what to hope for when Katya sat him down at the kitchen table, where the air still held the scent of the evening meal: wheatgrass boiled up with a few scraps of indefinable meat. Dima waited. He realised his heart was hammering, an exquisite mix of anxiety and excitement; on the other side of the room, near the stove, something clinked, and something else rattled. Then Katya was beside him again, placing something on the table with fastidious care.

"I wanted to give you something for your birthday that no one would have given you before," she said, her voice low and a little hesitant. "And I remembered what you said to Serezha that day – the day Masha did her play. So I wanted to give you colours."

Dima found he couldn't speak; he couldn't think of anything he could possibly say. He heard Katya's hands busy on the table in front of him, and then rising to hold something under his nose: the sweet, delicate scent of pine. He wanted to bury his face in it.

"This is green," Katya announced. "*Zeloniy.*"

Dima took a deep breath, cleared his throat. "I see," he said. His tone was neutral, and Katya rushed to explain.

"I know that you can't see them like I do, but I wanted to give you, to show you what the colours are to me..."

"I understand," Dima said. He laid his hand on her face, swift and sure. Her cheeks moved as she smiled. Dima could feel the minute tremble of her lips; it filled him with an indescribable tenderness. He had never known that it would hurt, to feel so much for someone. "Keep going."

She opened his hand, palm upwards, and placed into it feathery strands of grass; then his finger was placed on the silken surface of a leaf. Dima couldn't remember the last time he had touched an object just to be touching it, rather than as a way to work it into his understanding of the world. He had to concentrate, he had to remember this.

"Open your mouth," Katya instructed. She placed something on his tongue: a torn mint leaf, the richness of its flavour hitting the back of his throat and making him gasp.

"I wish I could have brought the orchestra here," she said, "but for me, green is an oboe."

For light blue, she gave him water, running his hand along the ripples in the top of a bowl. It was the cool night air on his face as she made him lean out the kitchen window; it was the middle notes of a piano. Red was a taste of the paprika that she had saved for seasoning, which made him draw back and swear, laughing, with the shock of it. It was the hum of a cello, and the soft scratch of felt in his hands. Katya offered him purple with a spray of some violet scent he had never known her to wear, and the touch of something deep and rich, the velvet at the collar of a dress she used to perform in. Brown was thick, scented earth from the courtyard, and Dima held it in his hands like something living. Yellow was the fragile warmth of a candle flame, a fingernail scraped along the smooth, bubbled paint along the windowsill. "I wanted to give you butter, for yellow," Katya said, and Dima nodded.

"This is enough," he said. "This is more than enough." He knew he could never make her understand, but he felt compelled to try and to try and to keep trying, with words that felt as clumsy as fists. Reaching out his hands, he touched again the grass, the earth, the supple give of the velvet. He had to remember this; it was vitally important he file it away in the same part of him where he kept his maps and his music. This was Katya, right there in this tiny, perfect gesture; this was why when he thought of her sometimes he felt dizzy with gratitude. "I don't think anyone – " His voice faltered. He started again. "No one has ever thought about anything so much, for me."

The fabric of her dress shivered against his skin as Katya leaned forward, pressing her lips against the pulse at the base of his throat. Dima's heart felt oddly swollen, almost uncomfortable, and he remembered with sudden, shocking clarity: this was what *sated* felt like.

CHAPTER TWENTY-FOUR

I: 1 August 1942, afternoon: Ulitsa Pravda

Another hour should do it," Marina said, knuckling her eyes and stretching. She was bent over the table, a sheaf of paper under her elbow and her fingertips ink-stained. Across the table Katya looked up from her own work, shrugging her hair out of her face.

"How come you're so much faster? I've barely started on the third movement."

"This is the fourth one I've done," Marina said. "You get used to it after a while."

"I could finish – " Trofim started, uneasy, but Marina shrugged him off.

"Don't be silly. I'm far quicker than you would be. Besides, you don't want the handwriting to change halfway through."

They had shared it out, the orchestra's civilians, the work of copying out the score, as it was generally accepted that the Crew had enough to do back at the Front without taking this on, too. Marina had proven both quick and neat, and so had taken on the work of others who were slower and sloppier; it was Trofim's own part she was copying out now, while Katya was working on the score for one of the trombonists, and Trofim had agreed to wait behind after rehearsal until they were ready. Practicality was the excuse, but the real reason, Trofim knew, was the lure of the apartment – Lidiya, yes, closeted in the bathroom washing the children's clothes and treating Marina with ill-disguised but lazy hostility – but more than that; the voices of Serezha and Masha playing in the bedroom, Dima pacing the floor, his hands alive on the fingerboard of his violin, practising in silence, and the still, warm air of somewhere that was a home, even though it wasn't his. It lulled him, his head against the back of the chair, his arms loose at his sides. If Trofim closed his eyes he could imagine himself out of his uniform, imagine himself into this life, as if it were a costume that he was trying on for size.

"You're quiet today." The voice was Dima's; Trofim opened his eyes to see Dima dropping into the chair next to his own, hauling up his violin case and putting his instrument away. There was something mesmeric about Dima's hands at work, deftly loosening the hairs of the bow, cleaning the rosin from the strings. Out of the edge of his eye Trofim caught Katya watching him too; at his glance she turned away, flushing, hiding a smile.

"I'm always quiet," Trofim said. It was nice just to be able to *say* that sometimes, without any need for bluster or bravado, without having to brace himself against anticipated insult. Dima grinned, shrugging.

"I suppose so. Katya would say it's because I never give anyone a chance to get a word in…"

"True," Katya said, her eyes on the score.

Dima waved a dismissive hand in her general direction, and without preamble asked: "So how is it, out there?"

How is it? It was a question that Trofim was asked rarely enough, and one that he never knew how to answer. He had listened as Vadim, talking to some of the more attentive women of the orchestra, had played up the danger and the bravery with a studied sang-froid; there was no need to do that here.

"Boring, a lot of the time," Trofim said at last. "Nothing much happens, for days and days and days. And then suddenly, just when you're starting to relax – "

"Do you still get scared?" Dima asked. It was a boy's question; the look on Dima's face showed that he knew it. Trofim was silent; he needed to decide how he felt before he could tell anyone else about it.

"I have a friend," he said at last, evasive; Trofim rarely mentioned Sasha, with a rigid certainty that his place was the battlefield, not the concert hall, tracking his way over it in his muddy boots. "My friend – he says that it's not that he wants to die, but he can't see as how it would make much difference either way."

There was a careful pause. Then: "He sounds like a bit of an idiot, your friend," Dima said cheerfully. From the table, Katya made a noise that could have been the start of a laugh; when Trofim looked up, even Marina was smiling. He knew, he had known even before he spoke that it was the sort of thing that sounded much better in his head, in Sasha's voice.

Trofim had grown up in an apartment like this – the two rooms shared with another family, of course; only people with some clout with the Party got places like this to themselves. It was dislocating, the similarity; Trofim half expected to see his father sitting in the corner, one sleeve pinned up over his abbreviated arm, toying restlessly with his pocket trumpet in his other hand. He had never played at home, and Trofim hadn't been allowed to either: his mother's flute had been just about acceptable, but the thinness of the walls meant that the trumpet was absolutely out of bounds. Trofim had stayed behind at school to practise, and hearing his father play was a treat that was accorded to holidays, out at the dacha that they shared with Trofim's mother's family, when Trofim's father would allow himself to be coaxed into offering a tune or two. It had made Trofim's heart hurt, the sound that his father had drawn from his instrument, small as it was and modified for a one-handed player; his father had never let him watch too closely, saying that he didn't want Trofim to pick up bad habits, but there had to be a trick to it, Trofim knew, because the sound that his father made was bright as gold and smooth as honey, and if only his father would show him then perhaps Trofim could play like that too. It had made his bones crack with wanting.

"When I was a boy," Trofim said, the words taking him by surprise, "during the school holidays, my parents used to send me out onto the street to practise." Beside him, Dima seemed to be sitting unusually still, like a country child not wanting to frighten away a wild animal come unexpectedly close. Was it really so rare for him to talk unprompted?

He closed his eyes again, tilting his head back. The only sounds were the scratch of Marina and Katya's pens from the table, and the distant clang and clatter of Lidiya in the bathroom. "It was far too loud for me to play in the apartment, of course. The family we lived with would have loathed us." It was a gift unasked for, when words came as easily as this; there was a temptation to make the most of it, to keep speaking until his mouth bled or his words ran dry, whichever came first. His untrustworthy tongue never seemed to matter so much at the Front, where he was probably best off keeping quiet in any case; he could never think of much he wanted to say out there, not even to Sasha. But the other musicians seemed to speak so easily – Dima, of course; there was barely anyone in the orchestra who didn't have chapter and verse on most details of Dima's life – but Marina, too, and even Katya; Trofim could have listed any number of facts about either of them: the names of Marina's sisters, the pieces that Katya had played for her graduation recital from the Conservatoire. What did any of them know about him? He imagined how it would feel, a blossoming or an unfolding. It would bring them back, a little, his parents and his sisters, vanished into the cold vast land on the other side of the Blockade. And just like that: it stopped, seized up, somewhere in his chest or in his throat. He couldn't say anything more.

"You should play something," Dima said idly. Trofim opened his eyes. At the table, Marina had turned towards them, her face open and pleased.

"Yes, Trofim, you should! Do you know, I don't think I've ever heard you play anything?"

She hadn't; he knew that for certain. As their energy had returned, many of the other musicians had started to show off, playing for one another or doing the sort of ostentatious solitary practise that was intended to be overheard – but not Trofim. It was part of the pact that he had made with himself, when the rehearsals started, taking to heart advice of Sasha's in a way that Sasha never would have intended: it was a job, nothing more. But he was *good* at it: he knew that with a gut-deep certainty, in the same way that he knew that he was an indifferent soldier at best – and suddenly, surgingly, that was what he wanted more than anything else he could think of: just to feel simply, indisputably *good* at something. Trofim opened his trumpet case and took out the instrument, taking care not to look anyone in the face. Standing, he lifted it to his lips; as he drew in breath, time felt suspended and provisional.

It was the Cadenza from the first movement of Haydn's trumpet concerto. As the first notes slid into the air, Trofim sensed – rather than saw – Dima sit up straighter. At the table, Katya laid down her pen and looked up; Marina beamed. It was the first piece that Trofim had ever played in public, at a concert when he was ten or eleven, and when he had opened his mouth to introduce the piece he hadn't been able to get the words out, not even close; his tongue lay like a dead thing in his mouth and his breath started to come in whistling gasps. It had been supposed to be the proudest moment in his life and yet he could feel it, second by second, ticking away into cringing humiliation. In the audience, a movement caught his eye: his father, waving – but not waving, gesturing something, his hand coming up to his mouth, fingers depressing invisible valves. *Start playing*. And he had. The music had come tumbling out of him, clear and bright and *right* – too fast, true; he had stumbled over some of the more complex passages, but he had done it, and when he had come to the end he had closed his eyes, taken a breath and spoken, perfectly, into the silent darkness: the name of the piece, and his own.

He lowered the trumpet, his ears still ringing with the sound of it. Marina clapped, still smiling, and Katya gave the table an appreciative volley of thumps. Sitting again, Trofim said, apologetic, "It's not the best instrument, of course. I lost mine, at the start of the war. This one – "

"That was *marvellous*," Dima said appreciatively. "I'd thought you must be good, but you get such a crisp sound out of that thing. Makes the violin feel…*flabby*, a bit. If there was a piano here, we could – "

"Hush, Dima," Katya said. Dima, surprisingly, hushed, lifting his hands in surrender and grinning. To Trofim, Katya said: "Will you play something more? Only if you've got the energy, but it would be nice to hear – "

"Play some jazz," Marina said, twitching her shoulders in an economical suggestion of a dance. "Do you know 'The Life is Full of Joy'?"

From the doorway to the kitchen came Lidiya's characteristic mirthless *ha*. "Never has a song been less appropriate," she said. Leaning on the doorjamb, drying her hands on a threadbare towel, she looked at Trofim, steady and expressionless; as he looked back, her mouth shivered into a reluctant smile, and she raised her hand in a half-mocking salute. "Go on, then," she said, nodding at Trofim. "We're waiting."

II: 1 August 1942, evening: Leningrad Front

It had become habit for Trofim to check in with Sasha once he was back at the Front, after rehearsal. He had become unwillingly superstitious about it, imagining what could have happened in the hours that he was away. Sometimes he would find Sasha alone, sometimes with the other men, sometimes vanished on an errand of his own, official or otherwise. Sometimes:

"Come and have a drink," Andrei said. There was a leaden flatness underneath the cheer of his words. Beside him, Sasha barely glanced up.

The things you learn to notice. There was blood under Sasha's nails, cut short, scrubbed clean, the fingertips raw and shining and yet a line of blood at the root of the nail. Andrei was slumped in his chair, his genial, pouchy face wearing an expression of utter weariness.

"What – " Trofim started to ask. He stopped. The sentence should start with *who*, but sentences like that were even harder for Trofim. Sasha's face was set into its accustomed expression of calm irony, but there was a tension around his eyes. As Trofim watched, one eyelid flickered, just a little.

"Viktor. There was some shelling, a few hours ago."

Viktor: Trofim had never quite managed to force himself to like him; Viktor's robust ignorance had seemed designed to throw Trofim's own education and awkwardness into starker relief. Sasha had liked him, though, or no, Sasha had been fond of him with a sort of prickly bafflement. More than that: since Viktor had aggressively befriended Sasha in that *izba* nearly a year before, Sasha had shouldered Viktor as a responsibility, in the same way that he had evidently shouldered Trofim himself. It felt different to Trofim, but perhaps he was deceived.

Andrei passed Trofim a bottle, and Trofim drank, mostly by reflex. For a long time they didn't speak; from the radio in the corner came the voice of a woman, low and steady, reading a poem or a story that Trofim couldn't make out. The bottle circled, glasses were filled up and knocked back, but neither Andrei nor Sasha could be bothered to toast, and Trofim didn't dare. After the third round Trofim felt his thinking start to soften, and he thought of Lidiya, then, the way she always seemed to sneak into his mind when it wasn't occupied by something more pressing. The grudging way that she had asked him to play, and that mock-salute: that could mean something, couldn't it? He thought of asking Sasha, and then, guiltily, remembered that this wasn't the time to ask about that sort of thing.

"What happened, exactly?"

"They'd got too complacent," Andrei said. Sasha was still staring at his hands. "All of us have. They thought – you know how it is. You go long enough without anything awful happening, and you think you're safe. A few of them got caught in the shelling and – " He shrugged. "Viktor was killed outright. Three more were taken to the field hospital with injuries. Two of them'll be fine, they think. Kostya might not last the night." Sighing, he rubbed his hands over his face. "Why don't you distract us, Trofim? Tell us about the rehearsals, about the Symphony."

"Oh – " Trofim cast about for something to say. People asked about it, often enough, and Trofim had become expert in evasion and elision; it was too difficult to marry the two worlds, and most of the time he hadn't the heart to try. Now, though, the idea of fobbing them off with something half-hearted felt shameful. "It's – I suppose it's going all right. But it's hard work, these days, now that we're just focusing on the Shostakovich. It's very complex, and there's so little time left to rehearse, now. One of the viola players has copied out my part for me, so at least I don't have to worry about that – "

"I hate writing the fucking letters," Sasha said abruptly, cutting across Trofim. He must be drunk; he was normally happy enough to surrender the burden of conversation to others. "Always the same fucking thing, all those words, *bravery* and *courage* and – what's that other one?"

"Valour?" Trofim suggested. It wouldn't do to tell Sasha the truth: that there was no need to bother with the letters, that no one else did these days; after the hundreds of thousands of deaths over the winter, the standard military condolence telegram was all most families got. Sasha still bothered; Trofim had the idea that he always would. Sasha shrugged, one-shouldered.

"They can't actually believe them, can they? The number of letters I've written, almost exactly the same. You'd think the mothers would recognise that I'm barely talking about their sons."

"It's what they want to – "

Sasha waved a hand in faint irritation. "Of course it's what they want to believe. Still. It would be nice to think that people weren't so easily duped. Just, it's *Viktor* I'm about to craft into some sort of ludicrous hero." Trofim could see his point; his own last memory of Viktor was of Viktor giving a minutely detailed description of a prostitute he'd slept with in Moscow before the war, complete with actions and sound-effects. Sasha smiled, humourless. "Sometimes I think about the letters I'd write if I could really say what I thought. I've already got yours planned out," he added, turning to Trofim. "It opens with: *he should have stayed at the Conservatoire.*"

"My mother'd love that," Trofim said. Perhaps he was getting into the spirit of this, whatever dismal, hectic spirit it was. He felt tougher, hard-headed and hard-hearted. "And yours – *he was a cantankerous old bastard, mostly useful for his accordion playing and his uncanny ability to procure alcohol in any given situation.*" The vodka made the floor of the dugout rise and fall like the deck of a ship. Trofim was unexpectedly enjoying the motion. "Who'd I send it to, anyway?"

His mouth asked the question before his brain had time to rein it in. *Stupid.* The grin was still on Sasha's face, but all animation dropped away behind it, leaving the smile an artefact. "You don't," Sasha said shortly. For a moment no one spoke; Trofim cast about for something to say, and Sasha hauled himself to his feet. "I need some air."

"Fuck," Trofim said to no one in particular. "That was fucking stupid."

Andrei blew out a breath, and a stream of smoke with it. In the doorway, Sasha stood, a silhouette but for the red gleam of his Belomor. He raised his left hand to his face, pressed the ball of his palm against his eye. "Leave him," Andrei said, as if Trofim was scrambling to his feet, making to follow; Sasha wasn't the sort of person you tried to comfort, after all. When Sasha came back inside, his eyes lowered, Andrei engineered a delicate change of subject, while Sasha, with a quiet and murderous energy, spirited up another bottle and turned his energies back to drinking. There was a thunderous feeling in the room; Trofim had the addled sense that Sasha was angry with him, but he couldn't think what for. They drifted once again into silence, and Trofim closed his eyes: the alcohol made him sentimental, and the refrain of 'Katiusha' floated into his head, the way it always did: *Katiusha was walking, singing a song about her true love, whose letters she was keeping.* Had Viktor ever mentioned someone, a girl, someone who would be keeping his letters? Trofim thought not. Seeking a good memory of Viktor, something well-suited to a silent send-off, all that came to mind was the incredibly wide variety of dirty jokes in Viktor's arsenal. Trofim supposed that was as much of a legacy as anything. Had Sasha been there, when Viktor died? Trofim thought so, with that blood on Sasha's hands. Perhaps that was why Sasha was angry, that Trofim had been off in the city, away from all of this, playing music rather than doing what he was supposed to be doing. Hardly meaning to speak out loud, Trofim heard himself say: "I should have been here, today, not messing about with – "

"My *god*, Trofim!" Sasha exploded. His hand hit the table, hard enough to rattle the bottles. Nonplussed, Trofim opened his eyes. "This is what makes me want to fucking punch you," Sasha said. His voice was low and steady, a fine, sharp edge honed to hurt. If Trofim hadn't watched Sasha consume the best part of a bottle of vodka, the relentlessness of Sasha's gaze would have made Trofim believe that he was sober.

"No one's punching anyone tonight," Andrei said, jovial and placatory. Sasha ignored him.

"You insist on thinking that *this* is important, *this* is what matters. That's bullshit. What the fuck does it matter if two countries line up their poor and stupid and violent young men and have them kill each other? It's fucking nonsense. And you – " Sasha said, pointing at Trofim, finger bare inches from his face, " – you think that this is more important than what you're doing with that orchestra, you think that blowing the shit out of some poor fucking arsehole just because he was born on the other side of a border, you think that's more important than *creating* something? All we're doing out here is *taking away*."

"Now, Sasha…" Andrei shifted, uncomfortable.

"Oh, I know, I'm no supporter of the Fascists. I'm the least likely deserter in this whole fucking army. I know what this means, this bullshit – it's a lie, but we have to fight on that lie. But do you think I would be doing this, if I could be doing anything else at all? You think *Viktor* would have? And whoever that is over there – " he said, flinging an arm out in the general direction of the German lines, " – that poor bastard Fritz, or whoever he is – he's not some hairy ogre with fangs. He's an idiot like Viktor, or a smug careerist like Andrei, or a stupid fucking should-be-at-the-Conservatoire boy like Trofim – "

"Or a bitter, drunken prick like you?" Trofim asked, unsure how much of his daring was attributable to the vodka. The night was sharp and rare, a breath away from dangerous. Sasha looked surprised, and then laughed.

"Now you're getting it. You ever wonder how they think about us? You know they call us Ivan, just like we call them Fritz?" Sasha sighed, a harsh, explosive sound. "Point is, you have to know what this is. Point *is*, Trofim, you still have no fucking idea." Experimentally, he stretched out one leg, hooked a foot around Trofim's trumpet case, and dragged it closer. "Go on, then," he said, eyes closing. "Play us something."

"*Now*?" Trofim asked. He couldn't quite bring his watch into focus, but he knew it was late; a heavy silence had swum up around them as they'd been sitting there, and outside the darkness was as thick as water.

"I don't know if that's a good idea…" Andrei began, but Sasha's eyes snapped open and he pushed back in his chair:

"Fuck your mother," he said clearly, pointing at Andrei, "and fuck *your* mother," he said to Trofim. He stood; behind his back, Trofim and Andrei exchanged alarmed glances. "Viktor deserves a decent fucking send-off," Sasha said, moving towards the doorway; unsteady and half-numb, Trofim pulled himself to his feet and followed.

Sasha had at least the sense to lead the three of them behind the lines, away from the dugouts – they would still be overheard, but the noise would perhaps seem like less of an affront. The gibbous moon lit up the mist that was rising off the ground; the long, lean shadows of the trees lent Sasha a hieratic air. Still holding the vodka bottle, he leaned against a tree trunk, squatting on the ground. Andrei, uncertain, settled behind Trofim, legs spaced widely, as if ready to run.

"Go on, then," Sasha said again. The edge had left his voice; in the moonlight he looked younger, tamer, more frightened. *No one here knows what they're doing*, Trofim thought. To his surprise, it helped. He didn't waste time deciding what to play; when he lifted the trumpet to his lips it was Telemann's 'L'Amour' that came out. The melody was like liquid: he had played drunk before but never as easily as this, a slow and easy fall. The stars wheeled and swung above and the damp summer earth smelled rich, loamy. When the piece came to an end and Trofim lowered his instrument, he fancied that he could feel the final shining notes vibrating through the soles of his feet.

For a long moment, no one spoke. Sasha straightened, stepped towards Trofim, and raised the vodka bottle, taking a swig. "To Viktor," he said, quietly, and passed the bottle to Trofim. "To Viktor," Trofim echoed, adding silently, *I'm sorry I never liked you much.* He passed the bottle on to Andrei, who drank swiftly, muttering the toast, anxious for it to be over. Taking the bottle back, Sasha upended it, pouring the remainder onto the ground.

"He'll complain we didn't leave him enough," he said, "but the living need it more than the dead."

III: 2 August 1942, morning: Leningrad Front

Trofim's headache had settled unpleasantly right behind his eyes, less painful than irritating. The morning was bright enough to wound, and he wasn't sure how he was going to make it through the walk to the trolleybus and its rattling journey into the city. His memory of the previous evening was fragmented at best, and he barely recalled rolling into bed, but he rather suspected he had left his trumpet and Marina's painstakingly copied score in Sasha's dugout.

The dugout was empty when he entered, the bed made with Sasha's customary precision. There was the trumpet, under the table, and there was the music, on top, slightly sticky with spilled vodka, but thankfully still legible. Next to it was an inky scrawl, bristling with crossings-out and smudges; Trofim knew he should leave it alone, but he caught sight of Viktor's name, and found himself gulping down the lines before he had made the decision to do so.

Your son was one of the laziest men I've ever met, and he practically shat himself at the sound of shelling. But he was even tempered, and told a decent dirty joke, and was good at remembering people's names and where they came from. That sort of thing's more important, most of the time, than courage and valour. His death didn't make much of a difference to anything, but at least it was quick, and he probably died thinking he was doing something that mattered.

I don't know you so this might be something you already know, but in case you don't, I want to tell you: at first, when you lose someone, it's like being in the centre of a storm, when you're blinded by snow and deafened by the wind and everything's blocked off and you can't find your way out. You know when you're so cold that even the idea of being warm seems impossible, like something someone invented, as a joke? And the worst thing about losing someone is that when you try to imagine feeling better you don't want to, because that horrible, lost, cold, blind feeling is all you have left of them. But you can learn to hold onto them and to hold onto yourself at the same time. You will be all right. You will remember him.

"I have the real one here," Sasha said. Trofim looked up, flushing; he hadn't heard Sasha come in. Sasha was neat and scrubbed, no sign on his face of the previous night's overindulgence other than the shadows under his eyes. He held a sheet of paper out to Trofim. "I wrote it over breakfast. Look it over, will you?"

Trofim took it; Sasha crossed to the table, picked up the scrawl and crumpled it, tossing it into the corner. The new letter was written in the careful script of someone who'd learned to write too late to ever be quite comfortable with it. It said all the right things.

"You spelled 'condolences' wrong," Trofim said tentatively.

"Did I?" Sasha asked, equable. "Well, mark down the correct way. I'll copy out a fresh version before sending it." He rubbed his forehead, wincing a little. "I'm sorry I was such a bastard last night, by the way. I was right, of course, and I meant every word, but I shouldn't have been such an arsehole about it."

"It's all right," Trofim said. Sasha's apology was so characteristic that he couldn't help grinning.

"You should get going. You'll be late for rehearsal," Sasha said. He eyed Trofim with unaccustomed envy. "The accordion's such an unfairly maligned instrument. I'll never know why Shostakovich didn't include an accordion line in his blasted Symphony."

"Maybe I'll write one," Trofim said.

"Duet for accordion and trumpet? It's bound to be a hit." Outside, the sun's glare was enough to make both of them flinch, and Sasha cursed. "Now that's just *cruel.*" He looked at his watch. "I've got to get over to the hospital. See how Kostya's doing."

"Sasha," Trofim said, before his traitor brain could step in and stop him. Sasha looked up. "The tickets," Trofim said. *Just get the words out*, he told himself viciously. *Just say it.* "For the Symphony. I can get you one, if you want. A ticket."

Sasha smiled. This wasn't the smile that Trofim had seen on Sasha's face a thousand times, that knowing, ironic half-mouthed smirk; this was different, open and clear, a smile that seemed to have been surprised out of him. Trofim had only seen that look on Sasha's face once or twice in the whole time he had known him, and it had always alarmed him a little, this indication that perhaps there was a whole other person behind the version of himself he chose to show. It was gone after a moment, but the shadow of it was in Sasha's voice when he spoke. "That'd be good," he said. "I'd like that."

"See you later," Trofim said. It always felt like a promise to him, or a pact.

"See you later," Sasha agreed. Trofim waited until he was out of sight and then, heart hammering, pushed open the heavy curtain that served as Sasha's front door. The first letter was where Sasha had thrown it, screwed into a ball, and Trofim bent, picked it up, and slipped it into his pocket. *You will be all right*, he thought. The words weighed heavy in his memory but there was beauty in their simplicity. *You will remember him.* He would smooth out the creases later.

CHAPTER TWENTY-FIVE

4 August 1942

The last chord shone on the air as Katya let her bowing arm fall. No one seemed to want to move, holding a collective breath, until Genya blew out a considering sigh.

"Well," he said carefully, "that wasn't *too* awful."

Beside Katya, Dima laughed softly, mostly to himself. Catching sight of his face, Katya found it held a mixture of pride, relief, and pure, untrammelled delight. It was the first time the string section had played the second movement all the way through, and Katya had been worried about how he would cope with it. She was well aware by now that Dima's memory was prodigious, but even so, playing a piece he had only heard once in its entirety, no matter how many times he had gone over individual lines with Katya, had struck her as near impossible; she had had enough difficulty keeping up herself, with the aid of her smudged, barely legible score. It was true that Dima had slipped up a couple of times, but no more than anyone else, and he had been remarkably quick to correct himself; even now, Katya could tell by his inward look of concentration that he was shoring up his memory, ensuring that he wouldn't make the same mistakes again. She reached out and squeezed his arm in silent congratulation.

Harried and distracted, Karl Ilych waved a hand to dismiss the strings, turning his attention to the brass section. "Their turn to be hauled over the coals," Marina murmured, coming up beside Katya, and shooting Trofim a commiserating look; he gave her a shy smile back. In front of them, heading for the cafeteria, Daniil and Dima, their heads bent towards each other, were deep in animated conversation, doubtless the prologue to the kind of row they both enjoyed. Marina leaned in closer to Katya. "How long do you think it's going to take before Lidiya makes it clear to that poor boy that he doesn't have a chance in hell with her?"

"Trofim?" Katya asked, surprised. She looked back at him, his trumpet lifted to his mouth, eyes screwed shut. Following her gaze, Marina smiled lazily.

"Of course Trofim. I've had my eye on him for weeks. Took me a while to realise how good looking he is, I admit, because he's got no idea what to do with it. It's rather endearing, actually. And as soon as Lidiya breaks his little heart – " Marina said, snapping her fingers, " – I'll be ready to swoop in and pick up the pieces. It's a rather good strategy, you know, following beautiful women around and scooping up their cast-offs."

Katya laughed. A year ago she would have found Marina shamefully frivolous; now, she couldn't help but be reluctantly charmed by her. At the door to the cafeteria, Marina paused. "You go on, Katya. I think I'm going to wait and eat with the brass section." She gave a salacious wink. In the cafeteria, Dima was already seated opposite Daniil, unconsciously combative; as Katya slipped into the empty seat beside him, touching his shoulder by way of greeting, Dima said with great certainty:

"He is a genius."

Daniil laughed, dismissive. "Of course you think that about your namesake."

"It's nothing to do with that. He – it's the way he puts sounds together. You can tell – absolutely – what it is that he's trying to say. With some other composers you know that they just want to create something melodious."

"And what's wrong with that?"

"Nothing, of course, if that's what you want. But I – " Dima made one of his characteristic gestures, lifting his hands in front of his eyes, palms facing outwards. "Music is not just background to me. It is *everything*. I want it to be more than *pretty*."

Daniil looked affronted. "It's not just background to me either, of course! But what is the good of music that you can only understand if you have studied harmony and counterpoint at the Conservatoire?"

"I've never been near the Conservatoire and I don't have any trouble with anything that Shostakovich has written."

Katya dipped her head to hide a hint of a smile. She loved Dima for his arrogance because there was nothing of a bluff in it; his belief in himself was that genuine.

"All right, then," Daniil shifted himself in his seat so that his shoulders were squared. Katya remembered this from the Conservatoire: the inevitable precursor to a fight. "Perhaps I should have said, what's the point of music that only other musicians can understand? Music – all art, in fact – should be…"

"Democratic," Dima finished for him, grinning. "Yes, I know. Nice, uncomplicated music with tunes that the proletariat can sing along to. I'm just disappointed, Daniil, that you have such a low opinion of the proletariat – speaking as one of them."

"Are you saying that I am not?" Daniil asked hotly. He shifted his shoulders again, and Katya heard him exhale sharply through his nose. She recalled, suddenly, the times she'd visited Daniil's apartment when they'd been playing in the quartet together, the mingled shame and pride with which he'd treated the once-fine furniture and the dim and delicate art that lined the walls.

"Of course not," Dima said easily. "We're all proletarians, aren't we? Otherwise we wouldn't be here. But I grew up in a house where the only music I ever heard was my father wheezing along to his accordion, and all I'm saying is that if I can appreciate – not just appreciate, can *love* the intricacies in Shostakovich's compositions, then perhaps we should give the non-musical proletarian a little more credit. Perhaps he would welcome a bit of a challenge." From the other end of the table, Genya, also from a peasant background, shot Dima a sly smile of collusion, seemingly forgetting that it would be lost on him.

Daniil's frustration at arguing with someone as even-tempered as Dima was evident; he argued best when he could goad his adversary into losing his temper first. "I'm not saying, of course, that Shostakovich has never written anything of any worth. His Fifth Symphony, for example… but I was at the premiere of *The Nose*, and that percussion – I honestly thought I would be deafened. And as for *Lady Macbeth of Mtsensk* – even you, Dima, even you couldn't argue that that was anything other than a complete mess?"

"'Muddle instead of music'," Dima quoted thoughtfully. "I haven't had the pleasure of hearing it, for obvious reasons. But that's what comes of putting bureaucrats in charge of music."

Daniil cleared his throat, nonplussed. "Dima, surely you cannot be saying that the Party…"

"Yes, that's exactly what I'm saying," Dima confirmed cheerfully.

"Dima," said Katya warningly, but Dima ploughed on regardless.

"I don't go about telling Stalin how to run the country, do I? So why should he be telling me – us – " he waved his arms expansively, nearly upsetting Katya's cup in the process, "why should he be telling us what music is worth playing or listening to?"

There was a shocked silence. Dima raised his eyebrows, awaiting a response, and then laughed. "Oh, come on! Is someone really going to report me to the NKVD in the middle of all this? Does the city really care about what I think, these days? I'm not inciting revolution. I just think that…that music should be in the hands of musicians. That's all."

~

"Let's not go straight home," Dima said, after the rehearsal was over. The day was uncertain, blue skies alternating with roiling banks of clouds surging in from the Baltic, threatening squalls and horizontal rain. Katya was exhausted, physically and mentally, from the Shostakovich, her arms rubbery and a metallic taste in her mouth. She longed for bed, to close her eyes and drift for an hour or two in that pleasant, cushioned state between sleeping and waking. But Dima had a restless look about him, and Katya had a fondness for these in-between times, neither at the apartment with Lidiya and the children and Ilya, nor at rehearsal with the other members of the orchestra. Katya still found the observation of others oppressive, even while Dima was utterly immune to it; it was a treat to be just the two of them.

"Where do you want to go?" Katya asked.

"If it was two years ago, I'd invite you to a café and buy you a slice of cake. And then maybe I'd take you to the cinema – "

"The cinema?"

"I always quite enjoy it, actually – Vasya and I used to go sometimes, and he'd whisper to me, to explain the bits I would have missed. And the music, too, of course. I was always so envious of anyone who'd had the chance to hear Shostakovich playing in the movie theatres in Leningrad. I used to go to every film that he scored, but it was never the same as hearing him play live would have been."

"We could go, if you want? I don't know what's playing, but the Molodyozhny Cinema's open." Katya thought she'd fall asleep in the close, warm dark, but that was rather appealing in itself. Dima shook his head.

"Another time. I want to walk a bit, if you don't mind." He smiled, his face lightening. "Shall we go and visit the horses?"

As they walked, Dima was unusually quiet. When they reached the bridge it was Katya who bent first, taking his hand, placing it on the horses wrought into the railings.

"There they are," Dima said.

"I don't know why they comfort me so much," Katya said, "but they do."

"I suppose – so much has changed here, since the start of the war, but they stay the same. And they'll be here after it's all over. Whether we are or not."

"When you were ill – " Katya had never spoken about this to Dima; the memory of his illness still made her a little dry-mouthed with remembered fear. "The first rehearsal after you'd been so sick, when we were walking together – my god, I was so frightened. You looked so weak. And when we passed here, I couldn't help touching one of the horses, like it was a good luck charm."

"Maybe it worked," Dima said. He was smiling, but he sounded distracted, distant. Katya touched his arm.

"What's wrong?"

"Nothing, really. Just…in a week it'll be over."

"*Oh.*" Suddenly understanding, Katya leaned into Dima's side; he had propped his elbows on the railing of the bridge and lifted his face into the breeze. Seagulls wheeled above; a memory, sharp as a blade, of seagulls in winter, wanting nothing more than to catch one and kill it for food. Katya was powerfully thankful that animals had stopped seeming like things only worth being eaten. "And then what?"

"And then what?" Dima echoed, nodding. "I shouldn't be ungrateful, I know. By some miracle, I've got what I always wanted – *more* than I always wanted," he nudged Katya gently, "and in the middle of all this horror, too. I should probably feel guilty about it. But I don't. And I don't – I don't want it to end. I'm twenty-three years old, and every scrap of sense I have tells me that this is the only chance I'm ever going to have to play in a normal orchestra, because they're desperate and they need me to make up the numbers."

Katya didn't say anything; there was nothing to say. She knew Dima was right.

"And until today," he went on, his voice low, "I thought maybe they had a point. Of course I knew I'd be fine playing all the stuff I'd played before, and I knew I could learn things quickly, but – honestly – I talked it up to Genya, right at the start. I didn't know if I could do it, something as complex as the Symphony, with so little rehearsal time, no recordings to listen to, and no braille music if it turned out I needed it. But I *can*. I did all right today, didn't I? I know I made a few mistakes, but it was no worse than anyone else, wasn't it?"

Katya wasn't sure if it was a genuine question; she answered anyway. "You were perfect," she said, inaccurate and truthful, and then, in a rush: "There's more to music than orchestras, you know. You would be a wonderful chamber musician, in a trio, or a quartet – "

"I know," Dima said. Katya loved that it didn't even occur to him to feign modesty; she wondered if she would ever tire of it. "I know that there are plenty of other things I can do. I'll work something out, and I was lucky even to get this chance." He rubbed his wrists absently, and Katya felt the answering ache in her own, a pleasurable complaint. "But my god," Dima said at last, his voice slightly unsteady, "the orchestra, the *weight* of it, the intricacy, the richness of sound – when I think about never being part of that again, it – " He drew in a sharp breath. "It breaks my fucking heart."

Katya couldn't remember him ever swearing in front of her before. She took his hand, running her thumb over the fine skin at the inside of his wrist. Dima was silent, his lips pressed tightly together; Katya could feel the tension strung through every joint of his body, and then, sighing, he seemed to let it go.

"So there we are," he said, lightly. "No use fretting about it. It's just such a strange time, now, despite the awfulness of it all, the bombs and the shelling and the starvation – I have this sense that things have… shifted. And it's hard to imagine how things are going to be, afterwards, when things have settled again."

"I know what you mean," Katya said. She had never meant to bring this up to Dima, she tried to avoid mentioning Yevgeny as much as possible, but now seemed to be the right time: she wanted to tell him, but also just to say the words out loud, to watch them solidify when they met the air. "Lida told me the other night that Yevgeny informed on her husband."

"I know. She told me," Dima said.

Katya opened her mouth, and then closed it again. A month ago she would have given room to the jealousy that rose up in her at the idea of Lidiya and Dima sharing confidences; now, she swallowed it down, waiting it out, and sure enough, after a couple of moments it flickered into nothingness.

"It was like the last thread of everything that I had *before*, everything I thought I knew, and now that's been cut too. I feel as if I have to reimagine everything, the way things were and the way *I* was. Everything has come apart, and I have to build it all up again. It's terrifying – I got it wrong before, I know I did. The girls were the only good part of what I had. And now – what if I get it wrong this time, as well?" She paused, thinking. "And yet – I told Lidiya I didn't know. And I didn't – but in some ways I did. Not exactly, but I remember how it used to be before, how people were scared of Yevgeny, of all of us. I mistook it for respect, but it was fear, wasn't it? And I liked it. I *liked* it."

Dima said nothing. The pause stretched on a little too long for Katya's taste. "Dima…"

"I'm thinking," he said, affronted.

"What about?"

"About how I was when I first went to school. Horrible, really. I told myself I wasn't a bully because so many of my fights were about protecting Piotr, but he wasn't the only person there who needed protecting. I liked the power, I think. I felt so powerless, so helpless most of the time that I enjoyed the fact that some of the other boys were scared of me." He squeezed Katya's hand. "It's human, Katya. It's not *nice*, but it's human."

"I don't want to be like that any more."

"You're not, now. You just need something else to take up that space inside you. I think about when I found music – it changed me, every part of me, from the atoms up. I became a different person. I had something to prop me up, and I was so full of excitement and happiness that there was no room for all that anger." He stretched luxuriantly. "It was such a relief. And of course Vasya helped, too, later. He was always completely *himself*, and so he helped me to be the same way. It made such a difference."

Dima spoke a lot about Vasya, these days. It had taken Katya a while to notice, picking out the threads of it from Dima's undiscriminating cascade of talk; Dima never came right out and said that he missed him, but it was clear in the way that he had started to try and wedge Vasya into conversation that it was a kind of summoning, rebuilding Vasya out of breath and words and repetition. Katya still had a lingering sense of guilt about her instinctive judgement of Vasya, the few times that she'd met him – she had thought of him as dull and thuggish, but nor could she forget Trofim's words: Dima would never have survived the winter without Vasya. The debt that she owed to Vasya made it easier to think of him kindly. She remembered, then, an image surfacing from early spring: she and Dima had been walking home after a rehearsal, and Vasya had met them near the Vladimirskaya Church, muffled in coats and scarves, looking half mad. What was it, in that memory? The way that Dima's face had blazed with pleasure at the sound of Vasya's voice? The way, when the two boys parted company with Katya, that Vasya had flung an arm over Dima's shoulder, abandoned and affectionate, their hips knocking together? A thought struck Katya, something that had tapped occasionally at the edges of her awareness but never been put into words.

"Dima, did you and Vasya ever…?" She didn't know how best to end the sentence, but Dima obviously understood. He flushed, but when he spoke his voice was calm.

"Well. Now and then." He cleared his throat a little. "Does that – does that bother you?"

"No," Katya said. She found that it wasn't even a lie; she wouldn't have guessed it before that moment, but now she knew, it fit.

"He'd been in Solovki for five years, and I'd been in school…Things happen." He shrugged. "I suppose it makes sense. We were close."

"You loved him," Katya said.

"Yes," Dima said, after a pause. "Not like – not like this. But yes."

Katya considered it, how hard she had worked to carefully circumscribe her world, and the lack of importance Dima put on the boundaries that she had always clung to.

"Doesn't it – didn't it get confusing? All of that, everything mixed up together?"

Dima laughed. "When you put it like that, then yes, I suppose so. But not in a bad way. Not in a bad way at all." Looping his arm around her shoulder, Dima pulled Katya against him, leaning down to kiss her, and then the expression on his face changed: still, watchful.

"What is it?" Katya asked, although there was only one thing it could be; Dima always heard it before she did.

"Planes are coming," he told her, gently but factually. Immediately it became harder for her to breathe. Moments later, there was the muffled thud of an explosion, and the earth shuddered as if in echo; then again, and again. People began to run in all directions. There seemed to be no sense to it. This was one thing that hadn't changed since the winter, the uncontrollable deluge of physical fear that descended on Katya at these moments.

"Where's the nearest shelter?" she demanded of Dima. It took him no more than a second to consult the map he kept in his head.

"There's one in the Anichkov Garden. Not far. Come on – "

They turned and started to walk. If she had been alone, Katya would have run, but Dima had tucked his arm into hers – for his sake or for her own, she wasn't quite sure – and it forced her to slow, matching his measured pace. When they reached the shelter they found the usual motley selection of people – an old woman clutching a bag containing some scraps of bread and a misshapen potato; a middle-aged woman with a boy, perhaps her son, but not necessarily, given the way relations had warped and shifted over the winter; two young Red Army soldiers; a young woman hugging a notebook, maybe a student; an elderly bearded man. Room was made for Dima and Katya on one of the wooden benches; they sat. Some of the people nodded to them in greeting, but no one spoke. The old woman had her eyes tightly shut and was praying constantly. As often happened, Katya's eagerness to reach the shelter evaporated as soon as she entered. It started to feel like a tomb, still and dank and dead, and she longed for the movement of air against her skin. A bomb dropped, almost overhead, and the whole world shrugged and shifted. For a moment it felt like it would never quite settle, as if everything was invisibly but irrevocably changed. The old woman's voice rose briefly to a wail, then died back down again. An aeroplane whined somewhere in the unseen sky. Another crash and a roar, and another. A spasm of shaking overtook Katya, rising in a wave from the soles of her feet. Convulsively, she opened and closed her hands. *The worst has already happened*, she told herself. It did no good. Her body feared for its own sake, and her mind could do little to persuade it otherwise. Her breathing stuttered and started, and her pulse hammered at her wrists. Looking at Dima only made her feel more frightened: the impassivity of his face, the terrifying delicacy of skin and flesh and bone. The worst had already happened, but there was always another worst. She looked down at her hands, then back up again. Her eyes couldn't settle on anything.

Dima took her hand, flattened it and pressed it against his thigh. He straightened her fingers, rubbing the knuckles and the knotted tendons with his thumb. "It's all right," he said, very quietly. Katya's mouth was too dry for her to answer. The fear was tangible, visceral; it made her feel possessed. Silence hung on the air, heavy like dust. Katya counted. Perhaps it was over; it was not over. Three sharp crashes, and then a long, slow grinding noise as something collapsed nearby. The sound of the aeroplanes was constant, and the young boy started to identify them: "That's a Messerschmidt. That's one of ours…" Another bomb fell. "That'd be over on Lomonosova Ulitsa," the boy said, authoritative. The woman who could have been his mother had her arms around him, her chin resting on his hair.

"No," said Dima, smiling. "Not as close as that. I'd say Apraksin Pereulok."

The boy stared at Dima, tilting his head in appraisal. "I bet you it's Lomonosova Ulitsa."

"What do you bet?"

The boy looked deflated. He had nothing. Dima relented. "All right. Whoever's wrong has to stand in the middle of Ploshchad Lomonosova for a full minute, shouting, 'I'm an idiot! I'm an idiot!' How's that?"

"All right," the boy said, giggling. Even the woman with him managed the ghost of a smile. Katya couldn't. The panic was stuck at the back of her throat, moving neither upwards nor downwards. She was afraid that if she opened her mouth she would scream, and if she moved any part of her body she would run out of the shelter into the street. Silence fell again, aside from the relentless tick of the metronome, coming out of the loudspeakers by the door. Then another barrage of crashes, further away, but closer together. Somewhere in the street outside came the ragged sound of a man screaming with horrible abandon. Even Dima winced, and Katya flinched violently. "*Oh*," she said. Her voice sounded tinny and small to her own ears.

"All right," said Dima, as if in answer. He squeezed her hand and put it back on her own knee, then bent down for his violin case. Flicking the clasps open, he lifted out the Guarneri, his touch light and firm in the trembling air. He had never done this before; if asked, Katya would have said that he valued the safety of his instrument above his own during raids. For a moment, surprise overtook terror.

"What are you doing?"

"What does it look like?" Dima asked blandly. He started to tune.

"But you can't – " Katya hissed.

"Why ever not? I need as much practise as I can get at the moment, we both do. And who knows how long we're going to be stuck here?"

Turning a peg minutely, Dima plucked the G string and smiled, satisfied. He began to play the first violin part from the Largo movement of Katya's favourite Bach concerto.

For a moment, it was just noise, too loud and too close in the too-small room, another series of nonsensical sounds no less oppressive than the clamour of destruction outside. Then it came into focus, a string of bright, blazing notes that floated through the darkness. Every face in the shelter lifted in unison, their expressions almost disbelieving. Dima played more slowly than normal, matching himself to the metronome. Katya's breath slowed. She loosened her fists. A complex series of emotions wound around each other: disapproval that Dima should be arrogant enough to push his music onto people who may not want it; fear, still, clouding her vision and roaring in her ears; sharp, reluctant pride in his boldness; irritation – irritation, because it sounded so wrong on its own. The piece needed two violins. Without the second, it limped, unbalanced. In her head, she heard the way the second violin buoyed up the first, turning a monologue into a conversation. It was an itch that demanded to be scratched. She picked up her own violin case and lifted it to her knee. "Don't think I don't know what you're doing," she muttered. Half of Dima's mouth quirked into a smile. "You're not *tricking* me into anything." He didn't slow, didn't stop.

Katya's hands were shaking too much to let her tune up, and her ears were ringing so much from the explosions that she wasn't sure she could have managed it anyway. Instead, she closed her eyes and launched in blind.

Immediately, Dima made room for her in the music. She was slightly out of tune, but not so much that anyone other than she or Dima would notice. Katya understood, suddenly, that technical perfection didn't matter. What mattered was the act of playing it, for her and for Dima and for everyone else around them.

A bomb fell. Katya's wrist twitched. Her instrument squealed. It would not do. Taking a deep breath, she pressed on. Now it was Katya's turn to take the melody, and she tried to play as if she were Dima, reaching for the part of herself that he would put into his music, rather than holding onto her customary reserve. It worked, after a fashion. They played it through to the end, and then Katya, surprising herself, started again from the beginning, taking the first violin part this time. It needed to be complete. Her eyes half closed, the music pulled her along of its own accord, slowing the beating of her heart, steadying her hands. It wasn't until they had finished that she realised that the metronome had stopped.

"Time to go," said Dima cheerfully. With brisk, spare movements he wiped the rosin off his instrument, put it back in its case, and stood. Katya was slower to shrug off the music. It was the first time, she thought, that she had ever played in front of people who had not explicitly or implicitly asked her to. It felt brash and boastful but also something else, something better and kinder.

Outside, a trolleybus was on its side, burning. The man who had been screaming was nowhere to be seen, having wandered off or been taken away or died, somewhere, alone and in silence. People had begun to move about again, as if the raid had only been a brief interruption to their day, a momentary annoyance. The old woman still clutched her potato, guarding it jealously. The boy pulled at Dima's elbow.

"What about our bet?"

"Oh, I haven't forgotten. I hope you're ready to lose. And by the way," he added sternly, "don't think you'll be able to fool me because I can't see. I've got other ways of working out which one of us is right. Katya can be our impartial observer, can't she? And – " he extended a hand to the woman who stood behind the boy.

"Polina," she said, smiling. "I'm Nikita's aunt."

The bomb that they had heard had fallen halfway between Lomonosova Ulitsa and Apraksin Pereulok. Dima and Nikita set out to decide whether it was minutely closer to one of their camps or the other, a convoluted method involving exaggerated striding, complex mathematics, and good-natured insults. Katya and Polina stood by the side of the street, leaning against a wall that was warmed by the sunshine. It still startled Katya how quickly things could return to normal, out of a maelstrom in which the very idea of *normal* was impossible.

"Thank you for playing," Polina said shyly. "It made me feel braver, somehow."

"It made me feel braver, too," Katya admitted. She wasn't sure if it was true; perhaps it had just blocked everything else out for a little while, and perhaps that was all bravery was. "Anyway. You're welcome."

"You're in the orchestra, then? You and your…" She paused minutely to give Katya the chance to supply the noun, and when Katya didn't: "…your friend."

"Yes."

"You'll be playing the Symphony?" There was a strange eagerness in Polina's voice. It sounded covetous, admiring. "I can't spare the money for a ticket, but they'll be broadcasting it, won't they?" On the opposite corner, Dima had evidently conceded the victory, and was fulfilling his part of the bargain, much to Nikita's delight. Polina was still gazing at Katya, expecting an answer, and Katya wanted to say: *it's impossible.* She wanted to say: *you have no idea the colossal effort it takes even to hold our instruments; despite the increased rations one of the clarinettists died of dystrophy only a week ago; we've hardly started working on it properly and we don't yet have the strength to play it all the way through.* She wanted to shake the woman who clearly thought of the Symphony as hers, just because she had suffered along with the city.

"Yes," she said instead.

CHAPTER TWENTY-SIX

9 August 1942: Midday

Leningrad had never meant much to Sasha – a staging point, a way station, little more. People spoke of its beauty in a way that didn't make sense to him: the streets like caverns, the buildings monoliths, the canals cold veins streaming towards the gnarled muscle of the city's heart. It had taken on a different tenor since the Blockade, something to be protected because it was under attack, but Sasha was still unconvinced that he would find it valuable in any other context. The city struck him as smug, too certain of its own importance; it alienated Sasha, who still thought of himself as a country boy at heart, but then he was by no means certain that the village where he had grown up would feel any more like a home to him these days. The army was its own city, its own family; it was futile to look for any belonging outside of that.

It made him smile, though, to see how the city changed Trofim – he doubted that Trofim himself noticed it, but he seemed to stand straighter, breathe easier. You could tell when someone was in their element, Sasha thought; he himself swam more easily through the army than anywhere else he'd ever been, while Trofim thrashed and struggled and did little but attract attention to how awkward the fit was. One of the rules that Sasha had chosen to live by was *never ask*; he knew that people came to the army along an unimaginable variety of paths, and the best you could do was shrug your shoulders and put out of your mind anything but the present. Trofim, though, was something else, something that sharpened a thin edge of anger inside Sasha whenever he allowed himself to think about it: the idea that Trofim had chosen something that Sasha himself had tumbled into, a refuge of last resort, as if the plain fact of the choice made it right. It had only become clearer since Trofim had started playing with the orchestra again, coming back from rehearsals clear-eyed and loose-limbed, words coming easily for once, only starting to snarl up again in the dense press of the dugouts. Sasha didn't know why it bothered him so much, with Trofim; it wasn't as if the army had any shortage of lives wasted, but it had come so that Sasha could barely look at Trofim without mentally enumerating the dozens of other places where he would be better off.

If it had been up to Sasha, he would have come straight from the Front to the performance; he felt himself untrustworthy in company, his charm unreliable, too given to sudden silences, losing his way in the midst of polite conversation, surrendering to the temptation to say something wildly inappropriate, or, worse, doing so unintentionally. This lunch struck him as a bad idea, even disrespectful: he hated the idea of two soldiers forgoing their own rations and eating the food of civilians. But Trofim had insisted, or rather, because Sasha was more than capable of resisting Trofim's entreaties, he had insisted that *Lidiya* had insisted, and so there he was, stiff and uncomfortable, trailing Trofim up the steps of a battered apartment block. Sasha could tell that the woman waiting at the door was Lidiya, just from the way the angles in Trofim's body seemed to soften at the sight of her, although their greetings were circumspect, almost perfunctory.

"Lidiya, this is my friend Sasha." It was a tone of voice that Sasha had never heard from Trofim before, eagerness and pride combined. Lidiya eyed Sasha, head cocked, half smiling, before extending her hand to shake; Sasha took in as much as he could, knowing he was sure to be quizzed about it later. Cropped fair hair, the firm and definite line of her jaw, the bones of her face under skin as clear as glass – beautiful, no doubt; perhaps a little too poised and elegant for Sasha's own taste. Everything about her radiated certainty and determination – the shape of her shoulders, the set of her lips. Silently, Sasha wished Trofim luck: he was going to need it.

"Pleased to meet you. Are you well?"

"Very well, thank you." Lidiya appeared to be scrutinising Sasha with equal intensity, but gave away nothing of her conclusions in her expression. She was alarmingly unreadable. "Please, come in."

"We brought you something." Trofim pulled a series of bundles out of his coat pocket: sugar, salt, barley, some scraps of dried fish. "It's not much, but we wanted to be able to contribute to lunch – "

Lidiya's face lit up in genuine pleasure. "Thank you! We'd practically run out of salt, I was worried that the borshch was going to be revoltingly bland. You may have saved it." She backed into the hallway; Trofim followed, Sasha lagging slightly behind. His skin prickled with discomfort that it took him a moment or two to identify: when was the last time he'd been in a home, the sort of place where normal people, normal families lived? It was true that there was no glass in the windows, that the walls were streaked with soot, that the floors were pitted where the boards had been dug up for firewood, but from one direction came the dusty clamour of the radio, and from the other came the sound of children's voices. *Children*: Sasha couldn't remember the last time he'd spoken to a child, other than the empty-eyed refugees they'd encountered on the retreat. They passed the kitchen, where an older man, lean and spare, was stirring something on the stove: Ilya, Lidiya explained; two children pushed through the door, the older of whom, a boy, Sergei, shook hands gravely with Sasha and Trofim, while the younger, Masha, hid behind Lidiya and wouldn't meet Sasha's eyes.

"The others are in the living room," Lidiya explained. "Couldn't *possibly* help in the kitchen when there's a concert to fret about." Her words were barbed but her voice was not. As Lidiya ushered them inside, Trofim announced him: "Sasha, these are some of my friends from the orchestra," and Sasha hid a smirk; Trofim's casual tone could barely have been further from the near-reverence with which he'd spoken Lidiya's name. By the window, two figures rose to their feet in greeting as Sasha stepped forward. The woman – she introduced herself as Katya – was mousy and nondescript, but with a pleasant air of openness about her; as she extended her right hand to Sasha, he saw that her left was clasped in the hand of the man next to her, who smiled easily in Sasha's general direction and –

"Good god," said Sasha. His lips felt clumsy and bloodless. His heart stumbled. "Dima?"

All colour vanished from the man's face. "Alik," he said. It was a statement, not a question.

~

Katya's mouth dropped open. She looked first at Trofim and then at Lida, to see if either of them understood the significance of what had just happened, but Lidiya only looked bemused, and Trofim slightly annoyed, as if he had just been upstaged. The moment seemed to lengthen, elastic: the breeze from the window was cool on the back of Katya's neck as Dima's grip tightened, almost convulsive, on her hand. His breathing faltered, stuttered. His brother took a step towards him and, as gently as possible, Katya untangled her fingers from Dima's, giving him a little push forward. Katya could see, now, the ghost shape of Dima's features under Sasha's own; his expression of dumbstruck astonishment was the mirror of Dima's. The two did not embrace. Neither spoke. Sasha simply stared and stared, as if he could never look long enough at Dima to be satisfied, while Dima let himself be looked at.

"What is it?" Trofim said at last, irritation giving way to concern. "Is something wrong?"

Sasha laughed a little, and then pressed his hand to his mouth, as if frightened by the wild sound of it. Neither he nor Dima seemed capable of explanation.

"Alik – Sasha – he's Dima's brother," Katya said simply. The look of disbelief on Trofim's face was so exaggerated that Katya could have laughed. Of all the many ways Trofim must have imagined this afternoon, this eventuality hadn't been on the list.

"I thought he was dead," Sasha said, seemingly to Trofim. He didn't – perhaps couldn't – move his eyes from Dima's face. Dima coloured, looking almost angry.

"Me? I thought *you* were dead!"

"Turns out neither of us is dead," Sasha said. His tone was matter-of-fact, but his voice shook a little. It was such a Dima thing to say, and the half smile on his face was so similar to the one Katya had seen so often on Dima's face that Katya's eyes filled with tears. She blinked them away crossly: this wasn't hers to cry over. Across the room, Katya watched Lidiya's face shift from bewilderment to shock to calm. If ever Katya had appreciated Lidiya's uncanny ability to accept and embrace the bizarre, now was the time.

"Well, this is unexpected," she said. Katya ducked her head to hide her smile at Lidiya's casual tone.

"I think – " Dima's voice was very small. He stopped, drawing in a deep breath. "I'm sorry, I think I need – "

"Will you give us a moment?" Katya asked, surprised at the steadiness of her own voice. Sasha nodded, sharp and decisive.

"Of course."

In the bedroom, Dima couldn't stand still. He paced, his hands a constant flurry of movement. Every so often he would take a breath as if he was about to start to talk, before closing his mouth again in silence. Katya sat on the bed, watching, waiting for him to be ready to speak. She didn't think she'd ever known him to spend so long silent.

"I keep thinking that it's impossible," he said at last. "It's as if every time my mind starts to accept it, it shuts down. How can it be? But it is. It *is*."

"It's astonishing," Katya said. She had the idea that it didn't really matter what words she chose, as long as she filled Dima's silences with something that sounded positive and encouraging.

"I assumed he was dead. She said, the woman who told me about my family, she said that she had heard that perhaps some of my brothers got out. But I didn't let myself think about it. The cost of hoping – it didn't seem worth it." He stopped, suddenly, looking helpless. "I'm scared of him, Katya. Isn't that crazy? My own brother, and I'm scared of him. It's all too big, somehow. I don't know how to talk to him."

"Dima. You don't have to rush it, but when you're ready – you'll find the words." She touched his arm. "If there's one thing you're good at, it's talking."

Under his breath, Dima muttered something that Katya didn't catch. She crossed to him and took his hands. "What did you say?"

"I said, there are *lots* of things I'm good at."

Katya laughed. "There you go." She put her arms around him. "*That's* how you talk to him," she whispered in his ear. "You don't have to impress him, you don't have to act any different with him than you do with anyone else. There are no right words or wrong words with this. You only have to talk to him."

In her embrace, Dima was still, finally, his eyes closed. He dropped his forehead to Katya's shoulder. "There are – so many lost things," he said at last.

"Not everything has to stay lost."

"The chances – "

"The world is full of people stumbling about in the dark," Katya said. "Perhaps it makes sense that sometimes the right ones stumble into each other."

~

In the living room, Lidiya eyed Trofim with sharp annoyance. After Dima and Katya had disappeared into the bedroom, Sasha had mumbled a confused excuse and gone outside, while Trofim seemed quite happy to continue sitting with her at the table by the window, making desultory attempts at conversation that she found she had little interest in reciprocating. After his third inconsequential remark – they had covered the weather, his nerves for the concert that evening, and the likelihood of its disruption by an enemy bombardment – Lidiya lost patience.

"Aren't you going to go and talk to him?" she demanded, tilting her head towards the door through which Sasha had left.

"I think he probably wants to be left alone," Trofim said uncertainly. "He doesn't – mostly he doesn't like to talk much. Certainly not about things like this."

Lidiya sighed, rolling her eyes. "Don't be ridiculous." Shooting Trofim a look of withering scorn, she got up and went out onto the landing. Sasha was sat on one of the steps, a cigarette in his hands. Sitting down on the step above him, Lidiya nudged his shoulder with her knee.

"Do you have a spare cigarette?"

Silently, Sasha reached into his pocket, passing her a crumpled packet of Belomors and some matches. Lidiya lit up, took a small puff and then held the cigarette between two fingers, watching the smoke climb. She didn't really enjoy smoking – certainly not Belomors, which hit the back of her throat like she was gulping down thorns – but she did like the way her hands and wrists looked while holding a cigarette.

"I think your brother's having a bit of a panic in there," she said at last.

"Him and me both." Sasha smiled a little. Under the cropped hair, there was a mobility to his face that Lidiya rather liked. How would it be, Lidiya wondered, if Lev were to appear, flesh conjured from air and breath and dust? It was something she hadn't let herself think about for so long – Lev for her, now, was ink on paper, a couple of photographs, a collection of memories curled up in the scent of clean cotton and the touch of a hand *just so* on her shoulder and a million other things, equally trivial. For him to be made real again – would he feel more revenant than man?

"Your friend Katya – " Sasha was saying; Lidiya shook off a cobweb of ghosts. "She and Dima – the two of them – "

"Oh, yes. Only for a few months now, but yes."

"And she's good to him?"

"Of course!" Lidiya found herself mildly, and unexpectedly, affronted.

"Good." Sasha nodded. "Good."

"Did you really think he was dead?"

"Sort of. I went to try and find him at his school, years ago, when he would have been sixteen or seventeen. They said he had left. I went to the blind ghettos in Leningrad, in Moscow, and he wasn't..." Sasha shrugged. "I couldn't think how I could possibly find him after that. And a blind boy, on his own, in this country...It was easier, I suppose, to think of him as – as gone. Vanished. He had been gone from us since he was seven, after all." He turned, casting a quick look at the closed door behind them. "Do you think he's going to want to talk to me?"

"I'd have thought so. Normally it's impossible to shut him up."

"That sounds about right." Sasha shivered suddenly, his smile dropping from his face. "Perhaps he needs some time to get used to it. Perhaps I should just go, come again another time, if he wants me to."

"Don't be stupid," Lidiya said sharply. "You must at least see him play."

"What do you – " Sasha stared at Lidiya. "He's in the orchestra? But he can't be. He *can't* be."

"He is. Hadn't you worked that out yet? I guess lack of brains must run in the family."

"How could I? Trofim never said – or perhaps he did, but I didn't think – what instrument?"

"Violin. By all accounts he's rather good." She shrugged. "Not that I'm one to judge, but Katya seems to think so."

"But how can he follow a conductor?"

"You'd have to ask him that. He did explain it to me once – something to do with listening to the other musicians – didn't make much sense to me. It seems to work, though. I've seen him perform with the orchestra a couple of times. You couldn't tell the difference between him and the other musicians. Or I couldn't, anyway."

Sasha shook his head, smiling. "I should have known. I should have known he'd survive, and I should have known he'd do something – something unexpected. He was the stubbornest kid I've ever known."

"He's never spoken much about his family. Not to me, in any case. I only knew that he'd lost them – lost you. I suppose he must have talked more to Katya – she seemed to know who you were, right away."

"There's – " Sasha cleared his throat. "There's a lot to tell him."

For some time neither of them spoke – and then Lidiya's cigarette, half-forgotten in her hand, burned low enough to singe her fingers. She yelped, dropping it, and Sasha got to his feet to stamp it out.

"I can't believe I wasted a cigarette on you. Did you actually smoke any of that?"

"It was a conversational gambit," Lidiya said, unconcerned. Sasha cocked his head and grinned. He regarded her for a long moment.

"You know, Trofim thinks he's in love with you."

Lidiya snorted. "He's out of luck. I'm a married woman."

"Pity."

"For him? Or for you?"

Sasha laughed. He opened his mouth to speak, but then his gaze shifted, staring over Lidiya's head. She turned, finding the door open and Katya standing, a little shy, in the doorway, Dima's shadow visible behind her.

"Lunch is ready."

Lunch went off with a surprising lack of awkwardness. Both Dima and Sasha spoke little, but Katya watched the way Sasha kept sneaking glances at Dima over his glass, smiling as if against his will, and it made her like him more and more. Katya, with the assistance of Ilya, who had been swiftly apprised of the situation, made masterful efforts at polite, impersonal conversation; Trofim, perhaps already aware that his luck had run out, made reckless and doomed attempts to charm Lidiya, while Lidiya rebuffed him with cheerful brutality. Although bulked out by the supplies Trofim and Sasha had brought, the spread was typically meagre, but extravagantly praised.

"And there's even saccharine sweets for pudding," Lidiya announced. Simultaneously, both Dima and Sasha leaned back in their chairs wearing identical expressions of blissful satiety. "I couldn't possibly fit another thing in," said Dima, as Sasha said, "I'm absolutely full to bursting." A delighted laugh escaped Lidiya, catching her unawares, and Sasha joined in, pleased and surprised. Slowly, tentatively, Dima extended his hand across the table to where his brother was sitting, and Sasha took it, pressing it hard, seemingly unwilling to let go. His eyes were wet. Katya looked away.

The children were a good excuse for allowing twice as long as they needed to walk to the Philharmonic: Masha, at least, was young enough to admit when her legs were hurting and she was too tired to keep going, but Serezha had demonstrated more than once his tendency to try and keep up appearances until he was so exhausted that his body gave out completely. The sun was still high when they left, late afternoon settling over the city in an eerie, unaccustomed silence; Dima moved to put his arm around Katya's shoulders, but Lidiya forestalled him: "Katya's walking with me today, Dimulya. You go and talk to your brother." The diminutive caught Katya by surprise; she didn't think she'd heard Lidiya use it to Dima before, but she found Lidiya looking at Dima with irritated tenderness. Katya gave Dima a little push. "Lida's right," she said.

Behind them, Ilya had already taken the children in hand. Katya could catch snatches of his voice: he seemed to be telling Masha the story of Marya Morevna and Koschei the Deathless, one which she had heard a dozen times before but still clamoured to be told. Katya watched as Dima, wearing an expression of mingled eagerness and terror, walked on ahead; Sasha reached out to touch his shoulder, a simple announcement of his presence, and they fell into step with one another. Trofim was still hovering at Lidiya's elbow, awkward and undecided, until Lidiya, with airy malice, said to Katya, confidingly: "Sasha's rather handsome, isn't he?"

Katya, who thought Sasha was a shorter, rougher, less interesting version of Dima, made an uncertain noise that could have been taken for assent, while Trofim purpled and, trying and failing to affect an air of unconcern, dropped back and joined Ilya. Katya felt a throb of pity for him. True, it had never been going to amount to anything – but did Lidiya have to be so heartless?

"Honestly, Lida, you are cruel."

"Perhaps I am," Lidiya said, off-hand. She tucked her arm into Katya's. "Perhaps I am."

~

The easy silence that had stretched between them when they were in company took on an awkward weight now that they were alone. What could you talk about after sixteen years, when even the lightest topic seemed too loaded with absence and memory? *If there's one thing you're good at*, Dima thought. He considered how he would talk to Sasha if Sasha really were just a friend of Trofim's he'd never met before. In his head, he heard the casual tone to aim for. He opened his mouth.

"So you're Sasha now, then?" he asked.

"I suppose so. It wasn't really deliberate, but of course I was only ever Alik because Papa was Sasha, and after – " He stopped, half choking. Barely two sentences, and they had already fallen into a conversational bear-trap. Dima reached out his hand, found and squeezed Sasha's arm.

"Alik, I know what happened."

"You do?" Sasha's relief was palpable. "My god, I didn't want to be the one to tell you. I thought I would have to, but before the concert, I didn't want to…I didn't know how long it would take you to ask. How – how did you find out?"

"I met a woman from one of the villages near home here in Leningrad, a few years back. We got talking, found out we were from the same area, and when she heard my name was Kaverin, she told me…about what happened. She did say that she had heard that one or two of my brothers got out, but I thought perhaps she was just being kind."

"No, she was right." Sasha's voice had thinned and tightened.

"You don't have to talk about it if you don't want to," Dima said.

"Don't be an idiot. You deserve to know how it was. If you want to, that is."

Dima was not at all sure he did want to, but he had the muddled idea that if Sasha could bear to live through it, the least he could do was bear to hear about it. "All right. Tell me."

Sasha didn't speak immediately. Dima could hear the click of his throat, as if he was searching for right words that couldn't exist. "It was Grisha who woke me," he said; Dima had the impression that he had decided to just launch into it, almost at random. "The fire must have started on the other side of the house; the room was already full of smoke, and Valya and Stepan couldn't be woken. I don't…remember so much. We got out, me and Grisha. I kept saying we should go back for Valya and Stepan, but he said no. I think he must have known that they were already dead. Perhaps Mama and Papa too. Papa had been drunk…" Dima heard the shrug in his pause. "But as we stood outside – we couldn't do anything. It was too far gone. We could only watch it burn. And then Grisha thought he saw Mama standing at the window, waving. Perhaps he did. Sometimes I think I saw her too, and sometimes I'm certain it was just a shadow, maybe something falling from the ceiling. He went back in to find her. By the time I knew he wasn't coming out, everyone from the village had come out to watch. They wouldn't come close, wouldn't help, just watched. I didn't put it together until days afterwards that one of them – or some of them – must have started the fire, but still, I was terrified. So I ran."

Dima said nothing. It hurt to hear about it, but also it felt somehow better, cleaner to know the bones of it. Now he did not have to imagine – now he knew the length and the breadth of it, it was easier to grasp. There was another question, about which of his brothers had beaten the boy and thus brought down disaster on their heads; in Dima's imagination it had always been Alik, but the idea of making that idea real was frightening. It didn't seem fair to either of them to ask.

"So it's just us, now," he said at last.

"And Zina. She married the year before it happened. They live in Vologda, in town. I saw her once or twice afterwards, but…we don't have much to say to each other. And I was never able to stay for long. Her husband, he's active in the Party, and he worries – you know, about our *social origins*."

"Bastard," Dima said absently. His mind was still filled with smoke.

"I'm sorry you had to find out from a stranger. That must have been…"

Dima shook his head. "No. It was better to know what had happened. I had assumed – well, I had assumed the Gulag. The truth wasn't much worse, really. At least I knew why – " He tried valiantly to keep his voice free of bitterness, tasting his failure as he spoke the words: "At least I knew why I never heard from any of you."

"Oh, *Dima*," Sasha said. His voice shook a little. "When you went away – when they sent you away – I was so angry. They hadn't told me beforehand what they were doing. I wanted to write. I wanted to come and get you, even. But Mama said it was best for you that way, to be away from us. I think she and Papa already had an idea of what was coming. Not exactly, of course, but already by then, she knew it wasn't going to be good for us. They wouldn't even tell me exactly where your school was. They said it would be easier for you if you weren't still connected to us."

"That's what my friend said," Dima said, surprised. "And they were probably right. School – it was horrible, in a lot of ways, but I found this." He raised his violin case. "And it's been…it's everything to me. I don't know that I would have found it otherwise." He nudged Sasha with his shoulder. "Anyway, what happened to you? You know. *After*."

"For a while I drifted. The first few weeks – I don't really remember. I walked to Vologda, thought about going to see Zina but I couldn't – for a while afterwards I hated to be indoors anywhere at night. And I thought – I had the idea that I could be putting Zina in danger, too, by going to her. So I kept walking – I'm not sure how long it was. That whole time – it's unclear. Sometimes people would give me food, sometimes I would steal it. I met up with some other boys like me after a while, boys who had lost their families in various ways. Every so often we'd get rounded up and put into a children's home, but I always got out at the earliest opportunity. Did some stupid things for a few years, and then…then I grew up. Joined the army. Lots of us did, the boys like me. Like finding family again."

"I shouldn't be surprised. You were always good at fighting."

"So were you!"

"Not any more. Have to watch the hands. Is it good for you, the army?"

"Well. I'm a Captain now," Sasha said with a little pride. "It seems to suit me."

"How did you get them to take you, anyway? What with your *social origins*."

"Oh, I go by Yelizarov, Mama's name. Fake papers are easy enough to come by."

"I suppose so. I had – I had a friend. Vasya. He was the one I lived with once I left school, and he knew about that sort of thing." It gave Dima a strange sense of vertigo to mention Vasya's name to Sasha – too many lives colliding. But Sasha's silence had the shape of curiosity, and Dima continued: "He was the brother of someone I was at school with. I needed to come to Leningrad, for music lessons mainly, and he took me in."

"When was that?"

"I was sixteen."

"So you were here from 1936?" Sasha asked. "That was when I went to look for you at your school, just before I joined the army. They told me you'd gone, and they didn't know where."

"You came? In 1936?" It was painful to ask, but he did so anyway. "Why – what took you so long?"

Sasha sighed. "I came earlier too, once. Just a few months – a few months *after.* I didn't have the address, but I got to Pervomaysk and I asked and asked and asked until someone told me where the school was. I got as far as the fence outside, but…I was twelve. What did I have to offer you? I had nowhere to live, nothing. I was supporting myself by stealing and begging. And I kept thinking of what Mama had said. For all I knew, you were settled and happy at school. All I would have done was go in there with bad news and…and mess everything up. So I left."

Dima thought of who he'd been at nine, that driven and obsessive boy who could barely conceive of a world outside the piano and the violin. He tried to imagine the effect it would have had on him, Alik turning up, ragged and half-crazy, with news of his family. He had never had to choose between music and his family; the choice had been made for him. Dima was glad of it. "You did the right thing," he told Sasha, touching his arm.

"Good." Sasha cleared his throat. "And what about you? If the school had known where you'd gone when you left, I could have found you."

"You know what the worst thing was when I was at school?" Dima asked. "It wasn't that none of you ever came. It was that I didn't know you were never going to come. So every time – " The thought of it still winded him, a clean punch to the gut. He took a deep breath, like a draught of water. "Every weekend, every holiday, no matter how much I told myself not to be stupid, I couldn't stop myself from thinking *maybe this time*. After a while, hoping starts to hurt more. So when I left school, I thought – no, I didn't think it so clearly. But I had to draw a line."

Sasha didn't answer. Under the heft of his silence, Dima felt shaky, disassembled. There were some conversations that couldn't – shouldn't – be had all at once, that needed to be circled around, feinted at, unpicked, retreated from, taken by surprise. The space between them was so large and so deep, an ocean that both of them were only dipping their toes into. This was going to take time, and Dima was unsure how much of it they had.

"Katya seems nice," Sasha said eventually. His voice was deliberately, carefully light, but Dima could hear the tentativeness underneath it.

"She's…" *Nice* wasn't right, nowhere near enough, but Dima chose not to push it. "She is."

"How long have the two of you been together?"

"Not long at all. Only since the spring."

"And you have…" Sasha paused, delicate. "You've been with other women?"

"Why do people always ask me this?" Dima demanded, aggrieved. "It's only my eyes that have got a problem, you know, nothing else. *Yes*, I have been with other women. *A lot*."

"Must run in the family."

Dima cuffed him, lightly, on the shoulder. "But nothing serious, before now. And you? I don't suppose I have a sister-in-law hidden away somewhere?"

Sasha snorted. "Not likely."

"Not going to make me an uncle anytime soon? I'd be excellent at it, you know."

Sasha didn't laugh. Even jokes, Dima sensed, could be rough-edged, difficult. "I wouldn't even know how to begin," Sasha said at last. "Family – I don't know how to think about it, without it being… frightening."

"I suppose not."

They walked on. From behind them came the low murmur of voices: Lidiya and Katya, although Dima couldn't pick out a word. Ahead, space unfolded in a way that Dima knew meant the Anichkov Bridge, the mutter of the Fontanka below. It struck him:

"You know, Alik – you've not once tried to take my arm since we've been walking. Or warned me that there's a street coming up, or told me to be careful."

"Do you *need* help?" Sasha's voice was anxious.

"God, no! Not at all. It's just that normally people are tripping over themselves to lead me into obstacles or pull me into traffic. It's nice not to have to bat someone's arm away."

"You used to punch me if I tried," Sasha said. There was the very edge of a smile in his voice. "Do you remember? You always used to insist you could get around by yourself, and you were furious when people didn't believe you. The number of times I had to watch you trip over things, run into walls, because you'd never let me help you."

"Well, I manage all right."

"I suppose you do."

"Made it through the winter alive."

"It makes me feel sick to think about it." Sasha sounded fervent.

Dima laughed. "This morning you thought I was dead, and now you're fretting because I was in Leningrad over the winter? I survived, obviously."

"I can't imagine how."

"I got lucky," Dima said, suddenly serious. "I got lucky, again, and again, and again."

CHAPTER TWENTY-SEVEN

I: 9 August 1942: Before

The Great Hall of the Philharmonic was nothing new to Katya, somewhere she had been dozens of times, to play or to listen, its glamour long since worn thin. It wasn't as if it was transformed: its windows were still patched with plywood, its chandeliers denuded of crystal, the air holding a deep cold that seemed borrowed from winter – and yet it was crammed full of so much anticipation and energy that it felt almost dangerous, as if a single false move could cause it to ignite and blow sky high. Even those musicians who had averred all along that they were interested in nothing but increased rations were silent and intent, going over their scribbled scores again and again. Daniil was in a muttered conclave with Genya; Marina's eyes were fixed on her music, her fingers moving incessantly, and she wore an expression of such uncharacteristic seriousness that Katya felt a swell of affection for her. Katya laid down her violin, unrolled her score and went to check on Dima, who was where she had left him: he and Sasha stood at the door between the foyer and the auditorium, seemingly emptied of conversation, while Dima dithered, caught between the two poles of music and his resurrected brother.

"It's time to come inside," Katya said gently, and Dima nodded, decisive.

"We'll talk more after," he said to Sasha, though the statement sounded rather more like a question.

"Of course," Sasha said. He took a half step towards Dima, hands held away from his body, as if uncertain what to do with them: to embrace Dima, to shake his hand? In the end he gripped Dima's arm just above the elbow, squeezing. To Katya, it looked more like a test of Dima's corporeality than anything else. She tried to catch Sasha's eye, wanting to offer him something, some comfort or reassurance – she found she was thinking of him as an extension of Dima, and thus a responsibility she was willing to shoulder. As the door closed behind them, Sasha's pale face, with its studied lack of expression, was imprinted on Katya's eye like the afterimage of an explosion.

Sasha's lungs felt as if they were drawn into fists. He couldn't get a full breath, and the paltry lunch he had eaten writhed in his stomach. Talking to Dima, just being near him, was an act of unpeeling, and it made him feel faintly sick. And at the same time, memories were passing through him like a cavalcade, most of which had been carefully, firmly set aside years ago: their physicality was startling. Sasha felt as rocked, as unsteady as after a bomb blast. The tingling palms and dry mouth he diagnosed as classic adrenaline overload. He couldn't stop thinking about the anxious look that had been on Dima's face when he left him, and it twisted and tore at him: he felt himself to be just as untrustworthy as Dima seemed to fear. At least when Dima had been with him, his actual presence had been a distraction from Sasha's own reaction to it, but now, left alone, there was nowhere he could hide from himself. He wanted nothing more than to carve out a little pocket of silence in the foyer, to gather himself together. Instead, he felt his shoulder seized, and as he turned it took a few blank moments before the greatcoat, the stubbled face and the sleek hair resolved themselves into Andrei.

"Sasha, what are you doing here? I wouldn't have thought this was your sort of thing."

"Oh – " Sasha cast about for an appropriate response. What would he have said a day ago, before any of this? That other person he'd been had had a gift for dry sarcasm and off-hand remarks; he wished he could shrug that man back on, but he was already feeling painfully ill-fitting. "Well, Trofim – Pavlenko, you know – he's playing."

"Ah yes, of course." Andrei nodded. His lack of interest was evident, and Sasha wondered why he was there, himself, the way that his eyes were roaming restlessly over the crowd. When Andrei raised a hand in somewhat humble greeting, Sasha followed his line of sight and saw Govorov over the other side of the room. That made more sense: Andrei was clearly treating the event as strategic.

"I didn't know you knew him."

"Not well. Not *yet.* Notice anything, by the way?"

Sasha was sufficiently rattled that for a moment he couldn't imagine what Andrei was referring to, until Andrei rolled his eyes, and pointed slowly to the sky, as if trying to signal something to a particularly slow-witted child. "Pretty quiet, isn't it?"

In a flash, Sasha understood. His smile felt feeble on his own lips as Andrei went on:

"We've been bombarding the Fascists all day, hard as you like, to keep the skies clear for the performance. And we've set up loudspeakers pointed towards their trenches, so they'll hear every note of the Symphony." He grinned, vulpine. "Should be quite a blow for the Fascists. Show them what's going on in the city, show them that they can't shut us up."

Sasha grinned back, uncomfortable. A day ago, perhaps, he could have respected the sound military sense of a propaganda strike like that one. Now, the idea of it nagged at him somehow, that even an event like this could be sharpened, hurled and used as a weapon, and he fished for the words to try and express this to Andrei, although he knew it wouldn't matter. He came up with nothing. He *liked* Andrei, that was the bitch of it: he was sly and ambitious and cozening but also good company, and until that moment the latter had clearly outweighed the former. Now, all of Sasha's judgement was unbalanced.

Clearly thinking that Sasha had transformed into some sort of imbecile, not worth wasting time on, Andrei gave him a distracted nod of dismissal, clapped him on the arm and moved on smoothly into the crowd. There were more of them now, Red Army uniforms and civilians, men in sober suits and women in an unlikely variety of colours. Sasha felt besieged. Claustrophobia rose up inside him like a cloud: he should get out of the hall, have a walk around, stretch his legs, have a Belomor or ten; there was still time before the performance started. And yet he was certain that if he walked out that door no power on earth could force him to walk back in. He looked down at his hands, counted his breaths on his fingers; there was a flash of red in his peripheral vision, and he looked up to see Lidiya watching him steadily.

~

When Sasha looked up at her, startled, there was something in his stance that reminded Lidiya of Serezha, a bumptious, desperate approximation of bravery. If she had been a man, she thought, she probably would have worried that he was going to take a swing at her. Instead, it aroused in her a tender sort of pity.

"Are you all right?"

"Oh, I…" For a fraction of a second his mask slipped, and Lidiya didn't think she'd ever seen somebody look so frightened. "I've felt better, to be quite honest."

"I'm sure." Lidiya wouldn't have said she understood his panic, but it was formidable, a third presence between them. She waited: there were some things, she knew, that you couldn't try and lure out of someone; the best you could do was to sit quietly and let them wrestle them out themselves.

"I thought I'd already lost everything I could lose, you see," Sasha said presently. His voice was so quiet that Lidiya had to strain to hear it over the clamour of voices; his smile was wretched. "And I don't want to – my god, right now, I feel that I'd rather mount a single-handed, unarmed expedition over enemy lines than go into that auditorium."

Lidiya nodded, unsmiling. She slipped her arm into his. "Why don't you escort me to my seat?"

Inside the auditorium, the air felt combustible. Ilya was seated in one of the middle rows, Masha and Serezha to his left and a spare seat waiting for Lidiya on his right – but when she appeared with Sasha in tow he didn't question it, simply moved down and made room for both of them. Seated, the tension radiating off Sasha was tangible. Ilya was speaking to Masha, making sure she had her pencils and paper at the ready, something to keep her attention during the performance; as Masha listed the various things she planned to draw, Lidiya was increasingly conscious of Sasha beside her, his silence concentrating him, until he had the certain, toppling gravity of a cresting wave. His hand was fisted on his thigh, worrying the skin around his thumbnail until it was close to bleeding. Lidiya could hear his breaths coming tight and fast. Keeping her face turned towards Ilya and the children, she reached out and curled her own hand around Sasha's larger one. For a moment he froze, and she was sure that he was going to pull away; she hung on, and as he relaxed fractionally, she took his fingers one by one, coaxing them straight, laying them out flat on the rough wool of his uniform trousers. Done, she gave the back of his hand a brisk, conclusive pat and withdrew her own. Sasha breathed out the the barest hint of a laugh, and Lidiya caught Ilya's meaningful look, eyebrows raised. She couldn't have said why she'd done it: to irritate, to tease, to comfort?

"Quiet," she said reprovingly to Ilya, although he hadn't spoken. "It's about to start."

The red dress that Lidiya was wearing was like a flag; it tugged Trofim's eyes towards her. She was sitting in the audience, bent slightly towards Ilya on her left hand side. On her right, Sasha sat awkwardly, looking as if he badly wanted to fidget and was forcing himself into a regimented stillness. His face was shuttered. For a moment, Trofim felt a dizzying sense of loss, entirely uncertain quite what he was losing. It had become harder and harder to trace the path back from where he was to where he'd started, the hall, the dugout, the guns, the snow, the smooth, cool feel of a trumpet in his hands. There was an abrupt sensation of a line ending, a trolleybus shuddering off its tracks. He ducked his head, and when he looked up again, Marina was offering him a reassuring smile.

"Are you all right?" she mouthed across the stage, and Trofim nodded. Perhaps he would be; perhaps he was.

~

"Be careful at the start of the third movement, Dima," Genya warned. "Karl Ilych will want to draw out the strings, make them…ponderous. If you're not sure, hold back, all right?"

"All right," Dima said. His tension was strung along his jawline and his lips. His fingers moved unceasingly. Katya couldn't stop watching him, his pent-up energy and the great, elated smiles that kept exploding across his face, as if he couldn't hold them back. He seemed illuminated.

"How many are there?" he whispered to Katya. His voice was shaking, and Katya couldn't answer. It was too much. Audiences had been full before now, but this was another thing altogether. It was electric. People leaned forward, seemingly unaware of what they were doing, reaching for the stage in anticipation of the music. They looked no less thin and ill than they had before, but their eagerness was new. And there was something else, something different:

"The lights are on," she told Dima. It was the first time that this had happened, and Katya couldn't imagine how it was possible. She had forgotten that electricity existed, she had become so accustomed to the sickly flicker of gas lamps and their feeble light, their sharp smell, their uncertain shadows. Recording equipment was clustered around the stage, and Katya decided not to tell Dima of this. She was nervous enough thinking of how far and wide the concert was being broadcast, and she didn't want to add Dima's nerves to her own. She would tell him afterwards.

"Do you see Alik?" Dima asked, his voice a poor attempt at casual. Katya squinted and looked. There was a clutch of Red Army uniforms towards the front, a knot of men talking and back-slapping, but Alik – Sasha – didn't seem to be among them. A few rows behind, Katya's eyes skated over a face she recognised: Nina, with a pair of girls who had the same attenuated look that she did, presumably dancers – and Katya couldn't help smiling at how little that mattered now. When she spotted Sasha at last, a tide of relief coursed through her; she hadn't realised the extent to which she had absorbed Dima's fear, palpable but unspoken, that Sasha would vanish as abruptly and miraculously as he had appeared.

"He's sitting with Lidiya and Ilya, about halfway back."

Dima's face relaxed a touch. As Karl Ilych climbed onto the rostrum, an incendiary hush settled over the hall. Time seemed to become elastic, speeding up and slowing down at once. Katya was conscious of the glint of the dusty air, the prickle of her hair at the back of her neck, the flutter of paper as Daniil adjusted the music on his stand. At the back of the hall someone coughed, and was hushed from three directions. The silence felt soft and welcoming. Karl Ilych raised his baton with careful authority, and dropped it with the weighted certainty of a heartbeat.

II: 9 August 1942: During

The first movement had always been the one that Trofim found himself humming to himself, its martial nature and its relentless swell; it felt like something you could hold in your hands, something you could sink your teeth into. Ever since he was a child, he would sometimes be assailed by a euphoric light-headedness when playing, a swooning sensation of falling headlong into the music. This happened now: he had a sense of himself outside himself, disembodied in the close warmth of the hall and the concentrated quiet of the audience. They were listening, there in the hall, and outside, in the empty streets of Leningrad, the shattered apartments, families clustered around the radio sets that were spilling out the music that had been written for the city. Further: the lines of trenches that bordered the city, the scarred and corrugated ground that held back the enemy, the dirt and the dark and the silence as the soldiers listened, the millions of Viktors and Sashas and Andreis – and the Germans, too, those anonymous Fritzes with the loudspeakers set up to bombard their trenches with the Symphony. Further still: Trofim's sisters, his mother and father in Moscow, an apartment unimagined, lives unimagined if they even existed at all, but Trofim saw them clearly, watched them crowding around the loudspeaker, somehow recognising him in the honeyed blare of the trumpet line as the country bent towards Leningrad, silent and tense with listening. The city's heart beat through the airwaves, and the war was translated into music. It moved through Trofim, in anger and in loss and in pride, as the city gathered the Symphony in its hands and threw it out to the world.

~

Towards the back of the hall, Lidiya felt the prickle of her silk dress skating across her collarbones, caught on the twin peaks of her hipbones. On her left, Ilya's hands picked compulsively at his trousers, removing invisible scraps of dirt. His face was tight, fervent with concentration. Beyond the children, a woman she didn't know turned in Lidiya's direction, caught her gaze with the corner of her eye and smiled. She looked incandescent. Even Masha and Serezha seemed transfixed.

Lidiya felt for it, reached, couldn't grasp it. She had never understood music, had never even come close and that was something she had shared with Lev, their unmoved bewilderment at something the rest of the world seemed to find entrancing. This music was a barrage, nothing more. A row ahead, a middle-aged man pressed his gloved hand to his mouth, his eyes narrowed with emotion. What was it that she couldn't hear, what was she missing? Something brushed the edge of her heart, tugging: a beat, a drum. That was something, nearly there, perhaps.

On the stage, she picked out Trofim, the burnished glow of his trumpet. When he played, he seemed to inhabit his body completely differently, with an easy, unquestioning confidence. On the other side of the stage Lidiya caught the muted gleam of Katya's hair and next to her, the flash of Dima's teeth as he grinned, breathless, every curve and angle of his body speaking of energy held back, longing to stand and to move. Instinctively she turned towards Sasha, but could see nothing but the outline of his smooth, dark head, his compact body. She couldn't imagine what he must be thinking.

Ilya took her fisted hand, swallowing it within his own. He squeezed it in time with the music, the deep, heaving pulse of the hall. Lidiya half smiled, biting her lip. Perhaps that was it, not the music at all, just the act of making it and listening to it and sitting in the stilled city under the emptied sky, a fixed point, a focus. *Liova*, she thought, and then breathed out a laugh. *No, you'd still probably hate this.*

Dima was used to picking out the sharp thread of his own line to stop himself from getting lost in the monumental sound of the orchestra, tying himself to it, his violin an anchor to keep from tumbling dizzily into the glorious wash of noise. This time was different. This time there was no difficulty in keeping hold of the idea of the audience, the serried ranks of them beyond the stage. If this was the last time, he owed it to himself to remember every minute detail of it. There was the warmth of Katya's presence on his right, the slide of her breath as she readied herself to play, and the tiny gasps she made at the end of particularly tricky passages. There was Karl Ilych ahead, the creak of the boards under his feet as he swayed forward, urging them on. There was Genya in front and to the left, as solid and reliable as a pulse. There was Alik, too, in the audience, beyond his reach – *Alik*, an impossibility that made Dima's heart trip over itself whenever he thought of it.

Sasha watched his brother. *You could just slip out afterwards*, he thought, unbidden. He saw himself, striding down the empty streets, back to – his imagination skipped over the details – just away, away from this. He wouldn't do it. His brother was on the stage, his brother, with a violin tucked under his chin and a bow in his hand and a look on his face as if he was crawling through enemy lines with a dagger in his teeth and loving every minute of it. Dima at seven, and Dima at twenty-three – Sasha found it hard to draw the lines to separate them. Seven-year-old Dima, though, he had had a habitual expression, halfway between grim and transfigured, a knife-blade of focus. He looked the way the music sounded, the slash of strings, a burst of light. Something brimmed inside Sasha; he rose to his feet, unthinking, barely realising that the people on either side of him were doing the same.

The final movement was too fast. They had barely managed to play it in rehearsals; even at the dress rehearsal, the first and only time they had played the Symphony the whole way through, the final movement had slipped and slithered out of their hands. The musicians could not catch it: it mocked them, hovering slightly out of their reach. But now, the music took the musicians with it. As Katya played, her arms felt light. The Symphony came into her embrace: it was easy, inevitable; every movement of her fingers and every swipe of her bow felt guided. Next to her, she could catch the edge of Dima's movements. She felt his smile although she couldn't see it. Her body felt too small and too fragile to hold the music that spilled from her hands. Joy crashed through Katya like a breaking wave: its intensity was violent. She knew, suddenly, that it was impossible for her to make a mistake, to play a wrong note, to lose the beat. The audience was playing with them, moving with the music as it got louder, swelled and burst around them like gunfire or storm clouds or fireworks.

And then it ended. Katya could not get her breath. The silence crashed down, thick and heavy as a curtain; she was instantly bereft. Glancing around, bewildered, Katya saw the same expression mirrored on the faces around her. The audience let out a great, held breath, and the applause began, one pair of hands and then another and then all of them, clapping with a strength that Katya wouldn't have thought that enfeebled crowd could possess. The sound was elemental, almost as great as the music had been. Beside her, Dima clutched Katya's arm convulsively; she wanted to embrace him, but in front of this audience it wouldn't do. Instead, she took hard hold of his hand. Behind the dazzle of the lights she made out Lidiya, her eyes narrowed, an expression on her face as if she was trying to puzzle something out. Next to her was Sasha: he didn't clap, his hands fisted at his sides, his face pale and blank. He was standing, Katya noticed; they were all standing: Lidiya and Sasha and Ilya and the children, Nina and her ballerina friends, the hundreds of people that she didn't know – and beyond them too, listening at home: Katya had a swift, sharp image of Nikita and his aunt Polina, the pair that they had met in the shelter, dumbstruck by the radio in their anonymous apartment.

A small girl appeared on stage: her dress as white as a miracle, her limbs as thin as twigs. She clutched flowers in her arms, and walked over to Karl Ilych with steps so slow and measured that it was clear she recognised the gravity of the occasion as much as anyone else. Katya imagined Masha; she imagined Tanya or Nadya, entrusted with so solemn a task. The girl handed the flowers to Karl Ilych, and Karl Ilych took them, his face half hidden behind the blooms. The orchestra stood, now; Katya barely felt that her legs could hold her. The applause came like a shell blast, a vast communal shout. None of the orchestra knew quite what to do; Marina, Katya saw, was unashamedly sobbing into a handkerchief. They stood, and sat, and stood again. Karl Ilych left the stage, and stumbled back on, pushed by unseen hands. He bowed again, and the audience roared.

III: 9 August 1942: After

None of them could talk about it: something too big and too close to be shaped and moulded by words. Marina wasn't the only one in tears; Katya noticed Vadim, a trombone player from the Crew whom she barely knew other than to greet, a mountain of a man who dwarfed his instrument to toylike proportions, mopping his face as unobtrusively as he could. Katya wanted to say something but couldn't imagine what it would be. Genya looked overcome, groping for words. Some of the Crew were shaking hands wordlessly, slapping each other on the back. Daniil cleared his throat.

"Towards the end of the first movement – " he started to say, his tone dry and clinical, before Dima tackled him, seizing him around the shoulders and slapping his hand over Daniil's mouth.

"*No*," he said, smiling and fierce. "Not this time. None of your criticisms, none of your notes, not yet. Just…just *let it be*."

Behind Dima's hand, Daniil laughed, shrugging. "All right," he said, muffled. "All right."

~

What food would be served at the reception had been a topic of intense debate for weeks: speculation about cake and meat, champagne and cognac had been engaged in with much more enthusiasm than any discussion about the Symphony itself, and in the immediate aftermath of the performance it was the only topic that could be agreed upon.

"Marina said there would be beefsteak," Dima said, besotted with the very idea.

"You'll be sick," Daniil said, quelling.

Dima nodded. "Very probably. And then I'll just keep right on eating."

"I don't know if my teeth could stand it," Katya said.

"It'll pull my teeth right out of my head," Dima said, with lugubrious joy. He could barely imagine it, meat that you had to bite into, meat that you had to chew, meat that hadn't been boiled to scant wisps in a pretence of a stew. "I don't care. I'll *suck* the goodness out of it."

But when it came to it, Dima found himself possessed by an uncomfortable restlessness, too keyed up to stand still long enough to eat. Katya handed him a plate: potatoes, cabbage, a comically small nugget of beef, but he couldn't do more than pick at it. Everyone seemed to want to talk to him, to embrace him or to shake his hand, but he felt as if all the words had leaked out of him. There was Nina, squeezing his hand and talking to him in a voice that sounded tear-choked; there was Pavel, sounding closer to impressed than Dima had ever imagined possible – but none of it mattered, when he was painfully aware that every moment that passed was a moment closer to Alik returning to the Front. He ached to talk to him, and yet he couldn't bring himself to ask Katya to take him to Alik, for fear that Alik had already gone.

~

Lidiya had lost sight of Sasha after the performance; he had been swallowed by a flood of Red Army uniforms, while she had been distracted by insisting to Masha that yes, she probably *did* need to visit the bathroom before going to tell Auntie Katya and Uncle Dima how much she had liked the performance. Now there he was, on the very edge of a group of soldiers, unspeaking and looking slightly stunned.

When he caught her eye he spread his fingers in an economical sketch of a wave.

"Why aren't you talking to Dima?" Lidiya demanded, by way of greeting. Casting a cautious glance over his shoulder, Sasha shifted slightly further away from the clutch of soldiers.

"He seems busy. I don't want to interrupt – "

"My god, you really are useless," Lidiya said, sighing. Taking him by the arm, she towed him through the crowd to where Dima, looking agonised, was limping through a stilted conversation with an older man whom Lidiya didn't recognise.

"Dima, Sasha wants to talk to you," Lidiya announced. The older man seemed somewhat offended at the interruption, but Dima himself looked nothing but thankful for rescue.

"I thought you might have gone," he said, quietly, to Sasha.

"You were – " Sasha began, and then smiled helplessly. "I don't know how to describe it. It was – "

"I feel the same way," Dima said, laughing. Lidiya left them to it.

It was still hard for him to look at Dima directly, this tall, bright-faced boy who was his brother. Instead, Sasha leaned against the wall beside Dima, his eyes on his hands, loose fists on his thighs. Part of him still shouted that this was a trick, something he needed to ward off before it wormed its way too deep inside him. But in his head, he imagined himself looping an arm around his brother's shoulders, casual and uncaring.

"I thought about leaving, while you were playing," Sasha said. He hadn't meant to tell Dima this, but it suddenly seemed important. "I could see it so clearly: out of the hall, down Nevsky, not looking back. Then – then nothing."

For a long time Dima said nothing. He bent, carefully, and placed his plate of food on the floor; then shifted closer to Sasha, leaning a little so that their hips and shoulders jostled together. Sasha froze, hating himself, waiting for Dima to move away. Dima stayed still, silent, and slowly Sasha found his muscles uncoiling. He felt it in his hands, the memory of Dima's small, hard head, prickly with too-short hair, his bony child's hips and scratched, flimsy wrists. *He used to complain that you elbowed him in the ribs every night.* The same elbows; the same ribs.

"I get it," Dima said at last. "I understand why you might want to leave. Just – just don't, all right?"

Sasha pressed his lips together. He nodded, briefly and uselessly.

"Just don't," Dima said again. He made it sound like an agreement.

~

Trofim had always found it hard to come back to himself after a performance. He felt undone, slightly dizzy, an awkward and reluctant inhabitant of his body. He couldn't have named his feelings: satisfaction, disappointment, relief? On the other side of the room, Dima and Sasha were standing side by side, heads down; it seemed astonishing, now, that he had never noticed before the similarities between them, the way their postures echoed one another, brackets open and closed. Nearby, Katya and Marina were in intense discussion, and as he watched, Marina looked over and offered Trofim a beaming smile. It disconcerted him so much that he didn't notice Lidiya until she was at his elbow.

"Well done," she said. It was refreshing, the clarity of it, after the mess of words that had come from so many others.

Trofim smiled. "Thank you."

"I can't claim that I enjoyed the music. But the rest of it – that was worth being here for."

She was so beautiful, the shape of her face and the lines of her neck, the steadiness of her gaze. Now that it didn't matter any more Trofim could look as much as he liked, no longer having to hide it for fear of what she would think if she caught him staring. Lidiya looked back, head tilted a little to one side, her eyes cool. He asked without deciding to ask.

"Did you ever – ? It felt sometimes like perhaps you did. But…did you?"

"I think I wanted to," Lidiya said quietly. At least she didn't do him the disservice of pretending she didn't understand what she meant. "I think perhaps I was trying it on, to see how it might fit. That was wrong of me, and I'm sorry." She looked at him carefully, that familiar squint of concentration. "But it was you, too, trying things on," she said. "You know that it was never really *me* that you were interested in, don't you?"

Trofim hadn't known it until she said the words, but once they were spoken he felt the truth of it, as certain as a key in a lock, tumblers falling with weighty certainty. "I suppose not."

She nodded, once. "So what will you do now?"

"What I always do. Back to work." He closed his eyes: the hard, frost-streaked ground, the guns, the butcher's-shop smell of blood. "After this is over," Trofim said, his eyes still closed, "I might do something else. I might go back to this."

Lidiya touched his cheek; again, the surprising toughness of her fingertips. Trofim opened his eyes to her looking at him searchingly, as if groping for words. "You need to stop grabbing onto people," she said at last. "Me, and Sasha – people and things, too. The army. You don't need any of it. You're old enough to just…just be who you are."

On the street outside, the sky cupped the city: wild, deep blue. The cool air felt as fresh as water. Masha's dress was a white flag in the gathering darkness; Lidiya wrapped her arms around herself and shivered.

"We must go," Sasha said. He seemed to have collected himself, Katya noticed; courteous, he kissed her cheek, then Lidiya's, shook Ilya's hand. Trofim, a little clumsily, followed suit. "I'll – I'll be in touch," he said to Dima, and Dima laughed unsteadily.

"You do that." He reached out and gripped Sasha's hand. A group of Red Army soldiers passed them, laughing, and Trofim and Sasha slipped among them.

"Masha's asleep on her feet," Lidiya said. She looked tired enough herself, leaning against the wall outside the Philharmonic, one hand on Masha's shoulder, the other on Serezha's. "It's past time for bed."

"We'll follow you," Katya said. Left alone, Katya raised her hand, tentative, to Dima's face; smiling, he turned into it and kissed her palm. Overhead, a ball of white light streaked across the sky, and then another, chased by sound: the anti-aircraft guns were starting up again. Nothing had changed and everything had changed, the way bones knit back stronger where they've broken. Katya thought of the endless roll of the earth, the stubborn push of plants through parched soil. She thought of a man writing music while bombs fell, she thought of hundreds of thousands of men facing one another across strips of scarred and empty ground, she thought of the millions dead, the thousands lost, the precious few found. These were the things you could never say; the best you could do was to try and parcel them up in something ephemeral, in music or in the light brush of hand on hand. Perhaps you could never get close enough to another person, perhaps you could never patch up damage or fill in holes completely, but perhaps there were some things that could act as a shelter, and perhaps there were other things that could be found in the act of huddling together beneath it.

In the final, tender shreds of light, they turned for home.

LYCHKOVO

18 August 1941, morning: Leningrad

There was a time before, a heart unknotted. You could scroll back, if you let yourself, past the summer after the winter that had smelled of gunpowder and ice on stone, past the cold and the hunger, past the people who had died, past the brightest day there had ever been, with the sun tossed high and the hum of hot metal and the railway platform slick with blood. You could go back, as if rifling through pages in a book, searching for the one passage you most wanted to remember. Memory can make and unmake, both.

Once, then, there had been two girls: the older long-limbed and plain, straight-backed and brave; the younger round-faced and trusting, who loved nothing more than her older sister. There had been two girls who had grown like weeds, who had had coughs in the winter and grazed knees in the summer, who had played with dolls and sledges and balls, who had read books and drawn pictures and been careful and careless and wicked and obedient. There had been two girls who had greeted the war with an excited solemnity, who had watched their city vanish under camouflage netting and sandbags, who had carefully pasted crosses of newspaper onto their windows to prevent the glass from shattering in case of bomb blasts they couldn't conceive of. On the morning of the evacuation they had hefted the bags that their mother had helped them pack, small enough for the girls to carry because their mother believed their father's promise that they would all be home before winter. They had walked out of the apartment where they had spent all their lives, the older girl holding hands with the younger, they had walked down the steps and out of the front door and turned their back on the home they were certain they were going to return to; they had waited for the trucks to take them to Rybatskoe, to join the train line. They had been well-behaved, accustomed to patience and waiting quietly, standing side by side, wide-eyed and watchful as their father strode about, puffed up on official business, as their mother tried to persuade herself that what they were doing was for the best. When it had come time to board the trucks, Katya had turned to take her daughters by the hand, but found that Tanya had drawn Nadya to one side, bending down in front of her, straightening the collar on Nadya's dress, brushing away invisible dust. Katya hadn't been able to hear them over the sound of the hundreds of other children who surged around them, the shouts and cries of the mothers who were unlucky enough to have to stay behind, but she saw Nadya's lips move, her brow furrowed. In answer, Tanya leant in closer, her mouth to her sister's ear, and Nadya's whole body seemed to soften with whatever words of reassurance Tanya was able to offer. Katya took a step, another, closer to her girls, called their names: *Tanya! Nadya!* The girls turned, Tanya taking her sister's hand in her own, eyes searching for their mother. *Mama*, Nadya said, and Tanya echoed her; buffeted by the crowd Tanya stumbled, and then her shoulder was under Katya's hand. The girls looked up, pale-faced, wide-eyed, but they were smiling.

They were smiling.

ACKNOWLEDGEMENTS

The writing of this book took literal years of background research, consulting too many sources to count. However I owe a particular debt to *Natasha's Dance*, by Orlando Figes, which provided the initial arresting image that inspired this book. I also relied greatly upon *The 900 Days* by Harrison Salisbury (the veritable bible of the Siege), Elizabeth Wilson's biography of Shostakovich, *Ivan's War* by Catherine Merridale, and *The Whisperers*, also by Orlando Figes. I'm particularly grateful to two incredible memoirs of blindness: *Touching the Rock: An Experience of Blindness*, by John M Hull, and *And There Was Light*, by Jacques Lusseyran. I am also grateful to the staff of the Museum of the Defence and Siege of Leningrad in St Petersburg.

This book was written over several years, in multiple countries, and over various periods when, quite frankly, I probably should have been focusing on other things. I'm therefore indebted to my various employers over the years for their indulgence, particularly Charlie Goldsmith and Aly Verjee, as well as to Richard Chown, who was instrumental in encouraging my fascination with twentieth century Russian culture.

Thanks are owed to my family, particularly my parents, Michael and Susan, my aunt Julia, my brothers Stephen and MJ, sisters in- and out-law, Linda and Ali, and nieces and nephews, Jack, Danny, Harry, Ellie and Molly. Thanks also to the various friends over the years who have supported me through blind enthusiasm, intense discussions, book recommendations, and not getting annoyed that I spent so much time in the evenings at a laptop with my door closed.

Particular thanks to Muhammad Al Fatih, Jay Bagaria, Claire Beston, Gabriel Beston, Awak Bior, Anne Pordes Bowers, Angela Bravo Chacon, Hannah Bryce, Jenn Cianca, Ben Cutner, Rachel Coldbreath, Devin Connolly, Sarah Cooke, Gemma Cossins, Ginevra Cucinotta, Sabine Eckle Nielsen, Angel Earle, Nuala Fahey, Emma Felber, Honor Flanagan, Zoë Flower, Susanna Forrest, Mark Freestone, Zavy Gabriel, Leda Glyptis, Hannah Graham, Laura Gonzalez, Tom Harkness, Jessica Hjarrand, Clare Hollowell, Penny Hollowell, Caroline D'Anna Horne, Kirstin Innes, Johanna Johnson, Kate Jones, Chris Jung, Anneli Kastberg, Sarah Kingstone, Kat Knight, Lucie Leclert, Andrew Lewis, Sarah Lewthwaite, Winnie Li, Judith Logan, Iain MacLeod, Alasdair Mackenzie, Tina MacLellan, Cait Macquarrie, Havra Marketwala, Honor McAdam, Helen McElhinney, Hannah McNeish, Marcia Munt, Nine, Becky Quinton, Nicholas Ramsden, Yogini Raste, Justin Sacks, Niall Saville, Neil Scott, Joshua Swiss, Rob Timson, Nich Underdown, Angela van der Lem, Joanna Webster, David Womble, and Kat Woods.

And finally, endless thanks to Angel Belsey, for taking a chance on this book.

ABOUT THE AUTHOR

Jessica Gregson was born in London in 1978. She is a humanitarian education specialist and a writer, with occasional forays into other careers. Her first novel, The Angel Makers, was published in 2007 and has since sold to nine international markets. Her second novel, The Ice Cream Army, was published in 2009. She has lived and worked in a variety of places, including South Sudan, Myanmar and Azerbaijan, and currently divides her time between Glasgow and everywhere else.

@khawajia

ABOUT DEIXIS PRESS

Deixis Press is an independent publisher of fiction, usually with a darker edge. Our aim is to discover, commission, and curate works of literary art. Every book published by Deixis Press is hand-picked and adored from submission to release and beyond.

www.deixis.press

Lightning Source UK Ltd.
Milton Keynes UK
UKHW011830290422
402248UK00002B/66